Please return to:

Doug Williams

4618 Dalwick Dr.

Durham, NC
27713

919-484-8067

doug.alan @ verizon.net

O9-BTN-978

# THE AGE OF REASON

# LES CHEMINS DE LA LIBERTÉ

## (*The Roads to Freedom*)

### I

L'ÂGE DE RAISON (*The Age of Reason,* 1947)

### II

LE SURSIS (*The Reprieve,* 1947)

### III

LA MORT DANS L'ÂME (*Troubled Sleep,* 1951)

### IV

LA DERNIÈRE CHANCE (*in preparation*)

# THE
# AGE OF REASON

*by Jean-Paul Sartre*

TRANSLATED FROM THE FRENCH BY

ERIC SUTTON

VINTAGE BOOKS

A Division of Random House, New York

VINTAGE BOOKS EDITION, January 1973

Copyright © 1947 by Eric Sutton

All rights reserved under International and Pan-American
Copyright Conventions. Published in the United States by
Random House, Inc., New York. Originally published
by Alfred A. Knopf in 1947.
Originally published in France as *Les Chemins de La
Liberté I: L'Âge De Raison.* Copyright by Librairie
Gallimard 1945.

Library of Congress Cataloging in Publication Data

Sartre, Jean Paul, 1905–
The age of reason.

Translation of L'âge de raison.
I. Title.
[PZ3.S2494Ag12]  [PQ2637.A82]  843'.9'14  72–4476
ISBN 0–394–71838–0 (pbk.)

Manufactured in the United States of America

# THE AGE OF REASON

# CHAPTER I

HALFWAY down the rue Vercingétorix a tall guy seized
Mathieu by the arm; a policeman was patrolling the
opposite pavement.

"Listen, chief, can you spare me a franc or two? I'm
hungry."

His eyes were close-set, his lips were thick, and he smelt
of drink.

"You mean you're thirsty?" asked Mathieu.

"Not on your life, kid," the guy muttered thickly, "not
on your life."

Mathieu found a five-franc piece in his pocket.

"I don't give a good God-damn," he said. "I was just
saying the usual." He gave him the five francs.

"You're a good sort," said the man, leaning against the
wall. "And now I'd like to wish you something in return.
Something you'll be really glad to have. What shall it be?"

They both pondered; then Mathieu said:

"Whatever you like."

"Well, I wish you good luck. There!"

He laughed triumphantly. Mathieu observed the policeman strolling towards them and felt sorry for the man.

"Right," said he. "So long."

He was about to pass on when the man clutched him.

"Good luck isn't enough," he said in a sodden voice; "not nearly enough."

"Well, what then?"

"I'd like to give you something . . ."

"I'll have you locked up for begging," said the policeman. He was a young, ruddy-cheeked cop, and he tried to look tough.

"You've been pestering the passers-by for the last half-hour," he added, but there was no menace in his voice.

"He wasn't begging," said Mathieu sharply, "we were having a little talk."

The policeman shrugged his shoulders and walked on. The man was swaying rather precariously; he did not even seem to have seen the policeman.

"I know what I'll give you. I'll give you a Madrid stamp."

He produced from his pocket a rectangular bit of green card and handed it to Mathieu. Mathieu read:

"C.N.T. Diario Confederal. Ejemplares 2. France. Anarcho-Syndicalist Committee, 41 rue de Belleville, Paris II." Beneath the address there was a stamp. It too was green, and bore the postmark: Madrid. Mathieu reached out a hand.

"Thanks very much."

"Ah, but look," said the man angrily. "It's—it's Madrid."

Mathieu looked at him: the man seemed excited and was plainly struggling to express what was in his mind. He gave it up and merely said:

"Madrid."

"Yes."

"I wanted to get there, and that's the truth. But it couldn't be fixed."

A gloomy look came over his face, and he said: "Wait a moment," and he slid a finger over the stamp.

"All right. You can have it."

"Thanks."

Mathieu began to walk on, but the man shouted after him.

"Well?" said Mathieu. The man was holding up the five-franc piece:

"Some guy has just slipped me a five-franc piece. I'll stand you a rum."

"Not this evening."

Mathieu moved off with a vague sense of regret. There had been a time in his life when he had strolled about the city and haunted bars in any sort of company, with anyone who cared to ask him. Now it was all over; that game never paid. The fellow had looked decent enough. He had wanted to fight in Spain. Mathieu quickened his step, and he thought irritably: "Anyway, we hadn't anything to talk about." He took the green card out of his pocket. "It comes from Madrid, but it isn't addressed to him. Somebody must have passed it on to him. He kept on fingering it before giving it to me, just because it came from Madrid." He recalled the man's face and the look with which he had eyed the stamp: an oddly ardent look. Mathieu in his turn eyed the stamp as he walked on, and then put the bit of cardboard back in his pocket. A railway engine whistled, and Mathieu thought: "I'm getting old."

It was twenty-five minutes past ten; Mathieu was early. Without stopping, without even turning his head, he passed the little blue house. But he looked at it out of the corner of his eye. All the windows were dark except in Mme Duffet's room. Marcelle hadn't yet had time to open the outer door: she was leaning over her mother, and those masculine hands of hers were tucking her up into the great canopied bed. Mathieu still felt gloomy; the thought in his mind was: "Five hundred francs until the 29th—thirty francs a day, or rather less. How shall I manage?" He swung round and retraced his steps.

The light had gone out in Mme Duffet's room. In a moment or two the light went up in Marcelle's window.

Mathieu crossed the road and slipped past the grocer's shop, trying to prevent his new shoes from squeaking. The door was ajar; he pushed it very gently and it creaked. "I'll bring my oilcan on Wednesday and drop a little oil into the hinges." He went in, closed the door, and took his shoes off in the darkness. The stairs creaked faintly: Mathieu walked cautiously upstairs, shoes in hand, testing each step with his toe before putting his foot down. "What a farce!" he thought.

Marcelle opened her door before he had reached the landing. A pink iris-scented haze from her room pervaded the staircase. She was wearing her green chemise. Through it Mathieu could see the soft rich curve of her hips. He went in: he always felt as though he were entering a huge sea-shell. Marcelle locked the door. Mathieu made his way to the large wall cupboard, opened it, and put his shoes inside; then he looked at Marcelle and saw that there was something the matter.

"What's wrong?" he asked in a low tone.

"Nothing," said Marcelle under her breath. "Are you all right, old boy?"

"I'm broke; otherwise all right."

He kissed her on the neck and on the lips. Her neck smelt of ambergris, her mouth smelt of cheap cigarettes. Marcelle sat down on the edge of the bed and gazed at her legs while Mathieu undressed.

"What's that?" asked Mathieu.

There was an unfamiliar photograph on the mantelpiece. He went up to look at it and saw an angular girl, wearing her hair cut like a boy's and a hard, nervous smile. She was dressed in a man's jacket and flat-heeled shoes.

"It's me," said Marcelle without raising her head.

Mathieu turned round: Marcelle had pulled her chemise up over her fleshy thighs: she was leaning forward and beneath her chemise Mathieu caught the soft outlines of her rounded breasts.

"Where did you find it?"

"In an album. It was taken in 1928."

Mathieu carefully folded up his jacket and put it in the cupboard beside his shoes. Then he asked:

"Do you still look at family albums?"

"No, but I had a sort of feeling today that I'd like to remind myself of those times and see what I was like before I knew you and when I was always well. Bring it here."

Mathieu brought it to her and she snatched it out of his hands. He sat down beside her. She shivered and drew back, eying the photograph with a vague smile.

"I *was* a scream in those days," she said.

The girl was standing stiffly upright, leaning against a garden railing. Her mouth was open; she too was just about to say: "It's a scream," with the pert assurance of the Marcelle of today. But—she was young and slim.

Marcelle shook her head.

"Such a scream! It was taken in the Luxembourg by a chemistry student. You see the blouse I'm wearing? I'd bought it that very day, for a trip to Fontainebleau we had fixed for the following Sunday. Good Lord! . . ."

There was certainly something wrong: her gestures had never been so brusque, nor her voice so curt and masculine. She was sitting on the edge of the bed, blankly naked and defenseless, like a great porcelain vase in that dim pink room, and it was almost painful to hear her speak in that masculine voice, and smell the dark, strong odor of her body. Mathieu grasped her shoulders and drew her towards him.

"Do you regret those days?"

"No," replied Marcelle acidly; "but I regret the life I might have had."

She had begun to study chemistry, and had to give it up owing to illness. "One would think she bears me a grudge for it," thought Mathieu. He opened his mouth to ask her some more questions, but caught her express'on and was silent. She was gazing at the photograph with a sad, intense expression.

"I've got fatter, haven't I?"

"Yes."

She shrugged her shoulders and flung the photograph on the bed. "It's true," thought Mathieu, "she's had a rather rotten life." He tried to kiss her on the cheek, but she drew back, quite gently, laughed nervously, and said:

"That's ten years ago."

And Mathieu thought: "I give her nothing." He came to see her four nights a week; he told her all his doings in the minutest detail. She gave him advice, in a grave and slightly maternal tone. She often used to say: "I live by proxy."

"What did you do yesterday?" he asked her. "Did you go out?"

Marcelle waved her hand wearily and answered: "No, I was tired. I read for a while, but Mother kept on interrupting me about the shop."

"And today?"

"I did go out today," said she gloomily. "I felt I ought to get some air and see some people in the street. So I walked down as far as the rue de la Gaîté, and enjoyed it; and I wanted to see Andrée."

"And did you?"

"Yes, for five minutes. Just as I was leaving her, it began to rain; it's a funny sort of day for June, and besides the people looked so hideous. So I took a taxi and came home. What did you do?" she asked nonchalantly.

Mathieu didn't want to tell her. "Yesterday," he said, "I took my last classes at the school. I dined with Jacques, which was as boring as usual. This morning I went to the bursar's office to see if they couldn't advance me something, but apparently it's not done. When I was at Beauvais

I always managed to fix it with the bursar. Then I saw Ivich."

Marcelle raised her eyebrows and looked at him. He didn't like talking to her about Ivich.

He added: "She's a bit under the weather just now."

"Why?"

Marcelle's voice was steadier, and a sage, masculine sort of look had come into her face. He said with lips half-closed:

"She'll flunk her exam."

"But you told me she'd been working hard."

"Well—I dare say she has, in her own way—that is, she no doubt sits for hours over a book. But you know what she's like. She has visions, almost like a lunatic. In October she was well up in botany, and the examiner was quite satisfied; and then she suddenly *saw* herself opposite a bald chap who was talking about Cœlenterata. This seemed to her just funny, and she thought: 'I don't give a damn for Cœlenterata,' and the chap couldn't get another word out of her."

"What an odd little creature she must be," said Marcelle dreamily.

"Anyway," said Mathieu, "I'm afraid she may do it again, or get some fantastic idea into her head."

His tone, which suggested a sort of protective detachment, was surely intended to mislead. Everything that could be expressed in words, he said. "But what are words?"

He paused, then hung his head despondently. Marcelle was well aware of his affection for Ivich; she would not in fact have minded if he had been her lover. On one thing only she insisted—that he should talk about Ivich in just that tone. Mathieu had kept on stroking Marcelle's back, and her eyelids began to droop; she liked having her back stroked, particularly at the level of her hips and between the shoulder-blades. But she suddenly drew back and her face hardened as Mathieu said:

"Look here, Marcelle, I don't care if Ivich is dropped, she isn't suited to be a doctor any more than I am. In any case, even if she passed the P.C.B., her first dissection would so revolt her that she would never set foot in the place again. But if it doesn't come off this time, she'll do some damn-fool thing. If she fails, her family won't let her start again."

"Just what kind of damn-fool thing do you mean?" Marcelle asked in a precise tone.

"I don't know," he replied, utterly at a loss.

"Ah, I know you only too well, my poor boy. You daren't admit it, but you're afraid that she'll put a bullet through her skin. And the creature pretends to loathe anything romantic. One really might suppose you'd never seen that skin of hers. I wouldn't dare touch it, for fear of scratching it. A doll with a skin like that isn't going to mess it up with a revolver-shot. I can quite well picture her prostrate on a chair with her hair all over her face, glaring at a neat little Browning in front of her, in the best Russian manner. But anything more—not on your life! Revolvers are meant for crocodile-skins like ours."

She laid her arms against Mathieu's. He had a whiter skin than hers.

"Just look, darling—especially at mine; it's like morocco leather." And she began to laugh. "I would puncture rather well, don't you think? I can picture a nice little round hole under my left breast, with neat, clean, red edges. It wouldn't be at all disfiguring."

She was still laughing. Mathieu laid a hand over her mouth.

"Be quiet, you'll waken the old lady."

She was silent, and he said:

"How nervous you are!"

She did not answer. Mathieu laid a hand on Marcelle's

leg and stroked it gently. He loved that soft and buttery skin, its silky down that sent a thousand delicate tremors through his fingers. Marcelle did not move: she looked at Mathieu's hand. And after a while Mathieu took his hand away.

"Look at me," he said.

For an instant he saw her circled eyes, and in them a flash of haughty desperation.

"What's the matter?"

"Nothing," she said, turning her head away.

It was always like that with her: she was emotionally constricted. The moment would come when she couldn't contain herself: then she would blurt it out. The only thing to do was to mark time until that moment did come. Mathieu dreaded those noiseless explosions: the whispered caution with which passion had to be expressed in that sea-shell room, in order not to awaken Mme Duffet, had always revolted him. Mathieu got up, walked to the cupboard, and took the square of cardboard out of his jacket pocket.

"Look at this."

"What is it?"

"A fellow gave it to me in the street not long ago. He looked like a decent sort, and I gave him a little money."

Marcelle took the card with an indifferent air. Mathieu felt a tie of something like complicity between himself and the fellow in the street. And he added: "It meant something to him, you know."

"Was he an anarchist?"

"I don't know. He wanted to stand me a drink."

"Did you refuse it?"

"Yes."

"Why?" asked Marcelle casually. "You might have found him amusing."

"Pah!" said Mathieu.

Marcelle raised her head and peered at the clock with a half smile.

"It's curious," she said, "but I hate you to tell me things like that; and God knows there are enough of them at the moment. Your life is full of missed opportunities."

"You call that a missed opportunity?"

"Yes. There was a time when you would go out of your way to meet such people."

"I dare say I've changed a bit," said Mathieu, good-humoredly. "What do you think? Am I getting old?"

"You're thirty-four," said Marcelle soberly.

Thirty-four. Mathieu thought of Ivich and was conscious of a slight shock of annoyance.

"Yes. . . . But I don't think it's age; it's a sort of fastidiousness. I wouldn't have been in the mood."

"You very seldom are, nowadays," said Marcelle.

"And he wouldn't have been either," added Mathieu briskly. "When a man gets drunk he gets sentimental. That's what I wanted to avoid."

And he thought: "That isn't altogether true. I didn't really look at it like that." He wanted to make an effort to be sincere. Mathieu and Marcelle had agreed that they would always tell each other everything.

"The fact is—" he began.

But Marcelle had begun to laugh—a low, rich, cooing laugh, as though she were stroking his hair and saying: "Poor old boy." But she did not look at all affectionate.

"That's very like you," said she. "You're so afraid of anything sentimental! Supposing you had got a little sentimental with that poor chap, would it have mattered?"

"Well, it wouldn't have done me any good."

He was trying to defend himself against himself.

Marcelle smiled a frosty smile. "She wants to draw me out," thought Mathieu, rather disconcerted. He was feeling peaceably inclined and puzzled; he was, in fact, in a good temper and didn't want an argument.

"Look here," said he. "You're wrong to catch me up like this. In the first place, I hadn't the time. I was on my way here."

"You're quite right," said Marcelle. "It's nothing. Absolutely nothing, really; not enough to get a cat into trouble. . . . But all the same it's symptomatic."

Mathieu started: if only she wouldn't use such tiresome words.

"Really, really," he said. "I can't imagine why it should interest you."

"Well, it's that same lucidity you fuss about so much. You're so absurdly scared of being your own dupe, my poor boy, that you would back out of the finest adventure in the world rather than risk telling yourself a lie."

"Quite true, and you know it," said Mathieu. "But that's an old story."

He thought her unfair. "Lucidity"—he detested the word, but Marcelle had acquired it some while back. The winter before, it had been "urgency" (words did not last her for much more than a season), they had grown into the habit of it together, they felt mutually responsible for maintaining it—indeed, it was, actually, the inner meaning of their love. When Mathieu had pledged himself to Marcelle, he had forever renounced all thoughts of solitude, those cool thoughts, a little shadowy and timorous, that used to dart into his mind with the furtive vivacity of fish. He could not love Marcelle save in complete lucidity: she *was* his lucidity embodied, his comrade, his witness, his counselor, and his critic.

"If I lied to myself," said he, "I should have the feeling I was lying to you as well. And I couldn't bear that."

"Yes," said Marcelle; but she did not look as if she believed him.

"You don't look as if you believed me."

"Oh yes I do," she said nonchalantly.

"You think I'm lying to myself?"

"No—anyway, one can't ever know. But I don't think so. Still, do you know what I do believe? That you are beginning to sterilize yourself a little. I thought that to-day. Everything is so neat and tidy in your mind; it smells of clean linen; it's as though you had just come out of a drying-room. But there's a want of shade. There's nothing useless, or hesitant, or underhand about you now. It's all high noon. And don't tell me this is all for my benefit. You're moving down your own incline; you've acquired the taste for self-analysis."

Mathieu was disconcerted. Marcelle was often rather hard; she remained always on guard, a little aggressive, a little suspicious, and if Mathieu didn't agree with her, she often thought he was trying to dominate her. But he had rarely met her in such a resolve to be disagreeable. And then there was that photo on the bed. He eyed Marcelle: the moment had not yet come when she could be induced to speak.

"I'm not so much interested in myself as all that," he said simply.

"I know," said Marcelle. "It isn't an aim, it's a means. It helps you to get rid of yourself; to contemplate and criticize yourself: that's the attitude you prefer. When you look at yourself, you imagine you aren't what you see, you imagine you are nothing. That is your ideal: you want to be nothing."

"To be nothing?" repeated Mathieu slowly. "No, it isn't. Listen. I—I recognize no allegiance except to myself."

"Yes—you want to be free. Absolutely free. It's your vice."

"It's not a vice," said Mathieu. "It's—what else can a man do?"

He was annoyed: he had explained all this to Marcelle a hundred times before, and she knew it was what he had most at heart.

"If I didn't try to assume responsibility for my own existence, it would seem utterly absurd to go on existing."

A look of smiling obstinacy had come into Marcelle's face.

"Yes, yes—it's your vice."

Mathieu thought: "She gets on my nerves when she puts on a coy act." But he repressed this and said merely:

"It's not a vice. It's how I'm *made*."

"Why aren't other people made like that, if it isn't a vice?"

"They are, only they don't know it."

Marcelle had stopped smiling, and a hard, grim line appeared at the corner of her lips.

"Well, I don't feel such a need to be free."

Mathieu eyed her bent neck and felt troubled: it was always this sense of remorse, absurd remorse, that haunted him in her company. He realized that he would never be able to put himself in Marcelle's place. "The freedom I talk about is the freedom of a sound and healthy man." He laid a hand on her neck and gently squeezed the luscious but no longer youthful flesh.

"Marcelle, are you feeling bored with life?"

She looked at him with faintly troubled eyes.

"No."

Silence fell. Mathieu felt a thrill at the tips of his fingers. Just at the tips of his fingers. He passed his hand slowly down Marcelle's back, and Marcelle's eyelids drooped; he could see her long black lashes. He drew her towards him. He had no actual desire for her at that moment, it was rather a longing to see that stubborn, angular spirit melt like an icicle in the sunshine. Marcelle let her head fall on Mathieu's shoulder, and he could see only too clearly her brown skin and the bluish, veined curves beneath her eyes. And he thought: "Good Lord, she's getting old." And he reflected, too, that he was old. He leaned over her with a feeling of uneasiness: he wished he could forget himself, and her. But time had passed since he forgot himself when making love to her. He kissed her on the lips; she had fine lips, firm and sharply cut. She slid gently backwards and lay on the bed with eyes closed, limp and prostrate. Mathieu got up, took off his trousers and his shirt, folded them up and placed them at the foot of the bed, and then lay down beside her. But he noticed that her eyes were wide and set, she was staring at the ceiling with her hands clasped beneath her head.

"Marcelle," he said.

She did not answer; there was a hard look in her eyes; and then she sat up abruptly. He sat down once more on the edge of the bed, irked by his own nakedness.

"You must now tell me what's the matter."

"There's nothing the matter," she said in a toneless voice.

"Yes, there is," he said affectionately. "There's something on your mind. Marcelle, didn't we agree to be quite frank with each other?"

"You can't do anything about it, and it will only upset you."

He stroked her hair lightly.

"Never mind, tell me all the same."

"Well, it's happened."

"What's happened?"

"*It* has happened!"

Mathieu made a wry face.

"Are you sure?"

"Quite sure. You know I never get panicky: I'm two months late."

"Hell!" said Mathieu.

And he thought: "She ought to have told me at least three weeks ago." He felt he must do something with his hands—fill his pipe, for instance; but his pipe was in the cupboard with his jacket. He took a cigarette from the night-table and put it down again.

"There, now you know what's the matter," said Marcelle. "What's to be done?"

"Well—I suppose one gets rid of it, eh?"

"Right. I've got an address," said Marcelle.

"Who gave it to you?"

"Andrée. She's been there."

"That old woman who messed her up last year? Why, it was six months before she was well again. I won't allow that."

"So you want to be a father?"

She drew back and sat down a little way from Mathieu. There was a hard look in her eyes, but it wasn't a masculine look. She had laid her hands flat on her thighs, her arms looked like the twin handles of an earthenware jar. Mathieu noticed that her face had grown gray. The air was pink and sickly; it smelt and tasted pink; her face was gray and set, and she looked as though she were trying to stifle a cough.

"Wait," said Mathieu, "you've rather sprung this on me; we must think."

Marcelle's hands began to quiver, and she said with sudden vehemence:

"I don't want you to think—it's not for you to think."

She had turned her head towards him and was looking at him. She looked at Mathieu's neck, shoulders, and hips and then lower down, with an air of astonishment. Mathieu blushed violently and set his legs together.

"You can't do anything," repeated Marcelle. And she added with painful irony: "It's a woman's business now."

Her mouth snapped out the last words: a varnished mauve-tinted mouth, like a crimson insect intent upon devouring that ashen visage. "She's feeling humiliated," thought Mathieu, "she hates me." He felt sick. The room seemed suddenly cleared of its pink haze; there were great blank spaces between the objects it contained. And Mathieu thought: "It is I who have done *this* to her!" The lamp, the mirror with its leaden reflections, the clock on the mantelpiece, the armchair, the half-opened wardrobe suddenly appeared to him like pitiless mechanisms, adrift and pursuing their tenuous existences in the void, rigidly insistent, like the under side of a gramophone record obstinately grinding out its tune. Mathieu shook himself, but could not detach himself from that sinister, raucous world. Marcelle had not moved, she was still looking at Mathieu's naked body and the guilty flower that lay so delicately on his thighs with a bland air of innocence. He knew she wanted to scream and sob, but she would not, for fear of waking Mme Duffet. He gripped Marcelle round the waist and drew her towards him. She collapsed on his shoulder, sobbed a little, but she did not cry. It was all that she could allow herself: a rainless storm.

When she raised her head, she was calmer. She said in an emphatic tone:

"Forgive me, darling, I needed to explode. I've been holding myself in all day. I'm not blaming you, of course."

"Quite natural," said Mathieu. "I feel bad about this. It's the first time . . . Oh Lord, what a mess! I've done this damn-fool thing and you're the one that has to pay. Well, it's happened, and that's that. Look here, who is this old woman, and where does she live?"

"Twenty-four rue Morère. I'm told she's an odd old party."

"I believe you. Are you going to say that Andrée sent you?"

"Yes. She only charges four hundred francs. I'm told that's absurdly cheap," said Marcelle in a suddenly even tone.

"Yes, I realize that," said Mathieu bitterly. "In short, it's a bargain."

He felt as awkward as a newly accepted suitor. A tall awkward fellow, completely naked, who had done something he should not, and was smiling amiably in the hope he might be overlooked. But it wasn't possible; she saw his white, sinewy, stocky thighs, his complacent and uncompromising nudity. It was a grotesque nightmare. "If I were her, I should want to get my nails into all that meat." He said:

"That's just exactly what worries me: she doesn't charge enough."

"My dear," said Marcelle, "it's lucky she asks so little: as it happens, I've got the four hundred francs. They were earmarked for my dressmaker, but she'll wait. And," she went on emphatically, "I'm perfectly certain I shall be looked after just as well as in one of those discreet clinics where they charge you four thousand francs as soon as look at you. Anyhow, we can't help ourselves."

"No, we can't help ourselves," repeated Mathieu. "When will you go?"

"Tomorrow, about midnight. I gather she only sees people at night. Rather a scream, isn't it? I think she's a bit cracked myself, but it suits me all right, on mother's account. She keeps a dry-goods shop in the daytime, and she hardly ever sleeps. You go in by a yard, and you see a light under a door—that's where it is."

"Right," said Mathieu. "I'll go."

Marcelle eyed him in amazement.

"Are you crazy? She'll shut the door in your face, she'll take you for a policeman."

"I shall go," repeated Mathieu.

"But why? What will you say to her?"

"I want to get a notion of what sort of place it is. If I don't like it, you shan't go. I won't have you messed up by some old harridan. I'll say that I've come from Andrée, that I've got a girl friend who's in trouble, but down with influenza at the moment—something of that kind."

"But where shall I go if it won't do?"

"We've got a few days to turn round in, haven't we? I'll
go and see Sarah tomorrow, she's sure to know somebody.
They didn't want any children at first, you remember."

Marcelle's excitement subsided a little, and she stroked
his neck.

"You're being very nice to me, darling. I'm not quite sure
what you're up to, but I understand that you want to do
something; perhaps you'd like her to operate on you instead of me?" She clasped her lovely arms round his neck
and added in a tone of comic resignation: "Anyone recommended by Sarah is sure to be a Yid."

Mathieu kissed her and she dimpled all over.

"Darling," she said. "Oh, darling!"

"Take off your slip."

She obeyed; he tipped her backwards on the bed and
began to caress her breasts. He loved their taut, leathery
nipples, each in its ring of raised red flesh. Marcelle sighed,
with eyes closed, passionate and eager. But her eyelids
were contracted. The dread thing lingered, laid like a
damp hand on Mathieu. Then, suddenly, the thought came
into Mathieu's mind: "She's pregnant." He sat up, his head
still buzzing with a shrill refrain.

"Look here, Marcelle, it's no good today. We're both of
us too upset. I'm sorry."

Marcelle uttered a sleepy little grunt, then got up
abruptly and began to rumple her hair with both hands.

"Just as you like," she said coldly. Then she added, more
amiably: "As a matter of fact, you're right, we're too upset. I wanted you to love me, but I was a bit frightened."

"Alas," said Mathieu, "the deed is done, we have nothing more to fear."

"I know, but I wasn't thinking sensibly. I don't know
how to tell you: but I'm rather afraid of you, darling."

Mathieu got up.

"Good. Well then, I'll go and see this old woman."

"Yes. And you might telephone me tomorrow and tell me what you thought of her."

"Can't I see you tomorrow evening? That would be simpler."

"No, not tomorrow evening. The day after, if you like."

Mathieu had put on his shirt and trousers. He kissed Marcelle on the eyes. "You aren't angry with me?"

"It isn't your fault. It's the first time in seven years, you needn't blame yourself. And you aren't sick of me, I hope?"

"Don't be silly."

"Well, I'm getting rather sick of myself, to tell the truth; I feel like a great heap of dough."

"My darling," said Mathieu, "my poor darling. It will all be put right in a week, I promise you."

He opened the door noiselessly and glided out, holding his shoes in his hand. On the landing he turned. Marcelle was still sitting on the bed. She smiled at him, but Mathieu had the feeling that she bore him a grudge.

The tension in his set eyes was now released and they revolved with normal ease and freedom in their orbits: she was no longer looking at him, and he owed her no account of his expression. Concealed by his dark garments and the night, his guilty flesh had found its needed shelter, it was gradually recovering its native warmth and innocence, and began to expand beneath its covering fabrics; the oilcan, how on earth was he going to remember to bring the oilcan the day after tomorrow? He was alone.

He stopped, transfixed: it wasn't true, he wasn't alone. Marcelle had not let him go: she was thinking of him, and this was what she thought: "The dirty dog, he's let me down. He forgot himself inside me like a little boy who wets his bed." It was no use striding along the dark, deserted street, anonymous, enveloped in his garments; he could not escape her. Marcelle's consciousness remained, full of woe and lamentation, and Mathieu had not left her: he was there, in the pink room, naked and defenseless against that crass transparency, so much more baffling than a look. "Only once," he said savagely to himself, and he repeated in an undertone, to convince Marcelle: "once, in seven years!" Marcelle refused to be convinced; she remained in the room and was thinking of Mathieu. It was intolerable to be judged, and hated, away back in that room, and in silence. Without power to defend himself, or even to hide his belly with his hands. If only, in the same second, he had been able to exist *for others* with the same intensity. . . . But Jacques and Odette were asleep. Daniel was drunk or in a stupor. Ivich never remembered people when they were not there. Boris perhaps. . . . But Boris's consciousness was no more than a dim flicker, it could not contend against that savage, stark lucidity which fascinated Mathieu from a distance. Night had engulfed most human consciousness: Mathieu was alone with Marcelle in the night, just the two of them.

There was a light at Camus's place. The proprietor was stacking the chairs; the waitress was fixing a wooden shutter against one side of the double door. Mathieu pushed open the other side and went in. He felt the need of being seen. Just to be seen. He planted his elbows on the counter.

"Good evening, everybody."

The proprietor saw him. There was also a bus-conductor, drinking an absinthe, his cap pulled down over his eyes. Two kindly, casual consciousnesses. The conductor jerked his cap back and looked at Mathieu. Marcelle's consciousness released him and dissolved into the night.

"Give me a beer."

"You're quite a stranger," said the proprietor.

"It isn't for want of being thirsty."

"Yes, it's thirsty weather," said the bus-conductor. "It might be midsummer."

They fell silent. The proprietor went on rinsing glasses,

the conductor whistled to himself. Mathieu felt at ease because they looked at him from time to time. He saw his head in the glass, a ghastly globe emerging from a sea of silver: at Camus's one always had the feeling that it was four in the morning, which was an effect of the light, a silvered haze that strained the eyes and bleached the drinkers' faces, hands, and thoughts. He drank; and he thought: "She's pregnant. It's fantastic; I can't feel it's true." It seemed to him shocking and grotesque, like the sight of an old man kissing an old woman on the lips: after seven years that sort of thing shouldn't happen. "She's pregnant"—there was a little vitreous tide within her, slowly swelling into the semblance of an eye. "It's opening out among all the muck inside her belly, it's alive." He saw a long pin moving hesitantly forward in the half-darkness; there was a muffled sound, the eye cracked and burst: nothing was left but an opaque, dry membrane. "She'll go to that old woman; she'll get herself messed up." He felt venomous. "All right, let her go." He shook himself: these were bleak thoughts, four a.m. thoughts.

"Good night."

He paid and went.

"What did I do?" He walked slowly, trying to remember. "Two months ago . . ." He couldn't remember anything. Yes, it must have been the day after the Easter holidays. He had taken Marcelle in his arms, as usual, in affection no doubt, rather than with any feeling of desire; and now . . . he'd got stung. "A baby. I meant to give her pleasure, and I've given her a baby. I didn't understand what I was doing. Neither in destroying nor in creating life did I know what I was doing." He laughed a short, dry laugh. "And what about the others? Those who have solemnly decided to become fathers and feel progenitively inclined when they look at their wives' bodies—do they understand any more than I do? They go blindly on—three flicks of a duck's tail. What follows is a gelatinous job done in a dark room, like photography. They have no part in it." He entered a yard and saw a light under a door. "It's here." He felt ashamed.

Mathieu knocked.

"What is it?" said a voice.

"I want to speak to you."

"This isn't a time to visit people."

"I have a message from Andrée Besnier."

The door opened slightly. Mathieu saw a wisp of yellow hair and a large nose.

"What do you want? Don't try to pull any police stuff on me, it's no good, everything's in order here. I can have the light on all night if I like. If you're an inspector, show me your card."

"I'm not from the police," said Mathieu. "I'm in a fix. And I was given your name."

"Come in."

Mathieu went in. The old woman was wearing trousers and a blouse with a zip fastener. She was very thin, and her eyes were set and hard.

"You know Andrée Besnier?"

She eyed him grimly.

"Yes," said Mathieu. "She came to see you last year about Christmas-time because she was in trouble; she was rather ill, and you came four times to give her treatment."

"Well?"

Mathieu looked at the old woman's hands. They were a man's hands, a strangler's hands, furrowed, cracked, with broken nails, and black with scars and gashes. On the first joint of the left thumb there were some purple warts and a large black scab. Mathieu shuddered as he thought of Marcelle's soft brown flesh.

"I've not come on her account," he said. "I've come for one of her friends."

The old woman laughed dryly. "It's the first time that

a man has had the cheek to turn up on my doorstep. I won't have any dealings with men, let me tell you that."

The room was dirty and in disorder. There were boxes everywhere and straw on the tiled floor. On a table Mathieu noticed a bottle of rum and a half-filled glass.

"I've come because my friend sent me. She can't come today, and she asked me to fix up a date."

At the other end of the room a door stood half-open. Mathieu could have sworn there was someone behind that door.

"Poor kids," said the old woman. "They're too silly. I've only got to look at you to see that you're born unlucky— you're the sort that upsets glasses and smashes mirrors. And women trust you. Well, they get what they deserve."

Mathieu remained polite.

"I should have liked to see where you operate."

The old woman flung him a baleful and suspicious look.

"Look here! Who told you that I operate? What are you talking about? Mind your own business. If your friend wants to see me, let her come herself. I won't deal with anyone else. You want to make inquiries, do you? Did she make any inquiries before she got into your grip? You've had an accident. All right. Then let us hope I shall be better at my job than you were at yours; that's all I have to say. Good night."

"Good night, madame," said Mathieu.

He went out, with a sense of deliverance. He turned, and walked slowly towards the avenue d'Orléans; for the first time since he had left her, he could think of Marcelle without pain, without horror, and with a sort of tender melancholy. "I'll go and see Sarah tomorrow," he said to himself.

# CHAPTER II

Boris eyed the red-checked tablecloth and thought of Mathieu Delarue. "He's a good chap." The orchestra was silent, the air was blue, and there was a buzz of talk. Boris knew everybody in the narrow little room: they weren't people who came for a good time; they came along together after their jobs were done, quietly and in need of food. The Negro opposite Lola was the singer from the Paradise; the six fellows at the far end with their girls were the band from the Nénette. Something had certainly happened to them, they had had a bit of unexpected luck, perhaps an engagement for the summer (they had been talking vaguely the evening before last about a cabaret at Constantinople), because they had ordered champagne, and they were usually pretty careful. Boris also noticed the fair-haired girl who danced in sailor's costume at the Java. The tall emaciated man in spectacles smoking a cigar was the manager of a cabaret in the rue Tholozé that had just been shut by the police. He said it would soon be reopened, as he had influence in high places. Boris bitterly regretted never having been there, he would certainly go if it reopened. The man was with a pansy who looked rather attractive from a distance, a fair-haired lad with delicate features, devoid of the usual mincing airs, and not without charm. Boris hadn't much use for homosexuals, because they always were pursuing him, but Ivich rather liked them; she said: "Well, at any rate they've got the courage not to be like everybody else." Boris had great respect for his sister's opinions, and he made the most conscientious efforts to think well of fairies. The Negro was eating a dish of sauerkraut, and Boris reflected that he didn't like sauerkraut. He wished he knew the name of the dish that had just been brought to the dancer from the Java: a brown mess that looked good. There was a stain of red wine on the tablecloth. An elegant stain, which gave the cloth a satiny sheen in just that place. Lola had spread a little salt on the stain, being a careful woman. The salt was pink. It isn't true that the salt soaks up stains. He ought to tell Lola that it didn't. But he would have had to speak, and Boris felt he could not speak. Lola was beside him, soft and very warm, and Boris could not bring himself to utter the slightest word, his voice was dead. "Just as though I were dumb." It was delicious, his voice was floating at the far end of his throat, soft as cotton, and could not emerge, for it was dead. "I like Delarue," thought Boris, and felt glad. He would have been even more glad if he had not been conscious, all down his right side, from head to hip, that Lola was looking at him. It would certainly be a passionate look, for Lola could scarcely look at him in any other way. It was rather annoying, for passionate looks demand the acknowledgment of a friendly gesture or a smile; and Boris couldn't have made the slightest movement. He was paralyzed. But it didn't really matter: he couldn't be supposed to have noticed Lola's look; he guessed it, but that was his affair. Sitting sideways, with his hair in his eyes, he couldn't get a glimpse of Lola, he could perfectly well suppose that she was looking at the room and the people. Boris didn't feel sleepy; indeed, he was in an excellent humor, as he knew everybody in the room; he noticed the Negro's pink tongue; Boris had a high opinion of that Negro: on one occasion the Negro had taken his shoes off, picked up a box of matches with his toes, opened it, extracted a match, and lit it, all with his toes. "He's a grand chap," thought Boris with admiration. "Everyone ought to be able to use his feet just like his hands." He had a pain in his right side as a consequence of being looked at: he knew that the moment was near when Lola would ask him what he was thinking about. It was absolutely impossible to delay that question, it didn't depend on him: Lola would ask it in due time, with a kind of fatality. Boris felt as though he had at his disposal a small but infinitely precious fraction of time. As a matter of fact, it was rather a pleasant sensation. Boris saw the tablecloth, he saw Lola's glass (Lola had had supper; she never dined before her singing act). She had drunk some Château Gruau, she did herself well, and indulged in a few caprices because she was so terrified of growing old. There was still a little wine in the glass, which looked like dusty blood. The jazz band began to play: *The Moon is Turning Green* and Boris found himself wondering if he could sing that song. He fancied himself strolling down the rue Pigalle in the moonlight, whistling a little tune. Delarue had told him that he whistled like a pig. Boris began to laugh silently, and thought: "Blast the fellow!" He was brimming with affection for Mathieu. He peered out of the corner of his eye, without turning around, and he saw Lola's heavy eyes beneath a luxurious tress of auburn hair. As a matter of fact, it was quite easy to withstand a look. The trouble was to get used to that special sort of ardent emanation which sets your face aflame when someone is watching you with passion in her eyes. Boris submissively yielded to Lola's observing eyes—his body, his slim neck, and the half-profile that she loved so much; this done, he could take refuge in the depths of his own self and savor the agreeable little thoughts that came into his mind.

"What are you thinking about?" asked Lola.

"Nothing."

"One is always thinking of something."

"I was thinking of nothing."

"Not even that you like the tune they are playing, or that you wished you could play the castanets?"

"Yes—things like that."

"There you are. Why don't you tell me? I want to know everything you think."

"They're not things one can talk about, they're too trivial."

"Trivial! One might suppose that your tongue had been given you simply to talk philosophy with your prof."

He looked at her and smiled. "I like her because she's got red hair and looks rather old."

"Funny kid," said Lola.

Boris blinked and assumed a pleading air. He didn't like people talking about himself; it was always so complicated, and he became bewildered. Lola looked as if she was angry, but it was simply because she loved him passionately and tormented herself about him. There were moments when it was more than she could bear, she would lose her temper for no reason and glare at Boris, not knowing how to take him, and her hands began to quiver. All this used to surprise Boris, but he was accustomed to it by this time. Lola laid her hand on Boris's head.

"I wonder what's inside it," she said. "I feel quite frightened sometimes."

"You needn't. All quite harmless, I assure you," said Boris laughing.

"Yes, those thoughts of yours are just so many ways of getting away from me." And she ruffled his hair.

"Don't," said Boris. "Please don't uncover my forehead."

He took her hand, stroked it for a minute or two, and laid it back on the table.

"You are there, and quite affectionate," said Lola. "I begin to think you're really fond of me, and then, suddenly, no one's there at all, and I wonder where you've gone."

"I'm here."

Lola eyed him narrowly. Her pallid face was marred by the sort of dewy, sentimental expression she assumed when singing *Les Écorchés*. She thrust out her lips, those large, drooping lips that he had at first loved so much. Since he had felt them on his mouth, they gave him the sense of a clammy, feverish nakedness set in the center of a plaster mask. At present he preferred Lola's skin, so white that it did not look real.

"You—you aren't fed up with me?" Lola asked timidly.

"I'm never fed up."

Lola sighed, and Boris thought with satisfaction: "It's fantastic how old she looks; she doesn't tell her age, but she must be well over forty." He preferred that people who liked him should look old, he found it reassuring. Added to which, it gave them a sort of awesomely fragile air, not apparent at the first encounter, because they all had leathery skins. He felt an impulse to kiss Lola's puzzled face, he said to himself that her day was done, that she had thrown away her life and was now alone, even more so perhaps since she had fallen in love with him. "I can't do anything for her," he thought with resignation. And he found her, in that thought, irresistibly attractive.

"I'm ashamed," said Lola.

Her voice was heavy and somber, like a red velvet curtain.

"Why?"

"Because you're such a kid."

"I like to hear you say the word—kid," said he. "It suits your voice. You say it twice in the *Écorchés* song, and I'd go and hear you just for that. Were there a lot of people tonight?"

"A moldy crowd. I don't know where they came from—they just sat and chattered. And they hadn't any use for me at all. Sarrunyan had to ask them to keep quiet; it got on my nerves, I felt like an eavesdropper. They cheered when I came in, though."

"That's normal."

"Well, I'm fed up," said Lola. "I loathe singing for fools of that kind. They were the sort who came there because they've got to return a family invitation. I wish you could see them come in together, all smiles. They bow, and they hold the good lady's chair while she sits down. So really you're interrupting them, and they just glare at you when you come along. Boris—" said Lola abruptly, "I sing for my living."

"That's so."

"If I'd thought I should finish like that, I would never have started."

"Well, however you look at it, when you sang at music halls, you earned your living by singing."

"That wasn't the same."

After a short silence Lola added hurriedly:

"By the way, this evening I talked to the new little chap who sings next after me. He's a very decent fellow, but he's no more Russian than I am."

"She thinks she's annoying me," thought Boris. He resolved to tell her once for all that she never could annoy him. Not today, but later on.

"Perhaps he has learned Russian."

"But you ought to be able to tell me if he has a good accent," said Lola.

"My parents left Russia in '17, when I was three months old."

"It's funny that you shouldn't know Russian," observed Lola with a pensive air.

"She's fantastic," thought Boris. "She's ashamed of being in love with me because she's older than I am. It seems perfectly natural to me—after all, one party must be older than the other." Above all, it was more moral: Boris wouldn't have known how to treat a girl of his own age. If both parties are young, they don't know how to behave, they muddle about and it always seems like playing house. With older people, it's quite different. They're reliable, they show you what to do, and there's solidity in their affection. When Boris was with Lola, he had the approval of his conscience, he felt himself justified. Of course he preferred Mathieu's company because Mathieu wasn't a girl: a man was more intriguing all the time. Besides, Mathieu taught him all sorts of tricks. But Boris often found himself wondering whether Mathieu had any real regard for him. Mathieu was casual and brusque, and of course it was right that people of their sort shouldn't be sentimental when they were together, but there were all sorts of ways in which a fellow could show he liked someone, and Boris felt that Mathieu might well have shown his affection by a word or a gesture now and then. With Ivich, Mathieu was quite different. Boris suddenly recalled Mathieu's face one day when he was helping Ivich put on her overcoat; he felt an unpleasant shrinking at the heart. Mathieu's smile: on those sardonic lips that Boris loved so much, that strange, appealing, and affectionate smile. But Boris's head soon filled with smoke and he thought of nothing at all.

"He's off again," said Lola.

She eyed him anxiously. "What were you thinking about?"

"I was thinking of Delarue," said Boris regretfully.

Lola smiled sadly. "Couldn't you think of me too sometimes?"

"I don't need to think of you, since you are there."

"Why are you always thinking of Delarue? Do you wish you were with him?"

"I'm glad to be here."

"Do you mean that you're glad to be here or glad to be with me?"

"It's the same thing."

"It's the same thing for you. Not for me. When I'm with you, I don't care where I am. Besides, I'm never *glad* to be with you."

"Aren't you?" asked Boris with some surprise.

"No, not glad. Don't pretend to be stupid, you know just what I mean: I've seen you with Delarue, you're all of a twitter when he's there."

"That's quite different."

Lola set her lovely, ravaged face quite close to his; there was an imploring expression in her eyes.

"Look at me, you little stiff, and tell me why you like him so much."

"I don't know. I don't like him as much as all that. He's a good chap. Lola, I hate talking to you about him, because you told me you couldn't stand him."

Lola smiled with a rather embarrassed air. "Now you're twisting. Bless the little creature, I didn't tell you I couldn't stand him. It was simply that I couldn't understand what you found in him. I wish you would explain. I want to understand."

And Boris thought: "It isn't true—she'd start yawning before I'd said three words."

"I find him likable," said he sedately.

"That's what you always say. It isn't precisely the word that I should choose. Tell me he's intelligent, well-read, and I'll agree; but not likable. Look here, I'll tell you what I think of him: likable is a word I should use about somebody like Maurice, a straight sort of fellow; but Mathieu makes everyone uncomfortable because he's neither fish nor fowl, you don't know how to take him. Look at his hands, for instance."

"What's the matter with his hands? I like them."

"They're workmen's hands. They're always quivering a little, as though he'd just finished some heavy job."

"Well, why not?"

"Yes, but the point is he's not a workman. When I see his great paw gripping a glass of whisky, he looks like a man who means to enjoy life, and I don't think the worse of him for that; but take care not to watch him drinking, with that odd mouth of his—why, it's a parson's mouth. I can't explain it, I get the feeling he's austere, and then if you look at his eyes, you can see he knows too much, he's the sort of fellow who can't enjoy anything in a simple way, either eating, or drinking, or sleeping with women; he has to think about everything, it's like that voice of his, the cutting voice of a gentleman who is never wrong—I know it goes with the job of having to explain things to small boys. I had a teacher who talked like him, but I'm not at school any more, and I find it tiresome: I can understand a man being completely one thing or the other, a genial brute or the intellectual type, a schoolmaster or a parson, but not both at the same time. I don't know if there are women who like that sort of thing—I suppose there are, but I tell you frankly, I couldn't bear a fellow like that to touch me, I shouldn't like to feel those ruffianly hands on me while he soused me with his icy look."

Lola paused to get her breath. "She *is* down on him," thought Boris. But he remained unruffled. The people who liked him were not obliged to like each other, and Boris thought it quite natural that each of them should try to get him down on the others.

"I understand you quite well," said Lola with a conciliatory air; "you don't see him with the same eyes as mine, because he has been your prof and you're prejudiced; I can see that from all sorts of little tricks; for instance, you're always so critical of the way people dress, you never think them smart enough, whereas he is always got up like a scarecrow, he wears ties that my hotel waiter wouldn't look at—but you don't mind."

Boris was not to be roused. "It doesn't matter," he explained, "if a man is badly dressed when he doesn't bother about his clothes at all. What is rotten is to try to make a splash and not pull it off."

"Well, you don't do that, my little tyke."

"I know what suits me," said Boris modestly. He reflected that he was wearing a blue ribbed sweater and was glad: it was a handsome sweater. Lola had taken his hand and was tossing it up and down between her own. Boris watched his hand rise and fall, and he thought: "It doesn't belong to me, it's a sort of pancake." It had in fact grown numb; this amused him, and he twitched a finger to bring it back to life. The finger touched the palm of Lola's hand, and Lola flung him a grateful look. "That's what makes me nervous," thought Boris irritably. He told himself that he would certainly have found it easier to show affection if Lola hadn't fallen so often into these appealing, melting moods. He didn't in the least mind letting his hands be played with in public by an aging woman. He had long thought that this was rather in his line: even when he was alone, in the metro, people looked at him rather quizzically, and the little shop girls on their way home laughed in his face.

"You still haven't told me why you think him such a fine fellow."

She was like that, she could never stop once she had begun. Boris was sure that she was hurting her own feelings, but she enjoyed it. He looked at her: the air around her was blue, and her face was whitish blue. But the eyes were feverish and hard.

"Why?—tell me."

"Because he *is* a fine fellow," groaned Boris. "Oh dear, how you pester me! He doesn't care about anything."

"Well, does that make a fine fellow? You don't care about anything, do you?"

"No."

"But you do care a little about me, don't you?"

"Yes, I care about you."

Lola looked unhappy, and Boris turned his head away. Anyhow, he didn't much like looking at Lola when she put on that expression. She was upset; he thought it silly of her, but he couldn't do anything about it. He did everything expected of him. He was faithful to Lola, he telephoned to her often, he went to call for her three times a week when she came out of the Sumatra, and on those evenings he slept in her flat. For the rest, it was a question of character, probably. A question of age, too—older people grow embittered and behave as though their lives were at stake. Once, when Boris was a little boy, he had dropped his spoon; on being told to pick it up, he had refused and flown into a passion. Then his father had said, in an unforgettably majestic tone: "Very well, then, *I* will pick it up." Boris had seen a tall body stiffly bending down, and a bald cranium, he heard sundry creaking sounds—the whole thing was an intolerable sacrilege, and he burst out sobbing. Since then Boris had regarded grown-ups as bulky and impotent divinities. If they bent down, they looked as though they were going to break; if they slipped and fell, the effect they produced in the on-looker was a desire to laugh and a sense of awe-stricken abhorrence. And if the tears came into their eyes, as into Lola's at that moment, one was simply at a loss. Grown-up people's tears were a mystical catastrophe, the sort of tears God sheds over the wickedness of mankind. From another point of view, of course, he respected Lola for being so passionate. Mathieu had explained to him that a human being ought to have passions, and Descartes had said so too.

"Delarue has his passions," he said, pursuing his reflections aloud, "but that doesn't prevent his caring for nothing. He is free."

"By that token I'm free too, I care for nothing but you."

Boris did not answer.

"Am I not free?" asked Lola.

"That's not the same thing."

Too difficult to explain. Lola was a victim, she had no luck, and she appealed too much to the emotions. Which was not in her favor. Besides, she took heroin. That wasn't a bad thing, in one sense; indeed, it was quite a good thing, in principle; Boris had talked to Ivich about it, and they had both agreed that it was a good thing. But there were ways of doing it: if one took it to destroy oneself, either in despair or by way of emphasizing one's freedom, that was entirely commendable. But Lola took it with greedy abandonment, it was her form of relaxation. It didn't even intoxicate her.

"You make me laugh," said Lola in a dry voice. "It's a habit of yours to put Delarue above everybody else as a matter of principle. Because you know, between ourselves, which is the freer, he or I: he has a home of his own, a fixed salary, and a definite pension; he lives like a petty official. And then, into the bargain, there's that affair of his you told me about, that female who never goes out —what more does he want? No one could be freer than that. As for me, I've just a few old frocks, I'm alone, I live in a hotel, and I don't even know whether I shall have a job for the summer."

"That's different," repeated Boris.

He was annoyed. Lola didn't bother about freedom. She was getting excited about it that evening because she wanted to defeat Mathieu on his own ground.

"I could skin you, you little beast, when you're like that. What's different, eh?"

"Well, you're free without wanting to be," he explained, "it just happens so, that's all. But Mathieu's freedom is based on reason."

"I still don't understand," said Lola, shaking her head.

"Well, he doesn't care a damn about his apartment; he lives there just as he would live anywhere else, and I've got the feeling that he doesn't care much about his girl. He stays with her because he must sleep with someone. His freedom isn't visible, it's inside him."

Lola had an absent air, he felt he must hurt her a bit just to jostle her around, and he went on:

"Look here, you're too fond of me; he would never let himself get caught like that."

"Oho!" cried Lola indignantly. "I'm too fond of you, am I?—you little toad. And don't you think he's a bit too fond of your sister, eh? You'd only got to watch him the other night at the Sumatra."

"Of Ivich? You make me sick."

Lola flung him a sneering grin, and the smoke suddenly went to Boris's head. A moment passed, and then the band happened to launch into the *St. James Infirmary*, and Boris wanted to dance.

"Shall we dance this?"

They danced. Lola had closed her eyes, and he could hear her quick breathing. The little pansy had got up and went across to ask the dancer from the Java for a dance. Boris reflected that he would soon see him from near by and was pleased. Lola was heavy in his arms; she danced well, and she smelt nice, but she was too heavy. Boris thought that he would sooner dance with Ivich. Ivich danced magnificently; he told himself that Ivich ought to learn the castanets. Then Lola's scent and smell banished all further thought. He pressed her to him and breathed hard. She opened her eyes and looked at him intently.

"Do you love me?"

"Yes," said Boris, making a face.

"Why do you make a face like that?"

"Because—oh, you annoy me."

"Why? It isn't true that you love me?"

"Yes it is."

"Why don't you ever tell me so yourself? I always have to ask you."

"Because I don't feel like it. It's all rot; it's the sort of thing that people don't say."

"Does it annoy you when I say I love you?"

"No, you can say it if you like, but you oughtn't to ask me if I love you."

"It's very seldom I ask you anything, darling. It's usually enough for me to look at you and feel I love you. But there are moments when I wish I could get at your own real feelings."

"I understand," said Boris seriously, "but you ought to wait till I feel like it. If it doesn't come naturally, there's no sense in it."

"But, you little fool, you yourself say you never do feel that way unless somebody asks you."

Boris began to laugh.

"It's true," he said, "you put me off. But one can feel affection for somebody and not want to say so."

Lola did not answer. They stopped, applauded, and the band began again. Boris was glad to observe that the pansy lad was dancing towards them; but when he eyed him from near by, he got a nasty shock: the creature was quite forty years old. His face retained the sheen of youth, but underneath it he had aged. He had large doll-like blue eyes and a boyish mouth, but there were pouches under his porcelain eyes, and wrinkles around his mouth, his nostrils were pinched like those of a dying man, and his hair, which looked from a distance like a golden haze, scarcely covered his cranium. Boris looked with horror at this el-

derly, shaven child. "He was once young," thought he.
There were fellows who seemed created to be thirty-five—
Mathieu, for instance—because they had never known
youth. But when a chap had really been young, he bore
the marks of it for the rest of his life. It might last till
twenty-five. After that—it was horrible. He set himself
to look at Lola and said abruptly:

"Lola, look at me, I love you."

Lola's eyes grew pink, and she stepped on Boris's foot.
She merely said:

"Darling!"

He felt like exclaiming: "Clasp me tighter, make me feel
I love you." But Lola said nothing, she in her turn was
alone, the moment had indeed come. There was a vague
smile on her face, her eyelids were drooping, her face had
again shut down upon her happiness. It was a calm, forlorn face. Boris felt desolate, and the thought, the grinding
thought, suddenly came upon him: "I won't, I won't grow
old." Last year he had been quite unperturbed, he had
never thought about that sort of thing; and now—it was
rather ominous that he should so constantly feel that his
youth was slipping between his fingers. Until twenty-five.
"I've got five years yet," thought Boris, "and after that I'll
blow my brains out." He could no longer endure the noise
of the band and the sense of all these people around him.

"Shall we go?" said he.

"At once, my lovely!"

They returned to their table. Lola called the waiter,
paid the bill, and flung her velvet cloak over her shoulders.

"Come along," she said.

They went out. Boris was no longer thinking of anything
very definite, but there was a sense of something fateful in
his mind. The rue Blanche was crowded with random
people, all looking harsh and old. They met the Maestro
Piranese from the Puss in Boots, and greeted him; his little
legs pattered along beneath his enormous belly. "Per-

haps," thought Boris, "I too shall grow a paunch." What would it be like never to be able to look at oneself in a glass, nor to feel the crisp, wooden snap of one's joints. . . . And every instant that passed, every instant, consumed a little more of his youth. "If only I could save myself up, live very quietly, at a slower pace, I should perhaps gain a few years. But to do that, I oughtn't to make a habit of going to bed at two a.m." He eyed Lola with detestation. "She's killing me."

"What's the matter?" asked Lola.

"Nothing."

Lola lived in a hotel in the rue Navarin. She took her key off the board and they walked silently upstairs. The room was bare, there was a trunk covered with labels in one corner, and on the farther wall a photograph of Boris stuck on it with thumb-tacks. It was an identification photograph that Lola had had enlarged. "Ah," thought Boris, "that will remain when I'm a wreck; in that I shall always look young." He felt an impulse to tear it up.

"There's something odd about you," said Lola; "what's the matter?"

"I'm all in," said Boris. "I've got a pain in the top of my head."

Lola looked anxious. "You aren't ill, dear? Would you like an aspirin?"

"No, it's nothing, I shall soon feel better."

Lola took his chin and raised his head.

"You look as if you were angry with me. You aren't, are you? Yes, you are. What have I done?"

She looked distraught.

"I'm not angry with you—don't be silly," protested Boris feebly.

"You are, but what have I done to you? You'd much better tell me, because then I shall be able to explain. It's sure to be some misunderstanding. It can't be anything serious. Boris, I implore you, tell me what's the matter."

"But there's nothing."

He put his arms round Lola's neck and kissed her on the lips. Lola quivered. Boris inhaled a perfumed breath and felt against his mouth the moist nakedness of her lips. His senses thrilled. Lola covered his face with kisses; she began to pant a little.

Boris realized that he desired Lola, and was glad: desire absorbed his black ideas, as it did ideas of any other kind. His head began to whirl, its contents sped upwards and were scattered. He had laid his hand on Lola's hip, he touched her flesh through the silken dress: he was, indeed, no more than a hand outstretched upon that silken flesh. He curved his hand slightly, and the stuff slipped between his fingers like an exquisite skin, delicate and dead; below lay the real skin, resistant, elastic, and glossy as a kid glove. Lola threw her cloak on the bed, flung out two bare arms, and clasped them round Boris's neck; she smelt delicious. Boris could see her shaven armpits, powdered with bluish black dots, minute but clearly visible, like the heads of splinters thrust deep into the skin. Boris and Lola remained standing, on the very spot where desire had come upon them, because they had no longer strength to move. Lola's legs began to tremble, and Boris wondered whether they would not both just sink down on the carpet. He pressed Lola to him and felt the rich softness of her breasts.

"Ah," murmured Lola.

She was leaning backwards, and he was fascinated by that pale head with swollen lips, a veritable Medusa's head. He thought: "These are her last good days." And he held her yet more tightly. "One of these mornings she will suddenly collapse." He detested her; he felt his body against hers, hard and gaunt and muscular, he clasped her in his arms and defended her against the years. Then there came upon him a moment of bewilderment and drowsiness: he looked at Lola's arms, white as an old woman's hair; it seemed to him that he held old age between his hands and that he must clasp it close and strangle it.

"Don't hold me so tight," murmured Lola happily; "you're hurting me. I want you."

Boris released her: he was a little shocked.

"Give me my pajamas; I'll go and undress in the bathroom."

He went into the bathroom and locked the door: he hated Lola to come in while he was undressing. He washed his face and his feet and amused himself by dusting talcum powder on his legs. He had quite recovered his composure, and he thought: "It's fantastic." His head was vague and heavy, and he hardly knew what he was thinking about. "I must talk to Delarue about it," he decided. Beyond the door she awaited him, she was certain to be undressed by now. But he did not feel inclined to hurry. A naked body, full of naked odors, was something rather overwhelming, which was what Lola would not understand. He was now about to be engulfed into an enveloping and strong-savored sensuality. Once in it, all would be well, but *before*—well, a fellow couldn't help feeling a bit nervous. "In any case," he reflected with annoyance, "I don't intend to get involved the way I did the other time." He combed his hair carefully over the basin, to see whether it was falling out. But not one hair dropped on the white porcelain. When he had put on his pajamas, he opened the door and went back into the bedroom.

Lola was outstretched on the bed, completely naked. It was another Lola, sluggish and menacing, watching him from beneath her eyelids. Her body, on the blue counterpane, was silvery white, like the belly of a fish, and on it a triangular tuft of reddish hair. She was beautiful. Boris approached the bed and eyed her with an eagerness not unmingled with disgust. She stretched out her arms.

"Wait," said Boris.

He switched off the light, and the room was promptly filled with a red glow: at the third story of the building opposite, an illuminated sign had been recently installed. Boris lay down beside Lola and began to stroke her shoulders and her breasts. Her skin was so soft that it felt exactly as though she had kept her silk wrap on. Her breasts were slackening, but Boris liked that: they were the breasts of a woman who has lived. It was in vain that he had turned out the light, he could still see, in the glare from the confounded sign, Lola's face, pale in the red glow, and black-lipped: she looked as though she was in pain, and her eyes were hard. Boris felt oppressed with the sense of tragedy to come, just as he had done at Nîmes when the first bull bounded into the arena: something was going to happen, something inevitable, awesome, and yet rather tedious, like the bull's ensanguined death.

"Take off your pajamas," pleaded Lola.

"No," said Boris.

This was a ritual. Every time Lola asked him to take off his pajamas and Boris was obliged to refuse. Lola's hands slipped under his jacket and caressed him gently. Boris began to laugh.

"You're tickling me."

They kissed. A moment passed; Lola took Boris's hand and laid it on her body, against the tuft of reddish hair: she always had odd caprices, and Boris had to protect himself sometimes. For an instant or two he let his hand inert against Lola's thighs, and then slid it gently upwards to her shoulders.

"Come," said Lola, pulling him on to her, "come, I adore you—come, come!"

She was beginning to moan, and Boris thought: "Now I'm for it." A clammy thrill ran up his body from waist to neck. "I won't," said Boris to himself, and he clenched his teeth. But then he had a sudden sense of being picked up by the neck, like a rabbit, and he sank upon Lola's body, lost in a red, voluptuous dazzlement of passion.

"Darling," said Lola.

She let him gently slip aside and got out of bed. Boris remained prostrate, his head on the pillow. He heard Lola open the bathroom door, and he thought: "When this is over, I don't want any more affairs. I loathe making love. No, to be honest, that isn't what I loathe most, it's the entanglement of it all, the sense of domination; and besides, what's the point of choosing a girl friend? It would be just the same with anyone, it's physiological." And he repeated with disgust: "physiological." Lola was getting ready for the night. The water ran into the basin with a pleasant, limpid gurgle that Boris rather enjoyed. Men suffering from the hallucinations of thirst, in the desert, heard just such sounds, the sound of running water. Boris tried to imagine that he was under a hallucination. The room, the red light, the splashes, these were hallucinations, he would soon find himself in the middle of the desert, lying on the sand with a cork helmet over his eyes. Mathieu's face suddenly appeared to him. "It's fantastic," he thought; "I like men better than girls. When I'm with a girl I'm not half so happy as with a man. And yet I wouldn't dream of going to bed with a man." He cheered himself with the thought: "A monk, that's what I'll be when I've left Lola." He felt arid and austere. Lola jumped into the bed and took him in her arms.

"My dear," she said, "my dear."

She stroked his hair, and there was a long moment of silence. Boris could already see stars circling when Lola began to speak. Her voice sounded unfamiliar in that crimson night.

"Boris, I've got no one but you, I'm alone in the world, you must love me, I can't think of anyone but you. If I think of my life, I want to throw myself into the river, I have to think of you all day. Don't be a beast, darling, you

must never hurt me, you're all I have left. I'm in your
hands, darling, don't hurt me: don't ever hurt me—I'm
all alone."

Boris awoke with a start and surveyed the situation with
precision.

"If you are alone, it's because you like to be so," he
said, speaking in a clear voice, "it's because you're proud.
Otherwise you would love an older man than me. I'm too
young, I can't prevent you from being alone. I believe
you chose me for that reason."

"I don't know," said Lola. "I love you to distraction—
that's all I know."

She flung her arms wildly around him. Boris heard her
once more saying: "I adore you," and then he fell fast
asleep.

# CHAPTER III

SUMMER. The air was warm and dank. Mathieu was walking in the middle of the road, under a lucid sky, swinging his arms, and thrusting his way through heavy golden tapestries. Summer. Other people's summer. For him a black day was beginning, which would move on a slow and tortuous course until the evening, like a funeral procession in the sunshine. An address. Money. He would have to run all over Paris. Sarah could provide the address. Daniel would lend the money. Or Jacques. He had dreamed that he was a murderer, and something of his dream still lurked in the depths of his eyes, crushed beneath the dazzling pressure of the light. 16 rue Delambre, here it was; Sarah lived on the sixth floor, and the elevator was of course out of order. Mathieu walked upstairs. Behind closed doors servants were at their housework, clad in aprons and with dusters knotted round their heads: for them, too, a day had started. What day? Mathieu was slightly out of breath when he rang, and he thought: "I ought to do some physical exercises," and he also thought with annoyance: "I say that to myself every time I walk upstairs." He heard a faint patter of footsteps; a short, bald man, with light eyes, opened the door with a smile. Mathieu recognized him, it was a German, a refugee, he had often seen him at the Dôme, ecstatically sipping a cup of *café crème,* or brooding over a chessboard, and licking his thick lips.

"I want to see Sarah," said Mathieu.

The little man grew grave, bowed, and clicked his heels; he had violet ears.

"Weymüller," said he in a formal tone.

"Delarue," said Mathieu unemotionally.

The little man resumed his genial smile. "Come in, come in," he said. "She's below, in the studio; she will be delighted."

He ushered him into the hall and trotted off. Mathieu pushed open the glazed door and went into Gomez's studio. On the landing of the inner staircase he stopped, dazzled by the glare that flooded through the great dusty skylights; Mathieu blinked, his head began to ache.

"What's the matter?" said Sarah's voice.

Mathieu leaned over the banisters. Sarah was sitting on the divan, in a yellow kimono, he could see her skull under the thin, stiff hair. Opposite her, a flaming torch: a red-haired, brachycephalic. . . . "It's Brunet," thought Mathieu with annoyance. He had not seen him for six months, but he wasn't at all pleased to run into him again at Sarah's. It was embarrassing, they had too much to say to each other, their fading friendship lay between them. Besides, Brunet brought with him an air of out of doors, a whole healthy universe, an abrupt and stubborn world of revolt and violence, of manual labor, of patient effort, and of discipline: he would not be interested in the shameful little bedroom secret that Mathieu was about to confide to Sarah. Sarah looked up and smiled.

"Good morning, good morning," she said.

Mathieu returned her smile: he looked down upon that flat, ill-favored countenance, marred by much benevolence, and beneath it the large slack breasts, half-emerging from the kimono. He hurried down.

"What good wind brings you here?" asked Sarah.

"There's something I want to ask you," said Mathieu.

Sarah's face flushed greedily. "Anything you like," she said. And she added, gleefully: "See who is here!"

Mathieu turned to Brunet and shook his hand. Sarah sat looking at them with a brooding, sentimental eye.

"How are you, my old social traitor?" said Brunet.

Mathieu was glad to hear that voice. Brunet was vast and solid, with a slow, bucolic face. He did not look particularly amiable.

"How are you?" said Mathieu. "I thought you were dead."

Brunet laughed, but did not reply.

"Sit down here beside me," said Sarah eagerly. She was going to do him a service, she knew that; for the moment he was her property. Mathieu sat down. Little Pablo was playing with building blocks under the table.

"And Gomez?" asked Mathieu.

"Just the same as usual. He's at Barcelona," said Sarah.

"Have you had any news of him?"

"Last week. A full account of his exploits," Sarah replied ironically.

Brunet's eyes gleamed. "You know he's a colonel now?"

Colonel. Mathieu thought of the man of yesterday, and his heart contracted. Gomez had actually gone. One day he had read of the fall of Irun, in *Paris-Soir*. He had paced up and down the studio for a long while, running his fingers through his black hair. And then he went out, bareheaded and without an overcoat, as though he were going to buy cigarettes at the Dôme. He had not returned. The room had remained exactly as he had left it: an unfinished canvas, a half-cut copperplate on the table, among phials of acid. The picture and the etching were of Mrs. Stimson. In the picture she was naked. Mathieu saw her in his mind's eye, resplendently tipsy on Gomez's

arm and singing raucously. He thought: "He was a beast
to Sarah all the same."

"Did the Minister let you in?" asked Sarah gaily.

She did not want to talk about Gomez. She had forgiven
him everything, his treacheries, escapades, and cruelty.
But not that. Not his departure for Spain: he had gone
away to kill men; he had killed men by now. For Sarah,
human life was sacred.

"What minister?" asked Mathieu in astonishment.

"The little red-eared mouse is a Minister," said Sarah
with naïve pride. "He was a member of the Socialist Government in Munich in '22. At present he is down and out."

"And you rescued him, of course."

Sarah began to laugh.

"He came along here with his suitcase. No, seriously,"
said she, "he has nowhere else to go. He was turned out of
his hotel because he couldn't pay the bill."

Mathieu reckoned on his fingers. "Annia, Lopez, and
Santi, that makes four pensioners for you," said he.

"Annia is leaving soon," said Sarah, with an apologetic
air. "She's got a job."

"It's ridiculous," said Brunet.

Mathieu started, and turned towards him. Brunet's indignation was ponderous and placid; he eyed Sarah with
his most bucolic air and repeated: "It's ridiculous."

"What? What is ridiculous?"

"Ah," said Sarah briskly, laying her hand on Mathieu's
arm. "You must stand by me, my dear Mathieu!"

"But what's the trouble?"

"It doesn't interest Mathieu," said Brunet to Sarah, with
a look of annoyance.

She was no longer listening.

"He wants me to turn my Minister out," she said
pathetically.

"Turn him out?"

"He says it's criminal of me to keep him."

"Sarah exaggerates," said Brunet mildly.

He turned to Mathieu and explained with something of an effort: "The fact is that we have had disquieting reports about the fellow. It seems that six months ago he was to be found hanging about the Germany Embassy. There's no need to be unduly malicious to guess what a Jewish refugee might be up to in such a place."

"You have no proofs," said Sarah.

"No, we haven't any proofs. If we had, he wouldn't be here. But even though there are only presumptions, Sarah is madly imprudent to have taken him in."

"But why? Why?" asked Sarah, passionately.

"Sarah," said Brunet affectionately, "you would blow up the whole of Paris to prevent anything unpleasant happening to your protégés."

Sarah smiled weakly. "Not the whole of Paris," she said, "but it's certain I'm not going to sacrifice Weymüller to your party intrigues. A party is so—so abstract."

"Just what I was saying," said Brunet.

Sarah shook her head vigorously. She had flushed, and her large green eyes had dimmed.

"The little Minister," she said with indignation. "You saw him, Mathieu. Could he hurt a fly?"

Brunet's serenity was enormous. It was the serenity of the ocean: suave and yet exasperating. He never appeared to be one sole person; he embodied the slow, silent, murmurous life of a crowd. He went on to explain: "Gomez sometimes sends us emissaries. They come here, and we meet them at Sarah's place; you can guess that the messages are confidential. Is this the place to house a fellow who has the reputation of being a spy?"

Mathieu did not answer. Brunet had used the interrogative form, but with purely rhetorical intent: he was not asking advice; indeed, it was a long time since Brunet had ceased taking Mathieu's advice on anything whatever.

"Mathieu, you shall decide: if I send Weymüller away,

he will throw himself into the Seine. Can one really drive a man to suicide for a mere suspicion?" she added desperately.

She was sitting upright, her ugly face aflame with kindliness. She inspired in Mathieu the rather squalid sympathy one feels for people who have been run over and hurt in an accident, or are suffering from boils and ulcers.

"Do you mean it?" he asked. "He'll throw himself in the Seine?"

"Certainly not," said Brunet. "He'll go back to the German Embassy and try to sell himself outright."

"It comes to the same thing," said Mathieu. "In any case he's done for."

Brunet shrugged his shoulders. "Yes, I suppose so," he said indifferently.

"Listen to him, Mathieu," said Sarah, eying him with distress. "Well? Who is right? Do say something."

Mathieu had nothing to say. Brunet did not ask his advice, he had no use for the advice of a bourgeois, a dirty intellectual, a watchdog. "He will listen to me with icy courtesy, he'll be quite immovable, he'll judge me by what I say, that's all." Mathieu did not want Brunet to judge him. There had been a time when, as a matter of principle, neither of the pair judged the other. "Friendship doesn't exist to criticize," Brunet used to say then. "Its function is to inspire confidence." He still said so, perhaps, but at the moment he was thinking of his comrades of the party.

"Mathieu!" said Sarah.

Brunet leaned towards her and touched her knee.

"Listen, Sarah," he said quietly. "I quite like Mathieu and I think highly of his intelligence. If it were a question of explaining a passage in Spinoza or Kant, I should apply to him. But this is a silly business, and I assure you I don't want any outside opinion, even from a teacher of philosophy. I've made up my mind."

Obviously, thought Mathieu, obviously. He felt sick at

heart, but not in the least angry with Brunet. "Who am I to give advice? And what have I done with my life?" Brunet had got up.

"I must hurry away," he said. "You will, of course, do as you like, Sarah. You don't belong to the party, and you have already done a great deal for us. But if you keep him, I would merely ask you to come to my place when Gomez sends any news."

"Certainly," said Sarah.

Her eyes were shining, as though a burden had been lifted from her.

"And don't leave things lying about. Burn everything," Brunet added.

"I promise."

Brunet turned to Mathieu. "Well, good-by, my dear fellow."

He did not hold out a hand, he eyed him narrowly, with a hard expression, like Marcelle's last evening, and with the same remorseless astonishment. He felt naked beneath that scrutiny, a tall and naked figure, molded out of dough. Clumsy, too. Who was he to give advice? He blinked: Brunet looked hard and knotty. "And I bear my futility written on my face."

Brunet spoke: not at all in the voice that Mathieu expected. "You're looking pretty rotten," he said gently. "What's the matter?"

Mathieu had got up also. "I've—I've got some lousy headaches. Nothing serious."

Brunet laid a hand on his shoulder and looked at him doubtfully.

"It's idiotic. I'm on the go all the time and everywhere and never have a moment for my old friends. If you croak, I should only hear of your death a month afterwards, and by accident."

"I'm not going to croak yet awhile," said Mathieu with a laugh.

He felt Brunet's fist on his shoulder; he thought: "He's not judging me," and was filled with a sense of humble gratitude.

Brunet remained serious. "No," said he, "not yet awhile. But—" He seemed to make up his mind at last. "Are you free about two o'clock? I've got a few minutes, I would look in on you and we might have a little talk, like old times."

"Like old times. I'm quite free, I shall expect you," said Mathieu.

Brunet smiled genially. He had kept his frank and vivid smile. He swung round and walked towards the staircase.

"I'll come with you," said Sarah.

Mathieu followed them with his eyes. Brunet ran up the stairs with surprising agility. "All is not lost," he said to himself. And something stirred inside his chest, something warm and homely, something that suggested hope. He stepped forward. The door slammed above his head. Little Pablo was eying him gravely. Mathieu picked up an etching-needle from the table. A fly that had alighted on the copperplate flew away. Pablo was still looking at him. Mathieu felt uneasy, without quite knowing why. He had the sense of being engulfed by the child's eyes. "Children are greedy little devils," he thought, "all their senses are mouths." Pablo's expression was not yet human, and yet it was already more than alive: the little creature had not long emerged from a womb, as indeed was plain: there he was, hesitant, minute, still displaying the unwholesome sheen of vomit; but behind the flickering humors that filled his eye-sockets lurked a greedy little consciousness. Mathieu toyed with the etching-needle. "How hot it is today!" he thought. The fly buzzed round him; in a pink room, within a female body, there was a blister, growing slowly larger.

"Do you know what I dreamed?" asked Pablo.

"Tell me."

"I dreamed I was a feather."

"And this thing thinks!" Mathieu reflected.

"And what did you do when you were a feather?"

"Nothing. I slept."

Mathieu flung the etching-needle back on the table; the frightened fly buzzed round and round and then alighted on the copperplate between two tiny grooves representing a woman's arm. There was no time to lose, for the blister was expanding, at that very moment; it was making obscure efforts to emerge, to extricate itself from darkness, and growing into something like *that*, a little pallid, flabby object that clung to the world and sucked its sap.

Mathieu took a few steps towards the staircase. He could hear Sarah's voice. She had opened the street door and was standing on the threshold, smiling at Brunet. What was she waiting for? Why didn't she come down again? He half turned, he looked at the child and he looked at the fly. A child. A bit of thinking flesh that screams and bleeds when it is killed. A fly is easier to kill than a child. He shrugged his shoulders. "I'm not going to kill anyone. I'm going to prevent a child from being born." Pablo was playing with his bricks once more; he had forgotten Mathieu. Mathieu reached out a hand and touched the table with his finger. He repeated to himself with a sense of astonishment: "Prevent its being born. . . ." It sounded as though there existed somewhere a completed child awaiting the hour to come out into the open, into the sunlight, and Mathieu was barring its passage. And, indeed, that was more or less the fact: there was a tiny human creature, conscious, furtive, deceitful, and pathetic, with a white skin, wide ears, and tiny flesh-marks, and all manner of distinctive signs such as are stamped on passports, a little man who would never run about the streets with one foot on the pavement and the other in the gutter; eyes, green like Mathieu's or black like Marcelle's, which would never see the vitreous skies

of winter, nor the sea, nor any human face, hands that
would never touch the snow, nor the flesh of women, nor
the bark of trees: an embodiment of the world, ensanguined, luminous, sullen, passionate, sinister, full of hopes,
an image populous with houses and gardens, tall delightful girls, and horrible insects; and a pin would pierce it
and explode it like a toy balloon.

"Here I am," said Sarah; "have I kept you waiting?"

Mathieu looked up and felt relieved: she was leaning
over the banisters, a heavy, amorphous figure; an adult
human being, aging flesh that looked as though it had
been lately pickled and not born at all; Sarah smiled at
him and hurried downstairs, her kimono fluttering round
her stocky legs.

"Now then: what is the matter?" she said eagerly.

Her large, clouded eyes were set on him insistently.
He turned away and said harshly: "Marcelle is going to
have a baby."

"Oh!"

Sarah looked really rather pleased. She added timidly:
"So you—you—?"

"No, no," said Mathieu briskly. "We don't want one."

"Ah yes," she said, "I see." She bent her head and remained silent. Mathieu was irritated by a distress that was
not even a reproach.

"I think the same thing happened to you some time ago.
Gomez told me," he retorted harshly.

"Yes; some time ago."

Suddenly she looked up and blurted out: "It's nothing
at all, you know, if it's taken in time."

She would not allow herself to criticize him, she abandoned her reserves, uttered no word to reproach; her sole
desire was to reassure him.

"It's nothing at all. . . ."

He must smile, he must view the future with confidence;
she alone would lament that secret little death.

"Look here, Sarah," said Mathieu angrily, "you must try to understand me. I won't marry. It isn't just selfishness: I regard marriage—"

He fell silent: Sarah was married, she had married Gomez five years before. He added after a pause: "Besides, Marcelle doesn't want a child."

"She doesn't like children?"

"They don't interest her."

Sarah seemed disconcerted.

"Yes," she said, "yes . . . very well, then."

She took his hands. "My poor Mathieu, how worried you must be! I wish I could help you."

"Well, that's just what you can do," said Mathieu. "When you were in the same sort of trouble, you went to see someone, a Russian, I think."

"Yes," said Sarah. (Her expression altered.) "It was horrible."

"Indeed!" said Mathieu in a strangled voice. "I suppose it's—it's very painful."

"Not particularly, but—" And she went on with a piteous air: "I was thinking of the child. It was Gomez who wanted it done, you know. And when he wanted anything in those days— But it was horrible, I would never—if he went down on his knees to me now, I would never have it done again." She looked at Mathieu with agonized eyes.

"They gave me a little parcel after the operation, and they said to me: 'You can throw that down a drain.' Down a drain! Like a dead rat! Mathieu," she said, gripping his arm, "you don't realize what you're going to do."

"And when you bring a child into the world, do you realize what you're going to do?" asked Mathieu wrathfully.

A child: another consciousness, a little center-point of light that would flutter round and round, dashing against the walls, and never be able to escape.

"No, but what I mean is—you don't know what you're

asking of Marcelle; I'm afraid she may hate you later on."
Mathieu had a vision of Marcelle's eyes—round, hard,
circled eyes.

"Do you hate Gomez?" he asked sharply.

Sarah made a piteous, helpless gesture: she could not
hate anyone, least of all Gomez.

"In any case," she said with a blank look, "I can't send
you to that Russian; he's still in practice, but he drinks
nowadays; I no longer trust him. There was a nasty episode two years ago."

"And you don't know anyone else?"

"No," said Sarah slowly. But suddenly all her kindliness
flooded into her face again and she exclaimed: "Yes, I do,
just the person—why didn't I think of it before? Wald-
mann. You haven't met him here? A Jew, a gynecologist.
He's a sort of specialist in abortion: you would be quite
safe with him. He had an immense practice in Berlin.
When the Nazis came into power, he set up in Vienna.
After that there was the Anschluss, and he arrived in
Paris with a suitcase. But he had sent all his money to
Zurich long before."

"Do you think he'll do it?"

"Of course. I'll go and see him this very day."

"I'm glad," said Mathieu, "I'm awfully glad. He isn't
too expensive, I hope."

"He used to charge up to two thousand marks."

Mathieu grew pale. "Ten thousand francs!"

"But that was sheer robbery," she added quickly. "He
was exploiting his reputation. No one knows him here, I'm
sure he'll be reasonable: I shall suggest three thousand
francs."

"Right," said Mathieu between clenched teeth. He was
wondering where he would find the money.

"Look here," said Sarah, "why shouldn't I go this very
morning? He lives in the rue Blaise-Desgoffe, quite near.

I'll slip on some clothes and go along. Will you wait for me?"

"No, I—I've got an appointment at half past ten. Sarah, you're a treasure," said Mathieu.

He took her by the shoulders and shook her, smiling as he did so. She had for his sake sacrificed her deepest repulsions, she had, in the kindness of her heart, become his accomplice in an act she loathed: she was beaming with delight.

"Where will you be about eleven o'clock?" she asked. "I might be able to phone you."

"I shall be at the Dupont Latin, boulevard Saint-Michel. I could stay there till you ring me up."

"At the Dupont Latin? Right."

Sarah's wrap had slipped back, exposing her clumsy breasts. Mathieu clasped her in his arms, in real affection, and also to avoid looking at her body.

"Good-by," said Sarah, "good-by, my dear Mathieu."

She raised her kind, ill-favored face to his. There was in that face an intriguing, almost voluptuous humility that evoked a mean desire to hurt her, to crush her with shame. "When I look at her," Daniel used to say, "I understand sadism." Mathieu kissed her on both cheeks.

"Summer!" The sky flooded the street with spectral effluence; the people hovered in the sky, and their faces were aflame. Mathieu breathed a green and living perfume, a youthful dust; he blinked and smiled. "Summer!" He walked a few paces; the black, melting asphalt, flecked with white, stuck to the soles of his shoes: Marcelle was pregnant—it was no longer the same summer.

She slept, her body swathed in the enveloping darkness, and as she slept she sweated. Her lovely brown and mauve breasts lay loose upon her, and their tips, salty and white as flowers, were encircled with oozing drops of moisture. She slept. She always slept until midday. But the pustule deep within her did not sleep, it had no time to sleep: it found nourishment and grew. Time passed with abrupt and fateful jerks. The pustule expanded and time passed. "I must find the money in forty-eight hours."

The Luxembourg, warm and white, statues and pigeons, children. The children ran about, the pigeons flew away. Racing children, white flashes, tiny turmoils. He sat down on an iron chair. "Where shall I find the money? Daniel won't lend me any. I'll ask him all the same . . . and then, as a last resort, I can always try Jacques." The grass rippled up to his feet, the youthful stone posterior of a statue caught his eye, the pigeons—birds of stone—were cooing: "After all, it's only a matter of a fortnight, this Jew fellow will surely wait until the end of the month, and on the 29th I shall get my pay."

Mathieu stopped abruptly: he *saw* himself think, and he loathed himself. "At this same hour Brunet is walking through the streets, enjoying the sunshine, lighthearted because he can look ahead, he walks through a city of threaded glass that he will soon destroy, he feels strong, he is walking with rather a mincing, cautious gait because the hour has not yet come to smash it all; he waits, he hopes. And what about me? Marcelle is with child. Will Sarah manage to get round that Jew? Where is the money to come from? That's what I think!" Suddenly he again saw once more two close-set eyes beneath black brows: "Madrid. I wanted to get there. And that's the truth. But it couldn't be fixed." And suddenly he thought: "I'm getting old."

"I'm getting old. Here I am, lounging in a chair, committed to my present life right up to the ears and believing in nothing. And yet I also wanted to set out for a Spain of mine. But it couldn't be fixed. Are there many Spains? I am there, absorbing the ancient taste of blood and iron-tainted water; I *am* my own taste, I exist. That's what existence means: draining one's own self dry without the sense of thirst. Thirty-four years. For thirty-four years I've been sipping at myself and I'm getting old. I have worked, I have waited, I have had my desire: Marcelle, Paris, independence; and now it's over. I look for nothing more." He gazed at that familiar garden, always new, always the same, just like the sea, swept for a hundred years by the same wavelets of colors and of sounds. Here it all was: scurrying children, the same for a hundred years past, the same sunshine on the broken-fingered plaster queens, and on all the trees; Sarah and her yellow kimono, Marcelle pregnant, money. All this was so natural, so *normal*, so monotonous, it was enough to fill a life, it *was* life. All the rest—the several Spains, the castles in Spain, was—what? "A tepid little lay religion for my benefit? A discreet and seraphic accompaniment to my real life? An alibi? That's how they view me—Daniel, Marcelle, Brunet, Jacques: the man who aspires to be free. He eats, he drinks, like everybody else, he is a government official, not interested in politics, he reads *L'Œuvre*, and *Le Populaire*, he is worried about money. Only he wants to be free, just as other people want a collection of stamps. Freedom, that is his secret garden, a little scheme with himself as sole accomplice. An idle, unresponsive fellow, rather chimerical, but ultimately quite sensible, who has dexterously constructed an undistinguished but solid happiness upon a basis of inertia and justifies himself from time to time on the highest moral grounds. Is that what I am?"

When he was seven years old he had been at Pithiviers, staying with his Uncle Jules, the dentist, and one day, when all alone in the waiting-room, he had played at ceasing to exist: the idea was to try not to swallow, as though he were holding on his tongue a drop of icy liquid by refraining from the little jerk of deglutition that would send it down his gullet. He had succeeded in completely emptying his head. But that emptiness still had a savor of its own. It had been a silly sort of day: the country round him sweltering in a haze that smelt of flies; indeed, he had just caught one and had torn its wings off. He had noticed that its head resembled the sulphured tip of a kitchen match, so he had fetched the scraper from the kitchen and rubbed it against the fly's head to see if it would catch fire. All this in an idle sort of mood; the feeble, lackadaisical sport of a bored little boy, who knew quite well that the fly would not catch fire. On the table there were some tattered magazines and a handsome Chinese vase, green and gray, with handles like parrots' claws. Uncle Jules had told him that the vase was three thousand years old. Mathieu had gone up to the vase, his hands behind his back, and stood, nervously a-tiptoe, looking at it: how frightening it was to be a little ball of bread crumb in this ancient fire-browned world, confronted by an impassive vase three thousand years old! He had turned his back on it, and stood grimacing and snuffling at the mirror without managing to divert his thoughts; then he had suddenly gone back to the table, picked up the vase, which was a heavy one, and dashed it on the floor—it had just happened like that, after which he had felt as light as gossamer. He had eyed the porcelain fragments in amazement: something had happened to that three-thousand-year-old vase within those fifty-year-old walls, under the ancient light of summer, something very disrespectful that was not unlike the air of morning. He had thought: "I did it," and felt quite proud, freed from the world, without ties or kin or origins, a stubborn little excrescence that had burst the terrestrial crust.

He was sixteen, a raffish youth, lying on the sand at Arcachon, looking at the long, flat ocean waves. He had just thrashed a lad from Bordeaux who had thrown stones at him, and he had forced him to eat sand. Seated in the shade of the pines, out of breath, his nostrils filled with the odor of resin, he felt somehow like a little explosive entity suspended in the atmosphere, spherical, compact, mysterious. He had said to himself: "I will be free," or rather he hadn't said anything at all, but that was what he wanted to say and it was in the nature of a bet; he had made a bet with himself that his whole life should be cast in the semblance of that unique moment. He was twenty-one, he was reading Spinoza in his room, on a Shrove Tuesday, gaily painted carts were passing down the street laden with cardboard figures; he had looked up and again made his bet, with that philosophic emphasis which Brunet and himself had recently assumed; he had said to himself: "I shall achieve my salvation!" Ten times, a hundred times, he had made that same bet. The words changed as his age increased, to suit his intellectual attitudes, but it was one and the same bet; and Mathieu was not, in his own eyes, a tall, rather ungainly fellow who taught philosophy in a public school, nor the brother of Jacques Delarue, the lawyer, nor Marcelle's lover, nor Daniel's and Brunet's friend: he was just that bet personified.

What bet? He passed his hands over his eyes, now wearied by the light; he no longer really knew; he was subject—more and more often now—to long moments of exile. To understand his bet, he had to be feeling exceptionally alert.

"Ball, please."

A tennis ball rolled up to his feet, a little boy ran towards him, racket in hand. Mathieu picked up the ball and threw it. He was certainly not particularly alert: he sweltered in that depressing heat, he could do no more than submit to the ancient and monotonous sensation of the daily round; in vain he repeated the once inspiring phrases: "I must be free. I must be self-impelled, and able to say: 'I am because I will; I am my own beginning.'" Empty, pompous words, the commonplaces of the intellectual.

He got up. An official got up, an official who was wor

ried about money and was going to visit the sister of one of his old pupils. He thought: "Are the stakes all set? Am I now just an official and nothing more?" He had waited so long; his latter years had been no more than a vigil. Oppressed with countless little daily cares, he had waited; of course he had run after girls all that time, he had traveled, and naturally he had had to earn his living. But through all that, his sole care had been to hold himself in readiness. For an act. A free, considered act that should pledge his whole life and stand at the beginning of a new existence. He had never been able to engage himself completely in any love-affair, or any pleasure, he had never been really unhappy; he always felt as though he were somewhere else, that he was not yet wholly born. He waited. And during all that time, gently, stealthily, the years had come, they had grasped him from behind; thirty-four of them. He ought to have made his decision at twenty-five. Like Brunet. Yes, but at that age one doesn't decide with proper motivation. One is liable to be fooled; and he didn't want to act in that way. He thought of going to Russia, of dropping his studies, of learning a manual trade. But what had restrained him each time on the brink of such a violent break was that he had no *reasons* for acting thus. Without reasons, such acts would have been mere impulses. And so he continued to wait. . . .

Sailboats sped over the Luxembourg pond, lashed from time to time by falling water from the fountain. He stopped to look at the miniature regatta. And he thought: "I'm no longer waiting. She is right: I have cleared myself out, sterilized myself into a being that can do nothing but wait. I am now empty, it is true, but I am waiting for nothing."

Near the fountain a little boat was in distress, and a laughing crowd looked on as a small boy tried to rescue it with a boat hook.

# CHAPTER IV

MATHIEU looked at his watch. "Twenty to eleven; she's late." He did not like her to be late, he was always afraid that she might have inadvertently died. She forgot everything, she fled herself, she forgot herself from one minute to the next, she forgot to eat, she forgot to sleep. One day she would forget to breathe, and that would be the end. Two young men had stopped beside him: they eyed a table with a disdainful air.

"Sit down," said one in English.

"I will," said the other. They laughed and did so. They had delicate hands, hard faces, and smooth skins. "Lousy little beasts," thought Mathieu irritably. Students or school-boys; young males, surrounded by gray females, looking like glittering, insistent insects. "Youth is fantastic," thought Mathieu, "so vivid on the surface, but no feeling inside it." Ivich was conscious of her youth, and so was Boris, but these were exceptions. Martyrs of youth. "I never knew I was young, nor did Brunet, nor did Daniel. We were only aware of it afterwards."

He reflected without much pleasure that he was going to take Ivich to the Gauguin exhibition. He liked to show her fine pictures, fine films, and fine things generally, because he was himself so unattractive; it was a form of self-excuse. Ivich did not excuse him: that morning, as on all occasions, she would look at the pictures with her wild, maniacal air; Mathieu would stand beside her, ugly, persistent, and forgotten. And yet he would not have liked to be good-looking—she was never more alone than when confronted with something to admire. He said to himself: "I don't know what I want from her." At that very moment he caught sight of her; she was walking down the boulevard beside a tall, shiny-haired young man in spectacles, she raised her face to his and offered him her brilliant smile; they were deep in animated talk. When she saw Mathieu, the light went out of her eyes, she parted from her companion with a brief good-by and crossed the rue des Écoles with a drowsy air. Mathieu got up.

"Glad I am to see you, Ivich."

"Good morning," said she.

Her face was largely hidden by her fair curls, which she had brought right forward to her nose, and her fringe reached down to her eyes. In winter the wind blew her hair about and exposed her large, pallid cheeks and the low forehead that she called "my Kalmuck forehead," revealing a broad face, pale, girlish, and sensual, like a moon between clouds. Today Mathieu could see no more than an artificially narrow and ingenuous countenance that she wore like a triangular mask over the real one. Mathieu's young neighbors eyed her; they were obviously thinking: What a pretty girl! Mathieu looked at her affectionately; he was the only one among all those people who knew that Ivich was plain. She sat down, composed and gloomy. She was not made up, because make-up spoils the skin.

"And what will Madame have?" asked the waiter.

Ivich smiled at him, she liked being called Madame; then she turned to Mathieu with a hesitant air.

"Have a peppermint," said Mathieu, "you know you like it."

"Do I?" she said with amusement. "All right. What is it?" she asked when the waiter had gone.

"It's green mint."

"That green, gluey stuff I drank the other day? Oh, I don't want that, it makes my mouth all sticky. I always take what I'm given, but I oughtn't to listen to you, we haven't got the same tastes."

"You told me you liked it," said Mathieu rather irritably.

"Yes, but then I remembered the taste." She shuddered, "I'll never touch it again."

"Waiter!" cried Mathieu.

"No, no, never mind, he'll bring it, and it's nice to look at. I won't touch it, that's all; I'm not thirsty."

She said no more. Mathieu did not know what to say to her: so few things interested Ivich; besides, he didn't feel like talking. Marcelle was there; he could not see her, he did not utter her name, but she was there. Ivich he saw, he could call her by her name or touch her on the shoulder; but she was out of reach, with her frail figure and her fine, firm throat; she looked painted and varnished, like a Tahitian woman on a canvas by Gauguin, not meant for use. Sarah would be telephoning very soon. The page-boy would call out: "Monsieur Delarue"; and Mathieu would hear a dark voice at the end of a wire: "He won't take a penny less than ten thousand francs." Hospital, surgery, the reek of ether, money difficulties. Mathieu made an effort and turned towards Ivich; she had closed her eyes and was passing a finger lightly over her eyelids. She opened her eyes again.

"I have the feeling that they keep open by themselves. But I shut them now and then when they get tired. Are they red?"

"No."

"It's the sun; I always have trouble with my eyes in summer. On days like this one oughtn't to go out until it gets dark; otherwise one gets into a wretched state, the sun pursues you everywhere. And people's hands are so clammy."

Mathieu felt the palm of his own hand under the table: it was quite dry. No doubt the tall shiny-haired young man had clammy hands. He looked at Ivich without emotion; he felt both remorseful and relieved because he was less attracted by her.

"Are you annoyed because I made you come out this morning?"

"I couldn't have stayed in my room, anyhow."

"Why not?" asked Mathieu in astonishment.

Ivich looked at him impatiently.

"You don't know what a women students' hostel is like. The young ladies are very thoroughly looked after, especially at examination time. Besides, the superintendent has taken a fancy to me, she invents all sorts of pretexts for coming into my room, and she strokes my hand; I loathe being touched."

Mathieu was scarcely listening to her: he knew that she was not thinking of what she was saying. Ivich shook her head with an air of irritation.

"The old party at the hostel likes me because I'm fair. But it makes no difference, she'll detest me in three months: she'll say I'm sly."

"So you are," said Mathieu.

"I dare say . . ." she said in a drawling voice, which somehow seemed to go with her sallow cheeks.

"And in the end everyone notices how you hide your cheeks and drop your eyes as though butter wouldn't melt in your mouth."

"Oh well, I suppose you like people to know what sort of person you are," she added with a faint contempt. "It's true you aren't susceptible to that sort of thing. And as for looking people in the face," she went on, "I just can't do it. My eyes begin to smart at once."

"You used often to annoy me in the early days," said Mathieu. "You used to look at me above the forehead, just at the level of the hair, and I've always been so nervous of getting bald. . . . I thought you had noticed a thinning patch and couldn't take your eyes off it."

"I look at everyone like that."

"Yes—or sideways: so . . ."

He flung a sly, quick glance at her. She laughed, amused and angry.

"Stop! I won't be imitated."

"There was nothing very mean about that."

"No, but it frightened me to see you put on my expressions."

"I can understand that," said Mathieu, with a smile.

"You don't look as if you did. However handsome you were, the effect on me would be just the same." And she added in an altered voice: "I do wish my eyes didn't hurt me so."

"Look here," said Mathieu, "I'll go to a druggist's and get you an aspirin. But I'm waiting for a telephone call. If anyone asks for me, would you mind telling the page-boy that I'll be back in a few minutes and that the caller is to ring again?"

"No, don't go," she said coldly. "Thank you very much, but nothing would do me any good, it's the sun."

They fell silent. "What a hell of a time I'm having!" thought Mathieu with a strange, grinding thrill of pleasure. Ivich was smoothing out her skirt with the palms of her hands, lifting her fingers a little as though she were about to strike the keys of a piano. Her hands were always rather red, because she had a poor circulation; she usually held them up and waved them to make them pale. They scarcely served her to take hold of anything: they were two small crude idols at the extremities of her arms; they fluttered over the surfaces of objects, feeling their shapes, instead of picking them up. Mathieu looked at Ivich's nails, long and tapering and loudly painted, almost in the Chinese manner. Indeed, these awkward, fragile adornments made it plain that Ivich could make no use of her ten fingers. One day one of her nails had dropped off by itself; she kept it in a little casket, inspecting it from time to time with a blend of disgust and satisfaction. Mathieu had seen it: it had retained its varnish, and looked like a dead beetle. "I wonder what is on her mind: never have I known her so tiresome. It must be her examination. Well, as long as she doesn't get bored with me; after all, I'm a grown-up, so to speak."

"I suppose this isn't how blindness starts," said Ivich suddenly with a dispassionate air.

"Certainly not," said Mathieu smiling. "You know what the doctor at Laon told you: you've got a touch of conjunctivitis."

He spoke gently, he smiled gently; with Ivich it was essential to smile and use slow, gentle gestures. "Like Daniel with his cats."

"My eyes hurt me so much," said Ivich. "The merest trifle is enough. . . ." She hesitated. "I—the pain is at the back of my eyes. Right at the back. Wasn't that the beginning of that nonsense you were telling me about?"

"That affair the other day?" asked Mathieu. "Look here, Ivich, last time it was your heart, you were afraid of a heart attack. What an odd little creature you are! You almost seem as if you wanted to torment yourself; and then another time you suddenly announce that you're as hard as nails; you must make up your mind."

His voice left a sugary taste in his mouth.

Ivich looked darkly at her feet.

"Something must be going to happen to me."

"I know," said Mathieu; "your line of life is broken. But you told me you didn't really believe in that sort of thing."

"No, I don't really. . . . But it is a fact that I just can't picture my future. It's a blank."

She said no more, and Mathieu eyed her in silence. Without a future . . . suddenly he was conscious of a bad taste in his mouth and he realized how deep was his attachment to Ivich. It was true that she had no future: Ivich at thirty, Ivich at forty, didn't make any sense. There was nothing ahead of her. When Mathieu was alone or when he was talking to Daniel or Marcelle, his life stretched out before him, plain and monotonous: a few women, a few holidays, a few books. A long and gentle slope, Mathieu was moving slowly, slowly down it; indeed, he often found himself wishing that the process could be speeded up. And suddenly, when he saw Ivich, he felt as though he were experiencing a catastrophe. Ivich was a voluptuous and tragic little embodiment of pain which had no morrow: she would depart, go mad, die of a heart attack, or her parents would keep her close at Laon. But Mathieu could not endure to live without her. He made a timid movement with his hand: he longed to grasp Ivich's arm above the elbow and squeeze it. "I loathe being touched." Mathieu's hand fell back. He said quickly:

"That's a very nice blouse you're wearing, Ivich."

It was a tactless remark: Ivich bent her head stiffly and tapped her blouse with an air of constraint. She regarded compliments with disgust, they made her feel as though a rather blatantly alluring image of herself were being hacked out with a hatchet, and she was afraid of being deluded by it. She alone could think with due propriety about her own appearance. And she did so without the use of words, with a sort of affectionate certitude, a caress. Mathieu looked diffidently at Ivich's slender shoulders, the straight, round neck. She often said: "I have a horror of people who are not conscious of their bodies." Mathieu was conscious of his body, but rather as though it were a large and embarrassing parcel.

"Do you still want to go and see the Gauguins?"

"What Gaugins? Oh yes, the exhibition you were talking about. Well, we might go."

"You don't look as if you wanted to."

"Yes, I do."

"But if you don't want to, Ivich, you must say so."

"But *you* want to go."

"I've been already, as you know. I should like to show it to you if it would amuse you, but if you don't care about it, I'm no longer interested."

"Very well, then, I would sooner go another day."

"But the exhibition closes tomorrow," said Mathieu in a disappointed tone.

"I'm sorry for that," said Ivich indifferently, "but it will come back." And she added briskly: "Things like that always come back, don't they?"

"Ivich," said Mathieu, kindly but with some irritation, "that's just like you. You had better say you no longer want to go, you know quite well that it won't come back for a long time."

"Oh well," she said amiably, "I don't want to go because I'm upset about this examination. It's hell to make us wait so long for the results."

"Aren't they to come out tomorrow?"

"That's just it." And she added, touching Mathieu's sleeve with the tips of her fingers: "You mustn't mind me today, I'm not myself. I'm dependent on other people, which is so degrading; I keep on seeing a vision of a little white paper stuck to a gray wall. I just can't help it. When I got up this morning, I felt as if it was tomorrow already; today isn't a day at all, it's a day canceled. They've robbed me of it, and I haven't so many left." And she added in a low, rapid voice: "I made a mess of my botany prelim."

"I can well understand that," said Mathieu.

He wished he could discover in his own recollections a time of trouble that would enable him to understand what Ivich was enduring. The day before his diploma test, per-

haps. No, that wasn't really the same thing. He had lived
a placid sort of life, one that involved no risks. At present
he felt precarious, beset by a menacing world, but that
sensation was reflected *through* Ivich.

"If I qualify," said Ivich, "I shall have a few drinks before going to the oral."

Mathieu did not reply.

"Just a few," repeated Ivich.

"You said that in February, before going up for the
intermediate, and you know what happened; you drank
four glasses of rum and you were completely tight."

"However, I shan't qualify."

"No doubt, but if, by chance, you do?"

"Well, I won't drink anything at all."

Mathieu did not insist; he was sure that she would turn
up drunk at the oral. "I wouldn't have done such a thing,
I was much too careful." He was annoyed with Ivich and
disgusted with himself. The waiter brought a stemmed
glass and half filled it with green mint.

"I'll bring you the ice-bowl right away."

"Thank you," said Ivich.

She looked at the glass, and Mathieu looked at her. A
violent and undefined desire had taken possession of him:
a desire to *be* for one instant that distracted consciousness
so pervaded by its own odor, to feel those long slender
arms from within, to feel, at the hollow of the elbow, the
skin of the forearm clinging like a lip to the skin of the
arm, to feel that body and all the discreet little kisses it
so ceaselessly imprinted on itself. To be Ivich and not
cease to be himself. Ivich took the bowl from the waiter's
hand and dropped a cube of ice into her glass.

"It's not to drink," she said, "but it's prettier like that."

She screwed up her eyes a little and smiled a girlish
smile. "How pretty it looks!"

Mathieu eyed the glass with irritation, he set himself
to observe the thick, ungraceful agitation of the liquid,

the turbid whiteness of the ice cube. In vain. For Ivich it was a little viscous delight that made her sticky down to her fingertips; for him it was nothing. Less than nothing: a glass full of mint. He could *think* what Ivich felt, but he never felt anything; for her, objects were oppressive, insinuating presences, eddies that entered into her very flesh, but Mathieu always saw them from a distance. He flung a glance at her and sighed: he was behindhand, as usual. Ivich was no longer looking at the glass; she wore a sad expression and was nervously tugging at one of her curls.

"I should like a cigarette."

Mathieu took a packet of Goldflake out of his pocket and handed it to her.

"I'll give you a light."

"Thank you, I prefer to light it myself."

She lit the cigarette and took a few whiffs. She held her hand close to her mouth and with a sort of crazily intent expression amused herself by making the smoke trickle along her palm. And she said, by way of explanation to herself:

"I wanted the smoke to look as though it came out of my hand. It would be funny to see a hand smoldering."

"It isn't possible, the smoke moves too quickly."

"I know, it's tiresome, but I can't help trying. I can feel my breath tickling my hand, right through the middle, as though it were divided by a wall."

She laughed lightly and fell silent, still breathing on her hand with a sort of peevish persistence. Then she threw her cigarette away and shook her head; the smell of her hair reached Mathieu's nostrils. A smell of cake and of vanilla-flavored sugar, from the egg-yolks that she used to wash her hair; but that pastried perfume left a fleshy taste behind it.

Mathieu began to think about Sarah.

"What are you thinking about, Ivich?" he asked.

She sat for a moment with her mouth open, disconcerted, then she resumed her meditative air and her face again became impenetrable. Mathieu found himself tired of looking at her, the corners of his eyes began to smart.

"What are you thinking about?" he repeated.

"I—" Ivich shook herself. "You're always asking me that. Nothing definite. Things that can't be expressed, there are no words for them."

"Still—what?"

"Well, I was looking at that fellow coming towards us, for instance. What do you want me to say? I should have to say: he's fat, he's wiping his forehead with a handkerchief, he's wearing a made-up tie—it's funny you should force me to tell you all this," she said, in sudden disgust and indignation, "it isn't worth saying."

"Yes it is—for me. If I could be granted a wish, it would be that you should be compelled to think aloud."

Ivich smiled involuntarily.

"That's morbid," she said. "Words aren't meant for that."

"It's fantastic, you've got a savage's respect for words; you apparently believe that they were made simply for announcing deaths and marriages and saying Mass. Besides, you don't look at people, Ivich, I've been watching you. You looked at your hand and then you looked at your foot. Anyway, I know what you're thinking."

"Then why ask? You don't need to be very clever to guess: I was thinking of the examination."

"You're afraid of being flunked, is that it?"

"Of course I'm afraid of being flunked. Or rather—no, I'm not afraid. I *know* I flunked."

Mathieu again sensed the savor of catastrophe in his mouth: "If she is flunked, I shan't see her again." She would certainly be flunked: that was plain enough.

"I won't go back to Laon," said Ivich desperately. "If I go back to Laon after having been flunked, I'll never get away again. They told me it was my last chance."

She fell to tugging at her hair again.

"If I had the courage—" she faltered.

"What would you do?" asked Mathieu anxiously.

"Anything and everything rather than go back to that place; I won't spend my life there, I just won't!"

"But you told me your father might sell the sawmill in a year or two from now and the whole family come and settle in Paris."

"Oh my God! That's what you're all like," said Ivich, turning towards him, her eyes glittering with rage. "I should like to see you there. Two years in that hole, two years of black endurance. Can't you get it into your head that those two years would be stolen from me? I've only got one life," she said passionately. "From the way you talk, you sound as though you believed yourself immortal. According to you, a year lost can be replaced." The tears came into her eyes. "That's not true, it's my youth that will be oozing out there, drop by drop. I want to live immediately, I haven't begun, and I haven't time to wait, I'm old already, I'm twenty-one."

"Ivich—please!" said Mathieu. "You frighten me. Do try for once at least to tell me clearly how you got on in the practical test. Sometimes you look quite pleased and sometimes you're in despair."

"I messed it all up," said Ivich gloomily.

"I thought you did all right in physics."

"I don't think!" said Ivich sardonically. "And then my chemistry was hopeless, I can't keep the formulæ in my head, they're so dismal."

"But why did you go in for it?"

"What?"

"The P.C.B.?"

"I had to get away from Laon," she said wildly.

Mathieu made a helpless gesture, and they fell silent. A woman emerged from the café and walked slowly past them; she was handsome, with a very small nose in a sleek face, and she seemed to be looking for somebody. Ivich must first have smelled her scent. She raised her brooding face, saw the woman, and her whole expression was transformed.

"What a magnificent creature!" she said in a low, deep voice. Mathieu hated that voice.

The woman stood motionless, blinking in the sunshine, she might have been about thirty-five, her long legs could be seen in outline through her thin silk frock; but Mathieu had no desire to look at them, he was looking at Ivich. Ivich had become almost ugly, she was squeezing her hands hard against each other. She had said to Mathieu one day: "Little noses always make me want to bite them." Mathieu leaned forward until he could see her in three-quarter profile; she looked somnolent and cruel, just, he thought, as though she would like to bite.

"Ivich," said Mathieu gently.

She did not answer; Mathieu knew that she could not answer: he no longer existed for her, she was quite alone.

"Ivich!"

It was at such moments that he was most attracted by her, when her charming, almost dainty little person was possessed by a gripping force, an ardent, uneasy, graceless love of human beauty. "I," he thought, "am no beauty," and he felt alone in his turn.

The woman departed. Ivich followed her with her eyes, and muttered passionately: "There are moments when I wish I were a man." She laughed a short dry laugh, and Mathieu eyed her regretfully.

"Monsieur Delarue is wanted on the telephone," cried the page-boy.

"Here!" said Mathieu.

He got up. "Excuse me, it's Sarah Gomez."

Ivich smiled coldly. He entered the café and went downstairs.

"Monsieur Delarue? First booth."

Mathieu picked up the receiver; the door would not shut.

"Hello, is that Sarah?"

"'Morning again," said Sarah's nasal voice. "Well, it's fixed up."

"I'm thankful to hear it."

"Only you must hurry: he's leaving for the United States on Sunday. He would like to do it the day after tomorrow at latest, so as to have time to treat the case during the first few days."

"Right. . . . Well then, I'll tell Marcelle this very day, only it catches me a bit short, I shall have to find the money. How much does he want?"

"I'm terribly sorry," said Sarah's voice, "but he wants four thousand francs, cash down. I did tell him that you were rather hard up at the moment, but he wouldn't budge. He's a dirty Jew," she added with a laugh.

Sarah was always brimming with superfluous compassion, but when she had undertaken to do anyone a service, she became as abrupt and bustling as a Sister of Charity. Mathieu was holding the receiver a little away from his ear. "Four thousand francs," he thought, and he heard Sarah's laugh crackle on the little black disk, with a positively nightmarish effect.

"In two days from now? Right, I—I'll fix it. Thank you, Sarah, you're a treasure. Will you be at home this evening before dinner?"

"All day."

"Good. I'll be along. There are one or two things to arrange."

"Till this evening."

Mathieu emerged from the booth.

"I want to telephone, mademoiselle. Oh, no, it doesn't matter, after all."

He threw a franc into a saucer and walked slowly upstairs. It wasn't worth while ringing up Marcelle before he had settled the money question. "I'll go and see Daniel at midday." He sat down again beside Ivich and looked at her without affection.

"My headache is gone," she said politely.

"I'm glad to hear it," said Mathieu.

His heart felt sooty.

Ivich threw a sidelong glance at him through her long eyelashes. There was a blurred, coquettish smile upon her face.

"We might—we might go and see the Gauguins after all."

"If you like," said Mathieu equably.

They got up and Mathieu noticed that Ivich's glass was empty.

"Taxi!" he cried.

"Not that one, it's open, we shall have the wind in our faces."

"No," said Mathieu to the chauffeur, "drive on, it wasn't for you."

"Stop that one," said Ivich; "it's as neat as a traveling tabernacle for the Holy Sacrament, and besides it's closed."

The taxi stopped, and Ivich got into it. "While I'm there," thought Mathieu, "I'll ask Daniel for an extra thousand francs—that will see me to the end of the month."

"Galerie des Beaux-Arts, faubourg Saint-Honoré."

He sat in silence beside Ivich. They were both ill at ease.

Mathieu noticed near his feet three half-smoked gold-tipped cigarettes.

"There's been someone all wrought up in this cab."

"How do you know?"

"It was a woman," said Ivich, "I can see the marks of lipstick."

They smiled and fell silent.

Mathieu said: "I once found a hundred francs in a taxi."

"You must have been pleased."

"Oh, I gave them to the chauffeur."

"Did you?" said Ivich. "I should have kept them. Why did you do that?"

"I don't know," said Mathieu.

The taxi crossed the Place Saint-Michel.

Mathieu was on the point of saying: "Look how green the Seine is," but he said nothing. Ivich suddenly remarked:

"Boris suggested we might all three go to the Sumatra this evening; I should rather like to. . . ."

She turned her head and was looking at Mathieu's hair, tilting her mouth towards him with a touch of affectionate coquetry. Ivich was not precisely a flirt, but from time to time she assumed an affectionate air for the pleasure of sensing the heavy, fruitlike sleekness of her face. Mathieu thought it an irritating and rather silly pose.

"I shall be glad to see Boris and to be with you," he said, "but what bothers me a little, as you know, is Lola; she can't stand me."

"What does that matter?"

A silence followed. It was as though they had both simultaneously realized that they were a man and a woman, enclosed together in a taxi. "It oughtn't to be so," he said to himself with annoyance. Ivich continued:

"I don't myself think that Lola is worth troubling about. She's good-looking, and she sings well, that's all."

"I think she's nice."

"Naturally. That's your attitude, you always must be perfect. The moment people dislike you, you do your best to discover virtues in them. I don't think she's nice," she added.

"She is charming to you."

"She can't behave otherwise; but I don't like her, she's always acting a part."

"Acting a part?" asked Mathieu, raising his eyebrows; "that's the last thing I should have accused her of doing."

"It's odd you shouldn't have noticed it: she heaves sighs as large as herself to make people believe she's in despair, and then orders herself a nice little dinner."

And she added with sly malice: "I should have thought that when people were in despair they wouldn't mind dying: I'm always surprised when I see her adding up every penny she spends, and saving money."

"That doesn't prevent her being desperate. It's just what people do when they're getting old: when they're sick of themselves and their life, they think of money and take care of themselves."

"Well, one oughtn't ever to get old," said Ivich dryly.

He looked at her with surprise and hurriedly added: "You're right, it isn't nice to be old."

"Oh, but you aren't any age," said Ivich. "I have the feeling that you have always been as you are now, you've got a kind of mineral youthfulness. I sometimes try to imagine what you were like as a boy, but I can't."

"I had curly hair," said Mathieu.

"Well, I picture you just as you are today, except for being a little smaller."

This time Ivich probably did not know that she was looking affectionate. Mathieu wanted to speak, but there was an odd irritation in his throat, and he suddenly lost all self-control. Away behind him were Marcelle, Sarah, and the interminable hospital corridors in which he had been wandering since morning; he was no longer anywhere at all, he felt free. The dense, warm mass of a summer day came close to him, and he longed to plunge headlong into it. For one more second he seemed suspended in the void, with an agonizing sense of freedom, and then, abruptly, he reached out his arm, took Ivich by the shoul-

ders, and clasped her to him. Ivich yielded stiffly, all of a
piece, as though she were losing her balance. She said
nothing; her face was utterly impassive.

The taxi had entered the rue de Rivoli, the arcades of
the Louvre lumbered past the windows, like great doves
in flight. It was hot—Mathieu felt a warm body against
his side; through the front window he could see trees and
a tricolor flag pendent from a mast. He remembered the
action of a man he had seen once in the rue Mouffetard.
A decently dressed guy with an absolutely gray face. The
guy had gone up to a provision-shop, he had gazed for a
long time at a slice of cold meat on a plate in the open
window, then he had reached out a hand and taken the
piece of meat; he did so with apparent ease, he too must
have felt free. The shopkeeper had yelled, a policeman
had appeared and removed the guy, who seemed surprised. Ivich was still silent.

"She's criticizing me," thought Mathieu irritably.

He leaned towards her; and to punish her, he laid his
lips lightly against a cold, closed mouth; he was feeling
defiant; Ivich was silent. Lifting his head, he saw her eyes,
and his passionate joy vanished. He thought: "A married
man messing about with a young girl in a taxi," and his
arm dropped, dead and flaccid; Ivich's body straightened
with a mechanical jerk, like a pendulum swinging back
to equilibrium. "Now I've done it," said Mathieu to himself, "she'll never forgive me." He sat huddled in his seat,
wishing he might disintegrate. A policeman raised his
baton, the taxi stopped. Mathieu looked straight in front
of him, but he could not see the trees; he was looking at
his love.

It was love. *This time* it was love. And Mathieu thought:
"What have I done?" Five minutes ago this love didn't
exist; there was between them a rare and precious feeling,
without a name and not expressible in gestures. And he
had, in fact, made a gesture, the only one that ought not

to have been made—it had come spontaneously. A gesture, and this love had appeared before Mathieu, like some insistent and already commonplace entity. Ivich would from now on think that he loved her, she would think him like the rest; from now on, Mathieu would love Ivich, like the other women he had loved. "What is she thinking?" She sat by his side, stiff and silent, and there was this gesture between them—"I hate being touched"— this clumsy, affectionate gesture, already marked with the impalpable insistence of things past. She was furious, she despised him, she thought him like the rest. "That wasn't what I wanted of her," he thought with despair. But even by this time he could no longer recall what he had wanted *before.* Love was there, compact and comfortable, with its simple desires and all its commonplace behavior, and it was Mathieu who had brought it into being, in absolute freedom. "It isn't true," he reflected vehemently; "I don't desire her, I never have desired her." But he already knew that he was going to desire her. It always finishes like that; he would look at her legs and her breasts, and then, one fine day. . . . In a flash he saw Marcelle outstretched on the bed, naked, with her eyes closed: he hated Marcelle.

The taxi had stopped; Ivich opened the door and stepped out into the street. Mathieu did not follow her at once: he was absorbed in wide-eyed contemplation of this love of his, so new and yet already old, a married man's love, sly, and shameful, humiliating for her, and, himself humiliated in advance, he already accepted it as a fatality. He got out at last, paid the fare, and rejoined Ivich, who was waiting in the entrance. "If only she could forget." He threw a furtive glance at her and caught a hard look on her face. "At the best, there is something between us that is over," he thought. But he had no wish to stop loving her. They went into the exhibition without exchanging a word.

# CHAPTER V

"THE archangel!" Marcelle yawned, sat up, shook her
head, and this was her first thought: "The archangel
is coming this evening." She liked his mysterious visits,
but that day she thought of them without much pleasure.
There was a fixed horror in the air about her, a midday
horror. The room was filled with stale heat, which had
spent its force outside and left its radiance in the folds of
the curtain and was stagnating there, inert and ominous
like a human destiny. "If he knew, he is so austere that
he would hate me." She had sat down on the edge of the
bed, just like yesterday, when Mathieu was sitting naked
at her side; she eyed her toes with distaste, and the previous evening lingered, impalpable, with its dead pink
light, like the faded fragrance of a scent. "I couldn't—I
just couldn't tell him." He would have said: "Right! Very
well, fix it," with a brisk and cheerful air, as though in the
act of swallowing a dose of medicine. She knew that she
could not have endured that face; it had stuck in her
throat. She thought: "Midday!" The ceiling was gray like
the sky at dawn, but the heat was of midday. Marcelle
went to bed late and was no longer acquainted with the
morning hours; she sometimes had the feeling that her

life had come to a stop one day at noon and she herself
was an embodied, eternal noontide brooding upon her
little world, a dank and rainy world, without hope or purpose. Outside, broad daylight and bright-colored frocks.
Mathieu was on the move outside, in the gay and dusty
whirl of a day that had begun without her and already
had a past. "He's thinking about me, he's doing all he
can," she thought without affection. She was annoyed
because she could imagine that robust, sunlit pity, the
bustling, clumsy pity of a healthy man. She felt languid
and clammy, still quite disheveled from sleep: the familiar
steel helmet gripped her head, there was a taste of blot-
ting-paper in her mouth, a lukewarm feeling down her
sides, and beneath her arms, tipping the black hairs, beads
of sweat. She felt sick, but restrained herself: her day had
not yet begun, it was there, propped precariously against
Marcelle, the least movement would bring it crashing
down like an avalanche. She laughed sardonically and
muttered: "Freedom!"

A human being who wakened in the morning with a
queasy stomach, with fifteen hours to kill before next bed-
time, had not much use for freedom. Freedom didn't help
a person to live. Delicate little feathers dipped in aloes
tickled the back of her throat, and then a sense of utter-
most disgust gathered upon her tongue and drew her lips
back. "I'm lucky, apparently some women are sick all day
at the second month; I bring up a little in the morning
and feel rather tired in the afternoon, but I keep going.
Mother knew women who couldn't stand the smell of
tobacco, and that would be the last straw." She got up
abruptly and ran to the basin; she vomited a foamy, turbid
liquid, which looked rather like the slightly beaten white
of an egg. Marcelle clutched the porcelain rim and gazed
at the frothing water. In the end it began to look like
semen. She smiled wryly and murmured: "A memento of
love." Then a vast metallic silence took possession of her

head, and her day began. She was no longer thinking of anything. She ran her hand through her hair and waited: "I'm always sick twice in the morning." And then, quite suddenly, she had a vision of Mathieu's face, his frank, determined look, when he had said: "Well, I suppose one gets rid of it, eh?" and a flash of hate shot through her.

It came. She first thought of butter and was revolted; she seemed to be chewing a bit of yellow, rancid butter, then she felt something like an insistent laugh at the back of her throat and leaned over the basin. A long filament hung from her lips, she had to cough it away. It did not disgust her, though she had been very ready to be disgusted with herself: last winter, when she was suffering from diarrhea, she would not let Mathieu touch her, she was sure she smelt unpleasantly. She watched the dabs of mucus sliding slowly towards the drain-hole, leaving glossy, viscous tracks behind them, like slugs. And she muttered: "It's fantastic!" She was not revolted; this was *life;* like the slimy efflorescences of spring, it was no more repulsive than the little dab of russet, odorous gum that tipped the buds. "It isn't *that* that's repulsive." She turned on a tap to sluice the basin, and slowly took off her slip. "If I were an animal, I should be left alone." She could sink into that living languor, as into the embrace of a glorious, enveloping fatigue. She was not a fool. "One gets rid of it, eh?" Since yesterday evening she felt like a hunted quarry.

The mirror reflected her image encircled by leaden gleams. She walked up to it. She looked at neither her shoulders nor her breasts: she disliked her body. She looked at her belly, her spacious fecund pelvis. Seven years ago—Mathieu had spent the night with her, for the first time—she had looked in the mirror one morning with the same hesitant astonishment, and she had then thought: "So it's true that someone loves me," and she contemplated her polished, silken skin, almost like a fabric, and her body just a surface made to reflect the sterile play of light and to ripple beneath caresses like water beneath the wind. Today this flesh was no longer the same flesh: she looked at her belly, and the placid abundance of those rich pastures revived her girlish impressions at the sight of women suckling their babies in the Luxembourg: and beyond her fear and disgust, a kind of hope. And she thought: "It's there." In that belly a little strawberry of blood was making haste to live, with a sort of guileless urgency, a besotted little strawberry, not even yet an animal, soon to be scraped out of existence by a knife. "There are others, at this very hour, who are looking at their bellies and also thinking: 'It's there.' But they, on the other hand, are glad." She shrugged her shoulders; yes, that foolish, burgeoning body was indeed created for maternity. But men had decided otherwise. She would go to the old woman: she need only imagine it was a tumor. "Indeed, at this moment *it is just a tumor.*" And then the affair would never again be mentioned, it would be no more than a sordid memory, such as plays a part in everybody's life. She would return to her pink room, she would continue to read, and feel rather uncomfortable inside. Mathieu would see her four nights a week, and would treat her, for some time still, with affectionate forbearance, as though she were a young mother, and when he made love to her he would redouble his precautions, and Daniel, Daniel the archangel, would also come from time to time. . . . An opportunity missed, eh? She caught sight of her eyes in the glass and turned abruptly away: she did not want to hate Mathieu. And she thought: "I must begin dressing all the same."

Her courage failed her. She sat down again on the bed, laid her hand lightly on her belly, just above the black hairs, and pressed it very gently, reflecting almost with affection: "It's there." But her hatred wouldn't let up. She said to herself with emphasis: "I won't hate him. He is

within his rights, we always said that in case of accident.
. . . He couldn't know, it's my fault, I never told him anything." For an instant she was able to believe that her
tense mood would relax, she dreaded having to despise
him. But then she quivered as she thought: "How could
I have told him? He never asks me anything." They had
indeed agreed, once for all, that they would tell each
other everything, but that worked out mainly in his favor.
He was very fond of talking about himself, of dilating on
his little struggles with his conscience, his moral scruples.
As for Marcelle, he confided in her: but in lethargy of
mind. He never worried about her, he said to himself:
"If there was anything the matter with her, she would tell
me." But she could not speak: it wouldn't come out. "And
yet he ought to know that I can't talk about myself, that
I don't like myself enough for that." Except with Daniel;
Daniel knew how to interest her in herself: he had such
a charming way of questioning her, as he gazed at her
with his fine, caressing eyes, and besides they had a mutual
secret. Daniel was so mysterious; he saw her secretly and
Mathieu was quite unaware of their intimacy; they did
nothing wrong, it was a sort of little comedy, but that
complicity established a light and charming bond between
them; and besides, Marcelle was not sorry to have a little
personal life, something that was really hers and she was
not obliged to share. "He had only to behave like Daniel,"
she thought. "Why is there no one but Daniel who knows
how to make me talk? If he had helped me a little . . ."
All yesterday the words had stuck in her throat; she would
have liked to say: "What about having it?" If he had hesitated, if only for a second, she would have said it. But he
had come, he had assumed his frank expression—"One
gets rid of it, eh?" And the words wouldn't come out. "He
was worried when he went away: he didn't want that old
woman to do me in. Oh yes, he'll inquire for addresses, it
will occupy his time now term is finished, and that's much

better than trailing about with Ivich. Besides, he really feels as angry as if he had broken a vase. But his conscience is, in fact, completely at ease. No doubt he has made up his mind to treat me with the utmost affection." She laughed curtly. "Well, well. Only he'd better hurry up. I shall soon have passed the age for love."

She clutched the sheets; she was afraid. "If I start detesting him, what would be left to me?" Did she even know if she wanted a child? She could see, in the distance, in the mirror, a dark limp mass: her body—the body of a barren odalisque. Would he even have lived? "For I am tainted." She would go to this old woman, under cover of night. And the old woman would stroke her hair, as she had stroked Andrée's, and call her dearie, with an air of vile complicity. "When a woman isn't married, pregnancy is as filthy as gonorrhea. I must try to make myself believe I've caught a venereal disease."

But she could not refrain from passing a hand over her belly, thinking: "It is there." Something living and unlucky, like herself. An absurd, superfluous life, just like her own. . . . Then she thought vehemently: "He would have been *mine*. Imbecile, or deformed, still mine." But that secret desire, that dark oath, were so remote, so utterly beyond avowal, and must be kept so carefully concealed from so many people, that she suddenly felt guilty and filled with self-contempt.

# CHAPTER VI

WHAT first met their eyes was the escutcheon above the door, bearing the letters "R.F." and the tricolor flags, which set the atmosphere at once. Then the visitor entered vast, empty halls, flooded by an academic light from frosted windows in the roof; a gilded light that soaked into the eyes, melted, and turned gray. White walls, beige velvet curtains; and Mathieu thought: "The French spirit." A visitation of the French spirit, it was indeed all-pervading—on Ivich's hair, on Mathieu's hands, in the muted sunshine and the official silence of these halls. Mathieu felt overwhelmed by a cloud of civic responsibilities. Visitors must talk in an undertone, not touch the exhibits, exercise their critical instinct with moderation, but also with decision, and not on any account forget the most French of all the virtues—Relevance. There were patches, of course, on the walls in the shape of pictures, but Mathieu no longer felt any wish to look at them. However, he took Ivich round and silently pointed out to her a Breton landscape with a calvary, a Crucifixion, a flower-piece, two Tahitian women kneeling on a beach, a dance of Maori horsemen. Ivich said nothing and Mathieu wondered what was in her mind. He made spasmodic efforts to look at the pictures, but they conveyed nothing to him. "Pictures," he thought with annoyance, "have no positive force, they are no more than suggestions; indeed, their existence depends on me, I am free as I confront them." Too free; he felt burdened by an additional responsibility, and somehow in fault.

"That," he said, "is Gauguin."

It was a small square canvas labeled: "Portrait of the Artist, by himself." Gauguin, pallid and sleek-haired, with an enormous jowl, combining an air of suave intelligence with the sullen conceit of a child. Ivich did not answer, and Mathieu flung her a further glance: he could only see her hair, tarnished by the false splendor of the day. The week before, when he had seen the portrait for the first time, Mathieu had thought it good. At present he felt desiccated. Besides, he didn't *see* the picture: Mathieu was oversaturated by reality and truth, permeated by the spirit of the Third Republic; he saw all that was real, he saw—he saw everything that that classic light could clarify, the walls, the canvases in their frames, the scumbled colors on the canvases. But not the pictures; the pictures had become extinct, and it appeared monstrous, in the depths of this little domain of relevance, that people could have been found to paint, to depict non-existent objects upon canvases.

A lady and a gentleman came in. The gentleman was tall and pink, with eyes like shoe-buttons, and soft white hair; the lady was of the gazelle-like type, and about forty. No sooner had they entered than they looked at home: no doubt a habit of theirs; indeed, there was an undeniable connection between their air of youthfulness and the quality of the light; the light of national exhibitions was clearly best fitted to preserve them. Mathieu pointed out to Ivich a large dark patch of muddy color on the side of the end wall.

"That's him again."

Gauguin, naked to the waist under a staring sky, glaring at them with the hard, false eyes of the hallucinated mind. Solitude and pride had eaten up his face, his body was transformed into a lush, limp, tropical fruit with pockets full of water. He had lost his Dignity—that Human Dignity which Mathieu still preserved without knowing how to use it—but he had kept his pride. Behind him loomed dark presences, a whole Sabbath of grim figures. The first time he had seen that foul and dreadful flesh, Mathieu had felt moved; but he was alone. Today there was a rancorous little body at his side, and Mathieu felt uneasily intrusive: a heap of refuse against a wall.

The lady and the gentleman approached; they took their stand opposite the picture. Ivich had to step aside, as they blocked her view. The gentleman tilted his head back and eyed the picture with critical intentness. Obviously a personage: he was wearing the rosette of the Legion of Honor.

"Dear, dear, dear," he observed, wagging his head. "I don't like that at all. He positively seems to have conceived himself as Christ. And that black angel—there, behind him—can't be seriously meant."

The lady began to laugh.

"Bless me, it's true," said she, in a flower-like voice, "it's such a terribly literary angel."

"I don't care for Gauguin when he tries to think," said the gentleman portentously. "The *real* Gauguin is the *decorator.*"

He looked at Gauguin with his doll's eyes, a neat slim figure in an elegant gray flannel suit, confronting that great naked body. Mathieu heard an odd gurgle and turned round. Ivich had been seized with a paroxysm of laughter and threw him a despairing look as she bit her lips. "She isn't angry with me any more," thought Mathieu with a flash of joy. He took her by the arm and led her, still convulsed, to a leather armchair in the center of the room. Ivich sank laughing on to the chair; her hair had tumbled all over her face.

"It's terrific," she said aloud. "Did you hear him say: 'I don't like Gauguin when he tries to think'? And the female—just the sort of female for a man like that."

The lady and the gentleman were standing very erect; they exchanged looks in apparent consultation on the proper line to take.

"There are more pictures in the side room," said Mathieu timidly.

Ivich stopped laughing.

"No," she said gloomily, "it's not the same now: there are people . . ."

"Would you like to go away?"

"Yes, I think so; all these pictures have brought my headache back. I should like to take a little walk."

She got up. Mathieu followed her, throwing a regretful glance at the large picture on the left-hand wall. He would have liked to show it to her. Two women were walking barefooted over pink grass. One of them was hooded like a sorceress, the other with an arm outstretched in prophetic impassivity. They were not quite alive. They looked as if they had been caught in the process of transforming themselves into objects.

Outside, the street was aflame; Mathieu had a sense of walking through an oven.

"Ivich," he said involuntarily.

Ivich grimaced, and raised her hands to her eyes.

"I feel as if they were being pricked with pins. Oh," she said vehemently, "how I hate the summer!"

They walked a few steps. Ivich swayed slightly, her hands still held against her eyes.

"Look out," said Mathieu. "You're on the edge of the sidewalk."

Ivich dropped her hand abruptly, and Mathieu saw her pale, staring eyes. They crossed the street in silence.

"They oughtn't to be public," said Ivich suddenly.

"You mean—exhibitions?" asked Mathieu in astonishment.

"Yes."

"If they weren't public"—he tried to resume the tone of gay familiarity in which they usually conversed—"I wonder how we should get there."

"Well, we wouldn't go," said Ivich curtly.

They were silent, and Mathieu thought: "She's still angry with me." And then suddenly a ghastly certainty flashed through his mind. "She wants to clear out. That's all she's thinking of. She's simply trying to find a polite way for saying good-by, and when she's found one, she'll leave me standing. I wish she wouldn't go," he thought despondently.

"You haven't got anything particular to do?" he asked.

"When?"

"Now."

"No, nothing."

"As you wanted to go for a walk, I thought—would it bore you to go with me as far as Daniel's place, in the rue Montmartre? We can say good-by outside his door, and you must let me stand you a taxi back to the hostel."

"If you like, but I'm not going back to the hostel, I'm going to see Boris."

So she didn't mean to leave him. That did not prove he was forgiven. Ivich had a horror of leaving places and people, even if she hated them, being afraid of what might come next. She acquiesced with sulky indolence in the most disagreeable situations, and ended by finding a sort of solace in them. Mathieu was glad all the same: as long as she stayed with him, he could stop her thinking. If he talked incessantly, if he asserted himself, he could for a little while delay the angry and contemptuous thoughts that would soon possess her mind. He must talk, and talk at once, about no matter what. But Mathieu could find nothing to say. In the end he asked sheepishly: "But you did enjoy those pictures, didn't you?"

Ivich shrugged her shoulders. "Of course I did."

Mathieu wanted to wipe his forehead, but didn't dare to do so. "In one hour she will be free, she will judge me without appeal, and I shall no longer be able to defend myself. I can't let her go like this," he decided. "I must explain."

He turned towards her, but when he saw her rather haggard eyes, the words would not come.

"Do you think he was mad?" asked Ivich suddenly.

"Gauguin? I don't know. Is it because of the portrait that you ask?"

"It's because of his eyes. And then there are those black figures behind him—they somehow suggest whispers."

She added with a sort of regret: "He was good-looking."

"Well," said Mathieu with surprise, "that's an idea that would not have entered my head."

Ivich had a way of talking about the illustrious dead that scandalized him slightly. She did not establish any relation between the great painters and their pictures. Pictures were things, beautiful objects to be appreciated and possessed; they seemed to her to have always existed; painters were men like other men. She felt no gratitude to them for their works and did not respect them. She asked if they had been pleasant, kindly, and whether they had had mistresses. One day Mathieu had asked her if she liked Toulouse-Lautrec's paintings, and she had answered: "Good heavens, no—he was horribly ugly!" And Mathieu had felt quite aggrieved.

"Yes, he was good-looking," Ivich said with conviction.

Mathieu shrugged his shoulders. The insignificant students of the Sorbonne, youths as trivial and fresh as girls —Ivich could devour them with her eyes as she pleased. And even Mathieu had found her charming one day when, after watching a girl from an orphanage school accompanied by two nuns, she had with rather uneasy gravity said: "I believe I'm becoming homosexual." Women, too, she might admire. But not Gauguin. Not that man of middle years who had made *for her* pictures that she liked.

"The trouble is," said he, "that to me he's not likable."

Ivich made a contemptuous grimace and said nothing.

"What is it, Ivich?" said Mathieu quickly. "You aren't cross with me for saying that he wasn't likable?"

"No, but I wonder why you said it."

"Just like that. Because it's my impression: that haughty air of his gives him the look of a boiled fish."

Ivich began to tug at a curl; she had assumed an expression of blank obstinacy.

"He has an air of distinction," she said in a nonchalant tone.

"Yes . . ." said Mathieu in the same tone, "he looks arrogant enough, if that's what you mean."

"Quite," said Ivich with a little laugh.

"Why do you say 'quite'?"

"Because I was sure you would call it arrogance."

"I don't mean to say anything against him," said Mathieu mildly. "I like people to think well of themselves."

For a while they were silent. Then Ivich said abruptly, with a set and foolish look:

"The French don't like anything aristocratic."

Ivich was rather fond of talking about the French temperament when she was angry, and always looked rather silly when she did so. But she added in an ingenuous tone:

"I can understand it, though. From the outside it must look so exaggerated."

Mathieu did not answer. Ivich's father came of an aristocratic family. But for the 1917 revolution, Ivich would have been educated in Moscow, at the academy for the daughters of the nobility. She would have been presented at court, she would have married a tall and handsome guards officer, with a narrow forehead and dead eyes.

Monsieur Serguine at present owned a sawmill at Laon. Ivich was in Paris, and going about Paris with Mathieu, a French bourgeois who disliked aristocracy.

"That's the man who—went away, isn't it?" asked Ivich suddenly.

"Yes," said Mathieu eagerly. "Would you like me to tell you the story of his life?"

"I think I know it: he was married, and he had children —isn't that so?"

"Yes. He had a job in a bank. And on Sunday he used to go out into the suburbs with an easel and a box of colors. He was what was called a Sunday painter."

"A Sunday painter?"

"Yes, that's what he was to begin with—it means an amateur who messes about with paints and canvases on Sunday; just as people take a rod and line and go out fishing. Partly for health reasons, too—painting landscapes gets a man out into the country, and good air."

Ivich began to laugh, but not with the expression that Mathieu expected.

"I suppose you think it funny that he should have begun as a Sunday painter," asked Mathieu uneasily.

"It wasn't him I was thinking about."

"What was it, then?"

"I was wondering whether people ever talked about Sunday writers, too."

Sunday writers: those petty bourgeois who wrote a short story or five or six poems every year to inject a little idealism into their lives. For health reasons. Mathieu shuddered.

"Do you mean that I'm one?" he asked gaily. "Well, it may lead to something. Perhaps I shall go off to Tahiti one of these days."

Ivich turned towards him and stared him full in the face. She looked malevolent and nervous; she was doubtless afraid of her own audacity.

"That would surprise me," she said in a toneless voice.

"Why shouldn't I?" said Mathieu. "Perhaps not to Tahiti, but to New York. I should much like to go to America."

Ivich tugged at her curls.

"I dare say," she said, "as one of a team—with other professors."

Mathieu eyed her in silence and she went on: "I may be wrong . . . I can very well imagine you delivering a lecture in a university to American students, but I can't see you on the deck of a ship among a crowd of emigrants. Perhaps it's because you're French."

"You think I need a luxury suite?" he asked with a blush.

"No," said Ivich curtly, "a second-class cabin."

He swallowed rather painfully. "I should like to see her on a ship's deck among a crowd of emigrants—she'd never stand it."

"Well," he said, "however that may be, I think it's odd of you to be so sure that I couldn't go. Besides, you're wrong, I used to want to very much in times gone by. I never did actually, because I thought it foolish. And it's especially comic that this should have come up in connection with Gauguin of all people, who remained a clerk until he was forty."

Ivich burst into an ironic laugh.

"Don't you believe it?" asked Mathieu.

"Of course—if you say so. Anyway, you've only got to look at his portrait—"

"Well?"

"Well, there can't be many clerks of his sort. He had a sort of—lost look."

Mathieu recalled a heavy face with an enormous jowl. Gauguin had lost his human dignity, and had done so willingly.

"I see," said he. "You mean the big picture at the end of the room. He was very ill at that time."

Ivich smiled contemptuously, "I mean the small picture, while he was still young. He looks capable of anything." She gazed into vacancy with a rather drawn expression, and Mathieu felt for the second time the bite of jealousy.

"Obviously, if that's what you mean, I'm not a lost man."

"Certainly not," said Ivich.

"I don't see why that should be an asset, anyway," said he, "or it may be because I don't understand what you mean."

"Oh well, let's drop the subject."

"Of course. You're always like that, you find fault with people in an indirect sort of way and then refuse to explain yourself—it's too easy."

"I'm not finding fault with anyone," she said indifferently.

Mathieu halted and looked at her. Ivich stopped too, with an air of irritation. She shifted from one foot to the other and evaded Mathieu's eye.

"Ivich, you must tell me what you meant."

"By what?" she asked with astonishment.

"When you spoke of a man being 'lost.'"

"Are we still discussing that?"

"It may seem silly," said Mathieu, "but I should like to know what you meant."

Ivich began to pull her hair again; this was exasperating.

"Nothing at all," she said, "it was just a word that came into my mind."

She stopped and seemed to be reflecting. From time to time she opened her mouth, and Mathieu thought she was going to speak; but nothing came. Then she said: "It's all the same to me whether people are like that or otherwise."

She had rolled a curl round a finger and was tugging it as though she meant to tear it out. Suddenly she added hurriedly, staring at the toes of her shoes:

"You're settled, and you won't change for all the money in the world."

"Indeed!" said Mathieu. "And how do you know?"

"It's an impression; and the impression is that your life and your ideas about everything are all set. You reach out to things when you think they're within your scope, but you don't trouble to go and get them."

"And how do you know?" repeated Mathieu. He could not find anything else to say: he felt she was right.

"I thought," said Ivich wearily, "I thought that you weren't prepared to risk anything, that you were too intelligent for that"; and she added with a sly look: "But of course if you tell me you aren't like that—"

Mathieu suddenly thought of Marcelle and was ashamed. "No," he said in a low voice, "I'm like that, just as you thought me."

"Ah!" said Ivich in a triumphant tone.

"You despise me for it?"

"On the contrary," said Ivich indulgently. "I approve. With Gauguin life must have been impossible." And she added, without the faintest trace of irony in her voice: "With you there's a sense of security, never any fear of the unexpected."

"True," said Mathieu dryly. "If you mean I don't act on impulse. . . . You know I could, like anybody else, but it seems sort of lousy to me."

"I know," said Ivich. "Everything you do is always so methodical. . . ."

Mathieu felt himself grow pale. "What are you referring to, Ivich?"

"Nothing at all."

"But you must have had something definite in mind."

"Every week," she muttered, without looking at him, "you used to turn up with the *Semaine à Paris* and make out a program . . ."

"Ivich!" said Mathieu impatiently, "it was for your benefit!"

"I know," said Ivich politely, "and I'm very grateful."

Mathieu was more surprised than hurt. "I don't understand. Didn't you like going to concerts or looking at pictures?"

"Of course I did."

"You don't say that with much conviction."

"I really did like it very much. But," she said with sudden violence, "I hate being made to feel obligations towards things I like."

"But you—you didn't like them," repeated Mathieu.

She had raised her head and flung her hair back, her broad pallid face had shed its mask, and her eyes glittered. Mathieu was dumbfounded; he looked at Ivich's thin, limp lips and wondered how he ever could have kissed them.

"You should have told me," he continued ruefully; "I would never have forced you to come."

He had dragged her to concerts and to exhibitions, he had explained the pictures to her, and while he was doing so she had hated him.

"What sort of use can pictures be to me," Ivich went on, not listening to what he said, "if I can't own them? I used to get so furious every time and long to take them away, but one can't even touch them. And I felt you beside me, so quiet and decorous. You behaved as if you were going to Mass."

They fell silent. Ivich still wore her hard expression. Mathieu suddenly felt a catch in his throat.

"Ivich, please forgive me for what happened this morning."

"This morning?" said Ivich. "I had quite forgotten it. I was thinking about Gauguin."

"It won't happen again," said Mathieu. "I still don't understand how it could have happened at all."

He spoke to clear his conscience: he knew his cause was lost. Ivich did not answer, and Mathieu continued with an effort:

"There were the museums and the concerts as well. . . . If you knew how sorry I am! One thinks one is in sympathy with someone—but you never said anything."

At every word he thought he had finished. And then another emerged from the far end of his throat and lifted his tongue. He spoke with disgust, and in short spasms. "I'll try to change," he continued. "I'm contemptible," he thought, and a desperate anger flushed his cheeks. Ivich shook her head.

"One can't change," she said. She now spoke in a matter-of-fact tone, and Mathieu frankly detested her. They walked in silence, side by side, immersed in sunlight and in mutual detestation. But at the same time Mathieu saw himself with Ivich's eyes and was filled with self-contempt. She raised her hand to her forehead and clasped her temples between her fingers.

"Is it much farther?"

"A quarter of an hour. Are you tired?"

"Yes. Forgive me, it's the pictures." She tapped her foot on the pavement and eyed Mathieu with a bewildered air. "They're out of my grasp already, and all getting mixed up in my head. It's just the same every time."

"Would you like to go home?" Mathieu felt almost relieved.

"I think it would be better."

Mathieu hailed a taxi. He was now eager to be alone.

"Good-by," said Ivich without looking at him.

Mathieu wondered whether he should go to the Sumatra just the same. But he did not even want to see her again.

"Good-by," said she.

The taxi drove off and for a few moments Mathieu watched it gloomily. Then a door slammed within him, the bolt clicked home, and he fell to thinking of Marcelle.

# CHAPTER VII

Naked to the waist, Daniel was shaving in front of his wardrobe mirror. "It's fixed for this morning; by twelve o'clock all will be over." It wasn't a simple scheme: the thing was already there, in the electric light, in the faint rasp of the razor; there was no chance of staving the event off, nor of hastening it, to get it over: it had to be gone through with, and that was all. Ten o'clock had only just struck, but midday was already present in the room, a compact and definite entity, like an eye. Beyond it there was nothing but an afternoon, writhing like a worm into vacancy. The backs of his eyes were smarting from want of sleep, and he had a pimple under his lip, a tiny red spot tipped with white: as always happened now when he had been drinking. Daniel listened: no, nothing but the noises in the street. He looked at the pimple, it was red and inflamed—there were also large bluish circles under his eyes—and he thought: "I'm ruining my health." He took great care to pass his razor all around the pimple without impinging on it; a little tuft of black hairs would remain, but that couldn't be helped: Daniel could not bear abrasions. All the while he listened: the door of his room was ajar, so that he could hear better; and he said to himself: "I won't miss her this time."

There was a faint, almost imperceptible rustle; Daniel had already dashed, razor in hand, to the door and flung it open. Too late, the child was too quick for him: she had fled, she must have huddled herself into an angle of the landing, where she stood with beating heart, holding her breath. Daniel noticed a little bunch of carnations on the mat at his feet. "Nasty little creature," he said loudly. It was the concierge's daughter, he was sure. He had only to look at her fried-fishy eyes when she said good-morning to him. This had been going on for a fortnight; every morning on her return from school she laid flowers outside his door. He kicked the flowers downstairs. He would have to stand and listen for a whole morning in the outer room, that was the only way he would catch her. He would emerge, naked to his belt, and fix her with a glassy eye. "It's my head that attracts her, my head and my shoulders, as she's a bit of an idealist. She'll get a shock when she sees the hair on my chest." He went back into his room and went on shaving. He observed in the mirror his dark, handsome, blue-jowled visage. "That's what excites them." An archangel's face; Marcelle called him her dear archangel, and now he must submit to the admiring gaze of this deplorable child, who was just at the puffy stage of puberty. "Horrid little creatures," thought Daniel angrily. He bent forward a little and with a neat stroke of the razor snipped the tip off his pimple. It wouldn't be a bad joke to deface the head they all admired. "Pah, a scarred face is still a face, it always *means* something: I should get tired of it all the sooner." He walked up close to the mirror and eyed himself distastefully. "Besides," he said to himself, "I like to be good-looking." He looked tired. He gripped himself at the level of the hips. He must get his weight down by a couple of pounds. Seven whiskies last evening all by himself at Johnny's. Until three o'clock he hadn't been able to make up his mind to go home because it gave him the shivers to put his head on the pillow and

feel himself slide away into the darkness, reflecting that
there must be a tomorrow. Daniel thought of the dogs at
Constantinople: they had been rounded up in the streets
and put into sacks, or even *baskets,* and then abandoned
on a deserted island; there they proceeded to devour one
another; and out at sea their howls were sometimes carried on the wind to the ears of passing sailors. "It wasn't
dogs that ought to have been put there." Daniel didn't
like dogs. He slipped on a cream silk shirt and a pair of
gray flannel trousers; he chose a tie with care: today he
would wear the green striped one, as he looked rather
washed-out. Then he opened the window, and the morning came into the room, a heavy, stifling morning, burdened with events to come. For one second he stood
lapped in the stagnant heat, then he looked about him:
he liked his room because it was impersonal and did not
give him away; indeed, it looked like a room in a hotel.
Four bare walls, two easy chairs, one straight chair, a
table, a wardrobe, a bed. Daniel possessed no mementos.
He observed the great wicker basket standing open in the
middle of the room and turned his eyes away: he thought
of what confronted him today.

By Daniel's watch the time was twenty-five minutes
past ten. He half-opened the door into the kitchen and
whistled. Scipio appeared first, white and sandy, with a
straggling beard. He eyed Daniel grimly, yawned fero-
ciously, and arched his back. Daniel knelt down gently
and began to stroke his nose. The cat, with eyes half-
closed, patted his sleeve with his paw. After a moment or
two Daniel picked him up by the scruff of his neck and
deposited him in the basket; Scipio lay motionless, prostrate and content. Malvina next; Daniel liked her less than
the two others, she was sly and servile. When she was
quite sure he had noticed her, she began to purr and at-
tudinize while still at a distance. She rubbed her head
against the edge of the door. Then Daniel caressed her

plump neck with one finger, she turned over on her back with stiffened paws, and he tickled the teats beneath the black fur. "Ha, ha!" he said in a sort of rhythmic chant. "Ha, ha!" and she swung from side to side, gracefully tilting her head. "Wait and see," he thought, "just wait till twelve o'clock." He picked her up by the paws and put her down beside Scipio. She looked slightly surprised, but curled herself up and, after a moment's hesitation, again began to purr.

"Poppæa!" cried Daniel. "Poppæa, Poppæa!" Poppæa hardly ever came when called; Daniel had to go and fetch her from the kitchen. When she saw him, she jumped on to the gas stove with a sharp, peevish growl. She was a stray cat, heavily scarred across her right side. Daniel had found her in the Luxembourg one winter evening, just before the garden closed, and had taken her home. She was imperious and bad-tempered, and she often bit Malvina: Daniel was fond of her. He took her in his arms, and she drew her head back, flattening her ears and arching her neck: she looked quite scandalized. He stroked her nose, and she nibbled the tip of one finger with angry playfulness; then he pinched her in the loose flesh of the neck, and she lifted a defiant little head. She did not purr—Poppæa never purred—but she looked at him, straight in the face, and Daniel thought, as indeed he often did: "A cat that looks you in the eyes is very rare." At the same time he felt an intolerable anguish take possession of him and had to turn his eyes away. "There, there," he said, "there, there, my beauty," and smiled at her with eyes averted. The two others had remained side by side, purring idiotically, like a grasshopper chorus. Daniel eyed them with a sort of malignant relief: "Rabbit stew," he thought. He remembered Malvina's pink teats. It was no end of a business to get Poppæa into the basket: he had to push her in head-first, but she turned and spat and tried to claw him. "Oh, would you now?" said Daniel.

He picked her up by the neck and hind quarters and crammed her forcibly into the basket, which creaked as Poppæa clawed it from within. Daniel took advantage of the cat's momentary stupor to slam down the lid and snap the two clasps.

"Ouf!" he ejaculated. His hand smarted slightly, with a dry little pain that was almost a tickle. He got up and looked at the basket with ironical satisfaction: safe and secure. On the back of his hand were two scratches, and in his innermost self an odd tickling sensation that promised to become unpleasant. He picked up the ball of string off the table and put it in his trouser pocket.

Then he hesitated. "It's a goodish way; I shall get pretty hot." He would have liked to wear his flannel jacket, but it was not a habit of his to yield easily to his inclinations, and besides it would be rather comical to march along in the bright sunshine, flushed and perspiring, with that burden in his arms. Comical and a trifle ridiculous: the vision made him smile and he chose his brown tweed jacket, which he had not been able to bear since the end of May. He lifted the basket by the handle and thought: "Curse the little brutes, how heavy they are!" He pictured their attitudes, humiliated and grotesque, their fury and their terror. "And that is what I was so fond of!" No sooner had he shut the three idols into a wicker basket than they became cats once more, just simply cats, small, vain, stupid mammals, stricken with panic—very far from being sacred. "Cats: merely cats." He began to laugh: he had the feeling that he was going to play an excellent trick on somebody. As he passed the outer door, his heart turned over, but the sensation soon passed: once on the staircase he felt hard and resolute, with an underside of strange sickliness, reminiscent of raw meat. The concierge was in her doorway, and she smiled at him. She liked Daniel because he was so ceremonious and polite.

"You are out early this morning, Monsieur Sereno."

"I was afraid you were ill, dear lady," replied Daniel with an air of concern. "I got back late last night, and I saw a light under the lodge door."

"Just imagine," said the concierge. "I was so done up that I fell asleep without turning the light off. Suddenly I heard the sound of your bell. 'Ah,' I said to myself, 'there's Monsieur Sereno coming in.' (You were the only tenant out.) I turned the light out immediately afterwards. I think it was about three o'clock."

"Just about. . . ."

"Well," she said, "that's a large basket you've got."

"They're my cats."

"Are they ill, poor little things?"

"No, but I'm taking them to my sister's at Meudon. The vet told me they needed air." And he added gravely: "Cats tend to become tubercular, you know."

"Tubercular!" said the concierge in a voice of consternation. "You must look after them carefully. All the same," she added, "they'll be missed in your apartment. I had got used to seeing the little dears when I was cleaning up. You will be sorry to lose them."

"I shall indeed, Madame Dupuy," said Daniel.

He smiled at her gravely and walked on. "The old mole, she gave herself away. She must have played about with them when I wasn't there; she'd much better have been attending to her daughter." Emerging from the archway, he was dazzled by the light, an unpleasant, scorching, stabbing light. It hurt his eyes, which was only to be expected: when a man has been drinking the night before, a misty morning suits him best. He could no longer see anything, he was afloat in the encompassing light, with a ring of iron round his skull. Suddenly he saw his shadow, a grotesque and stocky figure, with the shadow of the wicker basket dangling from the end of his arm. Daniel smiled: he was very tall. He drew himself up to his full height, but the shadow remained squat and misshapen, like that of a chimpanzee. "Doctor Jekyll and Mr. Hyde. No, I won't take a taxi," he said to himself; "I have plenty of time. I shall take Mr. Hyde for an airing as far as the 72 stop." The 72 would take him to Charenton. Half a mile from there Daniel knew a little solitary corner on the bank of the Seine. "At any rate," he said to himself, "I shan't be sick, that would be the last straw." The water of the Seine was particularly dark and dirty at that spot, being covered with greenish patches of oil from the Vitry factories. Daniel envisaged himself with disgust: he felt, within himself, so benevolent, so truly benevolent that it wasn't natural. "That," he thought, "is the real man," with a sort of satisfaction. His was a hard, forbidding character, but underneath it all was a shrinking victim pleading for mercy. It was odd, he thought, that a man could hate himself as though he were someone else. Not that that was really true: whatever he might do, there was only one Daniel. When he despised himself he had the feeling of detachment from his own being, as though he were poised like an impartial judge above a noisome turmoil; then suddenly he found himself plunging downwards, caught again in his own toils. "Damnation," he thought, "I must get a drink." He had to make a little detour for this purpose, he would stop at Championnet's, in the rue Tailledouce.

When he pushed open the door, the bar was deserted. The waiter was dusting the red wooden casklike tables. The darkness was grateful to Daniel's eyes. "I've got a cursed headache," he thought as he put down the basket and clambered on to one of the stools by the bar.

"A nice double whisky, I suppose," said the bartender.

"No," said Daniel curtly.

"God damn these fellows' mania for classifying human beings as though they were umbrellas or sewing-machines. I am *not* so-and-so; one isn't ever anything. But they pin you down as quick as look at you. One chap gives good

tips, another is always ready with a joke, and I am fond
of double whiskies."

"A gin fizz," said Daniel.

The bartender served him without comment: he was no
doubt offended. "So much the better," thought Daniel. He
would not enter the place again, the people were too familiar. Anyway, gin fizz tasted like a lemon-flavored purga-
tive. It scattered a sort of acidulated dust upon the tongue
and left a steely savor behind it. "It no longer has any
effect on me," thought Daniel.

"Give me a peppered vodka in a balloon glass."

He swallowed the vodka and remained for a moment
plunged in meditation, with a firework in his mouth.
"Won't it ever end?" he thought. But these were surface
thoughts, as usual, checks without funds to meet them.
"What won't ever end? What won't ever end?" Whereupon a shrill miaow was heard and the sound of scratching. The bartender gave a start.

"They are cats," said Daniel curtly.

He got off the stool, flung twenty francs on the counter,
and picked up the basket. As he lifted it, he noticed a tiny
red drop on the floor: blood. "What can they be up to inside there?" thought Daniel distressfully. But he could not
bring himself to lift the lid. For the moment the little
cage contained nothing but a solid, undifferentiated fear:
if he opened the basket, that fear would dissolve once
more into *his cats*, which Daniel could not have endured.
"You couldn't endure it, eh? And supposing I did lift that
lid?" But Daniel was already outside, and again the blindness fell, a clear and dewy blindness: your eyes itched, fire
seemed to fill the vision, then came the sudden realization
that for moments past you have been looking at houses,
houses a hundred yards ahead, airy and insubstantial,
edifices of smoke. At the end of the road stood a high blue
wall. "It's uncanny to see too clearly," thought Daniel. It
was thus that he imagined hell: a vision that penetrated

everything and saw to the very end of the world—the depths of a man's self. The basket shook at the extremity of his arm; the creatures inside it were clawing each other. The terror that he felt so near to his hand—Daniel wasn't sure whether it disgusted or delighted him; anyway, it came to the same thing. "There is always something to reassure them, they can smell me." And Daniel thought: "I am, indeed, for them, a smell." Patience, though: Daniel would soon be divested of that familiar smell, he would walk about without a smell, alone amid his fellow men, who haven't fine enough senses to spot a man by his smell. Without a smell or a shadow, without a past, nothing more than an invisible uprootment from the self towards the future. Daniel noticed that he was a few steps in advance of his body—yonder, at the level of the gas-jet—and that he was watching his own progress, hobbling a little under his burden, stiff-jointed and already soaked in sweat; he saw himself come, he was no more than a disembodied vision. But the shop-window of a dyeing establishment presented his reflection, and the illusion was dispelled. Daniel filled himself with viscous, vapid water: himself; the water of the Seine, vapid and viscous, would fill the basket, and they would claw one another to pieces. A vast revulsion came upon him; he thought: "This is a gratuitous act." He had stopped and set the basket on the ground. One could only damage oneself through the harm one did to others. One could never get directly at oneself. Once more he thought of Constantinople, where faithless spouses were put in a sack with hydrophobic cats, and the sack thrown into the Bosporus. Barrels, leather sacks, wicker baskets: prisons. "There are worse things." Daniel shrugged his shoulders: another thought without funds to meet it. He didn't want to adopt a tragic attitude, he had done that too often in the past. Besides, that meant taking oneself seriously. Never, never again would Daniel take himself seriously. The motor-bus suddenly appeared,

Daniel waved to the driver and got into the first-class compartment.

"As far as you go."

"Six tickets," said the conductor.

Seine water would drive them crazy. Coffee-colored water with violet gleams in it. A woman came in and sat opposite him, a prim, respectable female, with a little girl. The little girl observed the basket with interest: "Nasty little insect," thought Daniel. The basket miaowed, and Daniel started, as though he had been caught in the act of murder.

"What is it?" asked the little girl in a shrill voice.

"Hush," said her mother. "Don't annoy the gentleman."

"It's cats," said Daniel.

"Are they yours?" asked the little girl.

"Yes."

"Why are you taking them about in a basket?"

"Because they're ill," said Daniel mildly.

"May I see them?"

"Jeannine," said her mother, "mind what you're saying."

"I can't show them to you, they're ill, and rather savage."

"Oh," said the little girl in a calm, insinuating tone: "they'll be all right with me, the little darlings."

"Do you think so? Look here, my dear," said Daniel in a low, hurried voice, "I'm going to drown my cats, that's what I'm going to do, and do you know why? Because, no longer ago than this morning, they clawed the face of a pretty little girl like you, who came to bring me some flowers, and now she'll have to have a glass eye."

"Oh!" cried the little girl in consternation. She threw a terror-stricken glance at the basket and clung to her mother's skirts.

"There, there," said the mother, turning indignant eyes upon Daniel. "You must keep quiet, you see, and not chatter to everyone you meet. Don't be frightened, darling, the gentleman was only joking."

Daniel returned her look placidly. "She detests me," he thought with satisfaction. Behind the windows he could see the gray houses gliding by, and he knew that the good woman was looking at him. "An angry mother. She's looking for something to dislike in me. And it won't be my face." No one ever disliked Daniel's face. "Nor my suit, which is new and handsome. My hands, perhaps." His hands were short and strong, a little fleshy, with black hairs at the joints. He spread them out on his knees ("Look at them—just look at them"). But the woman had abandoned the encounter; she was staring straight ahead of her with a crass expression on her face; she was at rest. Daniel eyed her with a kind of eagerness: these people who rested—how did they manage it? She had let her whole person sag into herself and sat dissolved in it. There was nothing in that head of hers that resembled a frantic flight from self, neither curiosity, nor hatred, nor any motion, not the faintest undulation: nothing but the thick integument of sleep. Abruptly she awoke, and an air of animation took possession of her face.

"Why, we're there!" said she. "Come along! You bad little girl, you never notice anything."

She took her daughter by the hand and dragged her off. The bus restarted and then pulled up. People passed in front of Daniel laughing.

"All out," shouted the conductor.

Daniel started: the vehicle was empty. He got up and climbed out. It was a populous square containing a number of taverns; a group of workmen and women had gathered round a hand-cart. Women looked at him with surprise. Daniel quickened his step and turned down a dirty alley that led towards the Seine. On both sides of the road there were barrels and warehouses. The basket was now mewing incessantly, and Daniel almost ran: he was carrying a leaky bucket from which water oozed out drop by drop. Every mew was a drop of water. The bucket

was heavy. Daniel transferred it to his left hand and wiped
his forehead with his right. He must not think about the
cats. "Oh? So you don't want to think about the cats? Well,
that's just why you *must* think of them. You can't get away
with it so easily." Daniel recalled Poppæa's golden eyes
and quickly thought of whatever came first into his head
—of the Bourse, where he had made ten thousand francs
the day before, of Marcelle—he was going to see her that
evening, it was his day: "Archangel!" Daniel grinned: he
despised Marcelle profoundly. "They haven't the courage
to admit that they're no longer in love. If Mathieu saw
things as they were, he would have to make a decision.
But he doesn't want to: he doesn't want to lose his bear-
ings. He is a normal fellow," thought Daniel ironically.
The cats were mewing as though they had been scalded,
and Daniel felt he would soon lose his self-control. He put
the basket on the ground and gave it a couple of violent
kicks. This produced a tremendous commotion in the in-
terior, after which the cats were silent. Daniel stood for a
moment motionless, conscious of an odd shiver behind his
ears. Some workmen came out of a warehouse, and Daniel
resumed his journey. Here was the place. He made his
way down a stone stairway to the bank of the Seine and
sat down on the ground, beside an iron ring and between
a barrel of tar and a heap of paving-stones. The Seine was
yellow under a blue sky. Black barges loaded with casks
lay moored against the opposite quay. Daniel was sitting
in the sun and his temples ached. He looked at the rip-
pling stream, swollen with patches of opal iridescence.
He took the ball of string out of his pocket and cut off a
long strand with his clasp-knife; then, without getting up,
and with his left hand, he picked out a paving-stone. He
fastened one of the ends of the string to the handle of the
basket, rolled the rest of it round the stone, made several
knots, and replaced the stone on the ground. It looked a
singular contrivance. Daniel's idea was to carry the basket

in his right hand and the stone in his left hand; he would drop them into the water at the same moment. The basket would perhaps float for the tenth of a second, after which it would be forcibly dragged beneath the surface and abruptly disappear. Daniel felt hot and cursed his thick jacket, but did not want to take it off. Within him something throbbed, something pleaded for mercy, and Daniel, the hard and resolute Daniel, heard himself say in mournful tones: "When a man hasn't the courage to kill himself wholesale, he must do so retail." He would walk down to the water and say: "Farewell to what I love most in the world. . . ." He raised himself slightly on his hands and looked about him: on his right the bank was deserted; on his left, some distance away, he could see a fisherman, a black figure in the sunshine. The ripples would spread *under water* to the cork on the man's line. "He'll think he's had a bite." Daniel laughed and pulled out his handkerchief to wipe away the sweat that beaded his forehead. The hands of his wrist-watch stood at eleven twenty-five. "At half past eleven!" He must prolong that strange moment: Daniel had split into two entities; he felt himself *lost* in a scarlet cloud, under a leaden sky. He thought of Mathieu with a sort of pride. "It is *I* who am free," he said to himself. But it was an impersonal pride, for Daniel was no longer a person. At eleven twenty-nine he got up and felt so weak that he had to lean against the barrel. He got a smear of tar on to his tweed jacket and looked at it.

He saw the black smear on the brown material, and suddenly he felt that he was one person and no more. One only. A coward. A man who liked his cats and could not chuck them in the river. He picked up his pocket-knife, bent down, and cut the string. In silence; even within himself there was silence now, he was too ashamed to talk in his own presence. He picked up the basket again and climbed the stairway: it was as though he were walking with averted head past someone who regarded him with

contempt. Within himself desolation and silence still
reigned. When he reached the top of the steps he ventured
to speak his first words to himself: "What was that drop
of blood?" But he didn't dare open the basket; he walked
on, limping as he went. "It is I; it is I; it is I. The evil
thing." But in the depths of him there was an odd little
smile because he had saved Poppæa.

"Taxi!" he shouted.

The taxi stopped.

"Twenty-two rue Montmartre," said Daniel. "Will you
put this basket beside you?"

He swayed to the movement of the cab. He couldn't
even despise himself any longer. And then shame resumed
the upper hand, and again he began to see himself: it was
intolerable. "Neither wholesale nor retail," he reflected bitterly. When he took out his pocketbook to pay the chauffeur, he observed without satisfaction that it was stuffed
with notes. "Make money—oh yes, I can do that."

"So here you are again, Monsieur Sereno," said the concierge. "Someone has just gone up to your apartment. One
of your friends, a tall gentleman with high shoulders. I
told him you were out. 'Out,' says he, 'well, I'll leave a note
under his door.' "

She noticed the basket and exclaimed: "Why, you've
brought the little darlings back!"

"Ah well, Madame Dupuy," said Daniel, "I dare say it
was wrong of me, but I couldn't part with them."

"It's Mathieu," he thought as he went upstairs. "He's
always on the spot." He was glad to be able to hate another person.

He encountered Mathieu on the third-floor landing.

"Hello," said Mathieu, "I'd given you up."

"I've been taking my cats for an outing," said Daniel.
He was surprised to feel a sort of inner warmth. "Are you
coming in with me?" he asked abruptly.

"Yes, I want you to do something for me."

Daniel flung him a rapid glance and noticed that his face was drawn and ashen. "He looks damnably under the weather," he thought. He wanted to help the man. They went upstairs. Daniel put the key in the lock and pushed open the door. "Go along in," he said. He touched the other lightly on the shoulder and immediately withdrew his hand. Mathieu went into Daniel's room and sat down in an armchair.

"I couldn't make sense of what your concierge said," he remarked. "She told me that you had taken your cats to your sister's place. Have you made it up with your sister lately?"

Something within Daniel suddenly froze. "He would look sick enough if he knew where I had come from." He gazed unsympathetically into his friend's steady, penetrating eyes. "It's true," he thought, "he's quite normal." And he was conscious of the gulf between them. He laughed.

"Ah yes—my sister's place. That was an innocent little falsehood," he said. He knew that Mathieu would not press the point: Mathieu had the irritating habit of treating Daniel as a romancer, and he affected never to inquire into the motives that compelled him to lie. Mathieu accordingly glanced at the wicker receptacle with a perplexed air and fell silent.

"Will you excuse me?" said Daniel. He had become the man of action. His sole desire was to open the basket as soon as possible. What could that drop of blood have signified? He knelt down, thinking that they would probably fly in his face, and he bent his head over the lid, so that it was well within their reach. And he reflected, as he lifted the clasp: "A solid bit of worry wouldn't do him any harm. It would shake him out of his optimism and that complacent air of his." Poppæa slipped out of the basket snarling and fled into the kitchen. Scipio emerged in his turn: he had preserved his dignity, but did not seem in the least reassured. He proceeded with measured steps to the wardrobe, looked about him with a sly expression, stretched himself, and finally crawled under the bed. Malvina did not move. "She's hurt," thought Daniel. She lay full length at the bottom of the basket, prostrate. Daniel put a finger under her chin and pulled her head up: she had been deeply clawed on the nose, and her left eye was closed, but she was not bleeding. There was a blackish scab on her face, and round the scab the hairs were stiff and sticky.

"What's the matter?" asked Mathieu. He had got up and was looking at the cat politely. "He thinks me absurd because I'm worrying about a cat. It would seem to him quite natural if it was a baby."

"Malvina has a nasty wound," explained Daniel. "It must have been Poppæa that clawed her, she really is the limit. Excuse me, my dear fellow, while I see to her."

He produced a bottle of arnica and a packet of cotton wool from the cupboard. Mathieu followed him with his eyes without uttering a word; then he passed his hand over his forehead in a senile sort of gesture. Daniel began to bathe Malvina's nose, the cat resisting feebly.

"Now be a good little cat," said Daniel. "There, there—it will soon be over."

He thought he must be exasperating Mathieu, and that gave him heart for the job. But when he raised his head, he observed Mathieu staring grimly into vacancy.

"Forgive me, my dear fellow," said Daniel in his deepest voice; "I shan't be more than a couple of minutes. I simply had to wash the creature, you know, a wound gets so quickly infected. I hope it doesn't annoy you very much," he added, bestowing a frank smile on Mathieu. Mathieu shivered and then began to laugh.

"Now then, now then," said he, "don't you make your velvet eyes at me."

"Velvet eyes!" Mathieu's superiority was indeed offensive. "He thinks he knows me, he talks of *my* lies, *my* velvet eyes. He doesn't know me in the least, but he likes to label me as if I were an object."

Daniel laughed cordially, and carefully wiped Malvina's head. Malvina shut her eyes in an appearance of ecstasy, but Daniel knew very well that she was in pain. He gave her a little tap on the back.

"There," he said, getting up; "there won't be a sign of it tomorrow. But the other cat gave her a nasty clawing, you know."

"Poppæa? She's a vile creature," said Mathieu with an absent air. And then he said abruptly: "Marcelle is pregnant."

"Pregnant!"

Daniel's surprise was of short duration, but he had to struggle against a huge desire to laugh. That was it—so that was it. True enough, the creatures evacuate blood every lunar month, and they're as prolific as fish into the bargain. He reflected with disgust that he was going to see her that same evening. "I wonder if I shall have the courage to touch her hand."

"It's a ghastly business," said Mathieu with an objective air.

Daniel looked at him and said soberly: "I can quite understand that." Then he hurriedly turned his back on him on the pretext of replacing the bottle of arnica in the cupboard. He was afraid he would burst out laughing in his face. He set himself to think about his mother's death, which always answered upon these occasions; and but for two or three convulsive spasms, he did not betray himself. Mathieu went on gravely talking behind Daniel's back:

"The trouble is that it humiliates her," he said. "You haven't seen her often, so you can't quite understand, but she's a sort of Valkyrie. A bedroom Valkyrie," he added without malice. "For her it's an awful degradation."

"Yes," said Daniel with concern; "and it must be nearly as bad for you. Whatever you do, she of course hates the sight of you at the moment. I know that, in my own case, it would destroy love."

"I no longer feel any love for her," said Mathieu.

"Don't you?"

Daniel was profoundly astonished and amused. "We shall have some sport this evening," he thought.

"Have you told her so?" he asked.

"Of course I haven't."

"Why 'of course'? You'll have to tell her. I suppose you'll—"

"No, I'm not going to walk out on her, if that's what you mean."

"What, then?"

Daniel was solidly amused. He was now eager to see Marcelle again.

"Nothing," said Mathieu. "So much the worse for me. It isn't her fault if I no longer love her."

"Is it yours?"

"Yes," said Mathieu curtly.

"You'll continue to see her on the quiet and—"

"Well?"

"Well," said Daniel, "if you play that little game for any length of time you'll end up hating her."

"I don't want her to get into a mess," said Mathieu with a set and obstinate expression.

"If you prefer to sacrifice yourself—" said Daniel, with indifference. When Mathieu adopted a Quakerish attitude, Daniel hated him.

"What have I to sacrifice? I shall still teach at the lycée. I shall see Marcelle. I shall write a short story every two years, which is precisely what I have done until now." And he added with bitterness that Daniel had never seen in him before: "I am a Sunday writer. Besides," he went on, "I rather like her, and I couldn't bear not to see her any more. Except that it gives me the feeling of family ties."

A silence followed. Daniel came and sat down in the armchair opposite Mathieu.

"You must help me," said Mathieu. "I've got an address, but no money. Lend me five thousand."

"Five thousand," repeated Daniel with a hesitant air.

His swollen notecase, now bulging in his breast pocket, his pig-dealer's notecase—he had but to open it and take out five notes. Mathieu had often done him kindnesses in the old days.

"I'll pay back half at the end of the month," said Mathieu; "and the other half on July 14, because on that date I get my salary for both August and September."

Daniel looked at Mathieu's ashen visage and thought: "The fellow is all in." Then he thought of the cats and felt merciless.

"Five thousand francs!" said he in a melancholy tone, "I haven't got so much, my dear fellow, and I'm very much pressed—"

"You told me the other day that you were just going to pull off a very good piece of business."

"Well, my dear chap," said Daniel, "that same piece of business fell down on me; you know what the stock exchange is like. However, the plain fact is that I've got nothing but debts."

He had not imparted much sincerity to his voice, because he did not want to convince his companion. But when he saw that Mathieu did not believe him, he became angry: "Mathieu can go to hell. He thinks himself deep, he imagines he can see through me. Why on earth should I help him? He's only got to touch one of his own set." What he could not stand was that normal, placid aid which Mathieu never lost, even in trouble.

"Right," said Mathieu briskly, "then you really can't."

Daniel reflected that he must be in dire need to be so insistent.

"I really can't. I'm awfully sorry, my dear fellow."

He was embarrassed by Mathieu's embarrassment, but it was not a wholly disagreeable sensation; it had the feel of turning back a fingernail.

"Are you in urgent need?" he inquired with solicitude. "Is there nowhere else you can apply?"

"Well, you know, I did want to avoid touching Jacques."

"Ah yes," said Daniel, a little disappointed, "there's your brother. So you're sure of getting your money."

"Not by any means," said Mathieu rather gloomily. "He's got into his head that he oughtn't to lend me a penny, on the grounds that it would be doing me a bad turn. He told me I ought to be independent at my age."

"Oh, but in a case like this he's sure to let you have what you want," said Daniel emphatically. He slowly thrust out the tip of his tongue and began to lick his upper lip with satisfaction: he had succeeded at the first attempt in striking that note of light and cheery optimism which so infuriated his acquaintances.

Mathieu had blushed. "That's just the trouble. I can't tell him what it's for."

"True," said Daniel, and he reflected for a moment. "In any case, there are firms, you know, who lend to government officials. I ought to tell you that they're mostly sharks. But I dare say you won't bother about the amount of the interest, if you can only get hold of the money."

Mathieu looked interested, and Daniel realized with annoyance that he had reassured him slightly.

"What sort of people are they? Do they lend money on the spot?"

"Oh no," said Daniel briskly, "they take quite ten days: certain inquiries have to be made."

Mathieu fell silent and seemed to be reflecting; Daniel was suddenly aware of a faint shock: Malvina had jumped on to his knees, where she established herself and began to purr. "Here is someone who does not bear malice," thought Daniel with disgust. He began to stroke her with a light, indifferent touch. Animals and people never succeeded in hating him. They could not resist a sort of good-natured inertia he cultivated, or possibly his face. Mathieu had plunged into his pitiable little calculations: he, too, bore no malice. Daniel bent over Malvina and fell to scratching the top of her head; his hand shook.

"As a matter of fact," he said without looking at Mathieu, "I should be almost glad not to have the money. It has just occurred to me: you always want to be free; here is a superb opportunity of proclaiming your freedom."

"Proclaiming my freedom?" Mathieu didn't seem to understand. Daniel raised his head.

"Yes," said Daniel. "You have only to marry Marcelle."

Mathieu eyed him with a frown: he was probably wondering whether Daniel was serious. Daniel met his look with decorous gravity.

"Are you crazy?" asked Mathieu.

"Why should I be? Say one word and you can change your whole life, and that doesn't happen every day."

Mathieu began to laugh. "He has decided to laugh at the whole business," thought Daniel angrily.

"You won't persuade me to do any such thing," said Mathieu, "and especially not at this moment."

"Well, but—that's just it," said Daniel in the same light tone, "it must be very entertaining to do the exact opposite of what one wants to do. One feels oneself becoming some-one else."

"I don't fancy the prospect," said Mathieu. "Do you expect me to beget three brats for the pleasure of feeling like someone else when I take them for a walk in the Luxembourg? I can well imagine that I should alter if I became an utter wash-out."

"Not so much as all that," thought Daniel, "not so much as you think." "As a matter of fact," he said, "it can't be so very disagreeable to be a wash-out. I mean an utter and absolute wash-out, flat and finished. Married, with three children, just as you said. That would quiet a man down."

"It would indeed," said Mathieu. "I meet fellows like that every day: fathers of pupils who come to see me. Four children, unfaithful wives, members of the Parents' Association. They certainly look quiet enough—I might even say benign."

"They've got a kind of gaiety of their own, too," said Daniel. "They make me shudder. So the prospect doesn't tempt you? I can see you so well as a married man," he continued. "You'd be just like them, fleshy, neatly dressed, rather facetious, and with celluloid eyes. Not at all a bad type of fellow, I think."

"And not unlike yourself," said Mathieu blandly. "But I would, none the less, much prefer to ask my brother for five thousand francs."

He got up. Daniel put Malvina down and got up too. "He knows I've got the money, and he doesn't hate me: what on earth can one do to such people?"

The notecase was there; Daniel had only to put his hand in his pocket and say: "There you are, my dear chap, I was just putting you off for a bit—I wasn't serious." But he was afraid he might despise himself.

"I'm sorry," he said in a halting tone. "If I see any prospect, I'll write. . . ."

He had accompanied Mathieu to the outer door.

"Don't you worry," said Mathieu cheerfully. "I'll manage."

He shut the door behind him. As Daniel listened to his brisk step on the staircase, he thought: "That's final," and he caught his breath. But the feeling didn't last: "Not for a moment," he said to himself, "did Mathieu cease to be *balanced*, composed, and in perfect accord with himself. He's certainly upset, but that doesn't go very deep. Inside he's quite at ease." Daniel walked up to the mirror and inspected his dark and comely countenance, and thought: "All the same, it would be worth a thousand if he were forced to marry Marcelle."

# CHAPTER VIII

S HE had by now been awake a long time; she must be fretting. He ought to go and cheer her up and tell her that she would not go there *in any case*. Mathieu recalled with affection her poor ravaged face of the day before, and he suddenly envisaged her as pathetically fragile. He must telephone to her. But he decided to call on Jacques first. "In that way I might perhaps have some good news for her." He thought with annoyance of the attitude Jacques would adopt. An attitude of sage amusement, without a hint of reproach or tolerance, his head on one side, and his eyes half-closed. "What! In need of money again?" The prospect made Mathieu's flesh creep. He crossed the street, thinking of Daniel: he wasn't angry with him. That was how it was, one couldn't be angry with Daniel. He was angry with Jacques. He stopped outside a squat building in the rue Réaumur and read with irritation, as indeed he always did: "Jacques Delarue. Attorney and Counselor. Second floor." He went in and took the elevator, sincerely hoping that Odette would not be at home.

She was; Mathieu caught sight of her through the glass door of the little drawing-room, sitting on a divan, elegant, slim, and neat to the point of insignificance. She was reading. Jacques often said: "Odette is one of the few women in Paris who find time to read."

"Would you like to see Madame, sir?" asked Rose.

"Yes, just to say good-morning; but will you tell Monsieur that I shall be coming along to his office in a few minutes?"

He opened the door, and Odette looked up; it was a lovely face, impassive, much made up.

"Good morning, Thieu," she said pleasantly. "I hope this is *my* visit at last."

"Your visit?" said Mathieu.

It was with rather baffled appreciation that he observed that high calm forehead and those green eyes. She was beautiful beyond all doubt, but her beauty was of the kind that vanishes under observation. Accustomed to faces like Lola's, the sense of which was grossly obvious at once, Mathieu had on countless occasions tried to unify these fluid features, but they escaped him; as a face, Odette's always seemed to be dissolving, and thus retained its delusive bourgeois mystery.

"Indeed I wish it were *your* visit," he continued, "but I must see Jacques, I want to ask him to do something for me."

"You aren't in such a hurry as all that," said Odette. "Jacques won't run away. Sit down here." And she made room for him beside her. "Take care," she said with a smile. "One of these days I shall be angry. You neglect me. I have a right to my personal visit, you promised me one."

"You mean that you yourself promised to receive me one of these days."

"How polite you are!" she laughed. "Your conscience is uneasy."

Mathieu sat down. He liked Odette, but he never knew what to say to her.

"How are you getting on, Odette?" He imparted a little

warmth to his voice in order to disguise his rather clumsy question.

"Very well," she said. "Do you know where I've been this morning? To Saint-Germain, with the car, to see Françoise; it was delightful."

"And Jacques?"

"He is very busy these days; I see very little of him. But he's shockingly well, as usual."

Mathieu was suddenly aware of a profound sense of dissatisfaction. She belonged to Jacques. He looked distastefully at the long brown arm emerging from a very simple frock caught in at the waist with a scarlet cord, almost a girl's frock. The arm, the frock, and the body beneath the frock belonged to Jacques, as did the easy chair, the mahogany writing-table, and the divan. The discreet and modest lady was redolent of possession. A silence followed, after which Mathieu resumed the warm and rather nasal tone that he kept for Odette. "That's a nice frock of yours," he said.

"Oh come!" said Odette with a pettish laugh. "Leave my frock alone; every time you see me you talk about my frocks. Suppose you tell me what you've been doing this week."

Mathieu laughed too and began to feel more at ease. "In point of fact," said he, "I have something to say about that frock."

"Dear me," said Odette, "what can it be?"

"Well, I'm wondering whether you shouldn't wear earrings with it."

"Ear-rings?" Odette looked at him with a strange expression.

"I suppose you think them vulgar."

"Not at all. But they give one a rather forward look." She added brusquely, with a frank laugh: "You would certainly be much more at ease with me if I did wear them."

"Surely not—why should I?" said Mathieu vaguely.

He was surprised, and he realized that she was by no means stupid. Odette's intelligence was like her beauty—there was an elusive quality about it.

A silence fell. Mathieu could think of nothing else to say. And yet he had no desire to go, he enjoyed a sort of complacence in her company.

"But I mustn't keep you," said Odette kindly. "Run along to Jacques, you look as if you had something on your mind."

Mathieu got up. He remembered that he was going to ask Jacques for money, and felt the tips of his fingers tingle.

"Good-by, Odette," he said affectionately. "No, no, don't get up. I'll look in again on my way out."

Up to what point was she a victim, he wondered, knocking at Jacques's door. With that type of woman one never knew.

"Come in," said Jacques.

He rose, alert and erect, and approached Mathieu.

"Good morning, old man," he said cordially. "How are things?"

He looked much younger than Mathieu, although he was the elder of the two. Mathieu thought he was thickening round the hips, though he no doubt wore a body-belt.

"Good morning," said Mathieu, with a friendly smile.

He felt himself in fault; for twenty years he had felt himself in fault each time he recalled or met his brother.

"Well," said Jacques, "and what brings you here?"

Mathieu made a gesture of disgust.

"Something wrong?" asked Jacques. "Look here, take a chair. Would you care for a whisky?"

"A whisky would go down well," said Mathieu. He sat down, his throat felt dry. How about drinking his whisky and clearing out without uttering a word? No, it was too late. Jacques knew perfectly well what was up. He would simply think that his brother hadn't had the courage to ask him for a loan. Jacques remained standing; he produced a bottle of whisky and filled two glasses.

"It's my last bottle," he said, "but I shan't get in any more before the autumn. After all, a good gin fizz is a better drink for the hot weather, don't you think?"

Mathieu did not reply. There was no affection in his eyes as he looked at that fresh and ruddy face, a young man's face, and that cropped fair hair. Jacques smiled guilelessly; indeed, there was a guileless air about the man that morning. "That," thought Mathieu savagely, "is all put on; he knows why I have come, he is just choosing his attitude."

"You know quite well," said Mathieu harshly, "that I've come to touch you for money."

There, the die was cast. He couldn't draw back now; his brother had already raised his eyebrows in an expression of profound surprise. "He won't spare me anything," thought Mathieu with dismay.

"Certainly I didn't know," said Jacques, "how should I? Do you mean to insinuate that that's the sole object of your visits?"

He sat down, still very erect, and indeed a trifle stiff, and crossed his legs with an easy swing, as though to make up for the rigidity of his torso. He was wearing a smart sports suit of English tweed.

"I don't mean to insinuate anything at all," said Mathieu. He blinked and added, as he gripped his glass: "But I need four thousand francs by tomorrow." ("He's going to say no. I hope to goodness he refuses quickly so that I can clear out.") But Jacques was never in a hurry: he was a lawyer, and he had plenty of time.

"Four thousand," said he, wagging his head with a knowing air. "Well, well, well!"

He extended his legs and stared at his shoes with satisfaction.

"I find you amusing, Thieu," said he, "amusing and also instructive. Now, don't take offense at what I say to you," he said briskly, at a gesture from Mathieu; "I have no notion of criticizing your conduct, I'm just turning the thing over in my own mind, viewing it from above—indeed, I would say 'from a philosophic standpoint' if I wasn't talking to a philosopher. You see, when I think about you, I am the more convinced that one oughtn't to be a man of principles. You are stiff with them, you even invent them, but you don't stick to them. In theory, there's no one more independent, it's all quite admirable, you live above all class distinctions. Only I wonder what would become of you if I wasn't there. Please realize that I am only too happy, being a man without principles, to be able to help you from time to time. But I can't help feeling that with your ideas I should be rather chary of asking favors from a damned bourgeois. For I am a damned bourgeois," he added, laughing heartily. He went on, still laughing: "And what is worse, you, who despise the family, exploit our family ties to touch me for money. For, after all, you wouldn't apply to me if I wasn't your brother."

He assumed a cordial expression and added: "All this doesn't bore you, I hope."

"I can't very well avoid it," said Mathieu, laughing too.

He wasn't going to engage in an abstract discussion. Such discussions, with Jacques, always led to trouble. Mathieu soon lost his self-control.

"Yes, obviously," said Jacques coldly. "Don't you think that with a little organization—? But that's no doubt opposed to your ideas. I don't say it's your fault, mark you: in my view it's your principles that are to blame."

"Well," said Mathieu, by way of saying something, "the rejection of principles is in itself a principle."

"Not much of a one," said Jacques.

"At this moment," thought Mathieu, "he's in the mind to let go." But he looked at his brother's plump cheeks, his

florid complexion, his open but rather set expression, and
thought with a catch at the heart: "He looks hard on the
trigger." Fortunately Jacques was again speaking.

"Four thousand," he repeated. "It must be a sudden call,
for, after all, last week when you—when you came to ask
me a small service, there was no question of such a sum."

"That is so," said Mathieu. "I—it dates from yesterday."

He suddenly thought of Marcelle, he saw her in his
mind's eye, a sinister, naked figure in the pink room, and
he added in a pleading tone that took him by surprise:
"Jacques, I *need* this money."

Jacques eyed him with curiosity, and Mathieu bit his
lips; when they were together, the two brothers were not
in the habit of displaying their feelings with such emphasis.

"As bad as all that? I'm surprised. You are certainly not
the man— You—in the ordinary way you borrow a little
money from me because you either can't or won't manage
your affairs properly, but I would never have believed—
I'm not, of course, asking you any questions," he added in
a faintly interrogative tone.

Mathieu hesitated: should he tell him it was income-
tax? No. Jacques knew he had paid it in May.

"Marcelle is pregnant," he said curtly.

He felt himself blush and shook his shoulders; why not,
after all? Why this sudden and consuming shame? He
looked straight at his brother with aggressive eyes. Jacques
assumed an air of interest.

"Did you want a child?" He deliberately pretended not
to understand.

"No," said Mathieu curtly. "It was an accident."

"It would certainly have surprised me," said Jacques,
"but, after all, you might have wanted to carry your expe-
riences as far as possible outside the established order."

"Yes, but it isn't that at all."

A silence followed, and then Jacques continued blandly: "Then when is the wedding to be?"

Mathieu flushed with wrath: as always, Jacques refused to face the situation candidly, he obstinately revolved around it, and in so doing his mind was searching eagerly for an eyrie from which he could take a vertical view of other people's conduct. Whatever might be said or done to him, his first reaction was to get above the conflict, he could see nothing except from above, and he had a predilection for eyries.

"We have decided on an operation for abortion," said Mathieu brutally.

Jacques did not lift an eyebrow. "Have you found a doctor?" he asked with a noncommittal air.

"Yes."

"A reliable man? From what you have told me, the young lady's health is delicate."

"I have friends who assure me he's all right."

"Yes," said Jacques. "Yes, obviously."

He closed his eyes for an instant, reopened them, and laid the tips of his fingers together.

"In short," said he, "if I have properly understood you, what has happened is this: you have just heard that your girl is pregnant; you don't want to marry, being against your principles, but you consider yourself as pledged to her by ties as strict as those of marriage. Not wanting to marry her nor to damage her reputation, you have decided on an operation for abortion under the best possible conditions. Friends have recommended you a trustworthy doctor who charges a fee of four thousand francs, and there is nothing left for you to do but to get the money. Is that it?"

"Exactly," said Mathieu.

"And why do you want the money by tomorrow?"

"The fellow I have in view is leaving for America in a week."

"Right," said Jacques. "I understand."

He lifted his joined hands to the level of his eyes and contemplated them with the precise expression of one now in a position to draw conclusions from his words. But Mathieu had made no mistake: a lawyer doesn't conclude an affair so quickly. Jacques had dropped his hands and laid them one on each knee, he was sitting well back in his chair, and the light had gone out of his eyes. "The authorities are inclined to be severe on abortions at the moment."

"I know," said Mathieu, "they get a fit of doing so from time to time. They catch a few poor devils who can't protect themselves, but the great specialists don't have to worry."

"You mean that that's unjust," said Jacques. "I'm entirely of your opinion. But I don't wholly disapprove of the results. By force of circumstances, your poor devils are herbalists or clumsy old women who use dirty instruments; the attentions of the police do weed them out, and that's something."

"Well, there it is," said Mathieu wearily. "I have come to ask you for four thousand francs."

"And—" said Jacques, "are you quite sure that abortion is in accordance with your principles?"

"Why not?"

"I don't know, it's for you to say. You are a pacifist because you respect human life, and you intend to destroy a life."

"I have quite made up my mind," said Mathieu. "Moreover, though I may be a pacifist, I don't respect human life, there's no such implication."

"Indeed!" said Jacques. "I thought—" And he looked at Mathieu with amused complacency. "So here you are in the guise of an infanticide! It doesn't suit you at all, my poor Thieu."

"He's afraid I shall get caught," thought Mathieu. "He

won't give me a sou." It ought to have been possible to say to him: "If you let me have the money, you run no risk; I shall get in touch with a clever man who is not on the police records. If you refuse, I shall be obliged to send Marcelle to a low-down abortionist, and in that case I could guarantee nothing, because the police know them all and may pull them in any day." But these arguments were too direct to influence Jacques. Mathieu merely said: "Abortion is not infanticide."

Jacques picked up a cigarette and lit it. "True," he observed with detachment. "I agree, abortion is not infanticide, it is 'metaphysical' murder." He added gravely: "My dear Mathieu, I have no objections to metaphysical murder, any more than to any perfect crime. But that *you* should commit a metaphysical murder—you, being what you are—" He clicked his tongue disapprovingly. "No, that would be quite out of the picture."

It was all up, Jacques would refuse, and Mathieu might as well go away. However, he cleared his throat and, to salve his conscience, said: "Then you can't help me?"

"Please understand me," said Jacques. "I don't refuse to do you a service, but would this be *really* doing you a service? Added to which I'm quite sure you'll easily get the money you need. . . ." He rose abruptly, as though he had made a decision, went up to his brother, and put a friendly hand on his shoulder. "Listen, Thieu," he said cordially. "Assume I have refused. I don't want to help you to tell yourself a lie. But I have another suggestion to make. . . ."

Mathieu, who was about to get up, subsided into his chair, and the old fraternal resentment took possession of him once more. That firm but gentle pressure on his shoulder was more than he could stand; he threw his head back and saw Jacques's face foreshortened.

"Tell myself a lie! Look here, Jacques, say you don't want to be mixed up in a case of abortion, that you disapprovc of it, or that you haven't the ready money, and you're perfectly within your rights, nor shall I resent it. But this talk of lying is nonsense, there's no lying in it at all. I don't want a child: a child is coming, and I propose to suppress it; that's all."

Jacques withdrew his hand and took a few steps with a meditative air. "He's going to make me a speech," thought Mathieu. "I oughtn't to have let myself in for an argument."

"Mathieu," said Jacques in a calm tone, "I know you better than you think, and you distress me. I've long been afraid that something like this would happen: this coming child is the logical result of a situation into which you entered of your own free will, and you want to suppress it because you won't accept all the consequences of your acts. Come, shall I tell you the truth? I dare say you aren't lying to yourself at this precise moment: the trouble is that your whole life is built upon a lie."

"Carry on," said Mathieu. "I don't mind. Tell me what it is I'm trying to evade."

"You are trying," said Jacques, "to evade the fact that you're a bourgeois and ashamed of it. I myself reverted to bourgeoisie after many aberrations and contracted a marriage of convenience with the party, but you are a bourgeois by taste and temperament, and it's your temperament that's pushing you into marriage. For *you are married,* Mathieu," said he forcibly.

"First I heard of it," said Mathieu.

"Oh yes, you are, only you pretend you aren't because you are possessed by theories. You have fallen into a habit of life with this young woman: you go to see her quietly four days a week and you spend the night with her. That has been going on for seven years, and there's no adventure left in it; you respect her, you feel obligations towards her, you don't want to leave her. And I'm quite sure that your sole object isn't pleasure. I even imagine that, broadly speaking, however vivid the pleasure may have been, it has by now begun to fade. In fact, I expect you sit beside her in the evening and tell her long stories about the events of the day and ask her advice in difficulties."

"Of course," said Mathieu, shrugging his shoulders. He was furious with himself.

"Very well," said Jacques, "will you tell me how that differs from marriage—except for cohabitation?"

"Except for cohabitation?" said Mathieu ironically. "Excuse me, but that's a quibble."

"Oh," said Jacques, "being what you are, it probably doesn't cost you much to do without that."

"He has never said so much about my affairs," thought Mathieu, "he is taking his revenge." The thing to do was to go out and slam the door. But Mathieu was well aware that he would stay until the end: he was seized by an aggressive and malicious impulse to discover his brother's true opinion.

"But why do you say it probably doesn't cost me much, *being what I am?*"

"Because you get a comfortable life out of the situation, and an appearance of liberty: you have all the advantages of marriage and you exploit your principles to avoid its inconveniences. You refuse to regularize the position, which you find quite easy. If anyone suffers from all this, it isn't you."

"Marcelle shares my ideas on marriage," said Mathieu acidly; he heard himself pronounce each word and felt extremely ill at ease.

"Oh," said Jacques, "if she didn't share them she would no doubt be too proud to admit it to you. The fact is you're beyond my comprehension: you, so prompt with your indignation when you hear of an injustice, you keep this woman for years in a humiliating position, for the sole pleasure of telling yourself that you're respecting your principles. It wouldn't be so bad if it were true, if you really did adapt your life to your ideas. But I must tell you once more, you are as good as married, you have a delightful apartment, you get a competent salary at fixed intervals, you have no anxiety for the future because the State guarantees you a pension . . . and you like that sort of life—placid, orderly, the typical life of an official."

"Listen," said Mathieu, "there's a misunderstanding here; I care little whether I'm a bourgeois or whether I'm not. All I want is"—and he uttered the final words through clenched teeth and with a sort of shame—"to retain my freedom."

"I should myself have thought," said Jacques, "that freedom consisted in frankly confronting situations into which one has deliberately entered, and accepting all one's responsibilities. But that, no doubt, is not your view: you condemn capitalist society, and yet you are an official in that society; you display an abstract sympathy with Communists, but you take care not to commit yourself, you have never voted. You despise the bourgeois class, and yet you are a bourgeois, son and brother of a bour-geois, and you live like a bourgeois."

Mathieu waved a hand, but Jacques refused to be inter-rupted.

"You have, however, reached the age of reason, my poor Mathieu," said he, in a tone of pity and of warning. "But you try to dodge that fact too, you try to pretend you're younger than you are. Well—perhaps I'm doing you an injustice. Perhaps you haven't in fact reached the age of reason, it's really a moral age—perhaps I've got there sooner than you have."

"Now he's off," thought Mathieu, "he's going to tell me about his youth." Jacques was very proud of his youth; it was his moral guarantee, it permitted him to defend the cause of order with a good conscience; for five years he had assiduously aped all the fashionable dissipations, he had dallied with surrealism, conducted a few agreeable love-affairs, and occasionally, before making love, he had inhaled ethyl chloride from a handkerchief. One fine day he had reformed: Odette brought him a dowry of six hundred thousand francs. He had written to Mathieu: "A man must have the courage to act like everybody else, in order not to be like anybody." And he had bought a lawyer's practice.

"I'm not bringing your youth up against you," said he. "On the contrary: you had luck in avoiding certain misdemeanors. Nor, indeed, do I regret my own. The fact is we both had to work off the instincts we inherited from our old brigand of a grandfather. The difference is that I worked them off at one go, while you are dribbling them away; indeed, you haven't yet finished the process. I fancy that fundamentally you were much less of a brigand than I, and that is what is ruining you: your life is an incessant compromise between an ultimately slight inclination towards revolt and anarchy and your deeper impulses that direct you towards order, moral health, and I might almost say routine. The result is that you are still, at your age, an irresponsible student. My dear old chap, look yourself in the face: you are thirty-four years old, you are getting slightly bald—not so bald as I am, I admit—your youth has gone, and the bohemian life doesn't suit you at all. Besides, what is bohemianism, after all? It was amusing enough a hundred years ago, but today it is simply a name for a handful of eccentrics who are no danger to anybody and have missed the train. You have attained the age of reason, Mathieu, you have attained the age of reason, or you ought to have done so," he repeated with an abstracted air.

"Pah!" said Mathieu. "Your age of reason is the age of resignation, and I've no use for it."

But Jacques was not listening. His face suddenly cleared and brightened, and he went on briskly:

"Listen; as I said, I'm going to make you a proposal; if

you refuse, you won't find much difficulty in getting hold of four thousand francs, so I don't feel any compunction. I am prepared to put ten thousand francs at your disposal if you marry the girl."

Mathieu had foreseen this move; in any event, it provided him with a tolerable exit that would save his face.

"Thank you, Jacques," he said, getting up. "You are really too kind, but it won't do. I don't say you are wrong all along the line, but if I have to marry some day, it must be because I want to. At this moment it would just be a clumsy effort to get myself out of a mess."

Jacques got up too. "Think it over," said he, "take your time. Your wife would be very welcome here, as I need not tell you; I have confidence in your choice. Odette will be delighted to welcome her as a friend. Besides, my wife knows nothing of your private life."

"I have already thought it over," said Mathieu.

"As you please," said Jacques cordially—was he really much put out? And he added: "When shall we see you?"

"I'll come to lunch on Sunday," said Mathieu. "Good-by."

"Good-by," said Jacques, "and of course if you change your mind, my offer still holds."

Mathieu smiled and went out without replying. "It's all over," he thought, "it's all over." He ran down the stairs; he was not exactly in a cheerful mood, but he felt he wanted to burst into song. At this moment Jacques would be seated in his chair, staring into vacancy, and saying to himself with a sad, grave smile: "I'm worried about that boy, though he has reached the age of reason." Or perhaps he had looked in on Odette: "I'm distressed about Mathieu. I can't tell you why. But he isn't reasonable." What would she say? Would she play the part of the mature and thoughtful wife, or would she extricate herself with some brief words of commendation without looking up from her book?

Whereupon Mathieu remembered that he had forgotten to say good-by to Odette. He felt rather remorseful; indeed, he was in a remorseful mood. Was it true? Did he keep Marcelle in a humiliating position? He remembered Marcelle's violent tirades against marriage. He had indeed proposed it to her. Once. Five years ago. Rather vaguely, indeed, and Marcelle had laughed in his face. "Alas," he thought, "my brother always inspires me with an inferiority complex." But no, it wasn't really that; whatever his own sense of guilt, Mathieu had never failed to defend his position against Jacques. "But here is a damned fellow who makes me sick. When I cease to feel ashamed in his company, I'm ashamed for his sake. Well, well, one is never finished with one's family, it's like the smallpox that catches you as a child and leaves you marked for life." There was a cheap café at the corner of the rue Montorgueil. He went in and found the telephone booth in a dark recess. He felt his heart flutter as he unhooked the receiver.

"Hello! Hello! Marcelle?"

Marcelle had a telephone in her own room.

"Is that you?" said she.

"Yes."

"Well?"

"Well, the old woman is impossible."

"Hm," said Marcelle in a dubious tone.

"Absolutely. She was three parts drunk, her place stinks, and you should see her hands! Besides, she's an old brute."

"All right. And then—?"

"Well, I've got someone in view. Through Sarah. Someone *very* good."

"Ah!" said Marcelle with indifference. And she added: "How much?"

"Four thousand."

"How much?" repeated Marcelle, incredulously.

"Four thousand."

"You see! It's impossible, I shall have to go—"

"No you won't," said Mathieu forcibly. "I'll borrow it."

"From whom? From Jacques?"

"I've just left him. He refuses."

"Daniel?"

"He refuses too, the swine; I saw him this morning and I'm sure he was stuffed with money."

"You didn't tell him it was for—that?" asked Marcelle sharply.

"No," said Mathieu.

"What are you going to do?"

"I don't know." He realized that his voice lacked assurance, and he added firmly: "Don't get worked up. We have forty-eight hours. I'll get the money. The devil's in it if I can't get four thousand francs somewhere."

"Well, get it," said Marcelle in a queer tone, "get it."

"I'll telephone to you. Shall I be seeing you tomorrow?"

"Yes."

"Are you all right?"

"Perfectly."

"You—you aren't too—"

"Yes," said Marcelle hoarsely. "I'm in misery." And she added in a gentler tone: "Well, do the best you can, my poor old boy."

"I'll bring you the four thousand francs tomorrow evening," said Mathieu. He hesitated for a moment and then said with an effort: "I love you."

He emerged from the booth, and as he walked through the café he could still hear Marcelle's dry voice: "I'm in misery." She was angry with him. And yet he was doing the best he could. "In a humiliating position. Am I keeping her in a humiliating position? And if—" He stopped dead at the edge of the sidewalk. And if she wanted the child? That would burst up everything, he had but to think so for a second and everything acquired a different meaning, that was quite another story, and Mathieu, Mathieu himself, was transformed from head to heels, he had been telling himself lies all along and was playing a truly sordid role. Fortunately it wasn't true, it couldn't be true; "I have too often heard her laugh at her married friends when they were going to have children: sacred vessels, she used to call them, and say: 'They're bursting with pride because they're going to lay an egg.' A woman who says that hasn't the right to switch over to the sentimental view, that surely would be an abuse of confidence. And Marcelle is incapable of that; she would have told me, she would surely have told me, we told each other everything, and then—Oh hell!" He was sick of turning round and round in this inextricable tangle—Marcelle, Ivich, money, money, Ivich, Marcelle—"I'll do everything needful, but I don't want to think about it any more; for God's sake, I must now think of something else." He thought of Brunet, but that was an even gloomier subject: a dead friendship; he felt nervous and depressed because he was going to see him again. He caught sight of a newspaper kiosk and went up to it. "*Paris-Midi,* please."

There were none left, so he took a paper at random: it was the *Excelsior.* Mathieu produced his ten sous and carried it off. *Excelsior* wasn't an objectionable journal, it was printed on coarse paper, with a dull, velvety tapioca texture. It didn't succeed in making you lose your temper, it merely disgusted you with life while reading it. "Aerial bombardment of Valencia," Mathieu read, and looked up with a vague sense of irritation: the rue Réaumur, a street of blackened copper. Two o'clock, the moment of the day when the heat was most menacing, it curled and crackled down the center of the street like a long electric spark. "Forty airplanes circled over the center of the city for an hour and dropped a hundred and fifty bombs. The exact number of dead and wounded is not yet ascertained." He noticed out of the corner of his eye, beneath the headline, a horrid, huddled little paragraph in italics, which looked

very chatty and convincing: "From our Special Correspondent," and gave the figures. Mathieu turned over the
page, he did not want to know any more. A speech by
Monsieur Flandin at Bar-le-Duc. France crouching behind the Maginot Line. . . . A statement by Stokowski—I
shall never marry Greta Garbo. More about the Weid-
mann affair. The King of England's visit: Paris awaiting
her Prince Charming. All Frenchmen . . . Mathieu shuddered, and thought: "All Frenchmen are swine." Gomez
had once said so in a letter from Madrid. He closed the
paper and began to read the special correspondent's dis-
patch on the front page. Fifty dead and three hundred
wounded had already been counted, but that was not the
total, there were certainly corpses under the debris. No
airplanes, no A.A. guns. Mathieu felt vaguely guilty. Fifty
dead and three hundred wounded—what exactly did that
signify? A full hospital? Something like a bad railway
accident? Fifty dead. There were thousands of men in
France who had not been able to read their paper that
morning without feeling a clot of anger rise in their throat,
thousands of men who had clenched their fists and muttered: "Swine!" Mathieu clenched his fists and muttered:
"Swine!" and felt himself still more guilty. If at least he
had been able to discover in himself a trifling emotion that
was veritably if modestly alive, conscious of its limits. But
no: he was empty, he was confronted by a vast anger, a
desperate anger, he saw it and could almost have touched
it. But it was inert—if it were to live and find expression
and suffer, he must lend it his own body. It was other
people's anger. "Swine!" He clenched his fists, he strode
along, but nothing came, the anger remained external to
himself. He had been to Valencia, he had seen the Fiesta
in '34, and a great *corrida* in which Ortega and El Estu-
diante had taken part. His thought circled above the town,
seeking a church, a road, the façade of a house, of which
he could say: "I saw that, they've destroyed it, it no longer

stands." Ah! His thought swooped on to a darkened street, lying crushed under huge monuments. "I have been there, I used to walk there in the morning, stifling in the scorching shade, while the sky blazed far above the people's heads. That's it." *The bombs had fallen on that street, on the great gray monuments, the street had been enormously widened, it now extended into the interiors of the houses, there was no more shade in that street, the sky had dissolved and was pouring down upon the roadway, and the sun beat upon the debris.* Something was on the threshold of existence, a timorous dawn of anger. At last! But it dwindled and collapsed, he was left in solitude, walking with the measured and decorous gait of a man in a funeral procession in Paris, not Valencia, Paris, haunted by a phantom wrath. The windows were ablaze, the cars sped down the street, he was walking among little men dressed in light suits, Frenchmen, who did not look up at the sky and were not afraid of the sky. And yet it's all *real* down yonder, somewhere beneath the same sun, it's real, the cars have stopped, the windows have been smashed, poor dumb women sit huddled like dead chickens beside actual corpses, they lift their heads from time to time and look up at the sky, the poisonous sky—all Frenchmen are swine. Mathieu was hot, and the heat was *actual.* He wiped his forehead with his handkerchief and he thought: "One can't force one's deeper feelings." Yonder was a terrible and tragic state of affairs that ought to arouse one's deepest emotions. . . . "It's no use, the moment will not come. I am in Paris, in my own particular environment. Jacques behind his desk saying: 'No,' Daniel laughing derisively. Marcelle in the pink room, and Ivich whom I kissed this morning. Her actual presence, repellent by the very force of its actuality. Everyone has his own world, mine is a hospital containing a pregnant Marcelle, and a Jew who asks a fee of four thousand francs. There are other worlds." Gomez. He had seized his moment and had gone; he had been lucky in the draw. And the fellow of the day before. He had not gone; "he must be wandering about the streets, like me. But if he picks up a newspaper and reads: 'Bombardment of Valencia,' he will not need to put pressure on himself, he would suffer *there*, in the ruined town. Why am I caught in this loathsome world of noises, surgical instruments, furtive taxi-rides, in this world where Spain does not exist? Why am I not in the thick of it, with Gomez, with Brunet? Why haven't I wanted to go and fight? I could have chosen another world? Am I still free? I can go where I please, I meet with no resistance, but that's worse: I am in an unbarred cage, I am cut off from Spain by—by *nothing*, and yet I cannot pass." He looked at the last page of *Excelsior*: photographs by the special correspondent. Bodies outstretched on the pavement under a wall. In the middle of the roadway lay a buxom old wife, on her back, her skirts rucked up over her thighs, and without a head. Mathieu folded up the paper and threw it into the gutter.

Boris was waiting, outside the apartment house. When he saw Mathieu he assumed the chilly, rigid look that was intended to suggest that he was not quite all there.

"I've just rung your bell," he said, "but I think you were out."

"Are you quite sure?" asked Mathieu in the same tone. "Not absolutely," said Boris. "All I can say is that you didn't open the door."

Mathieu looked at him dubiously. It was scarcely two o'clock, and in any event Brunet wouldn't arrive for half an hour.

"Come along," said he. "Let us have a little talk."

They walked upstairs. On the way Boris said in his natural voice: "Is it all right about the Sumatra this evening?"

Mathieu turned away and pretended to be fumbling in

his pocket for his keys. "I don't know if I shall go," he said. "I've been thinking—perhaps Lola would rather have you all to herself."

"No doubt," said Boris, "but what does that matter? She'll be polite. And we shan't be alone in any case: Ivich will be there."

"You've seen Ivich?" asked Mathieu, opening the door.

"I've just left her," answered Boris.

"After you," said Mathieu, standing aside.

Boris went in before Mathieu and walked with easy familiarity into the living-room. Mathieu looked at his angular back with some aversion. "He has seen her," he thought.

"You'll come?" said Boris.

He had swung round and was looking at Mathieu with an expression of quizzical affection.

"Ivich didn't—didn't say anything about this evening?" asked Mathieu.

"This evening?"

"Yes. I was wondering if she meant to go: she looks quite taken up by her examination."

"She certainly means to go. She said it would be priceless for all four of us to make a party."

"All four of us?" repeated Mathieu. "Did she say all four of us?"

"Well, yes," said Boris ingenuously; "there's Lola."

"Then she reckons on my going?"

"Of course," said Boris with astonishment.

A silence fell. Boris was leaning over the balcony and looking at the street. Mathieu joined him and gave him a thump on the back.

"I like your street," said Boris, "but you must get bored with it in the long run. I'm always surprised that you live in an apartment."

"Why?"

"I don't know. Free as you are, you ought to auction

your furniture and live in a hotel. Don't you realize what life would be like? You could spend one month in a Montmartre pot-house, the next in the faubourg du Temple, and the next in the rue Mouffetard. . . ."

"Oh well," said Mathieu peevishly, "it's a matter of no importance."

"True," said Boris after an interval of meditation, "it's of no importance. There's a ring at the bell," he added with an air of annoyance.

Mathieu went to the door: it was Brunet.

"Good afternoon," said Mathieu. "You—you are before your time."

"Well, yes," said Brunet, with a smile. "Do you mind?"

"Not in the least."

"Who's that?" asked Brunet.

"Boris Serguine," said Mathieu.

"Ah—the famous disciple," said Brunet. "I don't know him."

Boris bowed coldly and withdrew to the far end of the room. Mathieu confronted Brunet, his arms hanging loose at his sides.

"He hates being taken for my disciple."

"Quite," said Brunet impassively.

He was rolling a cigarette between his fingers, a massive, indifferent figure, unperturbed by Boris's venomous gaze.

"Sit down," said Mathieu, "take the armchair."

Brunet sat on an ordinary chair. "No," he said with a smile, "your armchairs are too insidious," and he added: "Well, you old social traitor. I have to make my way into your lair to find you."

"That's not my fault," said Mathieu; "I have often tried to see you, but you were not to be found."

"True," said Brunet. "I have become a sort of traveling salesman. They keep me so much on the move that there are days when I can scarcely find myself." He continued sympathetically: "It's in your company that I find myself most easily, I have a feeling I must have left myself on deposit with you."

Mathieu flung him a grateful smile. "I have often thought that we ought to meet more often. I feel we should grow old less quickly if the three of us could forgather now and again."

Brunet eyed him with surprise. "All three of us?"

"Well, yes—Daniel, you, and I."

"True—Daniel," said Brunet in bewilderment. "So the fellow still exists—and you see him now and then, I suppose."

Mathieu's pleasure vanished: when he met Portal or Bourrelier, Brunet no doubt said to them in the same irritated tone: "Mathieu? He teaches at the Lycée Buffon, I still see him from time to time."

"Yes, I still see him, strange as it may seem," he said acidly.

A silence followed. Brunet had laid his hands flat on his knees. There he was, solid and substantial, sitting on one of Mathieu's chairs, looking rather grim as he leaned over a match-flame. The room was filled with his presence, with the smoke from his cigarette, and his measured gestures. Mathieu looked at his thick, bucolic hands and thought: "He has come." Confidence and joy were timidly reviving his heart.

"But apart from that," said Brunet, "what are you doing with yourself?"

Mathieu felt embarrassed: he was in fact doing nothing with himself. And he answered: "Nothing."

"I see. Fourteen hours' teaching each week, and a trip abroad during the long vacation."

"That's about it," said Mathieu with a laugh. He evaded Boris's eye.

"And your brother? Still a member of the Croix-de-Feu?"

"No," said Mathieu. "His views are changing. He says the Croix-de-Feu aren't dynamic enough."

"He sounds about ripe for Doriot," said Brunet.

"There's talk of that—in point of fact, I've just been having a row with him," added Mathieu, casually.

Brunet flung him a sharp, quick glance. "Why?"

"It's always the same. I ask him to do me a service and he answers with a sermon."

"And then you have a row. How odd you are!" said Brunet ironically. "Do you still think you can alter him?"

"Of course not," snapped Mathieu.

They fell silent for a moment, and Mathieu reflected sadly that the interview did not seem to progress. If only it would occur to Boris to go away. But he showed no signs of doing so, he stood bristling in his corner, looking like a sick greyhound. Brunet was sitting astride his chair, and he too was staring heavily at Boris. "He wants him to go away," thought Mathieu with satisfaction. He stared at Boris straight between the eyes; perhaps he would at last understand, exposed to the twin fires of both men's gaze.

Boris did not move. Brunet cleared his throat.

"Still working at philosophy, young man?" he asked.

Boris nodded—yes.

"How far have you got?"

"I'm just taking my degree," said Boris curtly.

"Your degree," said Brunet abstractedly. "Your degree —that's first-rate. . . ." And he added briskly: "Would you detest me if I took Mathieu away from you for a moment? You are lucky enough to see him every day, but I— Shall we take a turn outside?" he asked Mathieu.

Boris walked stiffly up to Brunet. "I understand," said he. "Please stay: I will go."

He bowed slightly: he was offended. Mathieu followed him to the outer door and said cordially: "This evening, then. I shall be there about eleven."

Boris returned a wry smile: "This evening."

Mathieu shut the door and came back to Brunet. "Well," he said, rubbing his hands, "you got him out!"

They laughed, and Brunet said: "Perhaps I went rather too far. You didn't mind?"

"On the contrary," laughed Mathieu. "It's a habit of his, and besides I'm so glad to see you alone."

"I was in a hurry for him to go," said Brunet in a calm tone, "because I've only got a quarter of an hour."

Mathieu's laugh broke off abruptly. "A quarter of an hour!" he added vehemently. "I know—I know, your time isn't your own. Indeed, it was very nice of you to come."

"As a matter of fact, I was actually engaged all day. But this morning, when I saw your dreary face, I thought I must absolutely have a word with you."

"Did I look awful?"

"You did indeed, my poor chap. Rather yellow, rather puffy, and your eyelids and the corners of your mouth were twitching. So I said to myself," he went on affectionately, "I must do what I can for him."

Mathieu coughed. "I didn't know I had such an expressive face. . . . I had slept badly," he went on with an effort. "I'm worried—just like everybody else, you know: just worried about money."

Brunet looked unconvinced. "So much the better, if that's the only trouble," he said; "you'll get out of that all right. But you looked much more like a fellow who had just realized that he had been living on ideas that don't pay."

"Oh, ideas!" said Mathieu, with a vague gesture. He looked with appealing gratitude at Brunet and he thought: "That is why he came. He had his day full, a number of important meetings, and he put himself out to help me." But all the same it would have been better if Brunet had come for the simple reason that he wanted to see him again.

"Look here," said Brunet, "I'll come straight to the point. I'm here to make you a proposal: will you join the party? If you agree, I'll take you along and it will all be settled in twenty minutes."

Mathieu started. "The party—Communist Party, you mean?"

Brunet burst out laughing, screwed up his eyes, and showed his brilliant teeth.

"Well, of course," said he, "you don't imagine that I want you to join La Rocque?"

A silence fell. "Brunet," asked Mathieu quietly, "why are you so keen on my becoming a Communist? Is it for my own good or for the good of the party?"

"For your own good," said Brunet. "You needn't look so suspicious. I haven't become a recruiting-sergeant for the Communist Party. And let us get this quite clear: the party doesn't need you. To the party you represent nothing but a little capital of intelligence—and we've got all the intellectuals we want. But you need the party."

"It's for my good," repeated Mathieu. "For my good. Listen," he repeated brusquely, "I wasn't expecting your —your proposal, I'm rather taken aback, but—but I should like you to tell me what you think. As you know, I live among schoolboys who think about nothing but themselves, and admire me on principle. No one ever talks to me about myself, and there are times when I can't seem to get hold of what I am. So you think I need to commit myself?"

"Yes," said Brunet emphatically. "Yes, you need to commit yourself. Don't you feel so yourself?"

Mathieu smiled sadly: he was thinking of Spain.

"You have gone your own way," said Brunet. "You are the son of a bourgeois, you couldn't come to us straight away, you had to free yourself first. And now it's done, you are free. But what's the use of that same freedom, if not to join us? You have spent thirty-five years cleaning yourself up, and the result is nil. You are an odd sort of creature, you know," he continued with a friendly smile. "You live in a void, you have cut your bourgeois connections, you have no tie with the proletariat, you're adrift, you're an abstraction, a man who is not there. It can't be an amusing sort of life."

"No," said Mathieu, "it isn't an amusing sort of life."

He went up to Brunet and shook him by the shoulders. He was very fond of Brunet. "You are, in fact, a blasted old recruiting-sergeant," said he. "I'm glad to have you say all that to me."

Brunet smiled an absent smile; he was still pursuing his idea. "You renounced everything in order to be free," he said. "Take one step further, renounce your own freedom: and everything shall be rendered unto you."

"You talk like a parson," said Mathieu laughing. "No, but seriously, old boy, it wouldn't be a sacrifice, you know. I know quite well that I shall get everything back—flesh, blood and genuine passions. You know, Brunet, I've finally lost all sense of reality: nothing now seems to be altogether true."

Brunet did not answer: he was meditating. He had a heavy, brick-colored face, drooping features, and reddish lashes, very pale and very long. A Prussian cast of countenance. Mathieu, every time he saw him, was conscious of a sort of uneasy curiosity in his nostrils, and he sniffed a little, in the expectation that he would suddenly inhale a strong animal smell. But Brunet had no smell.

"Now *you* are very real," said Mathieu. "Everything you touch looks real. Since you have been in my room, it seems to me an actual room, and it revolts me." He added abruptly: "You are a man."

"A man?" asked Brunet with surprise. "It would be awkward if I wasn't. What do you mean by that?"

"Exactly what I say: you have chosen to be a man."

A man with powerful, rather knotted muscles, who

deals in brief, stern truths, a man erect and self-enclosed, sure of himself, a man of this earth, impervious to the angelical allurements of art, psychology, and politics, a whole man, nothing but a man. And Mathieu was there, confronting him, irresolute, half his life gone, and still half-raw, assailed by all the vertigoes of non-humanity; and he thought: "I don't even look like a man."

Brunet got up and walked towards Mathieu. "Come, do as I did. What prevents you? Do you suppose you can live your whole life between parentheses?"

Mathieu eyed him dubiously. "Of course not," he said, "of course not. And if I choose, I must choose your side, there is no other choice."

"There is no other choice," repeated Brunet. He waited a few moments and then said: "Well?"

"Let me catch my breath," said Mathieu.

"Breathe by all means," said Brunet, "but make haste. Tomorrow you will be too old, you will have acquired your little habits, you will be the slave of your own freedom. And perhaps, too, the world will be too old."

"I don't understand," said Mathieu.

Brunet glanced at him and said quickly: "We shall be at war in September."

"You're joking," said Mathieu.

"You can believe me, the English know it, the French Government has been warned; in the second fortnight of September the Germans will enter Czechoslovakia."

"Gossip of that kind—" said Mathieu irritably.

"You don't seem to understand a thing," said Brunet with annoyance. But he recovered his composure and added mildly: "It is true that if you did understand, I shouldn't have to clamp everything down for you. Now listen: you are a footslogger like myself. Suppose you go in your present state of mind. You'll burst like a bubble. You'll have dreamed away your thirty-five years of life, and then one fine day a shell will blow your dreams to bits, and you will die without ever having waked up. You have been a hidebound official, you will make a ridiculous hero, and you will fall without having understood anything, solely to help Monsieur Schneider to maintain his interests in the Skoda works."

"And what about you?" asked Mathieu. He added with a smile: "I'm very much afraid, my dear fellow, that Marxism won't protect you from bullets."

"I'm afraid so too," said Brunet. "You know where they will send me? To the Maginot Line. That's a sure and certain knock-out."

"Well, then?"

"It's not the same thing, it's a deliberate risk. Nothing can now deprive my life of its meaning, nothing can prevent its being a destiny." And he added briskly: "Like every comrade's life, for that matter."

He sounded as though he dreaded the sin of pride.

Mathieu did not answer; he leaned his elbows on the balcony and thought: "That was well said." Brunet was right, his life was a destiny. His age, his class, his time—he had deliberately assumed them all, he had chosen the blackjack that would strike him on the temple, the German shell that would shatter him to pieces. He had joined up, he had renounced his freedom, he was nothing but a soldier. And everything had been rendered unto him, even his freedom. "He is freer than I: he is in harmony with himself and with the party." There he was, extremely real, with an actual savor of tobacco in his mouth, the colors and the forms with which he filled his eyes were more actual, more intense, than those which Mathieu could see, and yet, at the same moment, he reached across the whole earth, suffering and struggling with the proletarians of all countries. "At this moment, at this very moment, there are men firing point-blank at one another in the suburbs of Madrid, there are Austrian Jews agonizing in concentration camps, there are Chinese buried under the ruins of

Nanking, and here I am, in perfect health, I feel quite free, in a quarter of an hour I shall take my hat and go for a walk in the Luxembourg." He turned towards Brunet and looked at him with bitterness. "I am one of the *irresponsibles*," he thought.

"They've bombarded Valencia," he said suddenly.

"I know," said Brunet. "There wasn't an A.A. gun in the whole town. The bombs fell on a market."

He had not clenched his fists, he had not abandoned his measured tone, his rather sleepy attitude, and yet it was he who had been bombarded, it was his brothers and sisters, his children, who had been killed. Mathieu sat down in an armchair. "Your armchairs are insidious." He got up quickly and sat on the corner of the table.

"Well?" said Brunet. He seemed to be watching him.

"Well," said Mathieu, "you're lucky."

"Lucky to be a Communist?"

"Yes."

"What a thing to say! It's a matter of choice, old boy."

"I know. You're lucky to have been able to choose."

Brunet's face hardened a little. "That means that you aren't going to be equally lucky."

Well, an answer was expected. He is waiting. Yes or no. Join the party, inject a meaning into life, choose to be a man, to act and to believe. That would be salvation. Brunet kept his eyes on him.

"You refuse?"

"Yes," said Mathieu in desperation. "Yes, Brunet; I refuse."

And he thought: "He came to offer me the best thing in the world."—"It isn't final," he continued. "Later on—"

Brunet shrugged his shoulders. "Later on? If you're counting on an inner inspiration to make up your mind, you may have to wait a long time. Do you imagine that I was convinced when I joined the Communist Party? A conviction has to be created."

Mathieu smiled sadly. "I know that. Go down on your knees and you will believe. I dare say you are right. But I want to believe first."

"Naturally," ejaculated Brunet. "You're all the same, you intellectuals: everything is cracking and collapsing, the guns are on the point of going off, and you stand there calmly claiming the right to be convinced. If only you could see yourselves with my eyes, you would understand that time presses."

"Certainly, time presses; and what then?"

Brunet slapped his thigh indignantly. "There you are. You pretend to regret your skepticism, but you cling to it. It's your moral support. The moment it is attacked, you stick to it savagely, just as your brother sticks to his money."

To which Mathieu replied mildly: "Is there anything savage about my demeanor at this moment?"

"I don't say—" said Brunet.

A silence fell. Brunet seemed mollified. "If only he could understand me," thought Mathieu. He made an effort: to convince Brunet was his sole remaining chance of convincing himself.

"I have nothing to defend. I am not proud of my life, and I'm penniless. My freedom? It's a burden to me; for years past I have been free, and to no purpose. I simply long to exchange it for a good sound certainty. I would have asked nothing better than to work with you, it would take me out of myself, and I need to forget myself for a bit. Besides, I agree with you that no one can be a man who has not discovered something for which he is prepared to die."

Brunet had raised his head. "Well? And then?" he said, almost gaily.

"Well, there it is. I can't join, I haven't enough reasons for doing so. I am as angry as you are, and with the same people and the same things, but not violently enough. I can't help it. If I started parading, raising my fist and singing the *International*, and if I proclaimed myself satisfied with all that, I should be telling myself a lie."

Brunet had assumed his most massive and bucolic air, he stood like a great tower. Mathieu looked at him with despair.

"Do you understand me, Brunet? Do you really understand me?"

"I don't know if I understand you very well," said Brunet. "But, in any case, you have no need to justify yourself, no one is accusing you. You are waiting for a better opportunity, as you have a right to do. I hope it will come soon."

"I hope so too."

Brunet eyed him with curiosity. "Are you sure you do?"

"Certainly."

"Yes? Very well; so much the better. Only I'm afraid it won't come so very soon."

"That's what I've been thinking," said Mathieu. "I've been thinking that it may not come at all, or too late, or perhaps that *there is no such thing* as an opportunity."

"And then?"

"Well, in that case the loss is mine. That's all."

Brunet got up. "Then there we are," he said. "Well, my dear fellow, I'm very glad to have seen you, all the same."

Mathieu got up too. "You won't—you won't go off like that? Surely you have a minute or two to spare?"

Brunet looked at his watch. "I'm late already."

A silence fell. Brunet waited politely. "He mustn't go, I must talk to him," thought Mathieu. But he could not find anything to say to him.

"You mustn't be angry with me about this," said he hurriedly.

"Of course I'm not angry," said Brunet. "You aren't compelled to think as I do."

"That isn't true," said Mathieu drearily. "I know your sort: you do believe that a man is compelled to think as you do, if he isn't a rotter. You regard me as a rotter, but you won't tell me so, because you view the case as desperate."

Brunet smiled faintly. "I don't take you for a rotter," said he. "The plain fact is that you are less detached from your class than I thought."

Still talking, he had drawn nearer to the door.

"You can't think," said Mathieu, "how grateful I am to you for coming to see me and offering me your help, merely because I looked awful this morning. You are right, you know, I do need help. But it is your own help I want—not Karl Marx's help. I should like to see you often and talk to you—is that impossible?"

Brunet averted his eyes. "I would be very willing," he said, "but I haven't much time."

And Mathieu thought: "Obviously. He was sorry for me this morning and I put him off. And now we are strangers to each other once more. I have no claim on his time." But he said, despite himself: "Brunet, don't you remember? You were once my best friend."

Brunet was fiddling with the door-handle. "Why, then, do you think I came? If you had accepted my offer, we could have worked together. . . ."

They fell silent. Mathieu thought: "He is in a hurry, he is terribly anxious to get away."

Brunet added, without looking at him: "I still like you. I like your face, your hands, and your voice, and then there are the memories of old days. But that does not alter matters. My only friends, at present, are the comrades of the party, with them I have a whole world in common."

"And you think we no longer have anything in common?" asked Mathieu.

Brunet shrugged his shoulders and did not reply. One word would have sufficed, one sole word, and Mathieu would have recovered everything, Brunet's friendship, some reasons for being alive. A prospect as alluring as sleep. Mathieu straightened himself abruptly. "I mustn't keep you," said he. "Come and see me when you have the time."

"Certainly," said Brunet. "And if you should change your mind, send me word."

"Certainly," said Mathieu.

Brunet had opened the door. He smiled at Mathieu and was gone. Thought Mathieu: "He was my best friend."

He had departed. He was walking along the streets, with the pitching, rolling gait of a sailor, and the streets became real one by one. But with him the reality of the room had vanished. Mathieu looked at his green, insidious armchair, his straight chairs, his green curtains, and he thought:

"He won't sit on my chairs again, he won't look at my curtains as he rolls a cigarette," the room was no more than a patch of green light that quivered when a motor-bus passed. Mathieu went up to the window and leaned his elbows on the balcony. He thought: "I *could* not accept," and the room was behind him like a placid sheet of water, only his head emerged above the water, the insidious room was behind him, he kept his head above the water, he looked down into the street, thinking: "Is it true? Is it true I couldn't accept?" In the distance a little girl was skipping; the rope swung above her head like the handle of a basket and whipped the ground beneath her feet. A summer afternoon; the light spanned the street and the roofs, serene and smooth and cold, like an eternal verity. "Is it true I'm not a rotter? The armchair is green, the skipping-rope is like a basket-handle, that's beyond dispute. But where people are concerned, there's always matter for dispute, everything they do can be explained, from above or from below, according to choice. I refused because I want to remain free: that's what I can say. And

I can also say I was a coward. I like my green curtains, I like to take the air in the evening on my balcony, and I don't want any change. I enjoy railing against capitalism, and I don't want it suppressed, because I should no longer have any reasons for doing so, I enjoy feeling fastidious and aloof. I enjoy saying no, always no, and I should be afraid of any attempt to construct a finally habitable world, because I should merely have to say yes and act like other people. From above or below: who would decide? Brunet has decided: he thinks I am a rotter. So does Jacques; so does Daniel; they have all decided I'm a rotter. Poor Mathieu, he's a wash-out, he's a rotter. And how can I prevail against them all? I must decide: but what am I to decide?" When he had said no just now, he thought himself sincere, a bitter enthusiasm had suddenly arisen in his heart. But who, beneath that light, could have retained the smallest particle of enthusiasm? It was a light that extinguished hope, that eternalized everything it touched. The little girl would skip forever, the rope would forever swing above her head and forever whip the sidewalk beneath her feet, and Mathieu would look at her forever.

What was the use of skipping? What indeed! What was the use of choosing freedom? Under the same light, at Madrid, at Valencia, men were standing at their windows looking at deserted and eternal streets, and saying, "What's the use? What's the use of continuing the struggle?" Mathieu went back into the room, but the light pursued him there. "*My* armchair, *my* furniture." On the table there was a paperweight in the form of a crab. Mathieu picked it up by the back, as though it were alive. "*My* paperweight." What was the use? What was the use? He dropped the crab on the table and said emphatically to himself: "I am a lousy wash-out."

# CHAPTER IX

It was six o'clock. On leaving his office, Daniel had
surveyed himself in the lobby mirror and thought:
"It's starting again," and he had been afraid. He turned
into the rue Réaumur. A man could lose himself there, it
was just a mere tunnel standing open to the sky, a vast
antechamber. Evening had emptied the business premises
on either side; there was, at least, no inducement to imagine any intimacies behind their darkened windows.
Daniel's vision, now released, sped between those pierced
cliffs towards the patch of pink and stagnant sky that they
enclosed on the horizon.

It was not so easy to hide; even for the rue Réaumur
he was too conspicuous. The tall painted lasses who came
out of the shops made bold eyes at him, and he was conscious of his body. "Bitches," said he between his teeth.
He was afraid to breathe: however much women washed,
they always smelt. Fortunately, the women were, in fact,
not many, it was not a street for women, and the men
ignored him, they were reading their newspapers as they
walked along, or listlessly polishing their spectacles, or
smiling quizzically at nothing. It was indeed a crowd,
though not a dense one, moving slowly on its way, appar-

ently crushed beneath the destiny that prevails on crowds.
Daniel fell into step with this slow procession, he adopted
the men's somnolent smile, their vague and menacing
destiny, and he was lost; there was nothing left within
him but the dull thud of avalanches, he was now no more
than a sea-strand of forgotten light. "I shall arrive too
early at Marcelle's, I've got time to walk a bit."

He drew himself up, stiffened, and looked warily about
him: he had recovered himself; indeed, he never slipped
far beyond his own control. "I've got time to walk a bit."
That meant: "I'll look in at the fair," it was a long while
since Daniel had managed to deceive himself. Indeed,
what was the point of doing so? Did he want to go to the
fair? Well, he would go. He would go because he had not
the slightest wish to refrain from doing so. The morning
with the cats, Mathieu's visit, then four hours' pestilential
work, and, this evening, Marcelle: it was intolerable—"I
can very well allow myself a little distraction."

Marcelle was a morass. She listened for hours to what
she was told, she said yes, yes, nothing but yes, and ideas
disappeared into her head; she existed solely in appearance. It is all very well to play for a while with fools—
slacken the cord and they rise into the air, vast and im-
ponderable, like elephant balloons; pull the cord, and
down they drop to the level of the earth, where they
gyrate distractedly, or bounce about in response to every
jerk upon the string; but fools must be changed fairly
often or the entertainment becomes tiresome. Moreover,
Marcelle was in an unwholesome condition at the moment;
the air in her room was hardly fit to breathe. Indeed, it
was always difficult to refrain from sniffing when entering
that room. It didn't exactly smell, but it induced an uneasy
sensation at the base of the bronchial tubes, which often
resulted in a touch of asthma. "I shall go to the fair."
There was no need of such excuses; in any case, it was
quite an innocent project: he wanted to observe the ma-

neuvers of perverts on the trail. The fair on the boulevard
de Sébastopol was famous in its own line, it was there
that the Finance Ministry official Durat had collected the
little brute that did him in. The scamps who loafed round
the penny-in-the-slot machines awaiting custom were
much more amusing than their colleagues in Montparnasse: they were amateurs, half-baked little louts, brutal,
coarse, with raucous voices, and a sly cunning all their
own, on the look-out for ten francs and a dinner. Then
there were the paying clients, intensely comic creatures,
silkily affectionate, with honeyed voices and a furtive,
appealing, vague expression in their eyes. Daniel could
not stand their humility, they looked as if they were per-
petually pleading guilty. He wanted to knock them down,
just as one always wants to use violence on a man self-
condemned and smash up his small remaining dignity.
He usually leaned against a pillar and watched them as
they preened themselves under the bleared, derisive eyes
of their young admirers. The clients took him for a detective or for one of the boys' bullies: he spoiled all their
pleasure.

Daniel was seized with a sudden access of impatience
and quickened his step. "This is going to be amusing!"
His throat was dry, and the air was dry and torrid. He
could no longer see, there was a blur before his eyes, the
remembered vision of a turbid light like the yellow of an
egg-yolk, repellent and alluring, a noisome light that he
longed to see, but it was still far away, hovering between
low walls, like the smell of a cellar. The rue Réaumur
vanished, nothing was left confronting him but a perspec-
tive dotted with obstacles, in the shape of people: rather
like a nightmare. Only in real nightmares Daniel never
reached the end of the street. He turned into the boulevard de Sébastopol, which lay scorching under a clear
sky, and slackened his pace. "Fair": he looked up at the

sign, made sure that the faces of the passers-by were unknown to him, and went in.

It was a long narrow hall, with brown-washed walls,
and the gaunt ugliness and vinous reek of a warehouse.
Daniel plunged into the yellow light, it was gloomier and
murkier than usual, and the daylight drove it into the far
end of the hall; for Daniel, it was the light of seasickness:
it reminded him of the night of nausea he had passed in
the boat to Palermo: in the deserted engine-room there
had been just such a yellow murk, he dreamed of it sometimes and awakened with a start, thankful to find himself
in darkness. The hours he spent at the fair seemed to him
punctuated by the dull, rhythmic thud of crankshafts.

Along the walls stood a row of roughly constructed
boxes standing on four legs; these were the games. Daniel
knew them all: the football-players, sixteen little figures
of painted wood impaled on long brass wires, the polo-
players, the tin automobile that ran on a felt-covered track
between houses and fields, the five little black cats on the
moonlit roof and a revolver to shoot them off it, the electric rifle, and the chocolate and scent machines. At the far
end of the room there were three rows of "kineramas," the
titles of the films being displayed in large black letters:
*The Young Couple, Naughty Chambermaids, The Sun-
Bath, The Interrupted Wedding-Night.* A spectacled gentleman had unobtrusively approached one of these machines, slipped a franc into the slot, and was goggling
eagerly through the mica-covered eyeholes. Daniel was
choking: it was the dust and the heat, and the thud of
heavy blows that came at regular intervals from the other
side of the wall. On his left he observed the attraction:
some ragged youths had gathered around the Negro
boxer, a wooden figure six feet tall, with a leather pad
and a dial in the center of his stomach. There were four of
them, one blond, one red-haired, and two dark; they had

taken off their coats, rolled their shirt-sleeves up their skinny arms, and were pounding on the pad with all their might. A needle on the dial indicated the strength of their fists. They flung sly glances at Daniel and went on hitting savagely. Daniel glared back in response to indicate that there was nothing doing and turned his back on them. On the right, near the cash-desk, and against the light, he noticed a tall, gray-faced young man, wearing a crumpled suit, a nightshirt, and slippers. He was certainly not a homo like the others; besides, he did not appear to know them, he had come in quite by chance—Daniel was sure of that—and seemed wholly absorbed in the contemplation of a mechanical crane. After a moment or two, attracted no doubt by the electric lamp and the Kodak displayed behind the windows on a heap of candy, he approached noiselessly and with a knowing look slipped a piece of money into a slit in the apparatus, drew back a little, and seemed to plunge again into meditation, stroking his nostrils with a pensive finger. Daniel felt a familiar thrill run down the back of his neck. "Ah, the Narcissus type," thought Daniel; "he enjoys touching himself." That was the most alluring, the most romantic type: those whose lightest movement revealed an unconscious coquetry, a deep and stealthy love of self. The young man briskly seized the two handles of the apparatus and swung them with a knowing air. The crane revolved with a noise of locking gears, and its senile creaking shook the whole apparatus. Daniel wished he might win the electric lamp, but a slot ejected a spate of multicolored sweets that looked as mean and uninviting as dried beans. The young man did not appear to be disappointed; he felt in his pocket and produced another coin. "That's his last," said Daniel to himself; "he hasn't had a meal since yesterday." But this wouldn't do. He must not be lured into imagining, behind that lean, alluring body, so intent upon itself, a mysterious life of privation, freedom, and hope.

Not today. Not here in this inferno, under this sinister light, to the accompaniment of those dull blows upon the wall—"I swore I would resist." And yet Daniel understood so well how a man could be caught by one of those machines, lose his money bit by bit, and begin again and yet again, his throat dry from dizziness and rage: there were many sorts of dizziness, and Daniel knew them all. The crane began to revolve in cautious and deliberate fashion: the nickeled apparatus seemed content with its operations. Daniel was afraid: he had taken one step forward, he ached to put his hand on the young man's arm—he already felt the contact of the rough and threadbare stuff—and say to him: "Don't play any more." The nightmare was about to begin again, with its accompanying savor of eternity, the triumphant tomtom from the other side of the wall, and the surge of uncomplaining melancholy that rose within him, that infinite and familiar all-engulfing melancholy, days and nights would pass before he could shake it off. But a man came in and Daniel was delivered: he stood up and thought he was going to burst out laughing. "That is the man," he thought. He was a trifle bewildered, but all the same glad because he had resisted.

The man moved briskly down the hall; his knees sagged as he walked, but he kept his body stiff, though his legs moved easily beneath him. "You," thought Daniel, "Are wearing a corset." He was getting on for fifty, close-shaven, with a bland countenance gently molded by the years, a peach-colored complexion, white hair, a fine Florentine nose, and a rather harsher, more myopic expression in the eyes than seemed quite in character—and a roving eye. His entrance caused a sensation: the four little scamps turned around simultaneously, affecting the same air of vicious innocence, and then resumed their blows on the Negro's pelvis, but by no means with the same enthusiasm. The man surveyed them for a moment with an aloof and slightly disapproving air, then turned around and approached the football game. He twirled the metal wires and examined the little figures with smiling curiosity as though in amusement at the caprice that had brought him there. Daniel noticed that smile and felt a catch at his heart; all these pretenses and subterfuges appalled him and made him want to run away. But only for an instant: it was a familiar flush of feeling that soon passed. He set his back comfortably against a pillar and gazed steadily at the newcomer. On his right the young man in a nightshirt had produced a third coin from his pocket, and for the third time resumed his silent acrobatics around the crane.

The handsome gentleman leaned over the game and slid his forefinger over the slender bodies of the little wooden players: he was not going to lower himself to make advances, he no doubt considered that he was, with his white hair and summer suit, a sufficiently delectable dish to attract all these young flies. And in fact, after a few moments' confabulation, the blond youth detached himself from the group and, flinging his jacket around his shoulders without putting it on, strolled up to the prospective client with his hands in his pockets. He came up with a timorous, sniffling sort of air, and the expression in the eyes beneath the thick brows was doglike. Daniel looked disgustedly at his plump hips, his broad bucolic cheeks, gray and already begrimed with an incipient beard. "Female flesh," he thought, "as lush as dough." The gentleman would take him home, give him a bath, soap him, and perhaps scent him. At this thought, Daniel's rage revived. "Swine!" he murmured. The youth had stopped a few paces away from the old gentleman and in his turn pretended to be examining the apparatus. They were bent over the wires and inspected them without looking at each other, and with an air of absorption. Then the youth appeared to make a prompt decision: he grasped a knob

and one of the pegs spun round and round. Four little
players described a semicircle and stopped head-down-
wards.

"You know the game?" asked the gentleman in an
almond-paste voice. "Ah, indeed! Will you explain it to
me? I don't understand it."

"You put in twenty sous and then you pull. The balls
come out and you've got to get them into the hole."

"But there must be two to play, mustn't there? I try
to get the ball into the goal, and you have to stop me,
eh?"

"That's so," said the young man. And he added after a
brief pause: "One of us has to be at either end."

"Would you like to play a game with me?"

"Sure," said the youth.

They played. The gentleman said in a heady voice:
"But this young man is so clever! How does he do it? He
wins all the time. Do show me."

"It's just knowing how," said the youth modestly.

"Ah! You practice? You come here often, no doubt? I
happened to look in as I was passing, but I have never met
you before: I should have noticed you. Yes indeed, I
should have noticed you, I am something of a physiog-
nomist, and you have an interesting face. You come from
Touraine?"

"Yes—yes, I do," said the youth, rather taken aback.

The gentleman stopped playing and came up to him.

"But the game isn't finished," said the youth ingenuously. "You've got five balls left."

"True. Well, we can play later on," said the gentleman.
"I would sooner talk to you for a bit, if you don't mind."

The youth smiled a professional smile. The gentleman,
in order to join him, had to make a half-turn. He raised
his head, and as he slowly licked his thin lips, his look
encountered Daniel's. Daniel glared at him, the gentleman
hastily averted his eyes, looked upset, uneasy, and rubbed

his hands together like a priest. The youth had seen nothing; with open mouth and vacant and submissive eyes he waited until he was spoken to. A silence fell, then the gentleman began to talk to him in an unctuous, husky voice, but did not look at him. Daniel strained his ears, but could only catch the words "villa," and "billiards." The youth shook his head emphatically.

"It must be a swanky place," said he loudly.

The gentleman did not answer and flung a furtive glance in Daniel's direction. Daniel felt invigorated by a dry, delicious anger. He knew all the rites of departure: they would say good-by and the gentleman would go first, padding busily out of the hall. The boy would nonchalantly rejoin his little friends, deal another blow or two at the Negro's stomach, and then go too, shuffling out after a few casual good-bys: he was the one to follow. And the old gentleman, as he paced up and down in the next street, would suddenly see Daniel appear on the heels of the young beauty. What a moment! Daniel enjoyed it in anticipation, he devoured with magisterial gaze his victim's delicate, lined face, his hands shook, and his joy would have been complete had not his throat been so dry; indeed, he was agonizingly thirsty. If he saw a chance, he would impersonate a police detective assigned to morals: he could always take the old man's name and reduce him to a state of jitters. "If he asks me for my inspector's card I'll show him my prefecture pass."

"Good morning, Monsieur Lalique," said a timid voice.

Daniel recoiled: Lalique was a pseudonym he sometimes used. He turned abruptly around.

"What are you doing here?" he asked severely. "I had forbidden you to set foot inside the place."

It was Bobby. Daniel had got him a job with a druggist. He had become gross and fat, he was wearing a new ready-made suit and was no longer in the least interesting. Bobby tilted his head sideways, as a child might do; he looked at Daniel without replying, but with an ingenuous, sly smile, as though he had said: "Here we are again!" It was the smile that brought Daniel's wrath to boiling-point.

"Will you answer me!" said he.

"I've been looking for you for three days, Monsieur Lalique," said Bobby in his drawling voice. "I didn't know your address. I said to myself: one of these days Monsieur Daniel will be sure to come in here. . . ."

One of these days! Impertinent little beast! He dared to predict what Daniel might do, and lay his petty plans accordingly. "He thinks he knows me, he thinks he can exploit me." There was nothing to be done but crush him like a slug: Daniel's image was embedded in that narrow forehead, and there it would remain forever. Despite his repugnance, Daniel felt a bond between himself and that patch of flaccid, living flesh: *it was he* who thus lived in Bobby's consciousness.

"You are ugly," he said, "you have lost your figure, and that suit is a disgrace, where on earth did you pick it up? It's dreadful how your vulgarity comes out when you put on your best clothes."

Bobby did not seem disconcerted: he looked at Daniel with wide, affectionate eyes and continued to smile. Daniel detested the nerveless patience of poverty, its limp, tenacious indiarubber smile: even if an angry fist crashed on those lips, the smile would linger on the bleeding mouth. Daniel threw a furtive glance at the handsome gentleman: his look of uneasiness had vanished; he was leaning over the little blond ruffian, breathing into his hair and laughing genially. "It had to happen," thought Daniel wrathfully; "he sees me with this tart, he takes me for a colleague, my reputation's gone." He hated this free-masonry of the urinal. "They imagine that everyone is in it. I, for one, would sooner kill myself than look like that old sod."

"What do you want?" he asked brutally. "I'm in a hurry. And keep your distance, you reek of brilliantine."

"Excuse me," said Bobby placidly. "You were there leaning against the pillar, you didn't look in a hurry, and that's why I thought I would—"

"Dear me, how correctly you talk!" said Daniel with a burst of laughter. "I suppose you bought some ready-made speeches at the same time as your suit?"

These sarcasms were lost on Bobby: he had tilted his head back and was contemplating the ceiling with an air of modest enjoyment, through his half-closed eyelids. "He attracted me because he looked like a cat." At that thought Daniel could not repress a quiver of rage. Yes indeed; in days gone by, Bobby had then attracted him. Could he therefore make claims on Daniel for the rest of his life?

The old gentlemen had taken his young friend's hand and was holding it paternally between his own. Then he said good-by to him, tapped him on the cheek, threw a meaning glance at Daniel, and departed with long mincing strides. Daniel put out his tongue at him, but the man had already turned his back. Bobby began to laugh.

"What's the matter?" asked Daniel.

"It's because you put your tongue out at the old mamma," said Bobby. And he added in a fawning tone: "You're still the same, Monsieur Daniel, just as boyish as ever."

"Well, really!" said Daniel, quite dumbfounded. A suspicion seized him, and he said: "What about your druggist? Aren't you with him still?"

"I had no luck," said Bobby plaintively.

Daniel eyed him with disgust. "You've managed to get fat, though."

The blond boy was strolling casually out of the fair and brushed against Daniel as he passed. His three companions soon followed him, jostling each other as they went and laughing loudly. "What am I doing here?"

thought Daniel. He looked around in search of the stooping shoulders and thin neck of the young man in the nightshirt.

"Come, tell me," he said absently. "What did you do? Did you rob him?"

"It was the druggist's wife," said Bobby. "She was down on me."

The young man in the nightshirt was no longer there. Daniel felt bored and exhausted, he was afraid of finding himself alone.

"She got mad because I was seeing Ralph," pursued Bobby.

"I told you to give up seeing Ralph. He's a dirty little scab."

"Do you mean that a chap is to chuck his pals because he's had a bit of luck?" asked Bobby indignantly. "I was seeing less of him, but I wasn't going to drop him all at once. He's a thief—that's what she said: 'I forbid him to set foot in my shop.' What are you to do with a bitch like that? I used to meet him outside so that she shouldn't catch me. But the assistant saw us together. Dirty little beast, I believe he's one of them," said Bobby virtuously. "When I was first there, it was Bobby here and Bobby there, you bet I told him off. 'I'll get back at you,' he said. He went to the shop and spat it all out, how he'd seen us together, and we were misbehaving, and the people had to look the other way. And the druggist's wife, she said: 'What did I tell you? I forbid you to see him or you shan't stay in our place.' 'Madame, I said, it's you who give orders at the shop, but when I'm outside, what I do isn't your business'; so that was that!"

The fair was deserted, beyond the wall the hammering had ceased. The cashier got up—she was a tall blonde. She pattered up to a scent machine and admired herself in the glass and smiled. Seven o'clock struck.

"It's you who give orders in the shop, but when I'm outside, what I do isn't your business," repeated Bobby complacently.

Daniel shook himself.

"So they threw you out?" he asked indifferently.

"I went of my own accord," said Bobby with dignity. "I said: 'I prefer to go.' And without a penny in my pocket. They wouldn't even pay me what was due, but it can't be helped: I'm like that. I'm sleeping at Ralph's place. I sleep in the afternoon, because he receives a lady in the evening. It's an affair. I haven't had anything to eat since the day before yesterday." He looked at Daniel with an insinuating air. "I said to myself: 'I can always try to find Monsieur Lalique, he'll understand me.'"

"You're a little fool," said Daniel. "You don't interest me any more. I wear myself out to find you a job, and you get yourself sacked at the end of a month. Added to which, you know, don't imagine that I believe half you tell me. You lie like a dentist at a fair."

"You can ask," said Bobby. "You'll soon see if I'm not telling the truth."

"Ask? Ask whom?"

"The druggist's wife."

"Of course I shan't," said Daniel. "I should hear some fine stories. Anyway, I can't do anything for you."

He felt shaky, and he thought: "I must go away," but his legs were numb.

"We had the idea of going to work, Ralph and I . . ." said Bobby with an air of detachment. "We thought of setting up on our own."

"Indeed? And you've come to ask me to advance you the money needed for a start, eh? Keep those stories for other people. How much do you want?"

"You're a fine chap, Monsieur Lalique," said Bobby in a clammy voice. "I was just saying to Ralph this morning: 'If only I can find Monsieur Lalique, you'll see that he won't leave me in the lurch.'"

"How much do you want?" repeated Daniel.

Bobby began to wriggle. "Well, if you could lend the amount, perhaps—and I mean *lend*—I would repay you at the end of the first month."

"How much?"

"A hundred francs."

"Here's fifty," said Daniel, "as a gift. And now clear out."

Bobby pocketed the note without a word, and they stood face to face, irresolute.

"Go away," said Daniel weakly.

"Thank you, Monsieur Lalique," said Bobby. He made as though to go and then turned back. "If you want to see me or Ralph at any time, we live near by, 6 rue aux Ours, seventh floor. You're wrong about Ralph, you know, he likes you very much."

"Go away."

Bobby moved off, walking backwards, still smiling, then he swung around and went. Daniel went up to the crane and had a look at it. In addition to the Kodak and the electric lamp, there was a pair of binoculars he had never noticed. He slipped a franc into the appropriate slot and turned the knobs at random. The crane dropped its claws and began clumsily to rake about in the pile of candy. Daniel picked up five or six in the hollow of his hand and ate them.

The sun began to plaster gold on the great black buildings, the sky was filled with gold, but a soft and liquid shadow rose up from the street, and the people smiled at its caresses. Daniel was devoured by thirst, but he would not drink: die, then! die of thirst! "After all," he thought, "I haven't done anything wrong." But he had done worse: he had let the evil thing come very close to him, he had done everything except satisfy his senses, and that was merely because he had not dared. Now he carried the evil thing within himself, it tingled down his body head to

foot, he was infected, there was still that yellow after-
taste in his eyes; indeed, his eyes turned everything yellow. He would have done much better to let pleasure
strike him down, and thus strike down the evil thing
within him. It was true that it always revived. He swung
around. "He might be following me to see where I live.
Oh!" thought he, "I wish he had done so. I would give
him such a thrashing in the open street!" But Bobby did
not appear. He had made his day's wages and now he had
gone home. To Ralph's place, 6 rue aux Ours. Daniel
quivered. "If I could forget that address! If only I could
manage to forget that address! . . ." What was the use?
He would take care not to forget it.

People were chattering all around him, in amity and
peace. A man said to his wife: "Why, it goes back to before
the war. It was 1912. No. It was 1913. I was still with Paul
Lucas." Peace. The peace of good and honest folk, the
peace of men of goodwill. "Why is *their* will good and not
mine?" It couldn't be helped, it just was so. Something in
this sky, in this light, in this display of nature, had thus
decided. They knew, they knew that they were right, that
God, if He existed, was on their side. Daniel looked at
their faces: how hard they were, despite their uncon-
straint! At the merest sign these men would fall upon him
and tear him to pieces. And the sky, the light, the trees,
the whole of nature would be, as always, in league with
them: Daniel was a man of ill will.

Before his doorway a large and pallid concierge lay back
in his chair enjoying the fresh air. Daniel caught sight of
him from a distance, and he thought: "Goodwill personified." The concierge sat with his hands across his stomach,
Buddha-fashion, watching the passers-by, from time to
time nodding his approval. "Oh, to be a fellow like that,"
thought Daniel enviously. A truly serious character; and
responsive to the great natural forces, heat, cold, light, and
moisture. Daniel stopped, fascinated by those long, silky

eyelashes, by the sententious malice of those plump cheeks. He longed to sink his senses until he was no more than that, until there was nothing in his head but a white paste and a faint scent of shaving-cream. "Never misses a night's sleep," he thought. He no longer knew whether he wanted to destroy the man, or slip into the warm refuge of that ordered soul.

The large man lifted his head, and Daniel walked on. "Living the life I do, I can always expect to break up pretty soon."

He flung a dark look at his portfolio; he disliked carrying it in his hand: it made him look like a lawyer. But his ill humour vanished when he remembered he had not bought it unintentionally; and, indeed, it was going to be *tremendously* useful. He did not blink the fact that he was running risks, but he was calm and cold, merely a little more animated than usual. "If I reach the edge of the sidewalk in thirteen strides . . ." He took thirteen strides and stopped dead on the edge of the sidewalk, but the last stride had been noticeably longer than the others, he had lunged like a fencer. "However, no matter: whatever happens, the job is as good as done." It could not fail, it was fool-proof; indeed, the surprising thing was that no one had thought of it before. "The plain fact is," he reflected scornfully, "thieves are damn fools." He crossed the street, ruminating on his idea. "They ought to have organized themselves a long time since. Into a syndicate, like conjurers." An association for the dissemination and exploitation of technical methods—that is what they needed. With a registered office, a scale of awards, a code, and a library. A private cinema as well, and films that would analyze the more difficult actions in slow motion. Each new improvement would be filmed, and the theory recorded on phonograph disks, with the name of the inventor; each one being graded according to category; there would be,

for example, the shop-window theft by method 1673, or
the "Serguine method," also called the Christopher Colum-
bus egg (as being extremely simple, but yet to be discovered). Boris would gladly have presided over a little in-
structional film. "Yes," he thought, "and free instruction
on the psychology of theft, that is indispensable." His
method was based almost wholly on psychology. He
threw an approving glance at a little one-story café,
painted pumpkin color, and suddenly noticed that he was
halfway along the avenue d'Orléans. Strange how pleasant
all these people looked on the avenue d'Orléans between
seven and half past seven in the evening! The light ac-
counted for a good deal—a most becoming russet-muslin
light—and it was delightful to find oneself on the out-
skirts of Paris, near one of the gates, the streets speeding
underfoot towards the old commercial centers of the city,
the markets, and the dark alleys of Saint-Antoine, immersed where he was in the soft, religious seclusion of the
evening and the suburbs. The people look as if they have
come out to enjoy each other's company; they don't mind
being jostled; indeed, they look into the shop-windows
with a naïve, dispassionate interest. On the boulevard
Saint-Michel people also look into the shop-windows, but
they mean to buy. "I shall come back here every evening,"
Boris decided eagerly. Then next summer he would take
a room in one of those three-storied houses that looked so
like twin sisters and recalled the Revolution of '48. "But
I wonder how the good women of those days managed to
push the bolsters through such narrow windows on to the
heads of the soldiers below. The frames of the windows
are all blackened with smoke, they look as though they
had been scorched in a fire; but these bleak façades holed
by small black windows are not depressing; they look like
bursts of storm-sky under a blue heaven; as I look at the
windows, if I could climb on to the terrace roof of that
little café, I should see the glass-doored wardrobes at the

far end of the rooms, like pools up-ended; the crowds pass
through me and I find myself thinking of the municipal
guards, the gilded entrance gates of the Palais Royal, and
the 14th of July. What did that Communist fellow want
with Mathieu?" he suddenly asked himself. Boris did not
like Communists, they were so serious. Brunet in particular was intolerably magisterial. "He slung me out,"
chuckled Boris to himself; "damn him, he fairly pitched
me out." And then, quite suddenly, like a violent little
tornado inside his head, there came upon him the impulse
to smash something. "I dare say Mathieu has noticed that
he has got in completely wrong, and now he'll join the
Communist Party." For a moment he lingered over all the
incalculable results of such a conversion. But in a sudden
flush of fear he stood still. Surely Mathieu had not been
in the wrong, that would be too awful now that Boris was
committed: in the philosophy class there had been a good
deal of lively interest in Communism, and Mathieu had
evaded the issue by explaining what freedom was. Boris
had promptly understood: the individual's duty is to do
what he wants to do, to think whatever he likes, to be ac-
countable to no one but himself, to challenge every idea
and every person. Boris had constructed his life on this
basis, and he kept himself conscientiously free: indeed, he
always challenged everyone, excepting Mathieu and
Ivich; that would have been futile, for they were above
criticism. As for freedom, there was no sense in speculat-
ing on its nature, because in that case one was then no
longer free. Boris scratched his head in perplexity and
wondered what was the origin of these destructive impulses which gripped him from time to time. "Perhaps
I am naturally highly strung," he reflected, with amusement and surprise. Because, after all, taking a cool view
of matters, Mathieu was definitely not in the wrong:
Mathieu was not that sort. Boris felt reassured and
brandished the portfolio. He also wondered if it was moral

to be highly strung, he considered the pros and cons of the matter, but he refrained from pushing his inquiries any farther; he would ask Mathieu. Boris considered it indecent for a fellow of his age to aspire to think for himself. He had seen enough of such people at the Sorbonne, pretentious young wise-acres, bleak, bespectacled products of the Normal School, who always had a personal theory in reserve, and invariably ended by making fools of themselves somehow, and even so, their theories were repellent and crude. Boris had a horror of the ridiculous, he had no intention of making a fool of himself, he preferred to say nothing and let it be assumed that he had no ideas—this was much the more agreeable line to take. Later on, of course, things would be different, but for the moment he deferred to Mathieu, whose profession it was to solve problems. Besides, he always enjoyed watching Mathieu apply his mind to a subject: Mathieu flushed, stared at his fingers, stammered a little, but it was an honest and admirable effort. Sometimes, not indeed very often, some trifling idea came to Boris, much against his will, and he tried to prevent Mathieu noticing the fact, but the old toad always did notice it, and he would say: "You've got something at the back of your head," and promptly plied him with questions. Boris was in agony, he struggled to divert the conversation, but Mathieu was extremly tenacious; in the end Boris blurted the thing out, looking down at the floor, and the worst of it all was that Mathieu proceeded to abuse him, saying: "That's just rubbish, you can't think straight," precisely as if Boris had claimed to have conceived an inspired idea. "The old toad!" repeated Boris cheerfully. He stopped before the window of a fine, red-painted drugstore and impartially considered his reflection. "I'm a decent sort of chap," he thought. He liked his looks. He stepped on to the automatic weighing-machine to see if he had put on weight since the day before. A red bulb flashed, a mechanism began to function with a rattle and a whir, and Boris received a cardboard ticket: a hundred and twenty-seven. For a moment he was dismayed. "I've put on over a pound." Luckily he noticed he was still carrying his portfolio. He got off the machine and went on his way. A hundred and twenty-six for five feet seven was quite all right. He was in excellent humor and felt a genial glow within him. Around him, indeed, the tenuous melancholy of that decaying day was slowly sinking into darkness and, as it faded, touched him lightly with its amber radiance, its perfumes laden with regret. That day, that tropical sea, receding now and leaving him alone beneath a fading light, was a stage upon his progress, though not one of much significance. The night would come, he would go to the Sumatra, he would see Mathieu, he would see Ivich, and he would dance. But soon, exactly at the hinge of day and night, this masterly act of larceny would be committed. He drew himself up and quickened his step: he must be cautious; he must remember that those nondescript-looking fellows who stand solemnly turning over the pages of books are private detectives. Six of them were employed at the Garbure bookshop. Boris had this information from Picard, who had served in the shop for three days after failing in his geology examination; he had to do something, his parents having cut off supplies, but he soon cleared out in disgust. Not only did he have to spy on the customers, he also had orders to watch out for simple-minded people, wearers of pince-nez, for instance, who strolled nervously up to the shop-window, and suddenly leap out on them, accusing them of having tried to slip a book into their pocket. The wretched creatures were naturally terror-stricken, and having been conducted down a long corridor into a small dark office, a hundred francs were extorted from them under threat of prosecution. Boris felt intoxicated: he would avenge them all; *he* would not be caught. "Most of these fellows," he thought, "have no notion of defending themselves; of a hundred thieves, eighty are amateurs." He was no amateur; it was true that he did not know everything, but what he did know he had learned methodically, having always thought that a fellow who worked with his head should be familiar with some form of manual labor, to keep himself in touch with reality. Hitherto he had drawn no profit from his enterprises: he attached no importance to possessing seventeen tooth-brushes, some twenty ash-trays, a compass, a poker, and a darning-egg. What he took into consideration in each case was the technical difficulty. It was far better, as he had done in the previous week, to annex a little box of Blackoid liquorice tablets under the eyes of the druggist than a morocco pocketbook from an empty shop. The benefit of the theft was entirely moral; on this point Boris felt himself in complete agreement with the ancient Spartans; it was a test of character. And there was indeed a delicious moment when you said to yourself: "I shall count up to five, and at five the toothbrush must be in my pocket"; you caught your breath and were conscious of an extraordinary sensation of clarity and power. He smiled: he was going to make an exception to his principles; for the first time, his own interest should be the motive for the theft: in half an hour or later he would possess that jewel, that indispensable treasure. "The Thesaurus!" he muttered, for he liked the word "Thesaurus," as reminding him of the Middle Ages, Abélard, herbalists, Faust, and the chastity belts at the Cluny Museum. "It will be mine, I shall be able to consult it any hour of the day." Hitherto he had been obliged to look through it in the shop-window, in a hurry, and as the pages were not cut, the information he had acquired was often incomplete. He would put it, that very evening, on his night-table, and tomorrow when he awoke, it would be the first object that met his eye. "Alas, no," he thought peevishly: "I'm sleeping with Lola this evening." In any case he would take it to the Sorbonne library, and from time to time, interrupting his work of revision, he would glance into it to refresh his mind: he resolved to learn one phrase and perhaps even two every day; in six months that would make six times three, which was eighteen, multiplied by two: three hundred and sixty, with the five or six hundred that he knew already, adding up to pretty near a thousand, which might be described as a good average of achievement. He crossed the boulevard Raspail and turned into the rue Denfert-Rochereau with a faint sense of dislike. The rue Denfert-Rochereau always irritated him extremely, perhaps because of its chestnut trees; in any case, it was a characterless place, except for a black-painted dyeing establishment with blood-red curtains looped dismally across the window like two scalped heads of hair. Boris, on his way past, looked appreciatively at the dyeing shop and then plunged into the blond, fastidious silence of the street. Street, indeed! It was no more than a burrow with houses on each side. "Yes, but the metro passes underneath it," thought Boris, and he drew some comfort from this notion, conceiving himself for a minute or two as walking on a thin crust of bitumen, which might perhaps crack. "I must tell Mathieu about it," Boris said to himself; "he'll be furious." No. The blood suddenly rushed into his face, he would do nothing of the kind. Ivich, yes: she understood him, and if she did not herself steal, it was because she was not gifted that way. He would also tell Lola, just to infuriate her. But Mathieu was not too candid on the subject of these thefts. He grinned indulgently when Boris mentioned them, but Boris was not very sure that he approved. For instance, he found himself wondering what arguments Mathieu could use against him. Lola just got wild, but that was natural, she could not understand certain fine distinctions, and the more so because she was rather common.

"You would steal from your own mother," she would

say to him, "and you'll steal from me some day." Whereto
he answered: "I dare say I shall!" The suggestion was, of
course, silly: one didn't steal from one's intimates, it was
much too easy, he answered thus because he so detested
Lola's habit of relating everything to herself. But Mathieu.
. . . Yes, Mathieu, that was beyond comprehension. Why
should he object to theft, provided of course that it was
committed according to the rules? Mathieu's unuttered
disapproval distressed Boris for a few moments, then he
shook his head and said to himself: "What a drama!" In
five years, seven years, he would have his own ideas,
Mathieu's would seem to him pathetically antiquated, he
would be his own critic: "Indeed, we may no longer know
each other at all." Boris did not look forward to that day,
he felt perfectly happy, but he was sensible and he knew
that it must come: he would inevitably develop, he would
leave many things and people behind him, he was not yet
mature. Mathieu was a stage on the route, like Lola, and
even when Boris admired him most, his admiration was in
so far provisional that, extreme as it was, it never became
abject. Mathieu was as sound as a man could be, but he
could not develop as Boris would; indeed, he could no
longer develop at all, he was too complete. These reflections depressed Boris, and he was glad when he got to the
Place Edmond-Rostand: he enjoyed crossing it and evad-
ing the motor-buses that blundered through it like gigantic
turkeys, merely by drawing in his chest the needful inch
or two. "If only it hasn't occurred to them to take the book
out of the window on this very day!"

At the corner of the rue Monsieur-le-Prince and the
boulevard Saint-Michel he stopped; he wanted to mod-
erate his impatience, it would not have been wise to arrive
with cheeks flushed and predatory eyes. His principle was
to act in cold blood. He forced himself to remain motionless outside an umbrella and cutlery shop and to look
methodically, one by one, at the articles displayed—midget

umbrellas, green and red and oily, large umbrellas, ivory-handled umbrellas topped with bulldogs' heads, all so utterly depressing that Boris tried to picture the elderly customers who came to buy these objects. He was just attaining a condition of cold and joyless resolve when he suddenly caught sight of something that plunged him once more into jubilation: "A clasp-knife!" he murmured, and his hands trembled. It was a genuine clasp-knife, with a thin long blade, a cross-guard, a black horn haft, as elegant as a crescent moon; there were two spots of rust on the blade, which might well have been blood. "Oh!" groaned Boris, his heart constricted with desire. The knife lay, wide open, on a varnished slab of wood, between two umbrellas. Boris looked at it for a long while, and the world dislimned around him, everything but the cold radiance of that blade lost its value in his eyes, he wanted to fling everything aside, enter the shop, buy the knife, and escape no matter where, like a thief, carrying his plunder with him. "Picard will show me how to throw it," he said to himself. But his rigorous sense of duty soon prevailed: "Later on. I'll buy it later on, as a prize for myself if I bring off the job."

The Garbure bookshop formed the corner of the rue de Vaugirard and the boulevard Saint-Michel, and it had—which served Boris's designs—a doorway on each street. In front of the shop stood six long tables laden with books, for the most part second-hand. Boris espied out of the corner of his eye a gentleman with a red mustache who was often to be seen hanging about the district and whom he suspected of being a dick. He approached the third table, and behold: the book was there, enormous, so enormous, indeed, that for an instant Boris was discouraged by the sight of it: seven hundred pages, quarto, with deckle edges as broad as a little finger. "And I've got to get that into my portfolio," he reflected with some dismay. But a glance at the gold letters of the title glowing softly on the binding sufficed to revive his courage: *Historical and Etymological Dictionary of Cant and Slang from the Fourteenth Century to the Present Day.* "Historical!" Boris repeated ecstatically to himself. He touched the binding with the tips of his fingers, a gesture of affectionate familiarity that restored his contact with the volume. "It's not a book, it's a piece of furniture," he thought with admiration. Behind his back, without doubt, the mustachioed gentleman had turned around to watch him. He must start the performance, look through the volume, and play the part of an idler who hesitates and at last succumbs. Boris opened the dictionary at random. He read:

"A man for; to be inclined towards. A phrase now in fairly common use. Example: 'The parson was no end of a man for.' Render: The parson was much inclined towards . . . 'A man for men' or 'A man's man' is also used for 'invert.' This idiom apparently originates in southwestern France. . . ."

The succeeding pages were not cut. Boris read no further and began to laugh silently. He repeated with delight: "The parson was no end of a man for . . ." Then he became abruptly serious and began to count: "One; two; three; four," while a high, pure joy made his heart beat faster.

He felt a hand upon his shoulder. "I'm done," thought Boris, "but they've struck too soon, they can't prove anything against me." He turned around slowly and with composure. It was Daniel Sereno, a friend of Mathieu. Boris had seen him two or three times and thought him rather splendid, though at the moment he did not look too pleasant.

"Hello," said Sereno. "What are you reading? You look quite absorbed."

No, he didn't really look unpleasant, but there was no sense in taking risks; as a matter of fact, he seemed rather *too* agreeable, as though he had a nasty trick up his sleeve. And then, as ill luck would have it, he had come upon Boris just as he was looking at the slang dictionary, a fact that would certainly reach Mathieu's ears and give him much sardonic satisfaction.

"I just stopped as I was passing," he said rather awkwardly.

Sereno smiled; he picked up the volume in both hands and raised it to his eyes; he must be rather shortsighted. Boris admired his nonchalance: those who turned over the pages of books usually took care to leave them on the table, for fear of detectives. But it was clear that Sereno thought he could do as he pleased. Boris muttered hoarsely, with an assumed air of indifference:

"It's a curious work. . . ."

Sereno did not answer; he seemed absorbed in what he was reading. Boris became annoyed and scrutinized him narrowly. But he had fairly to recognize that Sereno presented an extremely elegant appearance. In point of fact, there was, in the almost pink tweed suit, the linen shirt and yellow necktie, a calculated bravado that rather shocked Boris. Boris liked a sober, slightly casual elegance. None the less, the total effect was irreproachable, though rather lusciously suggestive of fresh butter. Sereno burst out laughing. He had a warm, attractive laugh, and Boris liked him because he opened his mouth wide when he laughed.

"A man's man!" said Sereno. "A man's man! That's a grand phrase, I must use it whenever I can."

He replaced the book on the table.

"Are you a man's man, Serguine?"

"I—" began Boris, and his breath failed him.

"Don't blush," said Sereno—and Boris felt himself becoming scarlet—"and believe me when I tell you that the idea didn't even enter my head. I know how to recognize a man's man"—the expression obviously amused him—

"there's a soft rotundity in their movements that is quite unmistakable. Whereas you—I've been watching you for a moment or two and was greatly charmed: your movements are quick and graceful, but they are also angular. You must be clever with your hands."

Boris listened attentively: it is always interesting to hear someone explain his view of you. And Sereno had a very agreeable bass voice. His eyes, indeed, were baffling: at first sight they seemed to be brimming with friendly feeling, but a closer view discovered in them something hard and almost fanatic. "He's trying to pull my leg," thought Boris, and remained on the alert. He would have liked to ask Sereno what he meant by "angular movements," but he did not dare, he thought it would be better to talk as little as possible, and then, under that insistent gaze, he felt a strange and bewildered access of sensibility arise within him, and he longed to snort and stamp to dispel that dizzying impulse. He turned his head away and a rather painful silence followed. "He'll take me for a damn fool," thought Boris with resignation.

"You are studying philosophy, I believe," said Sereno.

"Yes, I'm studying philosophy," rejoined Boris.

He was glad of a pretext to break the silence. But at that moment one stroke sounded from the Sorbonne clock, and Boris paused in sudden horror. "A quarter past eight," he thought with anguish. "If he doesn't go away at once, it's all up." The Garbure bookshop closed at half past eight. Sereno did not in the least look as if he wanted to go away.

"I must admit," said he, "that I don't understand philosophy at all. You, of course, do. . . ."

"I don't know—to some extent, I think," said Boris, now in torment.

And he thought: "I'm sure I must seem rude, but why doesn't he go away?" Not but what Mathieu hadn't warned him that Sereno always appeared at the wrong moment, it was a part of his demoniac character.

"I suppose you like it," said Sereno.

"Yes," said Boris, who felt himself blushing for the second time. He hated talking about what he liked: it was indecent. He had the impression that Sereno guessed as much and was being deliberately tactless. Sereno eyed him with an air of penetrating intentness.

"Why?"

"I don't know," said Boris.

It was true: he didn't know. And yet he did like it very much. Even Kant.

Sereno smiled: "At any rate, there's nothing intellectual in your enthusiasm, that's quite clear."

Boris quivered, and Sereno added briskly: "I'm not serious. As a matter of fact, I think you're lucky. I myself have read some philosophy, like everybody else. But I couldn't be induced to like it. . . . I imagine it was Delarue who disgusted me with it: he's too clever for me. I sometimes used to ask him to explain a difficulty, but as soon as he started, I was completely at sea; indeed, I no longer understood my own question."

Boris was hurt by this bantering tone, and he suspected that Sereno's purpose was to inveigle him into saying something unpleasant about Mathieu, for the pleasure of repeating it to Mathieu afterwards. He admired Sereno for being so gratuitously objectionable, but he was becoming restive, and he answered curtly: "Mathieu explains things very well."

This time Sereno burst out laughing, and Boris bit his lips.

"I don't for a moment doubt it. Only we are friends of rather too long standing, and I imagine he reserves his pedagogical qualities for younger men. He usually recruits his disciples from among his pupils."

"I am not his disciple," said Boris.

"I wasn't thinking of you," said Daniel. "Indeed, you don't look like a disciple. I was thinking of Hourtiguère, a tall, blond fellow who went to Indo-China last year. You must have heard of him: that was the grand passion two years ago, they were always about together."

Boris had to admit that the stroke had been well aimed, and it increased his admiration of Sereno, but he would have liked to knock him down.

"Mathieu did mention him," he said.

He detested the man Hourtiguère, whom Mathieu had known before himself. Mathieu sometimes assumed a set expression when Boris came to meet him at the Dôme, and said: "I must write to Hourtiguère," whereupon he became for a while abstracted and intent, like a soldier writing to his girl at home, and describing circles in the air with a fountain pen above a sheet of paper. Boris set to work beside him, with loathing in his heart. He was not, of course, jealous of Hourtiguère. On the contrary, his feeling for the man was one of pity touched with slight repulsion (indeed, he knew nothing of him except a photograph, which depicted him as a tall, rather dismal-looking fellow in plus fours; and a wholly fatuous philosophic dissertation that still lay on Mathieu's desk). But he wouldn't for the world have Mathieu treat him later on as he treated Hourtiguère. He would have preferred never to see Mathieu again if he could have believed that he would one day observe, with a set, portentous air, to another young philosopher: "Ah, I must write to Serguine today." He would, if he must, accept the fact that Mathieu was no more than a stage in his life—and that, indeed, was rather galling—but he could not bear to be a stage in Mathieu's life.

Sereno showed no disposition to move. He was leaning with both hands on the table, in a negligent and easy attitude. "I often regret I am such an ignoramus on that subject. Students of philosophy seem to get a great deal of satisfaction out of it."

Boris did not answer.

"I should have needed someone to initiate me," said Sereno. "Someone of your sort. Not too much of an expert, but one who took the subject seriously." He laughed, as though a pleasant notion had crossed his mind. "Look here, it would be amusing if I took lessons from you. . . ."

Boris looked at him with mistrust. This must be another trap. He could not see himself in process of instructing Sereno, who must be much more intelligent than himself and who would certainly ask him all sorts of embarrassing questions. He would choke with nervousness. He reflected with cold resignation that the time must now be twenty-five minutes past eight. Sereno was still smiling, he looked as though he was delighted with his own idea. But he had curious eyes. Boris found it hard to look him in the face.

"I'm very lazy, you know," said Sereno. "You would have to be strict with me. . . ."

Boris could not help laughing, and said candidly: "I don't think I could manage that. . . ."

"Oh yes you could," said Sereno. "I am quite sure you could."

"I should be frightened of you," said Boris.

Sereno shrugged his shoulders. "Nonsense! . . . Look here, can you spare a minute? We might have a drink opposite, at the Harcourt, and discuss our scheme."

"Our" scheme. . . . It was with anguish that Boris watched one of the shop clerks begin to collect books into piles. He would indeed have liked to go to the Harcourt with Sereno: he was an odd fellow, he was extremely good-looking, and it was amusing to talk to him because of the need to be constantly on guard, the persistent sense of danger. He struggled against himself for a moment, but the sense of duty prevailed:

"As a fact, I'm in rather a hurry," he said, and his disappointment lent an edge to his voice.

Sereno's expression changed. "Oh, all right," said he. "I don't want to put you out. Forgive me for having kept you so long. Well—good-by, and give my regards to Mathieu."

He turned abruptly and departed. "Have I offended him?" thought Boris uncomfortably. It was with an uneasy look that he watched Sereno's broad shoulders as he made his way up the boulevard Saint-Michel. And then he suddenly realized that he had not a minute to spare. "One. Two. Three. Four. Five." At five he openly picked the volume up with his right hand and walked towards the bookshop without any attempt at concealment.

A throng of words flying no matter where; words in flight, Daniel himself in flight from a tall, frail, round-shouldered body, hazel-eyed, with an ascetic and charming face, a veritable little monk, a Russian monk, Aliosha. Footsteps, words, footsteps ringing inside his head, he longed to merge himself into those footsteps and those words, anything was better than silence. "The little fool, I had judged him rightly. My parents have forbidden me to talk to people I don't know. Would you like a candy, darling? My parents have forbidden me. . . . Ah, well! It's only a very small brain, I don't know, I don't know, do you like philosophy, I don't know, how could he know it, poor lamb! Mathieu acts the sultan in his class, he has thrown him the handkerchief, he takes him to a café, and the lad swallows everything, *café crème* and theories, as if they were sacred wafers: you needn't show off like a girl at her first communion, there he was, as solemn and sedate as a donkey loaded with relics. Oh, I understand, I wasn't going to lay a hand on you, I am not worthy; and the look he flung at me when I told him I didn't understand philosophy, he wasn't even taking the trouble to be polite towards the end. I am *sure*—I suspected as much at the time of Hourteguère—I am *sure* he puts them on their guard against me.—Well, well," said Daniel, with a complacent laugh, "it's an excellent lesson and a cheap one, too, I'm glad he packed me off; if I had been crazy

enough to take a little interest in him and talk to him con-
fidentially, he would have promptly reported it all to
Mathieu for both of them to gloat over." He stopped so
abruptly that a woman who was walking behind him
bumped into his back and emitted a faint shriek. "He has
discussed me with him!" That was an in-tol-er-able notion,
enough to make a man sweat with fury—picture the pair
of them, in excellent humor, glad to be together, the young
one gaping and goggling, with his hands behind his ears,
anxious to lose none of the divine manna, in some Montparnasse café, one of those noisesome little dens that smelt
of dirty linen. . . . "Mathieu must have peered at him
with a deep look on his face and explained what I was like
—oh, what a scream!" And Daniel repeated: "What a
scream!" and dug his nails into the palms of his hand.
They had judged him from behind, they had dismantled
and dissected him, he was defenseless, for all he knew, he
might have *existed* on that day as on other days, as though
he were no more than a transparency devoid of memory
or purpose, as though he were not, for *others*, a rather
corpulent personage with thickening cheeks, a waning
Oriental beauty, a cruel smile, and—who knows? . . .
"No, no one. Yes, Bobby knows, Ralph knows, Mathieu
doesn't. Bobby is a shrimp, not a conscious entity, he lives
at 6 rue aux Ours, with Ralph. Oh, to live among the
blind! He indeed isn't blind, and he is proud of it, he can
use his eyes, he is an astute psychologist, and he has the
*right* to talk about me, having known me fifteen years and
my best friend, and he won't give up that right; when he
meets someone, there are two people for whom I exist,
and then three, and then nine, and then a hundred. Sereno,
Sereno, the broker, the man of the Bourse, Sereno the . . .
Perish the man, but no, he walks around as he likes with
his opinion of me in his head, injecting it into all and
sundry—well, he must dash about and scratch, scratch,
scrub and swill, I have scratched Marcelle to the bone.

She gave me her hand, looked at me intently on the first occasion, and she said: 'Mathieu has so often spoken of you.' And I looked at her in my turn, fascinated, I was *inside* his woman, I existed in that flesh, behind that set forehead, in the depths of those eyes, the slut. At the moment she no longer believes a word he says about me."

He smiled with satisfaction; he was so proud of that victory that for a second he forgot to keep an eye on himself: a rent appeared in the web of words, which gradually increased and widened into silence. A heavy, empty silence. He ought not—he ought not to have stopped talking. The wind had fallen, anger paused. In the depths of that silence Serguine's face appeared, like a wound. A mild, dim face; much patience and ardor were needed to light it up a little. He thought: "I could have. . . ." That year, that day even, he could have done it. Afterwards. . . . "It's my last chance," he thought. It was his last chance, and Mathieu had hinted as much, rather casually. Ralphs and Bobbys—these were all he had. "And he'll transform that poor lad into a learned ape!" He walked on in silence, the solitary sound of his footsteps echoing inside his head, as in a deserted street, at dawn. His solitude was so complete, beneath a lovely sky as mellow and serene as a good conscience, amid that busy throng, that he was amazed at his own existence; he must be somebody else's nightmare, and whoever it was would certainly awaken soon. Fortunately, anger again surged forth and enveloped everything, the vigor of his wrath restored him, and the flight began again, the procession of words began again; he hated Mathieu. Here was a man who found it quite natural to exist, he did not ask himself any questions, that light, so Greek and so impartial, that uncorrupted sky, were made for him, he was at home, he had never been alone. "Upon my word," thought Daniel, "he takes himself for Goethe." He had raised his head, he was looking into the faces of the passers-by; he was cherishing his hatred: "Take care, train disciples if it amuses you, but not as instruments *against me*, because I shall get the better of you in the end." A fresh gust of rage laid hold of him, his feet no longer touched the ground, he flew, delighted in his consciousness of power, when suddenly an idea, edged and flashing, came upon him: "But, but, but . . . there might be a chance of helping him to think, to withdraw into himself, of ensuring that things should not be too easy for him, that would truly be a good deed done." He remembered the abrupt and masculine air with which Marcelle had once snapped at him over her shoulder: "When a woman is completely up against it, she can always get herself into the family way." It would be too amusing if they were not altogether agreed on the matter, if he went on haunting the herbalists' shops, while she, ensconced in her pink room, was pining to have a child. She would not have dared to tell him, only . . . If there were someone, a kindly common friend, to give her a little courage. "I am a truly evil man," he thought, with a flush of satisfaction. Evil—that must be this extraordinary sense of speed, which detaches you from your own self and flings you forward; speed took you by the neck, awful and ecstatic, gaining momentum every second, smashing into all manner of insubstantial obstacles that rose abruptly to the left and right—"Mathieu, poor devil, I really am a scoundrel, I shall wreck his life"—and snapped like rotten branches; how intoxicating was the fearful joy of it, sharp as an electric shock, joy irresistible. "I wonder whether he will still acquire disciples. A family man won't be quite so popular in such a part." Serguine's face when Mathieu came to announce his marriage, the lad's contempt, his devastating amazement. "You're going to be married?" And Mathieu would stammer in reply: "A man has some sort of duties." But young men didn't understand duties of that kind. There was something timidly struggling back to life—Mathieu's face, his honest, loyal face, but the race

at once resumed its headlong course: evil could only maintain its balance at full speed, like a bicycle. His thought
leaped ahead of him, alert and joyous. "He is a good fellow, Mathieu; no evil in him at all; he is of the race of
Abel, he has his own form of conscience. Well, he *ought*
to marry Marcelle. After that he can rest upon his laurels,
he is still young, he will have a whole life in which to
congratulate himself on a good deed."

There was something so dizzying in the languishing re-
pose of a pure conscience, a pure, unfathomable conscience beneath this genial and familiar sky, that he didn't
know whether he aspired to it for Mathieu's sake or for
his own. The fellow was set, resigned, and calm—yes,
perfectly calm. . . . "And if she wouldn't. . . . Ah, if
there's a chance, a single chance that she might want to
have the baby, I'll swear she'll ask him to marry her tomorrow evening." Monsieur and Madame Delarue . . .
Monsieur and Madame Delarue have the honor to inform you. . . . "After all, I am their guardian angel, the
angel of the hearth." It was an archangel, an archangel
of hatred, a very magisterial archangel, who turned into
the rue Vercingétorix. For one instant he saw before him
once again a lean visage bent over a book, but the vision
was immediately engulfed, and it was Bobby who reappeared. "6 rue aux Ours." He felt as free as air, he could
allow himself any sort of indulgence. The large grocer's
shop in the rue Vercingétorix was still open, and he went
in. When he emerged he was carrying in his right hand
St. Michael's sword of fire and in his left hand a box of
candy for Mme Duffet.

# CHAPTER X

THE little clock struck ten. Mme Duffet did not seem to hear. She looked intently at Daniel, but her eyes had reddened. "It won't be long before she goes," he thought. She threw him a wry smile, but little drifts of air still filtered through her half-closed lips. She was yawning beneath her smile. Suddenly she flung her head back and seemed to make up her mind; she said with an air of arch vivacity:

"Well, my children, it's time for me to go to bed. Don't keep her up too late, Daniel, I rely on you. If she stays up late, she sleeps next day till twelve o'clock."

She got up and tapped Marcelle on the shoulder with a small, brisk hand. Marcelle was sitting on the bed.

"You hear, ginger-cat," she said, amusing herself by speaking between clenched teeth; "you sleep too late, my girl, you sleep till midday, and you're getting fat."

"I promise faithfully to go away before midnight," said Daniel.

Marcelle smiled. "If I want you to."

He turned towards Mme Duffet with an elaborately helpless air. "What can I do?"

"Well, be sensible," said Mme Duffet. "And thank you for the delicious candy."

She lifted the ribboned box to the level of her eyes, with a rather menacing gesture. "You are *too* kind, you spoil me, I shall have to scold you soon."

"Nothing could give me greater pleasure than your appreciation of it," said Daniel gravely.

He leaned over Mme Duffet's hand and kissed it. Seen from near by, the skin was a network of mauve patches.

"Archangel!" said Mme Duffet with a melting look. "And now I'm off," she added, kissing Marcelle on the forehead.

Marcelle put an arm round her waist and held her close for a moment; Mme Duffet ruffled her hair and slipped quickly out of her embrace.

"I'll come and tuck you up later on," said Marcelle.

"No you won't, you bad girl; I leave you to your archangel."

She fled with the agility of a child, and Daniel followed her slim back with a cold eye: he had thought she would never go. The door closed, but he did not feel relieved: he was a little afraid of staying alone with Marcelle. He turned towards her and saw that she was smiling at him.

"What are you smiling at?" he asked.

"It always amuses me to see you with Mother," said Marcelle. "What a flatterer you are, my poor archangel! It's a shame, you simply can't help trying to fascinate people."

She eyed him with a proprietary affection, apparently well content to have him to herself. "She already has the mask of pregnancy," thought Daniel maliciously. He disliked her for looking so happy. He always felt a little apprehensive when he found himself on the brink of those long, whispered interviews, but he had to take the plunge. He cleared his throat. "I'm in for an attack of asthma," he thought. Marcelle was just a solid, dreary smell, deposited on the bed; a huddle of flesh that would disintegrate at the slightest movement.

She got up. "I have something to show you." She picked up a photograph from the mantelpiece. "You always wanted to know what I looked like when I was a girl . . ." she said, handing it to him.

Daniel took it: it was Marcelle at eighteen, she looked like a tart, with her slack mouth and hard eyes. And always the same limp flesh that hung about her like too loose a frock. But she was thin. Daniel looked up and caught her anxious look.

"You were charming," he said judiciously, "but you have scarcely changed."

Marcelle began to laugh. "Nonsense! You know very well that I have changed, you wicked flatterer; but you shouldn't trouble, you aren't talking to my mother." And she added: "Still, I was a fine, strapping lass, wasn't I?"

"I like you better as you are," said Daniel. "There was something rather slack about your mouth. . . . You now look so *much* more interesting."

"One never knows if you are serious," she said peevishly. But it was easy to see that she was flattered.

She stiffened a little and threw a brief glance at the mirror. This silly, naïve gesture annoyed Daniel: there was a childish and ingenuous candor in this coquetry of hers that clashed with her very ordinary female face. He smiled at her.

"And now I'm going to ask you why you're smiling," she said.

"Because you looked at yourself in the glass just as a little girl would do. I'm always touched when you happen to take notice of yourself."

Marcelle flushed, and tapped her foot on the floor. "He'll always be a flatterer!"

They both laughed, and Daniel thought rather timorously: "Now for it." The opportunity was good, this was the moment, but he felt blank and listless. He thought of Mathieu, to put heart into himself, and was glad to find his hatred unimpaired. Mathieu was as compact and dry as a bone, a man who could be hated. It was not possible to hate Marcelle.

"Marcelle, look at me."

He had thrust his chest forward and was eying her with a solicitous air.

"There," said Marcelle.

She returned his look, but her head was quivering: she found it difficult to meet a man's look.

"You seem tired."

Marcelle blinked. "I am rather under the weather," she said. "It's the heat."

Daniel leaned a little closer and repeated with an air of grieved reproach:

"*Very* tired. I was looking at you just now, while your mother was telling us about her trip to Rome: you seemed so preoccupied, so nervous—"

Marcelle interrupted him, with an indignant laugh: "Look here, Daniel, that's the third time she has told you about that trip, and you always listen with the same air of passionate interest; to be quite frank, it rather annoys me; I don't know what is in your mind at such moments."

"Your mother amuses me," said Daniel. "I know her stories, but I like to hear her tell them, there are certain little gestures of hers I find delightful."

He jerked his head slightly, and Marcelle burst out laughing: Daniel was an admirable mimic when he chose. But he promptly resumed his serious expression and Marcelle stopped laughing. She said: "It's you who are looking odd this evening. What's the matter with you?"

He paused before replying. A heavy silence weighed them down, the room was a veritable furnace. Marcelle laughed a nervous little laugh that died at once upon her lips. Daniel was enjoying himself.

"Marcelle," he said, "I oughtn't to tell you—"

She started. "What? What? For heaven's sake, what is it?"

"You won't be angry with Mathieu?"

She paled. "He— Oh the— He swore he wouldn't tell you."

"Marcelle, were you really going to keep me in ignorance of something so important! Am I no longer a friend of yours?"

"It's so disgusting!" she said.

Ah! At last: she was naked. No more question of archangels, nor of youthful photographs; she had shed her mask of laughing dignity. Here was just a large and pregnant woman, who smelt of flesh. Daniel felt hot, he passed a hand across his damp forehead.

"No," he said slowly, "no, it's not disgusting."

An abrupt movement of Marcelle's elbow and forearm streaked through the torrid air of the room.

"You find me repulsive," she said.

He laughed a youthful laugh. "Repulsive? My dear Marcelle, it would be a very long time before you could find anything that would make me think you repulsive."

Marcelle did not answer, her face was downcast. At last she said: "I so much wanted to keep you out of all this. . . ."

They fell silent. There was now a fresh bond between them: a vile, loose bond, like an umbilical cord.

"Have you seen Mathieu since he left me?" Daniel asked.

"He telephoned about one o'clock," said Marcelle curtly. She had recovered herself and stiffened, she now stood on the defensive, erect and with indrawn nostrils; she was in agony of mind.

"Did he tell you that I had refused him the money?"

"He told me you hadn't any."

"But I had."

"You had?" she repeated in astonishment.

"Yes, but I wouldn't lend him any. Not before having seen you, at any rate."

He paused and then added: "Marcelle, am I to lend him the money?"

"Well," she said with embarrassment, "I just don't know. It's for you to consider whether you can."

"I most certainly can. I have fifteen thousand francs that I can dispose of without inconveniencing myself in the slightest."

"Then—yes," said Marcelle. "Yes, my dear Daniel, you must lend us the money."

A silence fell. Marcelle crumpled the sheet between her fingers, and her heavy throat began to throb.

"You don't understand me," said Daniel. "What I mean is—do you honestly want me to lend him the money?"

Marcelle raised her head and looked at him with surprise. "How odd you are, Daniel! You have something in your mind."

"Well—I was merely wondering whether Mathieu had consulted you."

"Of course he did. Anyway," she said with a faint smile, "you know how it is with people like ourselves; we don't consult each other, one of us says we will do this or that, and the other objects if he or she doesn't agree."

"Yes," said Daniel. "Yes. Only that is wholly to the advantage of the person who had made up his mind: the other is bustled around and hasn't time to make it up."

"Possibly," said Marcelle.

"I know how much Mathieu respects your advice," he said. "But I can so well imagine the scene: it has haunted me all the afternoon. He must have got on the high horse, as he always does on these occasions, and then said as he swallowed his saliva: 'Ha! Very well, this calls for extreme measures.' He had no hesitations, and besides, he couldn't have any: he's a man. Only—wasn't it rather hasty? You yourself can hardly have known what you wanted to do?" Again he leaned towards Marcelle: "Isn't that what happened?"

Marcelle was not looking at him. She had turned her head towards the hand-basin, and Daniel viewed her in profile. She looked downcast.

"Something like that," she said. Then she blushed violently. "Oh, please don't let's talk any more about it, Daniel. It—it upsets me rather."

Daniel did not take his eyes off her. "She is trembling," he thought. But he no longer quite knew whether his enjoyment lay in humiliating her or himself with her. And he said to himself: "It will be easier than I thought."

"Marcelle," he said, "don't be so aloof, I beseech you: I know how disagreeable it must be to you to discuss all this. . . ."

"Especially with you," said Marcelle. "Daniel, you are so different!"

"Good heavens, I am her purity embodied!" he thought. Again she trembled and pressed her arms against her chest.

"I no longer dare look at you," she said. "Even if I don't disgust you, I feel as if I had lost you."

"I know," said Daniel bitterly. "An archangel is easily scared. Look here, Marcelle, don't go on making me play this ridiculous part. There's nothing archangelic about me; I am just your friend, your best friend. And there's something I intend to say anyway," he added firmly, "since I'm in a position to help you. Marcelle, are you really sure that you don't want a child?"

A faint and sudden shock thrilled through Marcelle's body, as though it were about to collapse. But the disintegrating impulse was abruptly arrested, and the body sank, a motionless bulk, on the edge of the bed. She turned her head towards Daniel; she was crimson; but she looked at him without malice, in helpless amazement. "She is desperate," thought Daniel.

"You have but to say one word: if you are sure of yourself, Mathieu shall have the money tomorrow morning."

He almost wanted her to say she was. He would send the money, and that would be that. But she said nothing, she had turned towards him, she looked expectant; he must persevere to the end. "My God!" thought Daniel, "she's actually looking grateful." Like Malvina after he had slapped her.

"You!" said she. "You actually asked yourself that question! And he!—Daniel, there's no one but you who takes any interest in me."

He got up, came and sat down beside her, and took her hand. The hand was as soft and fevered as a confidence; silently he held it in his own. Marcelle seemed to be struggling against her tears; she was looking at her knees.

"Marcelle, don't you really mind if the baby is got rid of?"

"What else is there to do?" said Marcelle with a weary gesture.

"I've won," thought Daniel; but he felt no pleasure at his victory. He was choking. At close quarters, Marcelle smelt a little, he could have sworn she did; so faintly that indeed it could not, perhaps, be properly described as an odor, it was a sort of impregnation of the air around her. And then there was this hand that lay sweating in his own. He forced himself to squeeze it harder, to make it exude all its sap.

"I don't know what can be done," he said in rather a dry voice; "we'll consider that later on. At this moment I am thinking solely of you. If you have this baby, it might be a disaster, but it might also be a chance of better things. Marcelle, you must not be able to accuse yourself later on of not having thought enough about all this."

"Yes—" said Marcelle. "Yes. . . ."

She stared into vacancy with a naïve air of candor that seemed to rejuvenate her. Daniel thought of the young student of the photograph. "It's true. She was once young. . . ." But on that unresponsive face even the reflections of youth had no attraction. He dropped the hand abruptly and drew back a little.

"Think," he said in an urgent tone. "Are you really *sure?*"

"I don't know," said Marcelle.

She got up. "Excuse me, I must go and tuck up Mamma."

Daniel bowed silently: it was a ritual. "I've won," he thought as the door closed. He wiped his hands on his handkerchief; then he got up briskly and opened the drawer in the night-table: it sometimes contained amusing letters, brief missives from Mathieu, quite conjugal in tone, or interminable lamentations from Andrée, who was not happy. The drawer was empty; Daniel sat down again in the easy chair and thought: "I've won, she's pining to lay an egg." He was glad to be alone: he could thus recover from his hatred. "I bet he'll marry her," he said to himself. "Besides, he has behaved very badly, he didn't even consult her. But," he continued with a curt laugh, "it's not worth the trouble of hating him for *good* motives: I've got my hands full with the others."

Marcelle returned with a distraught expression on her face.

"And even supposing I wanted the baby?" she said abruptly. "What good would that do me? I can't afford the luxury of being an unmarried mother, and there's no question of his marrying me, of course."

Daniel raised astonished eyebrows. "Why not?" he asked. "Why can't he marry you?"

Marcelle looked at him in bewilderment, then she decided to laugh. "But, Daniel! Surely you know how we stand together!"

"I know nothing at all," said Daniel. "I know only one thing: if he wants to, he has only to take the necessary steps, like everybody else, and in a month you are his wife. Was it *you*, Marcelle, who decided never to marry?"

"I should hate him to marry me in self-defense."

"That's not an answer."

Marcelle relaxed a little. She began to laugh, and Daniel realized that he had taken the wrong line.

"No, really," she said, "I don't in the least mind not being called Madame Delarue."

"I'm sure of that," said Daniel briskly. "What I meant was—if it were the only means of keeping the child? . . ."

Marcelle seemed overwhelmed. "But—I have never looked at things in that light."

That was doubtless true. It was very difficult to make her face facts; her nose would have to be kept down to it, otherwise she scattered herself in all directions.

"It's—it's a matter," she added, "that was just accepted between us: marriage is a form of slavery, and neither of us wanted that sort of thing."

"But you want the child?"

She did not answer. It was the decisive moment; Daniel repeated harshly:

"Isn't that so? You want the child?"

Marcelle leaned one hand on the pillow; she had laid the other on her thighs. She lifted it and laid it against her stomach, as though she felt a pain there; it was a grotesque, intriguing scene. Then she said in a forlorn voice:

"Yes. I want the child."

The game was won. Daniel said nothing. He could not take his eyes off that stomach. Enemy flesh, lush, fostering flesh, a veritable larder. He reflected that Mathieu had desired it, and a brief flash of satisfaction leaped up within him: a foretaste of his vengeance. The brown, ringed hand lay clenched on the silk frock, pressing against the body.

What did she feel inside her, this bulky female in her dis-
array? He would have liked to *be her*.

"Daniel," said Marcelle in a hollow voice, "you have
saved me. I—I couldn't say that to anyone, not to anyone in the world, I had come to believe it was wrong."
She looked at him anxiously. "It isn't wrong, is it?"

He could not help laughing. "Wrong? But that's a per-
verted point of view, Marcelle. Do you think your desires
wrong when they are natural?"

"No, I mean—as concerning Mathieu. It's like a breach
of contract."

"You must have a frank talk with him, that's all."

Marcelle did not answer; she looked as though she were
reflecting. Then she said suddenly, and with fervor:

"Ah, if I had a child, I swear I wouldn't let him spoil his
life as I have done."

"You haven't spoilt your life."

"I have."

"No, you haven't, Marcelle. Not yet."

"I have indeed. I have done nothing and nobody needs
me."

He did not answer: it was true.

"Mathieu doesn't need me. If I were to die—well, he
wouldn't feel it in his bones. Nor would you, Daniel. You
have a great affection for me, which is perhaps what I
most value in the world. But you don't need me; it is I
who need you."

Should he answer? Or protest? He must be careful:
Marcelle seemed to be possessed by one of her accesses of
cynical clairvoyance. He took her hand without saying a
word and squeezed it meaningly.

"A baby," Marcelle went on. "A baby certainly would
need me."

He stroked her hand. "It's to Mathieu that you ought to
be saying all this."

"I can't."

"But why?"

"I'm dumb. I wait for it to come from him."

"But you know it never will: he doesn't think of such a thing."

"Why doesn't he? You thought of it."

"I don't know."

"Very well, then, we must leave things as they are. You will lend us the money, and I will go to this doctor."

"You can't!" cried Daniel brusquely. "You can't!"

He stopped short, and glanced at her with mistrust: it was emotion that had forced that foolish exclamation out of him. The idea made him shiver, he loathed any sort of self-abandonment. He bit his lips, and raised one eyebrow in an attempt to look sarcastic. All in vain; he ought not to have seen her: she sat with shoulders bent, her arms hanging loosely at her sides; she waited, passive and exhausted, she would wait thus for years to come, until the end. "Her last chance," as he had thought in his own case a little while ago. Between thirty and forty, people staked on their last chance. She was going to wager and she would lose; in a few days she would be nothing but a lump of misery. This he must prevent.

"Suppose I discussed it with Mathieu myself?" A slime of pity had engulfed him. He had no sympathy for Marcelle, and he felt profoundly disgusted, but the pity was there, and not to be denied. He would have done anything to extricate himself. Marcelle raised her head, her expression suggested that she thought him crazy.

"Discuss it with him? You? Really, Daniel, what can you be thinking about?"

"One could tell him—that I've met you—"

"Where? I never go out. And even so, should I have been likely to tell you all this point-blank?"

"No. No, clearly not."

Marcelle laid a hand on his knee. "Daniel, I beg you not to take a hand in this affair. I'm very angry with Mathieu, he oughtn't to have told you. . . ."

But Daniel clung to his idea. "Listen, Marcelle, this is what we must do. Tell him the truth quite simply. I shall say: 'You must forgive us our little deception: Marcelle and I do see each other now and then, and we haven't told you.'"

"Daniel!" begged Marcelle, "it can't be done. I won't have you talking about me. I wouldn't for the world seem to make any claims. It's for him to understand." She added with a conjugal air: "And then, you know, he would not forgive me for not having told him myself. We always tell each other everything."

Daniel thought: "She is a good creature." But he did not want to laugh.

"But I should not speak in your name," he said. "I should tell him that I've seen you, that you looked distressed, and that things were possibly not so simple as he thought. All this as though coming from myself."

"I won't have it," said Marcelle doggedly. "I won't have it."

Daniel looked avidly at her shoulders and neck. This crass obstinacy annoyed him; he wanted to break it down. He was possessed by a vast and vile desire—to desecrate that conscience and with her plumb the depths of this humility. But it was not sadism: it was something more tentative and clinging, more a matter of the flesh. It was goodwill.

"It must be done, Marcelle. Marcelle, look at me."

He took her by the shoulders, and his fingers seemed to slide into soft butter.

"If I don't tell him, you never will, and—what will be the result? You will live beside him in silence, and come to hate him in the end."

Marcelle did not answer, but he understood from her peevish and deflated look that she was about to yield. Again she said:

"I won't have it."

He released her. "If you won't let me do as I say," he said angrily, "I shan't forgive you for a long while. You will have wrecked your life with your own hands."

Marcelle rubbed her toes on the bedside mat.

"You would—you would have to speak quite vaguely," she said, "just to make him take notice."

"Of course," said Daniel. And he added to himself: "You can rely on that."

Then Marcelle continued, with a gesture of vexation: "It isn't possible."

"Oh come! You were just going to be reasonable. . . . Why isn't it possible?"

"You will be obliged to tell him that we see each other."

"Well, yes," said Daniel irritably, "I said so just now. But I know him, he won't mind, he'll be a bit put out, for the sake of appearances, and then, as he begins to feel guilty, he will be only too glad to have something against you. Besides, I shall say that we have only been seeing each other during the last few months, and at long intervals. Anyway, we should have had to tell him some time."

"True."

She did not look convinced. "It was *our* secret," she said with profound regret. "Look here, Daniel, it was my private life, I have no other." And she added venomously: "All I have of my own is what I hide from him."

"We must try. For the child's sake."

She was on the point of giving way; he needed only to wait; she would slip, under her own momentum, into resignation and self-abandonment; in one moment all she was and had would stand exposed, and she would say: "Do as you like, I am in your hands." She fascinated him; that soft fire that devoured him—was it Evil or Good?

Good and Evil, *their* Good, *his* Evil—it was the same.
Here was this woman, and this repellent and intoxicating
communion of two selves.

Marcelle passed a hand over her hair. "Well, let us try,"
she said defiantly. "After all, it will be a test."

"A test?" asked Daniel. "A test for Mathieu, do you
mean?"

"Yes."

"Can you suppose that he will remain indifferent? That
he won't be eager to have an explanation with you?"

"I don't know." And she added curtly: "I want to respect him."

Daniel's heart began to throb violently. "Don't you
respect him any more?"

"Certainly. . . . But I'm no longer in confidence with
him since yesterday evening. He has been— You are
right: he has been too neglectful. He took no trouble about
me. And then what he said on the telephone today was
pitiable. He—" She blushed. "He felt impelled to tell me
that he loved me. Just as he was hanging up the receiver.
It stank of a bad conscience. I can't tell you the effect it
had on me. If ever I ceased to respect him— But I won't
think of that. When I happen to be angry with him, I'm
always so upset. If only he tries to make me talk a bit
tomorrow, if he would *ask* me once, and only once: 'What
is in your mind?'"

She was silent and sat shaking her head despondently.

"I'll talk to him," said Daniel. "When I leave you, I'll
drop a note in his letter-box and make an appointment for
tomorrow."

They were silent. Daniel began to think of tomorrow's
interview: it looked like being hard and heated, another
plunge into the clinging slime of pity.

"Daniel!" said Marcelle. "Dear Daniel."

He raised his head and met her eyes. The look in them
was heavy and hypnotic, brimming with sexual gratitude,

the look that follows love. He closed his eyes: there was between them something more than love. She stood open, he had entered into her, they were now one entity.

"Daniel!" Marcelle repeated.

Daniel opened his eyes and coughed; he had a touch of asthma. He took her hand and kissed it lingeringly, holding his breath.

"My archangel," said Marcelle over his head. He will spend his whole life bent over that odorous hand, and she will stroke his hair.

# CHAPTER XI

A GREAT mauve flower was rising towards the sky; it was the night. And in that night Mathieu was walking through the city, thinking: "I'm a wash-out." It was quite a new idea, he must turn it over in his mind and sniff at it with circumspection. From time to time Mathieu lost it, nothing remained but the words. The words were not devoid of a certain somber charm: "A wash-out." Imagination could conceive all manner of grand disasters—suicide, revolt, and other violent issues. But the idea quickly returned: no, nothing of that kind; what was here in question was a little quiet, modest misery, no matter for despair; on the contrary, a rather soothing state of mind. Mathieu had the impression that he had just been allowed any indulgence he fancied, like a sick man who cannot recover. "All I need do is to go on living," he thought. He read the name "Sumatra" in letters of fire, and the Negro hurried towards him, touching his cap. On the threshold Mathieu hesitated: he could hear confused sounds, a tango; his heart was still filled with lethargy and darkness. And then—it happened in an instant, just as a sleeper suddenly finds himself on his feet in the morning without knowing how he got there: he had pulled the

green curtain aside, walked down seventeen steps, and
emerged into a scarlet, echoing cellar, picked out with
patches of unwholesome white—the tablecloths. At the
far end of the cellar silk-shirted gauchos were playing
dance-music on a platform. Before him stood a throng of
people, motionless, decorous, and apparently expectant:
they were dancers; they looked like gloomy victims of an
interminable destiny. Mathieu surveyed the room listlessly, in search of Boris and Ivich.

"A table, sir?" A sleek young man bowed to him with
an insinuating air.

"I'm looking for someone," said Mathieu.

The young man recognized him. "Oh, it's you, sir," he
said cordially. "Mademoiselle Lola is dressing. Your
friends are at the far end, on the left—I'll take you along."

"No, thanks, I shall find them all right. You're very full
this evening."

"Yes, not so bad. Mostly Dutch. Rather noisy, but they
drink a good deal."

The young man vanished. There was no prospect of
threading a way between the dancing couples. Mathieu
waited; he listened to the tango and the shuffling feet,
watching the slow evolutions of that taciturn assemblage.
Bare shoulders, a Negro's head, some handsome women
getting on in years, and a number of elderly gentlemen
dancing with an apologetic air. The rasping notes of the
tango passed over their heads: the bandsmen did not appear to be playing for their benefit. "What on earth am I
doing here?" said Mathieu to himself. His jacket was
shiny at the elbows, his trousers had lost their creases, he
was a poor dancer, and he was incapable of amusing himself with the appropriate air of grave vacuity. He felt ill
at ease: in Montmartre, despite the benevolence of the
head waiters, one could never feel at one's ease; there was
a sense of anxious, restless cruelty in the air.

The white lights were switched on again. Mathieu advanced on to the dance-floor among a throng of retreating backs. In an alcove stood two tables. At one of them a man and a woman were talking intermittently, with eyes averted. At the other he saw Boris and Ivich leaning towards each other, looking very intent and quite charmingly austere. "Like two little monks." It was Ivich who was talking, and gesticulating vivaciously. Never, even in her confidential moments, had she presented such a face to Mathieu. "How young they are!" thought Mathieu. He felt inclined to turn around and go away. But he went on towards them, because he could no longer endure his solitude; he felt as though he were looking at them through a keyhole. Soon they would catch sight of him, they would turn towards him those impassive faces which they kept for their parents and important persons, and even in their very hearts there would be something changed. He was now quite near Ivich, but she had not seen him. She was leaning close to Boris's ear and whispering. She looked a little—just a very little—like an elder sister, and she was talking to Boris with an air of baffled tolerance. Mathieu felt a little cheered: even with her brother Ivich did not quite let herself go, she played the part of elder sister, she never forgot herself. Boris laughed shortly.

"Punk," was all he said.

Mathieu laid a hand on their table. "Punk." On that word their dialogue closed forever: it was like the last rejoinder in a novel or a play. Mathieu gazed at Boris and Ivich: they looked quite romantic, he thought.

"Hello," he said.

"Hello," said Boris, getting up.

Mathieu threw a brief glance at Ivich: she was leaning back in her chair. Her eyes were pale and mournful. The *real* Ivich had disappeared. "And why the *real* one?" he thought with irritation.

"How are you, Mathieu?" said Ivich.

She did not smile, nor did she look astonished or annoyed; she seemed to find Mathieu's presence quite natural. Boris jerked a hand towards the packed hall.

"Quite a crowd," he said with satisfaction.

"Yes," said Mathieu.

"Would you like my place?"

"No, don't trouble; you'll want it for Lola later on."

He sat down. The dance-floor was deserted, and there was no one on the band platform: the gauchos had finished their succession of tangos; the Negro jazz, "Hijito's band," would soon take their place.

"What are you drinking?" asked Mathieu.

People were buzzing around him, Ivich had not received him unamiably: a moist warmth ran through him, and he savored the agreeable intensification of existence that comes from the sense of being a man among other men.

"A vodka," said Ivich.

"Dear me! So you now like the stuff?"

"It's strong," she said, without committing herself.

"But what's that?" asked Mathieu, anxious to deal fairly, pointing to a white froth in Boris's glass.

Boris eyed him with jovial and open-mouthed admiration; Mathieu felt embarrassed.

"Its filthy," said Boris, "it's the bartender's cocktail."

"I suppose you ordered it for politeness' sake?"

"He's been pestering me for the last three weeks to try it. The fact is he doesn't know how to make cocktails. He became a bartender because he had been a conjurer. He says it's the same sort of job, but he's wrong."

"I suppose he's thinking of the shaker," said Mathieu. "And besides, breaking eggs calls for a light hand."

"In that case he'd better have become a juggler. Anyway, I wouldn't have touched his foul compound, but I borrowed a hundred from him this evening."

"A hundred francs," said Ivich, "but I had that amount."

"So had I," said Boris, "but it's just because he's the bartender. It's the *thing* to borrow money from a bartender," he explained in a faintly austere tone.

Mathieu looked at the bartender. He was standing behind his bar, all in white, arms folded, smoking a cigarette. He looked like a placid sort of man.

"I should like to have been a bartender," said Mathieu; "it must be great fun."

"It would have cost you a lot," said Boris, "you would have broken so many glasses."

Silence fell. Boris looked at Mathieu, and Ivich looked at Boris.

"I'm not wanted," said Mathieu sadly to himself.

The head waiter handed him the champagne list: he must be careful; he had under five hundred francs left.

"I'll have a whisky," said Mathieu.

He was seized with a sudden disgust for economy and the meager wad of notes languishing in his pocketbook. He called the head waiter back.

"One moment. I'll have some champagne."

He looked at the list again. Mumm cost three hundred francs.

"You'll drink some," he said to Ivich.

"No—yes," she said after brief reflection. "I do like it better."

"Bring a bottle of Mumm, *cordon rouge.*"

"I'm always glad to drink champagne," said Boris, "because I don't like it. One must get used to it."

"Well, you are a pair, you two," said Mathieu. "You're always drinking stuff you don't like."

Boris beamed: he adored Mathieu to talk to him in that tone. Ivich bit her lips. "One can't say anything to them," thought Mathieu a little testily. "One of them always takes offense." There they were, confronting him, intent and grave; they had each of them conceived their individual picture of Mathieu, and they each insisted that he should conform to it. The trouble was that the two pictures conflicted.

They sat in silence.

Mathieu stretched his legs and smiled contentedly. The notes of a trumpet, shrill and defiant, reached his ears in gusts; it did not occur to him to listen for a tune: it was there, that was all, it made a noise and gave him a rich, metallic thrill all over his skin. He realized, of course, that he was a wash-out: but, when all was said, in this dance-hall, at that table, among all those fellows who were also wash-outs, it did not seem to matter very much and was not at all unpleasant. He looked around: the bartender was still dreaming; on his right was a fellow wearing a monocle, alone, with a lined, drawn face; and another, farther off, also alone, and three drinks and a lady's hand-bag on the table before him; his wife and his friend were no doubt dancing, and he looked in fact rather relieved: he yawned heavily behind his hand, and his little eyes blinked with satisfaction. Smooth and smiling faces everywhere, but ruin in their eyes. Mathieu suddenly felt a kinship with all those creatures who would have done so much better to go home, but no longer had the power, and sat there smoking slender cigarettes, drinking steely-tasting compounds, smiling, as their ears oozed music, and dismally contemplating the wreckage of their destiny; he felt the discreet appeal of a humble and timorous happiness: "Fancy being one of that lot. . . ." Fear shook him, and he turned towards Ivich. Malicious and aloof as she was, in her lay his sole salvation. Ivich was peering rather dubiously at the transparent liquid remaining in her glass.

"You must drink it at one go," said Boris.

"Don't do that," said Mathieu; "you'll scorch your throat."

"Vodka ought to be drunk straight off," said Boris severely.

Ivich picked up her glass. "I would sooner drink it off,
I shall have finished it quicker."

"No, don't drink it, wait for the champagne."

"I *must* swallow the stuff," she said irritably; "I want to
enjoy myself."

She threw herself back in her chair, raised the glass to
her lips, and tipped its entire contents into her mouth,
rather as though she were filling a jug. She remained thus
for a second, not daring to swallow, with a little pool of
fire at the bottom of her gullet. Mathieu felt distressed.

"Swallow!" Boris said to her. "Imagine that it's water:
that's the only thing to do."

Ivich's neck swelled, and she laid down the glass with a
horrible grimace; her eyes were full of tears. The dark-
haired lady at the next table, emerging for an instant from
her morose abstraction, glanced at her indignantly.

"Pah!" said Ivich. "How it burns! It's fire!"

"I'll buy you a bottle to practice on," said Boris.

Ivich reflected for a moment. "It would be much better
for me to train on marc, it's stronger." And she added with
a rueful air: "I think I shall be able to enjoy myself now."

No one replied. She turned briskly towards Mathieu; it
was the first time she had looked at him.

"I suppose you can stand a lot of liquor?"

"He's a terror," said Boris. "I've seen him drink seven
whiskies one day when he was talking to me about Kant.
In the end I stopped listening, I was tight enough for the
two of us."

It was true: even in that way Mathieu could not sink
his consciousness. All the time he was drinking, he took
a stronger hold on—what? On what? Suddenly he saw a
vision of Gauguin, a broad, pallid face with desolate eyes.
"On my human dignity," he thought. He was afraid that if
he lost grip of himself for an instant, he would suddenly
find within his head, astray and drifting like a summer
haze, the thought of a fly or a cockroach.

"I have a horror of being tight," he explained apolo-
getically. "I drink, but my whole body revolts against
drunkenness."

"And yet you're obstinate," said Boris with admiration.
"As obstinate as an old mule."

"I'm not obstinate, I'm highly strung: I don't know how
to let myself go. I must always think of what is happening
to me—it's a form of self-protection." And he added ironically, as though to himself: "I'm a thinking reed."

*As though to himself.* But it wasn't true, he wasn't being
sincere: he really wanted to please Ivich. "So," he thought,
"I've got to that point." He had begun to exploit his own
downfall, he did not scorn to extract some small advantages from it, he used it to flatter young women. "Rotter!"
He stopped in consternation: when he used that epithet
to himself, he was not sincere either, he was not really
indignant. It was a trick to retrieve himself, he thought, to
save himself from humiliation by such "lucidity," but the
lucidity cost him nothing, rather it entertained him. And
the very judgment that he passed upon his own lucidity,
this dodge of climbing on to his own shoulders . . . "I
must transform myself to the very bones." But nothing
could help him to do that: all his thoughts were tainted
from their origin. Suddenly Mathieu began to open gently
like a wound; he saw himself exposed and as he was:
thoughts, thoughts about thoughts, thoughts about
thoughts of thoughts, he was transparent and corrupt beyond any finite vision. Then the vision vanished, he found
himself sitting opposite Ivich, who was eying him with a
rather quizzical expression.

"Well?" he said to her. "So you've been doing some
work lately."

Ivich shrugged her shoulders angrily. "I don't want to
talk about that. I'm sick of it, I'm here to enjoy myself."

"She spent the day curled up on her sofa, with eyes like
saucers." And Boris added with pride, ignoring the black

looks that his sister flung at him: "She's a queer girl, she could die of cold in the middle of the summer."

Ivich had been shivering for many a long hour, and sobbing too perhaps. But she showed no sign of it at the moment: she had dabbed a little blue on her eyelids and raspberry-red on her lips, her cheeks were flushed with alcohol; she looked resplendent.

"I want this to be a grand evening," she said, "as it's my last."

"Don't be absurd."

"Yes it is," she said doggedly, "I shall be flunked, I'm certain, and I shall go away immediately; I shan't be able to stay a day longer in Paris. Or possibly—"

She fell silent.

"Or possibly?"

"Nothing. Don't let's talk any more about it, please, it makes me feel ashamed. Ah, here's the champagne," she said gaily.

Mathieu looked at the bottle and thought: "Three hundred and fifty francs." The fellow who had spoken to him the day before in the rue Vercingétorix was a wash-out too, but on a modest footing—no champagne and agreeable follies; and, moreover, he was hungry. Mathieu was revolted by the bottle. It was heavy and black, with a white napkin round its neck. The waiter, bending over the ice-pail with a stiff and reverential air, twirled it dexterously with his fingertips. Mathieu was still looking at the bottle, he was still thinking of the fellow of the day before and felt his heart contract with genuine anguish; but at that moment a decorous young man appeared on the platform and chanted through a megaphone:

*"Oh yes, he threw a winner—*
*Did Emile."*

Here was that bottle revolving ceremoniously between those pallid fingers, and here were all those people stew-

ing in their juice without making any fuss at all. "Well,"
thought Mathieu, "he smelt of cheap red wine, so there's
really no difference. Anyway, I don't like champagne."
He saw the dance-hall as a miniature hell, as light as a
soap-bubble, and he smiled.

"What do you find so funny?" asked Boris, laughing in
anticipation.

"I've just remembered that I don't like champagne
either."

Thereupon they all three burst out laughing. Ivich's
laugh was rather shrill; the neighboring lady turned her
head and looked her up and down.

"We're very cheerful!" said Boris. And he added: "We
might empty it into the ice-pail when the waiter has
gone."

"Just as you like," said Mathieu.

"No," said Ivich, "I want to drink, I'll drink the whole
bottle if you don't want any."

The waiter filled their glasses, and Mathieu raised his
gloomily to his lips. Ivich looked at hers with an air of
perplexity.

"It wouldn't be bad," said Boris, "if it were served hot."

The white lights went out, the red lights came on, and a
roll of drums echoed through the room. A short, bald,
paunchy gentleman in a dinner-jacket jumped on to the
platform and began to smile into a megaphone.

"Ladies and gentlemen, the management of the Sumatra
has great pleasure in presenting to you Miss Ellinor on her
first appearance in Paris. Miss El-li-nor," he repeated.
"Ha!"

At the first chords from a dulcimer, a tall, blonde girl
entered the room. She was naked, and her body, in the
crimsoned air, looked like a long strip of cotton. Mathieu
turned to Ivich: she was gazing at the naked girl with her
pale, wide-open eyes; she had assumed her convulsed and
cruel expression.

"I know her," whispered Boris.

The girl danced, agonizing in the desire to please; she seemed amateurish; she flung her legs vehemently to and fro, and her feet stood out like fingers at the extremities of her legs.

"She can't keep that up," said Boris; "she'll collapse."

And in fact her long limbs looked disquietingly fragile; when she put her feet on the floor, her legs quivered from the ankles to the thighs. She came up to the edge of the platform and turned around. "Oh Lord," thought Mathieu wearily, "she's going to do the backside act." From time to time the music was drowned by bursts of conversation.

"She can't dance," said Ivich's neighbor with set lips. "With drinks at thirty-five francs, the show ought to be first-rate."

"They've got Lola Montero," said her large companion.

"That doesn't matter; it's a disgrace, they've picked that girl up in the street."

The woman sipped her cocktail and began to fidget with her rings. Mathieu looked around the room—all the faces were stern and critical; the audience were enjoying their own disfavor: the girl seemed to them doubly naked because she was so clumsy. She looked as though she sensed their hostility and yearned to placate them. Mathieu was struck by her wild desire to give satisfaction: she thrust out her parted buttocks in a frenzied effort that wrung the very heart.

"She's trying very hard," said Boris.

"It won't be any use," said Mathieu, "they want to be treated with respect."

"They want to see backsides."

"Yes, but that sort of thing needs to be neatly done."

For a moment the dancer's legs tapped the floor beneath that gay but ineffectual posterior, then she stood up, smiled, raised her arms and shook them: a shiver rippled down them, slid over the shoulder-blades, and vanished in the hollow of the back.

"Well, I never saw such a stick of a girl," said Boris.

Mathieu did not answer, he had been thinking about Ivich. He did not dare look at her, but he remembered her air of cruelty; when all was said, she was like the rest, the nasty little creature: doubly protected by her charm and her unassuming frock, she was possessed by all the sensations of the vilest of her kind, as her eyes devoured that poor naked flesh. A flood of bitterness rose to Mathieu's lips and brought a taint of poison to his mouth. "She needn't have troubled to make such a fuss this morning." He turned his head slightly and caught sight of Ivich's fist lying clenched upon the table. The thumbnail, scarlet and sharpened, pointed to the dance-floor like an arrow on a dial. "She is quite alone," he thought; "she is hiding her wrecked face under her hair, she is sitting with her thighs together, and having an orgasm!" The idea was more than he could bear, he nearly got up and went, but had not the strength of will and merely thought: "And I love that girl for her purity." The dancer, with her hands on her hips, was shifting sideways on her heels, she brushed her hip against the table; Mathieu wished his desires could have been aroused by that large and cheerful tail beneath the wriggling backbone, if only to distract him from his thoughts or to put Ivich out of countenance. The girl was now crouching, legs apart, slowly swaying to and fro, like one of those pale lanterns swung by night in wayside railway stations by an invisible arm.

"Pah!" said Ivich. "I shan't look at her any more."

Mathieu turned towards her with astonishment; he saw a triangular face, distorted by anger and disgust. "So she was not excited," he realized with thankfulness. Ivich shuddered, he tried to smile at her, but his head was echoing with the sound of fairy bells; Boris, Ivich, the obscene body, and the purple mist slid out of his ken. He was alone, there were Bengal lights in the distance, and, in the smoke, a four-legged monster turning cartwheels, and the festive strains of a band that reached him in gusts through a damp rustle of foliage. "What can be the matter with me?" he asked himself. It was like what had happened in the morning: all this was just a mere *performance;* Mathieu was somewhere else.

The band came to a stop, and the girl stood motionless, turning her face towards the hall. Above her smile were lovely, agonized eyes. No one applauded and there were a few jeers.

"Brutes!" said Boris.

He clapped loudly. Astonished faces turned towards him.

"Be quiet," said Ivich, "you mustn't applaud."

"She does her best," said Boris, applauding.

"All the more reason."

Boris shrugged his shoulders. "I know her," he said; "I've dined with her and Lola, she's a good sort of girl, but silly."

The girl disappeared, smiling and blowing kisses. A white light flooded the room, this was the moment of awakening: the audience were relieved to find themselves in their own company again after justice had been done. Ivich's neighbor lit a cigarette and smiled a winning smile solely for her benefit. Mathieu did not awaken, this was a white nightmare; faces aglow all round him with laughing, limp complacency; most of them apparently uninhabited—"mine must be like that, with the same alertness in the eyes and the corners of the mouth, and yet only too obviously hollow"; it was a nightmare figure of a man who jumped on to the platform and waved for silence; there was a foretaste of the surprise he expected and an affected nonchalance in his mere announcement into the megaphone of the celebrated name:

"Lola Montero!"

The hall thrilled with responsive enthusiasm, there was a crackle of applause, and Boris seemed delighted.

"There're in a good mood tonight—this is going to be some show!"

Lola was leaning against the door; from a distance her flattened, furrowed face looked like the mask of a lion, her shoulders, a quivering whiteness flecked with green, recalled a birch tree on a windy evening under the headlights of a car.

"How beautiful she is!" murmured Ivich.

She advanced with long, calm strides and a sort of nonchalant despair; she had the small hands and the sultry charms of a sultana, but there was a masculine lavishness in her approach.

"She's the goods," said Boris admiringly; "*she* won't get the bird."

It was true: the people in the front row were sitting back in their chairs quite awed, as though they hardly dared look too closely at that famous head. It was a head for a tribune, the large commanding head of a public personage, with something of a politician air that thickened the features: a practiced mouth, trained to open wide and spit horror and disgust through outthrust lips, in a voice that all can hear. Lola stiffened suddenly, Ivich's neighbor heaved a thrilled, admiring sigh. "She's got them," thought Mathieu.

He felt embarrassed: fundamentally, Lola was a noble and passionate character, but her face belied her a great deal; it merely simulated nobility and passion. She suffered; Boris drove her to desperation; but for five minutes in the day she took advantage of her singer's act to suffer beautifully. "Well, what about me? Am I not doing just the same in impersonating a wash-out to the accompaniment of a band? And yet," he thought, "it's quite true that I'm a wash-out." Around him it was just the same: there were people who did not exist at all, mere puffs of smoke, and others who existed rather too much. The bartender, for instance. A little while ago he had been smoking a cigarette, as vague and poetic as a flowering creeper; now he had awakened, he was rather *too much* the bartender, manipulating his shaker, opening it, and tipping yellow froth into glasses with slightly superfluous precision: he was impersonating a bartender. Mathieu thought of Brunet. "Perhaps it's inevitable; perhaps one has to choose between being nothing at all and impersonating what one is. That would be terrible," he said to himself; "it would mean that we were naturally bogus."

Lola, without hurrying herself, looked around the hall. Her melancholy mask had hardened and set, it seemed to cling forgotten to her face. But in the depths of her eyes, which alone showed signs of life, Mathieu thought he could descry a flame of harsh and menacing curiosity that was not feigned. She at last caught sight of Boris and Ivich and seemed reassured. She threw them a large, good-natured smile and then announced with an absent air:

"A sailor's song: *Johnny Palmer*."

"I like her voice," said Ivich; "it reminds one of thick ribbed velvet."

And Mathieu thought: "*Johnny Palmer* again."

The orchestra played a few opening phrases and Lola raised her heavy arms—there she was, standing in an attitude of crucifixion, and he watched a crimsoned mouth open.

> *"Who is it that's cruel, jealous, hard?*
> *Who cheats when he can't hold a card?"*

Mathieu was no longer listening, this image of grief made him feel ashamed. It was only an image, he knew that quite well, but none the less . . .

"I don't know how to suffer, I never suffer enough." The most painful thing about suffering was that it was a phantom, one spent one's time pursuing it, one always

hoped to catch it and plunge into it and suffer squarely
with clenched teeth; but in that instant it escaped, leaving
nothing behind but a scattering of words and countless
demented, pullulating arguments. "There's a chattering in
my head, and the chattering won't stop. Oh, how I wish I
could be silent!" He looked enviously at Boris; behind
that dogged forehead there must be vast silences.

> *"Who is it that's jealous, cruel, hard?*
> *Why, Johnny Palmer."*

"I'm lying!" His downfall, his lamentations, all were lies,
and from the void; he was thrust into the void, at the
surface of himself, to escape the unendurable pressure of
his veritable world. A black and torrid world that stank of
ether. In that world Mathieu was not a wash-out—not by
any means, it was worse than that: he was a cheery fellow
—a cheery doer of ill deeds. It was Marcelle who would
be washed out if he did not find five thousand francs
within two days. Washed out for good and all, and that
was that; which meant that she would lay her egg or run
the risk of dying under the hands of an abortionist. In that
world suffering was not a condition of the soul and words
were not needed to explain it: it was an aspect of things.
"Marry her, you shoddy little bohemian, marry her, my
dear fellow, why don't you marry her?—I bet it'll finish
her," thought Mathieu with horror. Everyone applauded
and Lola deigned to smile. She bowed and said:

"A song from a musical comedy: 'The Pirate's Be-
trothed.'"

"I don't like her when she sings that. Margo Lion was
much better. More temperamental. Lola is too sensible,
quite devoid of temperament. Besides, she's too nice. She
hates me, but with a good compact hatred, the healthy
hatred of an honest human being." He listened absently to
these light thoughts which scurried around like rats in a
barn. Beneath them lay a dense and mournful slumber, a

dense world that waited silently. Mathieu would drop back into it in due course. He saw Marcelle, he saw her hard mouth and distracted eyes. "Marry her, you shoddy bohemian, marry her, you have reached the age of reason, you must marry her."

"*A high-pooped thirty-gunner,*
*Rolling into port.*"

"Stop! Stop! I'll find some money, I'll find it somehow or I'll marry her, that's understood, I'm not a rotter—but for this evening, just for this evening, I want to be left in peace and forget it all; Marcelle doesn't forget, she's in the room, outstretched on the bed, she remembers everything, she SEES me, she listens to faint sounds, within her, and what then? My name will be hers, my whole life if need be, but this night is mine." He turned to Ivich and leaned eagerly towards her, and she smiled, but he felt as though his nose had come into contact with a glass wall, just as the applause broke out. "Encore!" they cried. "Encore!" Lola paid no attention to these appeals. She had another appearance to make at two o'clock in the morning, and she reserved herself accordingly. She bowed twice and approached Ivich. Heads were turned to Mathieu's table. Mathieu and Boris got up.

"How are you, my little Ivich?"

"How are you, Lola?" said Ivich in a toneless voice.

Lola tapped Boris on the chin with a light finger. "Well, you young rapscallion?"

Her calm, grave voice conferred a sort of dignity on the word "rapscallion." It seemed as though Lola had purposely chosen it among the odd, rather touching words of her songs.

"Good evening, madame," said Mathieu.

"Ah!" said she, "so you're here too?"

They sat down. Lola turned to Boris, apparently quite at ease.

"It seems they couldn't stick Ellinor."

"I gather so."

"She came to cry in my dressing-room. Sarrunyan was furious, it's the third time in a week."

"He isn't going to sack her?" asked Boris uneasily.

"He wanted to: she hasn't got a contract. So I said to him: if she goes, I go with her."

"What did he say?"

"That she could stay on another week."

She surveyed the room and said in a high voice: "It's a foul crowd this evening."

"Well," said Boris, "I wouldn't have said so."

Ivich's female neighbor, who was eying Lola with greedy, impudent eyes, gave a sudden start. Mathieu wanted to laugh; he was rather fond of Lola.

"It's because you're not used to the place," said Lola. "When I came in I saw at once that they had just done someone dirt, they looked so sheepish. You know," she added, "if that kid loses her job, she'll have to go on the streets."

Ivich raised her head suddenly, there was a wild look in her eyes. "Then let her go on the streets," she said savagely, "she'd do better there."

She was making an effort to keep her head erect and her dulled, pink eyes open. She had lost a little of her assurance and added with a deprecating, harassed air: "Of course I quite understand that she must earn her living."

No one answered, and Mathieu felt distressed on her behalf: it must be hard to keep one's head erect. Lola looked at her composedly. As though she were thinking: "Nasty little rich girl." Ivich laughed lightly.

"I don't want to dance," she said slyly.

Her laugh broke, and her head fell forward.

"I wonder what's biting her," said Boris quietly.

Lola gazed with curiosity at the top of Ivich's head. After a moment or two she stretched out her small, plump hand, grasped a shock of Ivich's hair, and lifted her head. And with the air of a hospital nurse she said:

"What's the matter, darling? Too much to drink?"

She drew aside Ivich's blond curls like a curtain, exposing a broad, pallid cheek. Ivich half-opened her expiring eyes and let her head roll back. "She's going to be sick," thought Mathieu indifferently. Lola was tugging at Ivich's hair.

"Open your eyes, will you! Open your eyes! Look at me!"

Ivich's eyes opened wide, and they shone with hatred. "There—I'm looking at you," she said in a curt and icy tone.

"Come," said Lola, "you aren't as tipsy as all that."

She let go Ivich's hair. Ivich quickly raised her hands and smoothed her curls back over her cheeks, she looked as though she were modeling a mask, and, indeed, her triangular visage reappeared beneath her fingers, but a pasty, worn look still lingered round her mouth and in her eyes. She remained for a moment motionless, with the rather awesome look of a sleepwalker, while the orchestra played a slow foxtrot.

"Are you going to ask me to dance?" asked Lola.

Boris got up, and they began to dance. Mathieu followed them with his eyes, he did not want to talk.

"That woman disapproves of me," said Ivich gloomily.

"Lola?"

"No, the woman at the next table. She disapproves of me."

Mathieu did not answer, and Ivich went on: "I so much wanted to enjoy myself this evening . . . and look what's happened! I hate champagne!"

"She must hate me too because it's I who made her drink it." He was surprised to see her take the bottle from the bucket and fill her glass."

"What are you doing?" he asked.

"I don't think I've drunk enough. There's a state one must get into after which one feels all right."

Mathieu thought he ought to have stopped her drinking, but he made no sign. Ivich raised the glass to her lips and grimaced disgustedly. "How nasty it is!" she said, putting down her glass.

Boris and Lola passed close to their table—they were laughing.

"All right, little girl?" cried Lola.

"Quite all right now," said Ivich, with a friendly smile. She again picked up the glass of champagne and drained it at a draught without taking her eyes off Lola. Lola returned her smile, and the pair moved away, still dancing. Ivich had a fascinated look.

"She's close up against him," she said in an almost unintelligible voice. "It's—it's ridiculous. She looks like an ogress."

"She's jealous," said Mathieu to himself; "but of which?"

She was half drunk, smiling convulsively, and intent upon Boris and Lola; she was barely conscious of his presence, except as an excuse for talking aloud: her smiles, her mimicry, and all the words she uttered were addressed to herself through him. "I ought to find it intolerable," thought Mathieu, "but I don't mind in the least."

"Let's dance," said Ivich abruptly.

Mathieu was startled. "But you don't like dancing with me."

"It doesn't matter," said Ivich, "I'm tight."

She tottered to her feet, nearly fell, and grabbed the edge of the table. Mathieu took her in his arms and swung her away; they plunged into a bath of vapor, and the dark and perfumed throng closed around them. For an instant Mathieu was engulfed. But he promptly recovered himself, he stood marking time behind a Negro, he was alone, during the opening bars Ivich had vanished, he no longer felt her presence.

"How light you are!"

He looked down and caught sight of his feet. "There are many who don't dance better than I do," he thought. He held Ivich at a distance, nearly at arm's length, and did not look at her.

"You dance correctly," she said, "but it's plain that you don't enjoy it."

"It makes me nervous," said Mathieu. He smiled. "You're amazing, just now you could hardly walk, and you're dancing like a professional."

"I can dance when I'm blind tight," said Ivich. "I can dance all night, it never tires me."

"I wish I were like that."

"You couldn't be."

"I know."

Ivich looked nervously about her. "I don't see the ogress anywhere," she said.

"Lola? On the left, behind you."

"Let's go up to them," she said.

They bumped into a nondescript-looking pair; the man apologized, and the woman threw them a black look. Ivich, with her head half-turned, was towing Mathieu backwards. Neither Boris nor Lola had seen them come, Lola had shut her eyes, and her eyelids were two blue patches on her drawn face, Boris was smiling, immersed in angelic solitude.

"What now?" asked Mathieu.

"Let's stay here, there's more room."

Ivich had become almost a weight in his arms, she was scarcely dancing, her eyes were fixed on her brother and on Lola. Mathieu could see nothing but the tip of an ear between two curls. Boris and Lola circled up to them. When they were quite near, Ivich pinched her brother just above the elbow.

"Hello, Hop-o'-my-thumb."

Boris stared at her, wide-eyed, with astonishment.

"Hi!" said he. "Ivich, don't run away! Why did you call me that?"

Ivich did not answer, she swung Mathieu round so that she had her back to Boris. Lola had opened her eyes.

"Do you understand why she called me Hop-o'-my-thumb?" Boris asked her.

"I think I can guess," said Lola.

Boris said something more, but the din of applause drowned his voice; the jazz band had stopped, and the Negroes were hurriedly packing up to make way for the Argentine band.

Ivich and Mathieu were back at their table.

"I'm really enjoying myself," said Ivich.

Lola was already seated. "You dance awfully well," said she to Ivich.

Ivich did not answer, she fixed a heavy look on Lola.

"You were pulling our legs," said Boris to Mathieu. "I thought you never danced."

"It was your sister who wanted to."

"A stout fellow like you," said Boris, "ought to take up acrobatic dancing."

A burdensome silence followed. Ivich sat without a word, aloof and insistent, and no one wanted to talk. A miniature local sky had gathered above their heads, a dry and stifling arc. The lights were switched on. At the first chords of the tango, Ivich leaned towards Lola.

"Come along," she said hoarsely.

"I don't know how to lead," said Lola.

"I'll do the leading," said Ivich. And she added, with a malicious look, as she bared her teeth: "Don't be afraid, I can lead like a man."

They got up. Ivich gripped Lola savagely and thrust her on to the dance-floor.

"How absurd they are!" said Boris, filling his pipe.

"Yes."

Lola was particularly absurd: she looked positively girlish.

"See here," said Boris.

He produced out of his pocket an enormous horn·hafted dagger and laid it on the table.

"It's a Basque knife," he explained, "with a stop-catch."

Mathieu politely took the knife and tried to open it.

"Not like that, you ass!" said Boris. "You'll slash your hand to bits!"

He took the knife back, opened it, and laid it beside his glass. "It's a kaid's knife," he said. "Do you see those brown stains? The chap who sold it to me swore they were blood."

They fell silent. Mathieu saw, some distance off, Lola's tragic head gliding over a dark sea. "I didn't know she was so tall." He turned his eyes away and read on Boris's face a naïve pleasure that struck at his heart. "He is pleased because he's with me," he reflected remorsefully, "and I never can find anything to say to him."

"Look at the good lady who has just arrived. On the right, at the third table," said Boris.

"The blonde with the pearls?"

"Yes, they're false. Take care, she's looking at us."

Mathieu stole a glance at a tall, handsome girl with a frigid face.

"What do you think of her?"

"Not so bad."

"I got off with her last Tuesday, she was pretty full up, she kept on asking me to dance. And she actually presented me with her cigarette case; Lola was wild, she told the waiter to take it back." He added meditatively: "It was silver, set with jewels."

"She can't take her eyes off you," said Mathieu.

"So I supposed."

"What are you going to do with her?"

"Nothing," he said contemptuously; "she's somebody's mistress."

"And what of that?" asked Mathieu with surprise. "You've become very puritanical all of a sudden."

"It's not that," said Boris, laughing. "It's not that—but dancers, singers, and tarts, they're all the same ultimately. When you've had one, you've had them all." He laid down his pipe and said gravely: "Besides, I lead a chaste life, I'm not like you."

"Indeed?" said Mathieu.

"You shall see," said Boris. "You shall see, I'll astonish you. I shall live like a monk when this affair with Lola is over."

He rubbed his hands with an air of satisfaction.

"It won't be over so very soon," said Mathieu.

"On the 1st of July. What will you bet?"

"Nothing. Every month you bet you'll break it off the following month, and you lose each time. You already owe me a hundred francs, five Corona-Coronas, and the boat in the bottle that we saw in the rue de Seine. You've never had any intention of breaking it off, you're much too fond of Lola."

"You needn't be so unpleasant about it," said Boris.

"But you can't do it," continued Mathieu, ignoring the interruption. "It's the feeling you're committed to do something that knocks you out."

"Shut up," said Boris, angry but amused. "You'll have some time to wait for the cigars and the boat."

"I know, you never pay your debts of honor. You're a young scamp."

"And you are a second-rater." His face lit up. "Don't you think it's a grand insult to say to a fellow: sir, you're a second-rater?"

"Not bad," said Mathieu.

"Or, better still: sir, you're a man of no account."

"No," said Mathieu, "that's far less effective."

Boris admitted as much with a good grace. "You are right," said he. "You are detestable, because you are always right."

He relit his pipe with care.

"To be frank with you, I've got my own idea," he said with a confused, distraught expression. "I should like to have a society woman."

"Really?" said Mathieu. "Why?"

"Well—I think it must be fun, they have such interesting little ways. Besides, it's gratifying to the pride, some of them get their names in *Vogue*. You know what I mean. You buy *Vogue*, you turn over the photos, and you see Madame la Comtesse de Rocamadour with her six greyhounds, and you think: 'I slept with that lady last night.' That must give you a kick."

"I say, she's smiling at you now," said Mathieu.

"Yes, she's tight. She's a nasty bit of work, really; she wants to pinch me from Lola because she loathes her. I'm going to turn my back on her," he said decisively.

"Who is the chap with her?"

"Just a pick-up. He dances at the Alcazar. Handsome, isn't he? Look at his face. He's a good thirty-five years old, and he gives himself the airs of a Cherubino."

"Ah well," said Mathieu, "you'll be like that when you're thirty-five."

"At thirty-five," said Boris soberly, "I shall have been dead a long while."

"You like to say so."

"I'm tubercular," he said.

"I know"—one day Boris had skinned his gums while cleaning his teeth and had spat blood—"I know. And what then?"

"I don't mind being tubercular," said Boris. "The point is it would revolt me to take care of myself. In my opinion

a man *ought* not to live beyond thirty; after that he's a
back number." He looked at Mathieu and added: "I'm
not referring to you."

"No," said Mathieu. "But you're right. After thirty a
man is certainly a back number."

"I should like to live two years longer and then remain
at that age all my life; that would be delightful."

Mathieu looked at him with a kind of shocked benig-
nity. Youth was for Boris not merely a perishable and
gratuitous quality, of which he must take cynical advantage, but also a moral virtue of which a man must show
himself worthy. More than that, it was a justification.
"Never mind," thought Mathieu, "he knows how to be
young." He alone perhaps in all that crowd was definitely
and entirely *there*, sitting on his chair. "After all, it's not a
bad notion: to live one's youth right out and go off at
thirty. Anyway, after thirty a man's dead."

"You look horribly worried," said Boris.

Mathieu gave a start. Boris was crimson with confusion,
but he looked at Mathieu with uneasy solicitude.

"Is it obvious?"

"Indeed it is."

"I'm worried about money."

"You don't manage your affairs properly," said Boris
severely. "If I had your salary, I shouldn't need to borrow.
Would you like the bartender's hundred francs?"

"Thank you, no—I need five thousand."

Boris whistled and looked knowing. "I beg your pardon," said he. "Won't your friend Daniel produce the
stuff?"

"He can't."

"And your brother?"

"He won't."

"Hell!" said Boris disconsolately. "If you liked—" he
added with embarrassment.

"What do you mean—if I liked?"

"Nothing. I was just thinking. It seems so silly, Lola has a trunk full of cash that she never uses."

"I don't want to borrow from Lola."

"But I tell you she never uses the money. If it were a question of her bank account, I should agree with you. She buys securities, she gambles on the Bourse, for which she obviously has to have the wherewithal. But she has been keeping seven thousand francs at her flat for the last four months which she hasn't touched, she hasn't even troubled to take it to the bank. I tell you the money is just packed away at the bottom of a trunk."

"You don't understand," said Mathieu irritably. "I don't want to borrow from Lola because she dislikes me."

Boris burst out laughing. "That's true enough," said he, "she can't stand you."

"Very well, then."

"It's silly, all the same," said Boris. "You're hellishly worried about how to get five thousand francs, there's the money ready to your hand, and you won't take it. Suppose I ask for it as for myself?"

"No, no. Don't you do anything," said Mathieu quickly. "She would find out the truth in the end. Seriously, now!" he added insistently. "I should be very much annoyed if you asked for the money."

Boris did not answer. He had picked up the knife with two fingers, and lifted it slowly to the level of his forehead, point-downwards. Mathieu felt uncomfortable. "I'm a poor sort of fellow," he thought. "I haven't the right to play the man of honor at Marcelle's expense." He turned to Boris, intending to say: "All right, ask Lola for the money." But he could not get a word out of himself, and his cheeks flushed. Boris spread out his fingers, and the knife fell. The blade stuck in the floor, and the haft quivered.

Ivich and Lola came back to their places. Boris picked up the knife and put it on the table.

"What's that beastly thing?" asked Lola.

"It's a kaid's knife," said Boris. "It's to keep you in order."

"You little monster!"

The band had launched into another tango. Boris looked darkly at Lola.

"Come and dance," he said between his teeth.

"You people will be the death of me," said Lola. But her face lit up, and she added with a beaming smile: "That's very nice of you."

Boris got up, and Mathieu thought: "He's going to ask her for the money all the same." He felt overwhelmingly ashamed, and rather meanly relieved. Ivich sat down beside him.

"She's marvelous," she said in a husky voice.

"Yes, she's a fine woman."

"And such a body! There's something strangely exciting about that tragic head on so superb a body. I felt time run on, I had the feeling she was going to wither in my arms."

Mathieu followed Boris and Lola with his eyes. Boris had not yet put the question. He looked as though he were joking, and Lola was smiling at him.

"She is a good sort," said Mathieu absently.

"Indeed she isn't," said Ivich dryly. "She is the usual nasty female." And she added in a tone of pride: "She was quite frightened of me."

"So I observed," said Mathieu. He nervously crossed and uncrossed his legs.

"Do you want to dance?" he asked.

"No," said Ivich, "I want to drink." She half filled her glass and continued: "It's a good thing to drink when dancing, because dancing stops you from getting drunk, and alcohol keeps you going." And she added with a drawn look: "I'm having a fine time—it's a grand finale."

"The moment has come," thought Mathieu, "he's talking

to her." Boris had assumed a serious air; he was talking, but not looking at Lola. Lola was saying nothing. Mathieu felt his face grow crimson, he was vexed with Boris. The shoulders of a gigantic Negro obscured Lola's head for a moment, she reappeared with a set expression on her face, then the music stopped, the crowd parted, and Boris emerged, looking haughty and ill-tempered. Lola followed him at a slight distance, with a rather disconcerted air. Boris leaned over Ivich.

"Do me a service: ask her to dance," he said hurriedly. Ivich rose without a sign of astonishment and ran to meet Lola.

"No," said Lola, "no, my little Ivich, I'm tired." They parleyed for a moment, then Ivich swept her away.

"She won't?" asked Mathieu.

"No," said Boris, "I'll pay her out for it."

He was pale, and his vaguely malevolent scowl made him look very like his sister. It was a confused and rather displeasing resemblance.

"Don't do anything foolish," said Mathieu uneasily.

"So you're angry with me, eh?" asked Boris. "You did forbid me to mention it to her. . . ."

"I should be a swine if I were angry with you. You know very well that I let you do what you suggested. . . . Why did she refuse?"

"Don't know," said Boris, shrugging his shoulders. "She looked pretty glum and said she needed her money. And that," he went on with baffled rage, "is the only time I've ever asked a favor of her. . . . She doesn't know what's what. A woman of her age ought to pay up if she wants a fellow of mine."

"How did you put it?"

"I said it was for a pal of mine who wanted to buy a garage. I mentioned his name: Picard. She knows him. It's *true* that he wants to buy a garage."

"I expect she didn't believe you."

"I don't know about that," said Boris, "but what I do know is that I'll pay her out for it right away."

"Don't get excited," exclaimed Mathieu.

"Never you mind," said Boris with a hostile air. "That's my business."

He went over and bowed to the tall blonde, who blushed faintly and got up. As they began to dance, Lola and Ivich passed close to Mathieu. The blonde was smiling complacently, but beneath her smile there was a wary look. Lola retained her composure, she moved majestically on her course, and the crowd fell back as she passed in token of respect. Ivich was walking backwards, eyes on the ceiling, oblivious. Mathieu picked up Boris's knife by the blade and began to tap the haft against the table. "There'll be bloodshed," he thought. However, he didn't give a damn, he was thinking of Marcelle. He said to himself: "Marcelle—my wife," and something inside him shut with a clash. "My wife, she will live in my apartment. And that's that." It was natural, perfectly natural, like breathing, or swallowing one's saliva. It touched him at every point—let yourself go, don't get hustled, relax and be natural. "In my apartment. I shall see her every day of my life." And he thought: "All is clear—I have a *life*."

A life. He looked at all those empurpled visages, those russet moons that slid across the cushionings of cloud. "They have lives. All of them. Each his own. Lives that reach through the walls of the dance-hall, along the streets of Paris, across France, they interlace and intersect, and they remain as vigorously personal as a toothbrush, a razor, and toilet articles that are never loaned. I knew. I knew that they each had their life. And I knew that I had one too. I had begun to think: 'I do nothing, I shall escape.' And now I'm damn well in the thick of it." He laid the knife on the table, took the bottle, and tipped it over his glass; it was empty. There was a little champagne in Ivich's glass; he picked up the glass and drank.

"I've yawned, I've read, I've made love. And all that *left its mark!* Every movement of mine evoked, beyond itself, and in the future, something that insistently waited and matured. And those waiting-points—they are *myself*, I am waiting for myself in the squares and at the crossroads, in the great hall of the *mairie* of the Fourteenth District, it is I who am waiting for myself on a red armchair, I am waiting for myself to come, clad in black, with a stiff collar, almost choking with heat, and say: 'Yes, yes, I consent to take her as my wife.'" He shook his head violently, but his life maintained itself around him. "Slowly, surely, as suited my humors and my fits of idleness, I have secreted my shell. And now it is finished, I am utterly immured in my own self! In the center there's my apartment with myself inside it, and my green leather armchairs; outside there's the rue de la Gaîté, one-way only, because I always walk down it, the avenue du Maine and all Paris encircling me, north in front, south behind, the Panthéon on my right hand, the Eiffel Tower on my left, the Clignancourt Gate opposite, and halfway down the rue Vercingétorix a small, pink, satined lair, Marcelle's room, my wife's room, and Marcelle inside it, naked, and awaiting me. And then all around Paris lies France, furrowed with one-way roads, and then the seas dyed blue or black, the Mediterranean blue, the North Sea black, the Channel coffee-colored, and then the foreign lands, Germany, Italy—Spain white, because I did not go and fight there—and all the round cities, at fixed distances from my room, Timbuktu, Toronto, Kazan, Nizhnii Novgorod, immutable as frontier points. I go, I go away, I walk, I wander, and I wander to no purpose: this is the university vacation, everywhere I go I bear my shell with me, I remain *at home* in my room, among my books, I do not approach an inch nearer to Marrakech or Timbuktu. Even if I took a train, a boat, or a motor-bus, if I went to Morocco for my holiday, if I suddenly arrived at Marrakech, I should be

always in my room, at home. And if I walked in the
squares and in the sooks, if I gripped an Arab's shoulder,
to *feel* Marrakech in his person—well, that Arab would
be at Marrakech, not I: I should still be seated in my
room, placid and meditative as is my chosen life, two
thousand miles away from the Moroccan and his burnoose.
In my room. Forever. Forever Marcelle's former lover,
now her husband, the professor, forever a man ignorant
of English, a man who has not joined the Communist
Party, who has not been to Spain—forever."

"My life." It hemmed him in. It was a singular entity,
without beginning or end, and yet not infinite. He surveyed it from one *mairie* to another, from the *mairie* of the
Eighteenth District, where he had registered with the re-
cruiting board in October 1923, to the *mairie* of the Fourteenth District, where he was going to marry Marcelle in
August or September 1938; it had, like natural objects, a
vague and hesitant purpose, a kind of insistent futility, a
smell of dust and violets.

"I have led a toothless life," he thought. "A toothless
life. I have never bitten into anything. I was waiting. I was
reserving myself for later on—and I have just noticed that
my teeth have gone. What's to be done? Break the shell?
That's easily said. Besides, what would remain? A little
viscous bit of rubber, oozing through the dust and leaving
a glistening trail behind it."

He looked up and saw Lola, with a malicious smile upon
her lips. He saw Ivich: she was dancing, her head thrown
back, ecstatic, without age or future: "She has no shell."
She was dancing, she was drunk, she was not thinking of
Mathieu. Not in the very least. No more than if he had
never existed. The orchestra had struck up an Argentine
tango. Mathieu knew that tango very well, it was *Mio
caballo murrio,* but he was looking at Ivich, and he felt as
though he were hearing that melancholy, raucous tune for
the first time. "She will never be mine, she will never

come into my shell." He smiled and was conscious of a timid but refreshing sense of regret, he looked affectionately at that passionate, frail body on which his freedom was aground. "Beloved Ivich, beloved freedom." And suddenly, above his besmirched body, and above his life, there hovered a pure consciousness, a consciousness without ego, no more than a mere puff of warm air; there it hovered, in the semblance of a look, it viewed the shoddy bohemian, the petty bourgeois clamped into his comforts, the futile intellectual, "not a revolutionary, merely a rebel," the listless dreamer immersed in his flaccid life, and the verdict of that consciousness was: "The fellow is a wash-out and deserves his fate." And that consciousness was unlinked to any person, it revolved in the revolving bubble, crushed, adrift, agonizing yonder on the face of Ivich, thrilling with the sound of music, ephemeral and forlorn. A red consciousness, a dark little lament, *mio caballo murrio*, it was capable of anything, of *real* desperation on behalf of the Spanish, of any wild decision. If only it could continue thus. But it could not: the consciousness swelled and swelled, the band stopped, and then it burst. Mathieu was once again alone with his own self, in the life that was his, compact and self-sufficing, he did not even criticize himself, nor did he accept himself, he *was* Mathieu, that was all: "Another ecstasy. And then?" Boris returned to his seat, not looking overpleased with himself. He said to Mathieu:

"Well, well, well!"

"What's up?" asked Mathieu.

"The blonde. She's a nasty bit of work."

"What did she do?"

Boris frowned, shuddered, and did not reply. Ivich came back and sat down beside Mathieu. She was alone. Mathieu looked carefully around the room and observed Lola near the band, talking to Sarrunyan. Sarrunyan seemed to be astonished, then he threw a sidelong glance

at the tall blonde, who was nonchalantly fanning herself.
Lola smiled at him and crossed the hall. When she sat
down, there was an odd expression on her face. Boris eyed
his right shoe with an affected air, and a burdensome
silence followed.

"Nonsense," exclaimed the blonde lady, "you can't do
such a thing, I shan't go."

Mathieu started, and everybody turned around. Sarrunyan was leaning obsequiously over the blonde lady
in the attitude of a head waiter taking an order. He was
speaking to her in an undertone, with a quiet, resolute air.
The blonde suddenly got up.

"Come along," she said to her companion.

She rummaged in her bag. The corners of her mouth
were trembling.

"No, no," said Sarrunyan, "you are my guest."

The blonde flung a crumpled hundred-franc note on to
the table. Her companion had got up and was looking
disapprovingly at the hundred-franc note. Then the lady
took his arm and they marched haughtily out, with the
same swaying gait.

Sarrunyan approached Lola, whistling to himself.

"She won't come back in a hurry," he said with a quizzical smile.

"Thank you," said Lola. "I wouldn't have believed it
would be so easy."

He departed. The Argentine orchestra had gone, the
Negroes with their instruments were returning one by
one. Boris flung Lola a look of angry admiration, then he
turned abruptly towards Ivich.

"Come and dance," said he.

Lola watched them placidly as they were getting out of
their seats. But when they had moved away, a sudden
savage look came into her face. Mathieu smiled at her.

"You do what you like in this place," he said.

"I've got them in my pocket," she said nonchalantly. "The people come because I'm here."

There was still an anxious look in her eyes, and she began to tap nervously on the table. Mathieu could not find anything more to say to her. Fortunately she got up a moment later.

"Excuse me," she said.

Mathieu watched her walk around the room and disappear. "Time for her dose," he thought. He was alone. Ivich and Boris were dancing, looking as pure as a melody and scarcely less pitiless. He turned his head away and looked at his feet. Time passed, to no effect. His mind was a blank. A sort of raucous lamentation made him jump. Lola had returned, her eyes were closed, and she was smiling. "She has had what she wanted," he thought. She opened her eyes and sat down, still smiling.

"Did you know that Boris was in need of five thousand francs?"

"No," he said, "I didn't. He needs five thousand francs, does he?"

Lola was still looking at him and swaying to and fro. Mathieu observed the pin-point pupils in her large green eyes.

"I've just refused him the money," said Lola. "He tells me it's for Picard, I thought he would have applied to you."

Mathieu burst out laughing. "He knows I never have a bean."

"So you hadn't heard about it?" asked Lola with an incredulous air.

"Well—no."

"H'm," said she. "That's odd."

She looked somehow like a derelict hulk about to capsize, or as though her mouth were just about to split and utter a terrifying shriek.

"He came to see you not long ago?" she asked.

"Yes, about three o'clock."

"And he didn't say anything?"

"There's nothing surprising in that. He may have met Picard this afternoon."

"That's what he told me."

"Well, then?"

Lola shrugged her shoulders. "Picard works all day at Argenteuil."

"Picard was in need of money," said Mathieu nonchalantly. "No doubt he went to Boris's hotel. Not finding him at home, he met him in the street as he was walking down the boulevard Saint-Michel."

Lola glanced at him ironically. "Do you imagine that Picard would ask five thousand francs from Boris, who has only three hundred francs a month pocket-money?"

"Well then, I don't know what did happen," said Mathieu in a tone of irritation.

He wanted to say to her: "The money was for me." That would have brought matters to a head at once. But that was not possible because of Boris. "She would be terribly angry with him, he would look like my accomplice." Lola tapped the table with the tips of her scarlet nails, the corners of her mouth lifted abruptly, quivered, and dropped once more. She looked at Mathieu with uneasy insistence, but beneath that watchful anger Mathieu defined a deep void of confusion. He felt like laughing.

Lola turned her eyes away. "Perhaps it may have been a sort of test?" she suggested.

"A test?" repeated Mathieu with astonishment.

"Well, that's what came into my mind."

"A test? What an odd idea!"

"Ivich is always telling him I'm stingy."

"Who told you so?"

"You're surprised I know it?" said Lola with a triumphant air. "He's a loyal lad. You mustn't imagine that anyone can abuse me without my hearing of it. I always know, simply from the way he looks at me. Or else he asks me questions in a detached sort of way. I can see it coming, you know. He just has to get it off his chest."

"Well?"

"He wanted to see if I really was stingy. He invented this business about Picard—unless someone put him up to it."

"And who, do you suppose, did that?"

"I don't know. There are lots of people who think that I'm an old hag and he's just a boy. Watch them goggle at us in this place when they see us together."

"Do you imagine he cares for what they say to him?"

"No, but there are people who think they're doing him a kindness by trying to work on his feelings."

"Look here," said Mathieu, "let us put our cards on the table. If you mean me, you're completely wrong."

"Ah," said Lola coldly. "It's quite possible." There was a silence, then she said abruptly: "Why are there always scenes when you come here with him?"

"I don't know. It isn't my fault. I didn't want to come today. . . . I imagine he likes each of us in a different way, and that it gets on his nerves when he sees us both together."

Lola stared in front of her with a somber, strained expression. Then she said: "Now listen to what I'm going to say. I won't have him taken away from me. I'm definitely not doing him any harm. When he's tired of me, he can leave me, and that will happen quite soon enough. But I won't let anyone else take him away."

"She's unpacking it tonight," thought Mathieu. It was, of course, the influence of the drug. But there was something else: Lola detested Mathieu, and yet what she was then saying to him she wouldn't have said to anyone else. Between her and him, in spite of their mutual hatred, there was a kind of link.

"I'm not going to take him away from you," he said.

"I thought you were," said Lola darkly.

"Well, you mustn't think so. Your relations with Boris are no affair of mine. And if they were, I should think they were perfectly all right."

"I imagined that Boris felt under obligations to you because you are his professor."

She was silent and Mathieu realized that he had not convinced her. She appeared to be choosing her words with care.

"I—I know I'm an old woman," she repeated painfully. "I didn't need you to tell me that. But that's why I can help him: there are things I can teach him," she added defiantly. "Besides, am I really too old for him? He loves me as I am, he's happy with me when people don't put these ideas into his head."

Mathieu did not reply, and Lola exclaimed with rather ill-assured vehemence: "Surely you must know he loves me. He must have told you, since he tells you everything."

"I think he loves you," said Mathieu.

Lola turned her heavy eyes upon him.

"I've had many affairs, and it's with open eyes I tell you—that boy is my last chance. And now do what you like."

Mathieu did not reply at once. He looked at Boris and Ivich dancing together, and he felt inclined to say to Lola: "Don't let us quarrel, you must surely see that we're very much alike." But this resemblance rather disgusted him; there was in Lola's love, despite its violence, despite its honesty, something clinging and voracious. But he said, through half-closed lips:

"No need to tell me that. . . . I know it as well as you do."

"What do you mean—as well as I do?"

"We're alike."

"What's the meaning of that?"

"Look at us," said he, "and look at them."

"We are not alike," said Lola, with a contemptuous grimace.

Mathieu shrugged his shoulders, and they lapsed into silence, still at cross-purposes. They both looked at Boris and Ivich. Boris and Ivich were dancing, they were cruel, but quite unconsciously so. Or perhaps they were faintly aware of being so. Mathieu was sitting beside Lola, they did not dance, feeling beyond the age for doing so. "People must take us for lovers," he thought. And he heard Lola murmur to herself: "If only I were sure it was for Picard."

Boris and Ivich were coming towards them. Lola got up with an effort. Mathieu thought she was going to fall, but she leaned against the table and drew a deep breath.

"Come," she said to Boris, "I want to talk to you."

Boris looked ill at ease.

"Can't you do it here?"

"No."

"Well, wait till the band starts and we'll dance."

"No," said Lola, "I'm tired. You must come to my dressing-room. You'll excuse me, Ivich darling?"

"I'm tight," said Ivich amiably.

"We won't be long," said Lola. "Anyway, I shall have to be singing again soon."

Lola moved away, and Boris followed her ungraciously. Ivich collapsed on her chair.

"I'm certainly tight," she said. "It came over me while I was dancing."

Mathieu did not answer.

"Why have they gone away?" asked Ivich.

"There's something they want to talk about. And Lola has just drugged herself. As you know, after the first dose people just hang on till the second one."

"I rather think I should like to take drugs," said Ivich meditatively.

"Of course."

"Well, and what about it?" she said, indignantly. "If I've got to stay in Laon all my life, I must have something to do."

Mathieu did not reply.

"Ah, I see," she said. "You're angry with me because I'm tight."

"Not in the least."

"Yes, you are—you disapprove."

"Well, naturally. However, you aren't so very tight."

"I am ex-ces-sive-ly tight," said Ivich complacently.

The crowd was beginning to thin. It was about two o'clock in the morning. In her dressing-room, a mean little room hung with red velvet, with an ancient gilt-framed mirror, Lola pleaded and threatened: "Boris! Boris! Boris! You're driving me mad." And Boris looked down his nose, with an air of nervous obstinacy. A long black dress swirling between red walls, the black glitter of the dress in the mirror, and lovely white arms flung upwards in anti-quated pathos. Then Lola would slip behind a screen, and, with head thrown back as though to stop her nose from bleeding, she would sniff two pinches of white powder.

Mathieu's forehead dripped with sweat, but he did not dare to wipe it, he was ashamed of perspiring in front of Ivich; she had danced without respite, she was still pale, she did not perspire. She had said that very morning: "I loathe all these damp hands." He no longer knew what to do with his hands. He felt weak and listless, without desire for anything; his mind was vacant. From time to time he told himself that the sun would soon rise, that he must now take further steps, telephone to Marcelle, and to Sarah, live through the whole extent of a new day from end to end, which seemed beyond his compass of belief. He longed to remain indefinitely at that table, be-neath those artificial lights, and beside Ivich.

"I'm enjoying myself," said Ivich in a tipsy voice.

Mathieu looked at her: she was in that state of gay exaltation which a trifle could transform into fury.

"I don't care a damn for examinations," said Ivich. "If I flunk, I shall be quite content. I'm burying my bachelor life this evening."

She smiled and said with an ecstatic air. "It shines like a little diamond."

"What does?"

"This moment. It is quite round, it hangs in empty space like a little diamond; I am eternal."

She picked up Boris's knife by the handle, laid the flat of the blade against the edge of the table, and amused herself by bending it.

"What's the matter with that woman?" she asked suddenly.

"Who."

"The creature in black at the next table. She's been glaring at me ever since she came in."

Mathieu turned his head: the woman in black was looking at Ivich out of the corner of her eye.

"Well," said Ivich, "isn't it true?"

"I think it is."

He looked at Ivich's pinched little face, now quite congested, her malicious, roving gaze, and he thought: "I should have done better to keep quiet." The woman in black was quite aware that they had been talking about her: she had assumed a majestic air, her husband had waked up and was staring at Ivich. "What a bore it all is!" thought Mathieu. He felt lethargic and indifferent, his sole desire was to avoid trouble.

"That woman despises me because she's respectable," muttered Ivich, addressing the knife. "I, on the contrary, am not respectable, I enjoy myself, I get tight, I'm going to fail in my exam. I hate respectability," she rapped out at the top of her voice.

"Do be quiet, Ivich."

Ivich gave him a glacial stare. "You were speaking to me, I believe? True, you too are respectable. Don't be afraid: when I've been ten years at Laon, in the society of my mother and my father, I shall be a great deal more respectable than you are."

She sat huddled in her chair, feverishly bending the knife-blade against the table. A heavy silence followed, then the woman in black turned towards her husband.

"I don't understand how anyone can behave like that girl," she said.

The husband looked apprehensively at Mathieu's shoulders. "Hum!" he observed.

"It isn't entirely her fault," pursued the woman; "the people who brought her are to blame."

"Now we're in for a row," thought Mathieu. Ivich had certainly heard, but she sat silent and sedate, she remained quiet. Rather too sedate: she appeared to be on the watch for something, she had raised her head, and a strangely wild and ecstatic expression came into her face.

"What's the matter?" asked Mathieu, uneasily.

Ivich had become very pale. "Nothing. I—I'm going to do just one more disrespectable thing, to amuse Madame. I wonder how she'll stand the sight of blood."

Ivich's neighbor uttered a faint shriek and blinked. Mathieu looked hurriedly at Ivich's hands. She was holding the knife in her right hand and slashing at the palm of her left hand. The flesh was laid open from the ball of the thumb to the root of the little finger, and the blood was oozing slowly from the wound.

"Ivich!" cried Mathieu. "Your poor hand!"

Ivich grinned vaguely. "Is she going to faint?" she asked. Mathieu reached a hand across the table and Ivich let him take the knife. Mathieu was dumbfounded; he looked at Ivich's slender fingers already spattered with blood, and he thought her hand must be hurting her.

"You're crazy," he said. "Come along with me to the washroom, the attendant will bandage your hand."

"Bandage my hand?" said Ivich, with an unpleasant laugh. "Do you realize what you're saying?"

"Come along at once, Ivich, please."

"It's a very agreeable sensation," said Ivich without getting up. "My hand felt like a pat of butter."

She had lifted her left hand to the level of her nose and was eying it judicially. The blood was trickling all over it, with the busy to and fro of ants in an ant-heap.

"It's my blood," she said. "I like seeing my blood."

"That's enough," said Mathieu.

He gripped Ivich by the shoulder, but she shook herself free, and a large drop of blood fell on the tablecloth. Ivich looked at Mathieu with hatred gleaming in her eyes.

"You've dared to touch me *again*," she said. And she added with a savage laugh: "I ought to have guessed that you would find that too much for you. You are shocked that anyone should enjoy the sight of his own blood."

Mathieu felt himself growing pale with rage. He sat down again, laid his left hand flat on the table, and said suavely:

"Too much for me? Certainly not, Ivich, I find it charming. It's a game for a noble lady, I suppose."

He jabbed the knife into his palm and felt almost nothing. When he took his hand away, the knife remained embedded in his flesh, straight up, with its haft in the air.

"Oh-h-h!" shrieked Ivich. "Pull it out! Pull it out at once!"

"You see," said Mathieu with clenched teeth; "anybody can do that."

He felt benignantly impressive and was a little afraid that he might faint. But a sort of dogged satisfaction and the malice of a silly schoolboy took possession of his mind. It was not only to defy Ivich that he had stuck the knife into his hand, it was as a challenge to Jacques, and Brunet, and Daniel, and to his whole life. "I'm a ghastly kind of fool," he thought. "Brunet was right in saying that I'm a grown-up child." But he couldn't help being pleased. Ivich looked at Mathieu's hand, nailed to the table, and the blood gathering round the blade. Then she looked at Mathieu; her expression had entirely changed.

"Why did you do that?" she said gently.

"Why did you?" asked Mathieu stiffly.

From their left came the mutter of a little tumult: this was public opinion. Mathieu ignored it, he was looking at Ivich.

"Oh!" said Ivich, "I—I'm so sorry."

The mutter grew, and the lady in black began to yelp: "They're drunk, they'll do themselves an injury. Stop them! I can't bear it."

Some heads were turned in their direction, and the waiter hurried up.

"Does Madame want anything?"

The woman in black pressed a handkerchief to her mouth, she pointed silently at Mathieu and Ivich without uttering a word. Mathieu quickly pulled the knife out of the wound, which hurt him a good deal.

"We've cut ourselves with this knife."

The waiter had seen many such incidents. "If you, sir, and Madame, would kindly go to the washroom," he said calmly, "the cloakroom attendant has everything required."

This time Ivich rose without protest. They crossed the dance-floor behind the waiter, each with a hand in the air; it was so comic that Mathieu burst out laughing. Ivich looked at him anxiously, and then she too began to laugh. She laughed so violently that her hand shook. Two drops of blood fell on the floor.

"This is fun," said Ivich.

"Dear, dear!" exclaimed the cloakroom woman. "My

poor young lady, what have you done to yourself! And the poor gentleman, too!"

"We were playing with a knife," said Ivich.

"Well, I never!" said the attendant reproachfully. "An accident can happen in no time. Was it one of our knives?"

"No."

"Ah, I didn't think so. . . . It's deep too," she said, examining Ivich's hand. "Don't worry, I can fix you up all right."

She opened a cupboard, and half her body disappeared inside it. Mathieu and Ivich smiled at each other. Ivich seemed to have recovered her sobriety.

"I wouldn't have believed you could do it," she said to Mathieu.

"You see that all is not lost," said Mathieu.

"It's hurting me now," said Ivich.

"Me too," said Mathieu.

He felt quite happy. He read "Ladies," then "Gentlemen" in gold letters on two creamy-gray enameled doors, he looked at the white tiled floor, he breathed the aniseed odor of disinfectant, and his heart dilated.

"A cloakroom lady's job can't be so very disagreeable," said he gaily.

"Indeed no," said Ivich amiably. She was looking at him with an affectionately fierce expression; she hesitated for a moment and then suddenly applied the palm of her left hand to Mathieu's wounded palm, with a sticky, smacking sound.

"That's the mingling of the blood," she explained.

Mathieu pressed her hand without saying a word, and felt a stinging pain; he had the feeling that a mouth was opening in his hand.

"You're hurting me," said Ivich.

"I know."

The cloakroom lady had emerged from the cupboard, rather flushed. She opened a tin box.

"Here we are," she said.

Mathieu observed a bottle of iodine tincture, some needles, a pair of scissors, and a roll of bandage.

"You are well provided," he said.

She wagged her head gravely.

"Indeed, sir, there are days when my job is no joke. Two days ago a lady threw her glass at the head of one of our best clients. How he did bleed, poor gentleman! I was afraid for his eyes, I took a great splinter of glass out of his eyebrow."

"Good Lord!" said Mathieu.

The cloakroom dame was busy with Ivich.

"Patience, deary, it will smart a bit, that's the iodine; there, that's done."

"You—you will tell me if I'm indiscreet?" asked Ivich in an undertone.

"Yes."

"I want to know what you were thinking about when I was dancing with Lola."

"Just now?"

"Yes, just when Boris asked the blonde to dance. You were alone in your corner."

"I believe I was thinking about myself," said Mathieu.

"I was watching you, you were—almost handsome. If only you could always look like that!"

"One can't be always thinking of oneself."

Ivich laughed. "I believe I'm always thinking of myself."

"Now your hand, sir," said the cloakroom lady. "Steady! It will sting. There—that's over."

Mathieu felt a sharp, scorching pain, but he ignored it, he was watching Ivich tidying her hair rather awkwardly before the mirror and holding her curls in her bandaged hand. In the end she flung her hair back, leaving her broad face exposed to view. Mathieu felt a sharp and desperate desire grow great within him.

"You are beautiful," said he.

"No, I'm not," said Ivich, laughing. "On the contrary, I'm disgustingly plain. This is my private face."

"I think I prefer it to the other one," said Mathieu.

"I'll do my hair like this tomorrow," she said.

Mathieu could find no reply. He nodded and said nothing.

"That's done," said the cloakroom lady.

Mathieu noticed she had a gray mustache.

"Thank you very much, madame—you're as clever as a nurse."

The lady of the lavatory blushed with gratification.

"Oh," she said, "that's natural enough. In our job we have lots of tricky things to do."

Mathieu put ten francs in a saucer and they went out. They looked with satisfaction at their stiff, swathed hands.

"I feel as though my hand was made of wood," said Ivich.

The hall was now almost deserted. Lola, standing in the center of the dance-floor, was just about to sing. Boris was sitting at their table, waiting for them. The lady in black and her husband had disappeared. There remained on their table two half-filled glasses and a dozen cigarettes in an open box.

"It's a rout," said Mathieu.

"Yes," said Ivich, "and for me too."

Boris looked at them with a bantering air.

"You've been properly messing yourselves up," he said.

"It's your beastly knife," said Ivich angrily.

"The said knife seems very sharp," said Boris, with an appraising look at their hands.

"What about Lola?" asked Mathieu.

Boris looked depressed. "As bad as it could be. I pulled a boner."

"How?"

"I said that Picard had come to my place, and that I

had talked to him in my room. It seems that I said something else on the first occasion—God knows what."

"You said you had met him in the boulevard Saint-Michel."

"Oh dear!" said Boris.

"She's savage, I suppose."

"Indeed she is—as savage as a sow. You've only got to look at her."

Mathieu looked at Lola. Her face was angry and distraught.

"I'm sorry," said Mathieu.

"There's nothing to be sorry about: it's my fault. Besides, it will turn out all right. I know how to manage these things. They always do turn out all right in the end."

Silence fell. Ivich looked affectionately at her bandaged hand. Sleep, cool air, and a gray dawn had glided impalpably into the hall, which smelt of early morning.

"A diamond," thought Mathieu, "that's what she said—'a little diamond.'" He was content, he thought no more about himself, he felt as though he were sitting outside on a bench: outside—outside the dance-hall, outside his life. He smiled. "And she also said: 'I am eternal.' . . ."

Lola began to sing.

# CHAPTER XII

"THE Dôme, at ten o'clock." Mathieu awoke. That little hillock of white gauze on the bed was his left hand. It was smarting, but his body was alert. "The Dôme, at ten o'clock." She had said: "I shall be there before you are, I shan't be able to close my eyes all night." It was nine o'clock; he jumped out of bed. "She'll have done her hair differently," he thought.

He flung open the shutters: the street was deserted, the sky lowering and gray, it was cooler than the day before— a veritable morning. He turned a faucet on the wash-basin and plunged his head in water: "I too am a man of the morning." His life had fallen at his feet and lay there massed, it still enveloped him and enmeshed his ankles, he must step over it, he would leave it lying like a dead skin. The bed, the desk, the lamp, the green armchair: these were no longer his accomplices, they were anonymous objects of iron and wood, mere utensils, he had spent the night in a hotel bedroom. He slipped into his clothes and went downstairs whistling.

"There's an express letter for you," said the concierge.

Marcelle! A sour taste came into Mathieu's mouth: he had forgotten Marcelle. The concierge handed him a yellow envelope: it was Daniel.

"My dear Mathieu," Daniel wrote, "I have tried every-thing, but I just can't raise the sum in question. Believe me, I am very sorry. Could you look in tomorrow at twelve o'clock? I want to talk to you about your affair. Sincerely yours."

"Good," thought Mathieu, "I'll go: he won't part with his own money, but I expect he's got some suggestion to make." Life seemed easy to him, it *must* be made easy; in any case, Sarah would induce the doctor to wait a few days; if need be, the money could be sent to him in America.

Ivich was there, in a dark corner. What he first caught sight of was her bandaged hand.

"Ivich!" he said, softly.

She raised her eyes; the face was her deceptive, triangu-lar face, with its air of faint, malicious purity, her cheeks half-hidden by her curls; she had not lifted her hair.

"Did you sleep at all?" asked Mathieu gloomily.

"Very little."

He sat down. She noticed that he was looking at their two bandaged hands; she withdrew hers slowly and hid it under the table. The waiter came up, he knew Mathieu.

"I hope you're well, sir?" he said.

"Very well," said Mathieu. "Get me some tea and two apples."

A silence fell, of which Mathieu took advantage to bury his recollections of the night. When he felt that his heart was empty, he looked up.

"You look rather depressed. Is it the examination?"

Ivich's reply was a disdainful grimace, and Mathieu said no more, he sat looking at the empty seats. A kneeling woman was swilling water over the tiled floor. The Dôme was barely awake. Fifteen hours to go before there could be any prospect of sleep! Ivich began to talk in an under-tone, with a distraught expression on her face.

"It's at two o'clock," she said. "And nine o'clock has just

struck. I can feel the hours melting away underneath me."

She was tugging at her curls again with a wild look in her eyes; how was she to last out? "Do you think," she said, "I could get a job as a saleswoman in a big store?"

"You can't be serious, Ivich, it's a killing life."

"Or as a mannequin?"

"You're rather short, but we might try. . . ."

"I would do anything to avoid staying at Laon. I'd take a job as scullery-maid." And she added with an anxious elderly look: "Doesn't one put advertisements in the papers in such cases?"

"Look here, Ivich, we've got time to turn around. In any case, you've not flunked yet."

Ivich shrugged her shoulders, and Mathieu went on briskly: "But even if you had, you wouldn't be done for. You might, for instance, go home for two months, and I'll have a look around, I'm sure to find something."

He spoke with an air of genial conviction, but he had no hope: even if he got her a job, she would get herself fired at the end of a week.

"Two months at Laon," said Ivich angrily. "It's quite clear you don't know what you're talking about. It's—it's intolerable."

"But you would have spent your vacations there, in any case."

"Yes, but what sort of welcome will they give me now?"

She fell silent. He looked at her without saying a word: she wore her usual sallow morning face, the face of all her mornings. The night seemed to have glided over her. "Nothing leaves a mark on her," he thought. He could not help saying: "You haven't put up your hair?"

"As you see," said Ivich curtly.

"You promised last evening that you would," said he, rather irritably.

"I was tight," she said; and she added forcibly, as though to impress herself upon him: "I was completely tight."

"You didn't look so very tight when you promised."

"Well, well," she said impatiently, "and what then? People make very odd promises."

Mathieu did not answer. He had a sense of being plied with a succession of urgent questions: How to find five thousand francs before evening? How to get Ivich to Paris next year? What attitude to adopt towards Marcelle now? He hadn't the time to compose his mind, to return to the queries that had formed the basis of his thoughts since the previous day: Who am I? What have I done with my life? As he turned his head to shake off this fresh anxiety he saw in the distance the tall, hesitant silhouette of Boris, who appeared to be looking for them outside.

"There's Boris," he said with vexation. And, seized with an unpleasant suspicion, he asked: "Did you tell him to come?"

"Certainly not," said Ivich, utterly taken aback. "I was going to meet him at twelve o'clock, because—because he was spending the night with Lola. And look at his face!"

Boris had caught sight of them. He came towards them. His eyes were wide and staring, and his complexion livid. He smiled.

"Hello!" said Mathieu.

Boris lifted two fingers towards his temple in his usual salutation, but could not make the gesture. He dropped his two hands on the table and began to sway to and fro on his heels without uttering a word. He was still smiling.

"What's the matter?" asked Ivich. "You look like Frankenstein."

"Lola is dead," said Boris.

He was staring stupidly into vacancy. Mathieu sat for a moment or two dumbfounded, then a sense of shocked amazement came upon him.

"What on earth—?"

He looked at Boris: it was plainly no use to question him then and there. He gripped him by the arm and forced him to sit down beside Ivich. Boris repeated mechanically: "Lola is dead."

Ivich gazed wide-eyed at her brother. She had edged away from him as though she feared his contact. "Did she kill herself?" she asked.

Boris did not answer, and his hands began to tremble.

"Tell us," repeated Ivich nervously. "Did she kill herself? Did she kill herself?"

Boris's smile widened in unnerving fashion, his lips twitched. Ivich eyed him fixedly, tugging at her curls. "She doesn't realize anything," thought Mathieu with vexation.

"Never mind," he said. "You will tell us later on. Don't talk."

Boris began to laugh. He said: "If you—if you—"

Mathieu smacked his face with a sharp, noiseless flip of the fingers. Boris stopped laughing, looked at him, muttered something, then subsided and stood quiet, his mouth agape, and still with a stupid air. All three were silent, there was death among them, anonymous and sacred. It was not an event, it was an enveloping, yeasty substance through which Mathieu saw his cup of tea, the marble-topped table, and Ivich's delicate, malicious face.

"And for you, sir?" asked the waiter. He was standing by their table, looking ironically at Boris.

"Bring a cognac quick," and he added with a casual air: "My friend is in a hurry."

The waiter departed and soon returned with a bottle and a glass. Mathieu felt limp and exhausted, he was only just beginning to feel the fatigues of the night.

"Drink that up," he said to Boris.

Boris drank obediently. He put down the glass and said, as though to himself:

"It's a bad show."

"Dear old boy," said Ivich, going up to him. "Dear old boy."

She smiled affectionately, took hold of his hair, and shook his head.

"I'm glad you're here—how hot your hands are!" gasped Boris with relief.

"Now tell us all about it," said Ivich. "Are you sure she's dead?"

"She took that drug last night," said Boris painfully. "We'd had a row."

"So she poisoned herself?" said Ivich briskly.

"I don't know," said Boris.

Mathieu looked at Ivich with amazement: she was affectionately stroking her brother's hand, but her upper lip was oddly curled over her small teeth. Boris went on speaking in an undertone. He did not seem to be addressing them:

"We went up to her room, and she took some of the stuff. She had taken the first dose in her dressing-room while we were having an argument."

"In point of fact, that must have been the second time," said Mathieu. "I fancy she took some while you were dancing with Ivich."

"Very well," said Boris wearily. "Then that makes three times. She never used to take as much as that. We went to bed without saying a word. She tossed about in bed, and I couldn't sleep. And then suddenly she became quiet and I got to sleep."

He drained his glass and continued:

"This morning I woke up feeling stifled. It was her arm, which was lying on the sheet across me. I said to her: 'Take your arm away, you're stifling me.' She did not move. I thought she wanted to make up our quarrel, so I took her arm, and it was cold. I said to her: 'What's the matter?' She did not answer. So then I shoved her arm away, and she nearly fell down between the bed and the wall. I got out of bed, took her wrist, and tried to pull her straight.

Her eyes were open. I saw her eyes," he said with a kind of anger, "and I'll never be able to forget them."

"My poor old boy," said Ivich.

Mathieu tried to feel sorry for Boris, but could not succeed. Boris disconcerted him even more than Ivich did. He looked almost as if he was angry with Lola for having died.

"I picked up my clothes and dressed," Boris went on in a monotonous voice. "I didn't want to be found in her room. They didn't see me go out, there was no one in the office. I took a taxi and came along here."

"Are you sorry?" asked Ivich gently. She was leaning towards him, but not with much sympathy: she had the air of someone asking for information. "Look at me," she said. "Are you sorry?"

"I—" said Boris. He looked at her and said abruptly: "It's so repulsive."

The waiter passed; Boris hailed him: "Another brandy, please."

"In a hurry again?" smiled the waiter.

"Bring it at once," said Mathieu curtly.

Boris inspired him with a faint disgust. There was nothing left of the lad's dry, angular charm. His latest face was too like Ivich's. Mathieu began to think of Lola's body, prostrate on the bed in a hotel bedroom. Men in derby hats would enter that room, they would look at that sumptuous body with combined concupiscence and professional interest, they would pull down the bedclothes and lift the nightgown in search of injuries, reflecting that the profession of police inspector is not without its compensations. He shuddered.

"Is she all alone there?" he said.

"Yes, I expect she'll be discovered about twelve o'clock," said Boris with an anxious look. "The maid always wakes her up about that time."

"In two hours, then," said Ivich.

She had resumed her airs of elder sister. She was strok-ing her brother's hair with an expression of pity and of exultation. Boris appeared to respond to her caresses and then suddenly exclaimed:

"Good God!"

Ivich started. Boris often used slang, but he was never profane.

"What have you done?" she asked apprehensively.

"My letters," said Boris.

"What?"

"All my letters—what a ghastly fool I am! I've left them in her room."

Mathieu did not understand. "Letters you wrote to her?"

"Yes."

"Well?"

"Well—the doctor will come, and it will be known that she died of poison."

"Did you mention the drug in your letters?"

"Yes, I did," said Boris dismally. Mathieu had the im-pression that he was playing a part.

"Did you ever take it yourself?" he asked. He was rather vexed because Boris had never told him.

"I—well, it did so happen. Once or twice, from curi-osity. And I mentioned a fellow who sold it, a fellow from the Boule-Blanche, I bought some from him for Lola on one occasion. I wouldn't like him to get into trouble on my account."

"Boris, you're crazy," said Ivich. "How could you have written such things?"

Boris raised his head. "I expect you have lapses some-times!"

"But perhaps they won't be found," said Mathieu.

"It's the first thing they'll find. The best that can happen is that I shall be called as a witness."

"Oh dear—how Father will blow up!" said Ivich.

"He's quite equal to calling me back to Laon and sticking me into a bank."

"You'll be able to keep me company," said Ivich darkly.

Mathieu looked at them with pity. "This is what they're really like!" Ivich had shed her victorious air: clutched in each other's arms, pallid and stricken, they looked like two little old women. There was silence, and then Mathieu noticed that Boris was looking at him sidelong; the set of his lips suggested that he had some scheme in mind, some pitifully futile scheme. "He's up to something," thought Mathieu with annoyance.

"You say that the servant comes to wake her up at twelve o'clock?" he asked.

"Yes. She knocks until Lola answers."

"Well, it's half past ten. You've got time to go back quietly and get your letters. Take a taxi if you like, but you could do it in a bus."

Boris averted his eyes. "I can't go back."

"So that's how it is," thought Mathieu. "Don't you feel up to it?" he asked.

"No."

Mathieu noticed that Ivich was looking at him. "Where are your letters?" he asked.

"In a small black suitcase under the window. There's a valise on the suitcase, you've only got to push it off. You'll see—there's a pile of letters. Mine are tied up with yellow ribbon." He paused and then added nonchalantly: "There's also some cash—in small bills."

Small bills. Mathieu whistled softly as he thought: "The lad has got his wits about him, he has thought of everything, even of the money I need."

"Is the suitcase locked?"

"Yes, the key is in Lola's bag, on the night-table. You will find a bunch of keys, and then a small flat key. That's the one."

"What's the number of the room?"

"Twenty-one, third floor, second room on the left."

"Good," said Mathieu. "I'll go."

He got up. Ivich was still looking at him; Boris wore an air of deliverance; he flung his hair back with a resumption of the familiar charm and said with a watery smile: "If you're stopped, just say you're going to see Bolivar, the Negro from Kamchatka, I know him. He lives on the third floor too."

"You will both wait for me here," said Mathieu. He had unconsciously assumed a tone of command. He added more gently: "I shall be back in an hour."

"We'll wait for you," said Boris. And he added with an air of admiration and exaggerated gratitude: "You're a grand fellow, Mathieu."

Mathieu walked out on the boulevard Montparnasse, he was glad to be alone. Behind him Boris and Ivich would soon be whispering together, reconstituting their unbreathable and precious world. But he did not care. All around him, and in full force, there were his anxieties of the day before, his love for Ivich, Marcelle's pregnancy, money, and then, in the center, a blind spot—death. He gasped several times, passing his hands over his face and rubbing his cheeks. "Poor Lola," he thought, "I really liked her." But it was not for him to regret her: this death was unhallowed because it had received no sanction, and it was not for him to sanction it. It had plunged like a stone into a little crazy soul and was making circles there. On that small soul alone would fall the crushing responsibility of facing and redeeming it. If only Boris had displayed a gleam of grief. . . . But he had felt nothing but disgust. Lola's death would remain forever somewhere outside the world, despised, like a deed of disrepute. "She died like a dog." What an awful thought!

"Taxi!" cried Mathieu.

When he had sat down in the cab, he felt calmer. He had even a sense of quiet superiority, as though he had suddenly achieved forgiveness for no longer being Ivich's age, or rather as if youth had suddenly lost its value. "They depend on me," he said to himself with acid pride. It was better that the taxi should not stop outside the hotel.

"The corner of the rue Navarin and the rue des Martyrs."

Mathieu watched the procession of the tall, gloomy buildings in the boulevard Raspail. Again he said to himself: "They depend on me." He felt solid and even a trifle weighty. Then the windows of the cab darkened as it swung into the narrow gulley of the rue du Bac, and suddenly Mathieu realized that Lola was dead, that he was going to enter her room, see her large open eyes and her white body. "I shan't look at her," he decided. She was dead. Her consciousness was destroyed. But not her life. Abandoned by the soft affectionate creature that had for so long inhabited it, that derelict life had merely stopped, it floated, filled with unechoed cries and ineffectual hopes, with somber splendors, antiquated faces and perfumes, it floated at the outer edge of the world, between parentheses, unforgettable and self-subsistent, more indestructible than a mineral, and nothing could prevent it from having *been*, it had just undergone its ultimate metamorphosis: its future was determined. "A life," thought Mathieu, "is formed from the future just as bodies are compounded from the void." He bent his head; he thought of his own life. The future had made way into his heart, where everything was in process and suspense. The far-off days of childhood, the day when he had said: "I will be free," the day when he had said: "I will be famous," appeared to him even now with their individual future, like a small, circled individual sky above them all, and that future was himself, *himself* just as he was at present, weary and a little overripe, they had claims upon him across the passage of time past, they maintained their insistencies, and he was often visited by attacks of devastating remorse, because

his casual, cynical present was the original future of those
past days. It was he whom they had awaited for twenty
years, it was he, this tired man, who was pestered by a
remorseless child to realize his hopes; on him it depended
whether these childish pledges should remain forever
childish or whether they should become the first announce-
ments of a destiny. His past was in continual process of
retouching by the present; every day belied yet further
those old dreams of fame, and every day had a fresh future; from one period of waiting to the next, from future
to future, Mathieu's life was gliding—towards what?

Towards nothing. He thought of Lola: she was dead, and
her life, like Mathieu's, had been no more than a time of
waiting. In some long-past summer there had surely been a
little girl with russet curls who had sworn to be a great
singer, and about 1923 a young singer eager to appear first
on the concert bill. And her love for Boris, the great love of
an aging woman, which had caused her so much suffering,
had potentially existed since the first day. Even yesterday,
on its now obscure and unsteady course, her love expected
to receive its meaning from the future, even yesterday she
thought that she would live and that Boris would love her
some day; the fullest, the most loaded moments, the nights
of love that had seemed the most eternal, were but periods
of waiting.

There had been nothing to wait for: death had moved
backwards into all those periods of waiting and brought
them to a halt, they remained motionless and mute, aimless
and absurd. There had been nothing to wait for: no one
would ever know whether Lola would have made Boris
love her, the question was now meaningless. Lola was
dead—gestures, caresses, prayers, all were now in vain;
nothing remained but periods of waiting, each waiting for
the next, nothing but a life devitalized, blurred, and sinking back upon itself. "If I died today," thought Mathieu
abruptly, "no one would ever know whether I was a wash-

out or whether I still had a chance of self-salvation."

The taxi stopped and Mathieu got out. "Wait for me," he said to the driver. He crossed the street at an angle, pushed open the hotel door, and entered a dark and heavily scented hall. Over a glass door on his left there was an enameled rectangle bearing the legend: "Management." Mathieu glanced through the door: the room seemed to be empty, nothing was audible but the ticking of a clock. The ordinary clientele—singers, dancers, jazz-band Negroes, came in late and got up late: the place was still asleep. "I mustn't be in too much of a hurry," thought Mathieu. His heart began to throb, and his legs felt limp. He stopped on the third-floor landing and looked about him. The key was in the door. "Suppose there is someone inside." He listened for a moment and knocked. No one answered. On the fourth floor someone pulled a plug, Mathieu heard the rush of water, followed by a little fluted trickle. He opened the door and went in.

The room was dark; the moist odor of sleep still hung about it. Mathieu surveyed the semi-darkness, he was eager to read death in Lola's features, as though it had been a human emotion. The bed was on the right at the far end of the room. Mathieu saw Lola, an all-white figure, looking at him. "Lola!" he said in a low voice. Lola did not answer. She had a marvelously expressive but impenetrable face; her breasts were bare, one of her lovely arms lay stiff across the bed, the other was under the bedclothes. "Lola!" repeated Mathieu, advancing towards the bed. He could not take his eyes off that proud bosom—he longed to touch it. He stood for a few instants beside the bed, hesitant, uneasy, his body poisoned by a sour desire, then he turned and hurriedly picked up Lola's bag from the night-table. The flat key was in the bag; Mathieu took it and walked to the window. A gray day was filtering through the curtains, the room was filled with a motionless presence; Mathieu knelt down beside the suitcase, the inexorable presence was there, it weighed upon his back, like watching eyes. He inserted the key in the lock. He lifted the lid, slipped both hands into the trunk, and a mass of paper crackled under his fingers. The paper was banknotes —a quantity of them. Thousand-franc notes. Under a pile of receipts and notes Lola had hidden a packet of letters tied with yellow ribbon. Mathieu raised the packet to the light, examined the handwriting, and whispered to himself: "Here they are," and put the packet into his pocket. But he could not go away, he remained kneeling, his eyes fixed on the banknotes. After a moment or two he rummaged nervously among the papers, sorting them by touch with eyes averted. "I've got the money," he thought. Behind him lay that long, white woman with the astonished face, whose arms seemed still able to reach out, and her red nails still to scratch. He got up and brushed his knees with the flat of his right hand. In his left hand was a bundle of banknotes. And he thought: "Now we're all right," dubiously eying the notes. "Now we're all right. . . ." Despite himself he stood on the alert, he listened to Lola's silent body and felt clamped to the floor. "Very well," he murmured with resignation. Fingers opened and the banknotes fluttered down into the suitcase. Mathieu closed the lid, turned the key, put the key in his pocket, and padded out of the room.

The light dazzled him. "I haven't taken the money," he said to himself in amazement.

He stood motionless, his hand on the banisters, and he thought: "What a feeble fool I am!" He did his best to tremble with rage, but one can never be really angry with oneself. Suddenly he thought of Marcelle, the vile old woman with the strangler's hands, and a real fear gripped him: "Nothing—nothing was needed but a motion of the hands to save her pain and preserve her from a sordid business that would leave her marked for life. And I couldn't do it: I am too fastidious. What a fine fellow I must be! After this," he thought, looking at his bandaged hand, "it won't be much use my shoving a knife through my hand to impress my dark and fateful personality upon young ladies; I shall never be able to take myself seriously again." She must go to the old woman, there was no help for it: she must now show her courage, contend with anguish and horror, while he spent his time cheering himself up by drinking rum in a tavern. "No," he thought, as fear laid hold of him, "she shan't go. I'll marry her, since that's all I'm good for." He thought: "I'll marry her," and as he pressed his wounded hand heavily against the banister, he felt like a drowning man. "No, no!" he muttered, flinging his head back; then he took a deep breath, swung around, crossed the corridor, and re-entered the room. He stood with his back to the door as on the first occasion and tried to accustom his eyes to the half-light.

He was not even sure whether he had the courage to steal. He took two or three faltering steps into the room and finally made out Lola's gray face and her wide eyes looking at him.

"Who's that?" asked Lola.

It was a weak but angry voice. Mathieu shuddered from head to foot. "The little idiot!" he thought.

"It's Mathieu."

There was a long silence, and then Lola said: "What's the time?"

"A quarter to eleven."

"I've got a headache," she said. She pulled the bed-clothes up to her chin and lay motionless, her eyes fixed on Mathieu. She looked as though she were still dead.

"Where is Boris?" she asked. "What are you doing here?"

"You've been ill," explained Mathieu hurriedly.

"What was the matter with me?"

"You were quite stiff, and your eyes were wide open. When Boris spoke to you, you didn't answer, and he got frightened."

Lola looked as though she did not hear. Then suddenly she burst into a curt, harsh laugh and said with an effort: "So he thought I was dead?"

Mathieu did not answer.

"Well? That was it, I suppose? He thought I was dead?"

"He was frightened," said Mathieu evasively.

"Pah!" said Lola.

There was a fresh silence. She had shut her eyes, her jaws were quivering. She seemed to be making a violent effort to recover herself. Then she said, with eyes still closed: "Give me my bag, it's on the night-table."

Mathieu handed her the bag; she took a powder-box out of it and looked at her face with disgust.

"It's true—I do look as if I were dead," she said.

She put the bag down on the bed with a sign of exhaustion and added: "I'm not much more use than if I was dead."

"Do you feel ill?"

"Rather ill. But I know what it is, it will pass off during the day."

"Do you want anything? Would you like me to fetch the doctor?"

"No. Don't worry. So it was Boris who sent you?"

"Yes. He was in a dreadful state."

"Is he downstairs?" asked Lola, hoisting herself up in bed.

"No. . . . I—I was at the Dôme, you understand, he came to look for me there. I jumped into a taxi, and here I am."

Lola's head fell back on to the pillow.

"Thanks all the same."

She began to laugh, a gasping, labored laugh.

"I see, he got frightened, bless his heart. He bolted and sent you to make sure I was really dead."

"Lola!" said Mathieu.

"That's all right. No need to tell a tale."

She shut her eyes again, and Mathieu thought she was going to faint. But in a moment or two she continued in a rasping tone:

"Please tell him not to worry. I'm not in danger. I get these attacks sometimes when I—anyway, he'll know why. It's my heart that goes a bit wrong. Tell him to come along here at once—I'll be waiting for him. I shall stay here till this evening."

"Very well," said Mathieu. "There's really nothing you need?"

"No. I shall be all right by this evening, I have to sing at that place." And she added: "He hasn't done with me yet."

"Then good-by."

He made his way to the door, but Lola called him back. She said in an imploring voice: "You promise to make him come? We—we had a little argument last evening, tell him I'm not angry with him any more, that everything is all right. But he must come. Please, he must come! I can't bear the idea that he should think me dead."

Mathieu was touched. "Of course," he said. "I'll send him along."

He went out. The packet of letters, which he had slipped into his breast pocket, weighed heavily against his chest. "He'll be pretty sick," thought Mathieu, "I shall have to give him the key, he'll find some means of getting it back into the bag." He tried to say to himself cheerfully: "It was clever of me not to take the money!" But he wasn't cheerful, it was a matter of no moment that his cowardice should have had fortunate results, the real point was that he *hadn't been able* to take the money. "All the same," he thought, "I'm glad she's not dead."

"Hello, sir!" shouted the chauffeur. "This way!"

Mathieu turned around in bewilderment.

"Eh? Oh, it's you," said he, recognizing the taxi. "All right, drive me to the Dôme."

He sat down, and the taxi started. He wanted to dispel the thought of his humiliating defeat. He took out the packet of letters, untied the knot, and began to read. They were curt little missives that Boris had written from Laon during the Easter vacation. There was an occasional reference to cocaine, but in such veiled terms that Mathieu said to himself with surprise: "I didn't know he could be so careful." The letters all began: "My dear Lola," and continued as brief narratives of the day's doings. "I bathe. I've had a row with my father. I've made the acquaintance of a retired wrestler who is going to teach me the catch-as-catch-can style. I smoked a Henry Clay right to the end without dropping the ash." Boris concluded each letter with the words: "Love and kisses, Boris." Mathieu found it easy to imagine the state of mind in which Lola must have read these letters, her renewed but always anguished disappointment, and her constant effort to reassure herself: "He does really love me; the trouble is he doesn't know how to say so." And he thought: "She kept them, all the same." He carefully tied the packet up again and put it back in his pocket. "Boris must manage to replace it in the trunk without her seeing him." When the taxi stopped, it seemed to Mathieu that he was Lola's natural ally. But he could not think of her otherwise than as belonging to the past. As he entered the Dôme, he had the impression that he was about to defend a dead woman's memory.

Boris looked as though he had not moved since Mathieu's departure. He was sitting sideways, his shoulders hunched, his mouth open, and his nostrils indrawn. Ivich was talking animatedly into his ear, but she fell silent when she saw Mathieu enter. Mathieu came up and threw the packet of letters on the table.

"There you are," said he.

Boris picked up the letters and promptly slipped them into his pocket. Mathieu looked at him with no very friendly air.

"I hope it wasn't very difficult," asked Boris.

"It wasn't difficult at all, but look here: Lola isn't dead."

Boris raised his eyes, he looked as though he did not understand. "Lola isn't dead," he repeated idiotically. He sank deeper into his chair, he seemed utterly crushed.

"Good Lord," thought Mathieu, "he had begun to get accustomed to it."

Ivich looked at Mathieu with a glitter in her eye. "I would have bet on it!" she said. "What was the matter with her?"

"She had merely fainted," replied Mathieu stiffly.

They were silent. Boris and Ivich took their time to digest the news. "What a farce!" thought Mathieu. Boris finally raised his head. His eyes were glassy.

"Then—then she gave you the letters?" he asked.

"No. She was still unconscious when I took them."

Boris drank a mouthful of cognac and put the glass down on the table. "Well!" he said, as though speaking to himself.

"She says she gets these attacks sometimes when she takes the stuff; and she told me you ought to have known it."

Boris did not answer. Ivich seemed quite restored.

"What did she say?" she asked with curiosity. "She must have been surprised when she saw you at the foot of the bed?"

"Not particularly. I told her Boris had been frightened and that he had come to ask my help. Naturally I said I had come to see what was the matter. You will remember that," he said to Boris. "Try not to give yourself away. And then you must manage to put the letters back without her seeing you."

Boris passed a hand over his forehead. "It's more than I can stand," he said, "I see her lying dead."

Mathieu had had enough of this. "She wants you to go and see her at once."

"I—I believed she was dead," repeated Boris, as though to excuse himself.

"Well, she isn't!" said Mathieu with exasperation. "Take a taxi and go to her."

Boris did not move.

"Do you understand?" said Mathieu. "The poor woman is in great distress." He stretched out a hand to grasp Boris's arm, but Boris jerked himself violently out of reach. "No," he exclaimed in a voice so loud that a woman sitting outside turned around. He went on in a lower tone, but with a weak man's dogged obstinacy: "I shan't go."

"But," said Mathieu with astonishment, "yesterday's troubles are all over. She promised that there wouldn't be any further mention of them."

"Yesterday's troubles, indeed!" said Boris, with a shrug of his shoulders.

"Well then?"

Boris eyed him malevolently. "She revolts me."

"Because you believed she was dead? Look here, Boris, pull yourself together, this is becoming ludicrous. You made a mistake; well then, that's the end of it."

"I think Boris is right," said Ivich briskly. She added, and her voice was charged with a meaning that Mathieu did not understand: "I—in his place I would do just the same."

"But can't you understand? He'll be the death of her in good earnest."

Ivich shook her head, there was a look of vexation on her sinister little face. Mathieu threw a hostile look at her. "She's trying to get at him," he thought.

"If he goes back to her it will be from a motive of pity," said Ivich. "You can't ask him to do it: there's nothing more repugnant, even to her."

"He should try at least to see her. He'll soon find out what he feels."

Ivich grimaced impatiently. "There are things that you just can't grasp," she said.

Mathieu remained at a loss, and Boris took advantage of

the pause. "I won't see her again," he said in a determined voice. "For me, she is dead."

"But this is idiotic," exclaimed Mathieu.

Boris looked at him darkly: "I didn't want to say it, but if I see her again, I shall have to *touch* her. And that," he added with disgust, "I could not do."

Mathieu felt his impotence. Wearily he looked at these two hostile little heads.

"Very well, then," he said, "wait awhile—until the first reaction has faded. Promise me you'll go and see her to-morrow or the day after."

Boris seemed relieved. "That's the idea," he said shiftily, "tomorrow."

Mathieu was on the point of saying to him: "You might at least telephone to her to say you can't come." But he refrained, thinking: "He won't do it. I'll telephone." He got up.

"I must go and see Daniel," he said to Ivich. "When do your results come out? Two o'clock?"

"Yes."

"Would you like me to go and look at them?"

"No, thanks. Boris will go."

"When shall I see you again?"

"I don't know."

"Send me an express at once to say if you're through."

"I will."

"Don't forget," said Mathieu, departing. "Good-by."

"Good-by," they answered simultaneously.

Mathieu went down to the Dôme basement to consult a Bottin. Poor Lola! Tomorrow, no doubt, Boris would return to the Sumatra. "But there's this whole day that she'll be waiting for him. . . . I shouldn't like to be in her skin."

"Will you get me Trudaine 00-35," he said to the large telephone woman.

"Both booths are occupied," she answered. "You'll have to wait."

Mathieu waited; through two open doors he could see the white tiles of the lavatories. Yesterday evening, outside certain other "Toilets" . . . An odd recollection for a lover.

He felt very bitter against Ivich. "They're afraid of death," he said to himself. "They may be fresh and neat, but there's something sinister about their little souls, because they're afraid. Afraid of death, of illness, of old age. They cling to their youth like a dying man to life. How many times have I seen Ivich making up her face at a mirror! She shudders at the possibility of wrinkles. They spend their time brooding on their youth, their plans are never more than short-term ones, as though they had only five or six years to live. And then—and then Ivich talks about killing herself, but I don't worry, she would never dare: they'll just rake over the ashes. When all is said, my face is wrinkled, I've got the skin of a crocodile and cramp in my muscles, but I still have years to live. . . . I begin to believe that it's the likes of us who have been young. We tried to be men, and very silly we were, but I wonder whether the sole means of preserving one's youth isn't to forget it." But he remained ill at ease, he was aware of them *up there,* their heads together in whispering complicity; but they were fascinating, none the less.

"Have you got my number yet?" he asked.

"You must wait a moment, sir," replied the large woman acidly. "I have a customer calling Amsterdam."

Mathieu turned away and walked a few steps. "I could not take the money." A woman came down the stairs, light and lively, one of those who say with girlish faces: "I am going to take a pee." She caught sight of Mathieu, hesitated, and then continued on her way with long, gliding strides, the very embodiment of spirit and of perfume as she skimmed into the w.c.'s "I couldn't take the money; my freedom is a myth. A myth—Brunet was right—and my life is built up from below with mechanical precision. A void, the proud and sinister dream of being nothing, of being always something other than I am. It is to escape my age that I've been playing about with those young creatures for the past year; in vain: I am a man, a grown-up person, it is a grown-up person and a man of the world who kissed little Ivich in a taxi. It is to escape from my class that I write for Left reviews; in vain: I am a bourgeois, I couldn't take Lola's money, I was scared by their taboos. It is to escape from my life that I sleep with all and sundry, by grace of Marcelle, and that I obstinately refuse to appear before the mayor; in vain: I am married, I live a domestic life." He had got hold of the Bottin, and as he abstractedly turned over its pages, he read: "Holle-becque, dramatist, Nord 77-80." He felt sick, and he said to himself: "There, the sole freedom left to me is the desire to be what I am. My sole freedom is—to want to marry Marcelle." He was so weary of being tossed about among conflicting currents that he almost felt relieved. He clenched his fists, and addressing himself with all the grav-ity of a grown-up person, a bourgeois, a man of the world, and a family man, said: "I *want* to marry Marcelle."

Pah! These were words, it was a childish, empty choice. "This, too," he thought, "this too is a lie. I need no will-power to get married: I have but to acquiesce." He closed the Bottin and gazed in horror at the wreckage of his hu-man dignity. And suddenly it seemed to him that he could *see* his freedom. It was out of reach, as cruel, youthful, and capricious as the quality of charm: in measured terms it bade him throw Marcelle over. Only for an instant; he caught but a glimpse of this inexplicable freedom that wore the aspect of a crime; indeed, it frightened him, and it was so remote. He remained buttressed on his all too human will, on these all too human words: "I will marry her."

"Your number, sir," said the telephonist. "Second booth."

"Thank you," said Mathieu.

He entered the booth.

"You must unhook the receiver, sir."

Mathieu obediently did so.

"Hello! Trudaine 00-35? It's a message for Madame Montero. No, don't disturb her. You can give it to her later on. It's from Monsieur Boris; he can't come."

"Monsieur Maurice?" said the voice.

"No, not Maurice: Boris. B for Bernard, O for Octave. He can't come. Yes. That's right. Thank you, good-by, madame."

He went out, thinking as he scratched his head: "Marcelle must be in desperation, I ought to telephone to her while I'm about it." And he looked at the telephone lady with a hesitant air.

"Do you want another number?" she asked.

"Yes—get me Ségur 25–64."

It was Sarah's number.

"Hello, Sarah, it's Mathieu," he said.

"Good morning," said Sarah's harsh voice. "Well? Has it been arranged?"

"Indeed it hasn't," said Mathieu. "People are so stingy. Look, I wanted to ask you if you could go round to that fellow and get him to give me credit until the end of the month."

"But he will have gone at the end of the month."

"I'll send him his money to America."

A brief silence followed.

"I can always try," said Sarah dubiously. "But it won't be easy. He's an old skinflint, and besides he's going through a crisis of hyper-Zionism, he detests everything non-Jewish since he was thrown out of Vienna."

"Have a try, anyway, if it isn't too much of a bother."

"It isn't a bother at all. I'll go immediately after lunch."

"Thank you, Sarah, you're a noble lady!" said Mathieu.

# CHAPTER XIII

H E's very unfair," said Boris.
"Yes," said Ivich, "if he imagines he has done a
service to Lola!"

She laughed a short, dry laugh, and Boris relapsed into complacent silence. No one understood him like Ivich. He turned his head towards the lavatory staircase and thought grimly: "He went too far over that affair. One *ought not* to talk to anyone as he did to me. I'm not Hourtiguère." He looked at the staircase, he hoped that Mathieu would smile at them as he came up again. Mathieu reappeared and went out without even glancing at them; Boris's heart turned over.

"He's looking very haughty," he said.

"Who?"

"Mathieu. He has just gone out."

Ivich did not answer. She wore a noncommittal look and was contemplating her bandaged hand.

"He's angry with me," said Boris. "He thinks I'm not moral."

"Yes," said Ivich, "but it won't last." She shrugged her shoulders. "I don't like him when he's moral."

"I do," said Boris. And he added, after reflection: "But I'm more moral than he is."

"Pff!" said Ivich. She swayed a little on her seat, she was looking rather plump and ingenuous. She said in a rasping voice: "I don't care a damn for morality. Not one damn."

Boris felt very solitary. He would have liked to get near to Ivich, but Mathieu was still between them. "He's very unfair," he said. "He didn't give me time to explain myself."

Ivich replied judicially: "There are some things that you can't explain to him."

Boris, from habit, did not protest, but he thought that everything could be explained to Mathieu if you got him in the right mood. He always felt as though they were not talking of the same Mathieu: Ivich's Mathieu was a much more colorless personality.

Ivich laughed rather diffidently. "You do look like an obstinate little mule," she said.

Boris did not answer, he was ruminating on what he ought to have said to Mathieu: that he was not a selfish little brute, and that he had had a terrible shock when he had believed that Lola was dead. He had even suspected for a moment that he was likely to suffer for this business, and this had upset him. He regarded suffering as immoral and could not, in fact, endure it. So he had tried to prevail over himself. But something had got jammed and produced a breakdown, he must wait until the situation reverted to normal.

"It's funny," he said, "when I now think of Lola I see her as a nice old thing."

Ivich laughed shortly and Boris was shocked. He added, in an attempt to be fair: "She can't be feeling very cheerful just now."

"That's quite certain."

"I don't want her to suffer," he said.

"Then you'd better go and see her," said Ivich in a sing-song voice.

He realized that she was setting a trap for him and

answered briskly: "I shan't go. In the first place, she—I always picture her as dead. And then I don't want Mathieu to imagine that he can just whistle and I'll come."

On this point he would not give way, he was not Hourtiguère. And Ivich said quietly:

"He does rather treat you like that, in fact."

It was nastily said, as Boris realized, but without anger; Ivich had excellent intentions, she wanted to make him break with Lola. It was for his good. Everybody always had Boris's good in view. But it varied with each individual.

"I let him think I'm that sort of fellow," he said placidly. "Those are my tactics in dealing with him."

But he had been touched to the quick and was furious with Mathieu accordingly. He fidgeted a little on his seat, and Ivich eyed him uneasily.

"Dear old boy, you think too much," she said. "You have only got to imagine that she's dead for good and all."

"Yes, that would be convenient, but I can't," said Boris.

Ivich seemed amused. "That's odd," she said, "because I can. When I no longer see people, they don't exist."

Boris felt full of admiration for his sister and said nothing; he didn't think himself capable of such strongmindedness. After a pause he said: "I wonder if he took the money. That would mean trouble!"

"What money?"

"At Lola's. He needed five thousand francs."

"Did he!"

Ivich looked puzzled and annoyed. Boris wondered whether he wouldn't have done better to hold his tongue. It was understood that they told each other everything, but from time to time there could be exceptions to that rule.

"You look as if you didn't much like Mathieu," he said.

"He gets on my nerves," she said. "This morning he was being *manly* for my benefit."

"Yes—" said Boris.

He wondered what Ivich meant, but concealed the fact:
they must be assumed to understand each other's allusions
or the charm would be broken. There was a silence, then
Ivich added abruptly:

"Let's go. I can't stand the Dôme."

"Nor can I," said Boris.

They got up and went out. Ivich took Boris's arm. Boris
had a faint but persistent feeling that he wanted to vomit.

"Do you think he'll go on loathing us for long?" he asked.

"Of course not," said Ivich impatiently.

Boris said treacherously: "He loathes you too."

Ivich burst out laughing. "That's quite possible, but I
shan't let that depress me yet. I've got other troubles on
my mind."

"True," said Boris, disconcerted. "You're worried, of
course."

"Horribly."

"Over your examination?"

Ivich shrugged her shoulders and did not reply. They
walked a few steps in silence. He wondered whether it was
*really* about her examination. He wished, indeed, that it
was: it would have been more moral.

He looked up; it happened that the boulevard Montparnasse looked its best under that gray light. The season
might have been October. Boris was very fond of the
month of October. He thought: "Last October I did not
know Lola." At the same moment he experienced a sense
of deliverance: "She's alive." For the first time since he had
abandoned her corpse in the darkened room, he felt that
she was alive, it was like a resurrection. "Mathieu can't be
angry with me for long, as she isn't dead." Up to that minute he knew that she must be in distress, that she was
awaiting him in anguish, but that distress and that anguish
seemed to him irremediable and final, as in the case of
those who had died despairing. But there had been a mis-
deal: Lola was alive, she was lying in her bed with open

eyes, possessed by a little living anger, just as when he arrived late for their appointments. An anger that was no more nor less deserving of respect than others; a trifle more intense, perhaps. He did not owe her any of those vague, portentous obligations imposed upon us by the dead, but he had solid duties towards her—domestic duties, as they might be deemed. Now at last Boris could evoke Lola's face without disgust. It was not the face of a dead woman who responded to the call, but the youthful, angry face that she had turned to him last evening when she cried: "You told me a lie, you haven't seen Picard!" At the same time he felt definitely angry with this spuriously dead woman who had provoked all these disturbances.

"I shan't go back to my hotel; she is capable of coming there," he said.

"Go and sleep at Claude's place."

"I will."

Ivich was seized with an idea. "You ought to write to her—it's more correct."

"To Lola? Certainly not."

"But you should."

"I wouldn't know what to say to her."

"Silly boy—I'll write the letter for you."

"But what is there to say to her?"

Ivich looked at him with astonishment. "Don't you want to break with her?"

"I don't know."

Ivich seemed annoyed, but she did not insist. She never insisted; it was one of her qualities. But in any case, as between Mathieu and Ivich, Boris would have to be extremely cautious: for the moment he no more wanted to lose Lola than to see her again.

"We shall see," he said. "There's no point in thinking about it."

It was pleasant on the boulevard; the people wore amiable faces, he knew them nearly all by sight, and a little

ray of cheerful sunshine caressed the windows of the
Closerie des Lilas.

"I'm hungry," said Ivich. "I must get some lunch."

She went into Demaria's. Boris waited outside. He felt
weak and sentimental, rather like a convalescent, and he
found himself searching for a pleasant thought or two to
occupy his mind. His choice fell abruptly on the *Historical
and Etymological Dictionary of Slang.* Just what was
needed! The dictionary now reposed on his night-table
and was the chief object in his room. "It's a *piece of furniture,*" he thought in a glow of satisfaction. "That was a
master-stroke of mine." And then, as good fortunes never
came singly, he thought of his knife, took it out of his
pocket, and opened it. "I must be tight!" He had bought
it the day before, and the knife already had a history, it
had slit the skin of the two beings whom he loved most.
"It cuts damned well," he thought.

A woman passed and looked at him insistently. She was
*terribly* smart. He turned to look at her from behind; she
had turned too, and they exchanged a friendly look.

"Here I am," said Ivich.

She was holding two large Canadian apples in her hands.
She rubbed one of them on her behind, and when it was
well polished she bit into it, offering the other to Boris.

"No, thank you," said Boris. "I'm not hungry." And he
added: "You really shock me."

"Why?"

"By rubbing apples on your behind."

"It's to polish them," said Ivich.

"See that woman walking away?" said Boris. "I clicked
with her."

Ivich went on amiably munching.

"Again?" she said, with her mouth full.

"Not there," said Boris. "Behind you."

Ivich turned and raised her eyebrows.

"She's pretty," she said simply.

"Did you notice her dress? I don't want to die before I've had a woman like that. A society woman. It must be a delightful experience."

Ivich was still looking at the departing lady. She had an apple in each hand and looked as though she were holding them out to him.

"When I'm tired of her, I'll pass her on to you," said Boris generously.

Ivich bit into her apple.

"Indeed!" said she.

She took his arm and drew him abruptly away. On the other side of the boulevard Montparnasse there was a Japanese shop. They crossed over and looked into the window.

"Do you see those little cups?" said Ivich.

"They're for saki," said Boris.

"What's that?"

"Rice brandy."

"I'll come and buy some. I'll use them for teacups."

"They're much too small."

"I can go on filling them."

"Or you might fill six at a time."

"Yes," said Ivich overjoyed. "I shall have six little full cups in front of me, and I'll drink out of one or another just as I choose."

She drew back a little, clenched her teeth, and said passionately: "I'd like to buy the whole shop."

Boris disapproved of his sister's taste for such trifles. But he was about to enter the shop when Ivich held him back.

"Not today. Come along."

They walked back up the rue Denfert-Rochereau, and Ivich said: "I would sell myself to an old gentleman so as to be able to buy a lot of little things like that."

"You wouldn't know how," said Boris severely. "It's a profession. It has to be learned."

They walked quietly along, it was an instant of happiness; Ivich had certainly forgotten her examination, she looked positively gay. In those moments Boris had the impression that they had merged into one identity. In the sky there were large patches of blue behind a scurry of white clouds; the foliage was heavy with rain, and there was an odor of wood fires, as in a village street.

"I like this sort of weather," said Ivich, biting her second apple. "It's rather damp, but it's not muggy. I feel I could walk ten miles."

Boris discreetly made sure that there were cafés within reach. When Ivich talked of walking ten miles it invariably meant that she would want to sit down very soon.

She looked at the Belfort lion and said ecstatically: "I like that lion. He's a wizard."

"Hum!" said Boris.

He respected his sister's tastes, even though he didn't share them. Moreover, Mathieu had vouched for them when he said one day: "Your sister's taste is bad, but it's better than impeccable good taste: it's *profoundly* bad taste." In those conditions there could be no difference of opinion. But Boris personally was more inclined to classic beauty.

"Shall we go down the boulevard Arago?" he asked.

"Where is it?"

"Over yonder."

"All right," said Ivich. "It looks nice and bright."

They walked in silence. Boris noticed that his sister was becoming depressed and nervous, and she deliberately twisted her feet as they walked. "The agony is going to begin," he thought despondently. Ivich fell into an agony every time she waited for the results of an examination. He raised his eyes and noticed four young workmen approaching, who laughed as they looked at the pair. Boris was used to this sort of derision; indeed, he regarded it with sympathy. Ivich bent her head and seemed not to have seen them. When the youths came up to them, they divided: two of them passed on Boris's left and the other two on Ivich's right.

"What about a threesome?"

"Stinker," said Boris politely.

At that moment Ivich gave a jump and uttered a piercing scream, which she promptly stifled by putting her hand to her mouth.

"I'm behaving like a kitchen-maid," she said, crimson with confusion. The young workmen were already at a distance.

"What's the matter?" asked Boris, with astonishment.

"He touched me," said Ivich with disgust. "The filthy fellow." And she added sharply: "Never mind, I oughtn't to have screamed."

"Which was it?" asked Boris indignantly.

Ivich held him back. "Please don't do anything. There are four of them. And I've made myself ridiculous enough already."

"It isn't because he touched you," Boris explained. "But I can't bear that sort of thing happening when I'm with you. When you are with Mathieu, no one touches you. What do I look like?"

"That's how it is, my dear boy," said Ivich sadly. "Nor am I any protection for you. We don't inspire respect."

It was true, and it often surprised Boris: when he looked in the glass, he thought himself quite impressive.

"We don't inspire respect," he repeated.

They drew together, feeling like a pair of orphans.

"What's that?" asked Ivich after a moment or two.

She pointed to a long wall, black through the green of the chestnut trees.

"It's the Santé," said Boris. "A prison."

"It's grand," said Ivich. "I've never seen anything more sinister. Do people escape from it?"

"Not often," said Boris. "I read somewhere that a

prisoner jumped off the top of the wall. He got caught on the branch of a chestnut tree and was found strangled."

Ivich reflected, and pointed to one of the trees. "It must have been that one," she said. "Shall we sit on the bench beside it? I'm tired. Perhaps we shall see another prisoner jump."

"Perhaps," said Boris without conviction. "They usually do it at night, you know."

They crossed the street and sat down. The bench was wet and Ivich said with satisfaction: "It's nice and cool."

But in a moment or two she began to fidget and tug at her hair. Boris had to slap her hand to prevent her pulling out her curls.

"Feel my hand," said Ivich, "it's frozen."

It was true. Ivich was livid, she looked as though she were in pain, her whole body was shaken by convulsive quivers. She looked so wretched that Boris tried, out of sympathy, to think of Lola.

Ivich looked up abruptly and said, with an air of dark resolve: "Have you got your dice?"

"Yes."

Mathieu had presented Ivich with a set of poker dice in a little leather case. Ivich had given them to Boris. They often played together.

"Let's have a game," she said.

Boris took the dice out of the bag. Ivich added: "Best out of three. You throw first."

They drew apart. Boris sat astride the bench and tipped the dice on to it. A full house, kings high.

"I'll stand," said he.

"I hate you," said Ivich.

She frowned and, before shaking the dice, blew on her fingers and muttered something. It was an incantation. "This is serious," thought Boris. "She's playing for success in the exam." Ivich threw and lost: three queens.

"Second game," she said, looking at Boris with glittering eyes. This time she threw three aces.

"I'll stand," she announced in her turn.

Boris flung the dice and was on the point of getting four aces. But before the dice had settled, he put out a hand as though to pick them up and surreptitiously tipped two of them over with his first and middle fingers. Two kings appeared in place of the ace of hearts and the joker.

"Two pairs," he announced with an air of vexation.

"My game," said Ivich triumphantly. "Now for the final."

Boris wondered if she had seen him cheat; but, after all, it was of no great importance: Ivich only took account of the result. She won the final with two pairs against one, without his having to interfere.

"Good," she said simply.

"Another game?"

"No—no," she said, "that's enough. I was playing to see if I should pass, you know."

"I didn't know," said Boris. "Well, you have passed."

Ivich shrugged her shoulders. "I don't believe in that sort of thing," she said.

They fell silent and remained sitting side by side, staring at the pavement. Boris did not look at Ivich, but he felt her tremble.

"I'm hot," said Ivich, "how dreadful! My hands are damp. I'm so wretched that I'm damp all over."

And in fact her right hand, which had been so cold, was now burning. Her left hand, inert and bandaged, lay on her knees.

"I'm sick of this bandage," she said. "I look like a war casualty; I've a good mind to tear it off."

Boris did not reply. A clock in the distance struck one stroke. Ivich gave a start. "Is—is it half past twelve?" she asked with a bewildered look.

"It's half past one," said Boris, consulting his watch. They looked at each other, and Boris said: "Well, it's time for me to go now."

Ivich snuggled against him and put her arms round his shoulders. "Don't go, Boris, my dear old boy, I don't want to know anything about it, I shall go back to Laon this evening, and I—I don't want to know anything at all."

"Nonsense," said Boris gently. "Of course you must know how you stand when you see the parents."

Ivich let her arms drop. "All right, go," she said. "But come back as soon as you can; I'll be waiting for you here."

"Here?" said Boris with astonishment. "Wouldn't you rather we walked there together? You could wait for me in a café in the Latin Quarter."

"No, no," said Ivich. "I'll wait for you here."

"As you like. Suppose it rains?"

"Boris, please don't torment me—be quick. I shall stay here even it it rains, even it there's an earthquake; I can't get on my legs again, I haven't the strength left to raise a finger."

Boris got up and strode away. When he had crossed the street, he turned. He now saw Ivich from behind: huddled on the bench, her head sunk between her shoulders, she looked like an old beggar-woman. "After all, she may pass," he said to himself. He walked on a few steps and suddenly saw a vision of Lola's face. The real one. "She is unhappy," he thought, and his heart began to throb violently.

# CHAPTER XIV

IN ONE moment. In one moment he would resume his
futile quest; in one moment, haunted by Marcelle's
rancorous and weary eyes, by Ivich's sly face, by Lola's
mortuary mask, he would again feel the taste of fever at
the back of his mouth, and misery would come and turn
his stomach. In one moment. He lay back in his armchair
and lit his pipe; he was solitary and calm, and he sat
luxuriating in the dim coolness of the bar. Yonder was the
varnished cask that served as a table, actresses' photographs and sailors' berets hanging on the walls, the invisible radio installation muttering like a fountain, sundry
resplendent, large, rich gentlemen at the far end of the
room smoking cigars and drinking port—the only customers left, businessmen, all the rest having gone to lunch
long ago; it must be about half past one, but one could
easily imagine that it was still morning, the day lingered
stagnant, like a placid ocean. Mathieu sat awash in that
passionless, waveless sea until what remained of his existence was merged into a barely audible Negro spiritual,
a buzz of agreeable voices, an amber light, and the soft
gestures of those fine surgical hands, which, wielding their
cigars, swayed like caravels loaded with spices. This in-

finitesimal fragment of comfortable living—he knew it was merely a loan, which he would soon have to return, but he savored it without any sense of bitterness: the world provides the unlucky wash-out with many trivial little satisfactions, and indeed it is for them that the world reserves its passing favors, on condition that they enjoy them with discretion. Daniel was seated at his left, grave and silent. Mathieu could view at leisure his handsome sheiklike countenance, and the contemplation of it was one of those same trivial satisfactions. Mathieu extended his legs and smiled to himself.

"I recommend the sherry," said Daniel.

"Good; but you must stand me a glass: I'm broke."

"Certainly," said Daniel. "But look here: can I lend you two hundred francs? I'm ashamed to suggest so little. . . ."

"Bah!" said Mathieu, "it isn't even worth the trouble."

Daniel had turned his large, caressing eyes upon him. "Please," he urged. "I've got four hundred francs to finish the week; we'll go shares."

He must be careful not to accept, it was not in the rules of the game.

"No," said Mathieu. "No, really—though it's very nice of you."

Daniel fixed him with a heavy, solicitous gaze. "You're not actually in need of anything?"

"Yes, I am," said Mathieu. "I'm in need of five thousand francs. But not at this moment. What I need at this moment is a glass of sherry and your conversation."

"I wish my conversation could equal the sherry," said Daniel. He had not so much as mentioned the express letter, nor the reasons that had impelled him to get hold of Mathieu. For which Mathieu was rather grateful: that would come quite soon enough.

"Did you know," he said, "that I saw Brunet yesterday?"

"Indeed?" said Daniel politely.

"I think all is over between us this time."

"Did you have a quarrel?"

"Not a quarrel. Worse than that."

Daniel had assumed a pained expression. Mathieu could not help smiling. "You don't give a damn for Brunet, eh?" he asked.

"Well, you know—I was never as intimate with him as you were," said Daniel. "I respect him greatly, but if I had my way, I would have him stuffed and exhibited in the Museum of Humanity, twentieth-century department."

"And he would look pretty well there," said Mathieu. Daniel was lying: he had been much attached to Brunet at one time.

Mathieu sipped his sherry and said:

"It's excellent."

"Yes," said Daniel, "it's the best drink they have. But their stocks are running out and can't be renewed because of the war in Spain."

He put down his empty glass and took an olive from a saucer.

"Look here, I have a confession to make."

It was over: this moment of modest little enjoyment had slipped into the past. Mathieu looked at Daniel out of the corner of an eye: there was a high, intense expression on Daniel's face.

"Go ahead," said Mathieu.

"I wonder how it will affect you," Daniel continued in a hesitant tone. "I should be wretched if you took offense."

"Tell me what it is, and you'll soon know," smiled Mathieu.

"Well—guess whom I saw yesterday evening?"

"Whom you saw yesterday evening?" repeated Mathieu in a disappointed tone. "I don't know—all sort of people, no doubt."

"Marcelle Duffet."

"Marcelle? Did you, indeed?"

Mathieu was not very surprised: Daniel and Marcelle had not seen each other often, but Marcelle had seemed rather attracted to Daniel.

"You're lucky," he said. "She never goes out. Where did you meet?"

"At her home," said Daniel with a smile. "Where else could it be, since she never goes out?" And he added, discreetly lowering his eyelids: "To tell you the truth, we do see each other now and then."

A silence followed. Mathieu looked at Daniel's long black eyelashes, which had begun to quiver. A clock struck twice, and a Negro voice chanted in an undertone: *"There's a cradle in Carolina."* We do see each other now and then. Mathieu averted his eyes, and fixed them on the red pompon on a sailor's cap.

"You see each other," he repeated in a puzzled tone. "But—where?"

"At her home, as I've just told you," said Daniel with a touch of irritation.

"At her home? You mean you go and see her?"

Daniel did not reply, and Mathieu went on: "What was the idea? How did it happen?"

"Quite simply. I have always had a deep regard for Marcelle Duffet. I greatly admired her courage and her generosity." He paused, and Mathieu repeated with surprise:

"Marcelle's courage—her generosity?" These were not the qualities that he most respected in her.

Daniel continued: "One day when I was feeling bored, I had an impulse to go and call on her, and she received me very kindly. That's all; and we have gone on seeing each other ever since. We were only wrong in not telling you."

Mathieu plunged into the loaded perfume, the wadded air of the pink room: Daniel sitting in the easy chair, looking at Marcelle with great doe-like eyes, and Marcelle smiling awkwardly as though posing for a photograph. Mathieu shook his head: it didn't make sense, it was absurd, it was unseemly, these two had absolutely nothing in common, they could not have understood each other.

"You visit her, and she didn't tell me?" And he added calmly: "You can't be serious."

Daniel raised his eyes and looked at Mathieu gloomily. "Mathieu," he said in his deepest tones, "you must in all fairness admit that I have never permitted myself any sort of light remark about your relations with Marcelle, they are too precious."

"I dare say," said Mathieu, "I dare say. That doesn't alter the fact that you're pulling my leg."

Daniel dropped his eyes with a gesture of discouragement. "All right," he said sadly, "let us leave it at that."

"No, no," said Mathieu. "Go on, you are very amusing: I'm not taken in, that's all."

"You don't make things any easier for me," said Daniel reproachfully. "I find it painful enough to have to accuse myself in this way." He sighed. "I would have preferred you to take my word. But since you insist on proof—"

He had produced a pocketbook stuffed with bills. Mathieu saw the bills and thought: "Swine." But idly, and for form's sake.

"Look," said Daniel.

He held out a letter to Mathieu. Mathieu took the letter; it was in Marcelle's handwriting. He read:

*You are right, as you always are, my dear Archangel. They were certainly periwinkles. But I don't understand a word of your letter. Saturday is all right, as you aren't free tomorrow. Mamma says she will scold you seriously about the candy. Come soon, dear Archangel: we await your visitation with impatience.*

*Marcelle*

Mathieu looked at Daniel. "Then—it's true?" he said.

Daniel nodded. He was sitting very straight, with the funereal decorum of a second in a duel. Mathieu reread the letter from beginning to end. It was dated April 20. "She wrote that." That mannered, sprightly style was so unlike her. He rubbed his nose perplexedly, then he burst out laughing.

"Archangel. She calls you archangel. I should never have thought of that. A fallen archangel, I imagine; something of the type of Lucifer. And you see the old lady too: that puts the lid on it."

Daniel seemed disconcerted. "Good," he said dryly. "I was rather afraid you might be angry. . . ."

Mathieu turned towards him and looked at him dubiously; it was quite clear that Daniel had been convinced he would be angry.

"True," he said, "I ought to be angry, it would be the normal reaction. And take note: it may so happen. But for the moment I'm just bewildered."

He drained his glass, in his turn astonished that he was not more annoyed.

"Do you see her often?"

"At irregular intervals; say about twice a month."

"But what on earth can you find to say to each other?"

Daniel started, and his eyes flashed. He said in a rather silky voice: "Have you any subjects of conversation to suggest?"

"Now, don't lose your temper," said Mathieu in a conciliatory tone. "It's all so sudden, so unexpected—it seems, somehow, funny. But I'm not feeling unfriendly. So it's true? You enjoy talking to each other? But—now do keep calm: I'm trying to understand—but what do you talk about?"

"All sorts of things," said Daniel coldly. "Of course, Marcelle doesn't expect a very elevated style of conversation. But she finds me soothing."

"It's incredible, you are so different."

He could not rid himself of the ridiculous vision: Daniel, the man of ceremony, of high, insinuating charm, with his Cagliostro airs and his long, African smile, and Marcelle, face to face with him, stiff, awkward, and loyal. . . . Loyal? Stiff? She couldn't be so stiff after all: "Come, Archangel, we await your visitation." It was Marcelle who had written *that*, it was she who was attempting these heavy-handed courtesies. For the first time Mathieu felt a flicker of something like anger. "She has deceived me," he thought with amazement. "She has been deceiving me for six months." He went on:

"I'm so astonished that Marcelle should have kept anything from me."

Daniel did not answer.

"Was it you who asked her to say nothing?" asked Mathieu.

"Yes. I didn't want you to take charge of our relations. At present I've known her for some while, so it doesn't matter so much."

"It was you who asked her," repeated Mathieu in a milder tone. And he added: "But didn't she object?"

"She was greatly surprised."

"Yes, but she didn't refuse."

"No, she couldn't have thought it very wrong. She laughed, I remember, she said: 'It's a personal matter.' She thinks I like to surround myself with mystery." And he added, with a veiled irony that annoyed Mathieu extremely: "She began by calling me Lohengrin. Then, as you see, she chose Archangel."

"Yes," said Mathieu. He thought: "He's making fun of her," and he felt ashamed for Marcelle's sake. His pipe had gone out; mechanically he reached out a hand and picked up an olive. This was serious: he did not feel *sufficiently* upset. Mentally bewildered, yes, just as when one discovers one has been completely mistaken. . . .

But awhile ago there had been something alive within him that would have bled. He merely said in a melancholy voice:

"We used to tell each other everything."

"You imagined you did," said Daniel. "Can people tell each other everything?"

Mathieu shrugged his shoulders irritably. But he was mainly angry with himself.

"And that letter!" he said. " 'We await your visitation.' I seem to be discovering another Marcelle."

Daniel looked alarmed. "Another Marcelle, indeed! Look here, you're not going to let a bit of nonsense—"

"You were reproaching me just now for not taking things seriously enough."

"The fact is you pass from one extreme to the other," said Daniel. And he continued with an air of affectionate understanding: "And what is more, you are inclined to rely too much on your judgments of people. This little affair merely goes to show that Marcelle is more complicated than you thought."

"Perhaps," said Mathieu. "But there is more in it than that."

Marcelle had put herself in the wrong, and he was afraid of being angry with her: he *must* not lose his confidence in her, today—today, when he would be perhaps obliged to sacrifice his freedom for her sake. He needed to respect her; otherwise the task would be too hard.

"Besides," said Daniel, "we always intended to tell you, but we found our little conspiracy so amusing that we put off doing so from day to day."

"We!" He said: "We." Here was someone who could say "we" when speaking to Mathieu about Marcelle. Mathieu looked at Daniel with no friendly eye: this would have been the moment to hate him. But Daniel was as disarming as ever. Mathieu said to him abruptly:

"Daniel, why did she do it?"

"Well, I told you," replied Daniel. "Because I asked her to. And then it must have entertained her to have a secret."

Mathieu shook his head. "No. There's something else. She knew quite well what she was doing. Why did she do it?"

"But—" said Daniel, "I imagine it can't always be very comfortable to live within your orbit. She wanted to find a shady corner."

"She finds me too dominating?"

"She didn't exactly say so, but that is what I gathered. After all, you are rather compelling," he added with a smile. "But don't forget that she admires you, she admires your habit of living in a glass house and announcing to the world what one usually keeps to oneself; but it gets her down. She didn't tell you about my visits because she was afraid you might put pressure on her feelings for me, that you might force her to give them a name, that you might dissect them and return them to her in small pieces. They need to be kept in a half-light, you know—they are rather nebulous and ill-defined. . . ."

"She told you so?"

"Yes, she did. She said to me: 'What amuses me in your company is that I don't in the least know where I am going. With Mathieu I always know.'"

"With Mathieu I always know." And Ivich: "With you one never has to fear anything unexpected." He felt a little sick.

"Why didn't she speak to me about all this?"

"She says it's because you never asked her."

It was true; Mathieu bowed his head: each time when it was a question of getting at Marcelle's feelings, an invincible lethargy weighed him down. When sometimes he thought he noticed a shadow in her eyes, he had shrugged his shoulders. "Nonsense! If there was anything, she would tell me, she tells me everything." ("And that is

what I called my confidence in her. I've ruined everything.")

He shook himself and said abruptly: "Why are you
telling me this *today?*"

"I had to tell you one day or another."

This evasive air was intended to stimulate curiosity;
Mathieu was not duped by it.

"Why *today,* and why *you?*" he went on. "It would have
been more—normal that she should mention it first."

"Well," said Daniel, with an assumption of embarrassment, "I may have been mistaken, but I—I thought it was
in the best interests of you both."

Good. Mathieu stiffened. "Look out for the real attack,
it will be coming now." And Daniel added:

"I'm going to tell you the truth: Marcelle doesn't know
I've spoken to you, and only yesterday she didn't look as
though she had made up her mind to make it known to
you so soon. You will do me the favor of saying nothing to
her about our conversation."

Mathieu laughed despite himself. "How truly Satanic!
You sow secrets everywhere. Only yesterday you were
conspiring with Marcelle against me, and today you ask
for my collusion against her. A peculiar brand of
treachery."

Daniel smiled. "There's nothing Satanic about me," he
said. "What impelled me to speak was a genuine feeling
of anxiety that came over me yesterday evening. It
seemed to me that you were both involved in a serious
misunderstanding. Naturally Marcelle is too proud to
mention it to you herself."

Mathieu took a firm grip of his glass: he began to understand.

"It's about your—" Daniel struggled with his modesty,
and continued: "your accident."

"Ah," said Mathieu. "Did you tell her you knew?"

"Certainly not. It was she who mentioned it first."

"Ah."

"Only yesterday, on the telephone," he thought, "she seemed to be afraid I should refer to it. And in the evening she told him everything. Another little comedy." And he added: "Well, what then?"

"Look here, all is not well; something has gone wrong."

"What makes you say so?" asked Mathieu hoarsely.

"Nothing definite, it's rather—the way in which she put things to me."

"What's the matter? Is she angry with me for having got her with child?"

"I don't think so. No, it's not that. It's your attitude yesterday, rather. She spoke of it with bitterness."

"What did I do?"

"I couldn't tell you exactly. But there's something she said to me, among other things: 'It's always that he decides, and if I am not in agreement with him, it is understood that I am to object. But that is entirely to his advantage, because he always has his mind made up, and he never leaves me the time to make up mine'—I won't guarantee the exact words."

"But I have never had a decision to make," said Mathieu with a puzzled look. "We have always been in agreement on what had to be done in such cases."

"Yes, but did you worry about what she might think, the day before yesterday?"

"Certainly not. I was sure she thought as I did."

"Yes, the point being that you didn't ask. When did you last consider this—eventuality?"

"I don't know—two or three years ago."

"Two or three years. And you don't think she may have changed her mind in the interval?"

At the far end of the room the men had got up, they were laughing with genial familiarity, a boy brought their hats, three black felts and a derby. They went out with a friendly salute to the bartender, and the waiter switched off the radio. The bar sank into arid silence; there was a savor of disaster in the air.

"This is going to end badly," thought Mathieu. He did not exactly know what was going to end badly: this stormy day, this abortion business, his relations with Marcelle? No, it was something vaguer and more comprehensive: his life, Europe, this ineffectual, ominous peace. He had a vision of Brunet's red hair: "There will be war in September." At that moment, in the dim, deserted bar, one could almost believe it. There had been something tainted in his life that summer.

"Is she afraid of the operation?" he asked.

"I don't know," said Daniel with a distant air.

"She wants me to marry her?"

Daniel burst out laughing: "I don't know at all, that's asking me too much. Anyway, it can't be as simple as all that. Look here, you ought to have a talk with her this evening. Without mentioning me, of course: as though you had been attacked by scruples. From her manner yesterday, I should be surprised if she doesn't tell you everything; she looked as though she wanted to unburden herself."

"Very well. I'll try to make her talk."

A silence followed, then Daniel added with an embarrassed air: "Well, I've warned you."

"Yes, thanks all the same," said Mathieu.

"Are you annoyed with me?"

"Not at all. It is so very much the sort of service that you favor: it drops on a fellow's head as plumb as a tile."

Daniel laughed heartily, opening his mouth wide, exposing his brilliant teeth and the back of his throat.

"I oughtn't to have done it," she thought, with her hand on the receiver; "I oughtn't to have done it, we always told each other everything. He is thinking: 'Marcelle used to tell me everything'—— oh, he thinks it, he *knows*, by now he knows; shocked amazement in his head and this little voice in his head: 'Marcelle always told me everything,' it is there, at this moment—it *is there* in his head. Oh, it's beyond bearing; I would a hundred times rather he hated me, but there he was, sitting on the café sofa, his arms dangling as though he had just dropped something, and his eyes fixed on the floor as though something lay there broken. It's done, the conversation *has taken place*. Neither seen nor heard, I was not there, I knew nothing; but it has happened, the words have been spoken, and I know nothing; the grave voice rises like smoke to the café ceiling, the voice will come from *there*, the fine, grave voice that always makes the disk of the receiver quiver; it will come from there and say that it is done; oh God, oh God, what will it say? I am naked, I am pregnant, and that voice will come out fully clad from the white disk; we oughtn't to have done it, we oughtn't to have done it." She could almost have been angry with Daniel if it had been possible to be angry with him; "he has been so generous, so good; he is the only person who ever bothered about me. He took up my cause, the Archangel did, and he devoted his grand voice to it. A woman, a weak woman, utterly weak, and *protected* in the world of men and of the living by a dark, warm voice. The voice will come from there, and it will say: 'Marcelle used to tell me everything, poor Mathieu, dear Archangel!" At the thought of the Archangel her eyes melted into soft tears, tears of abundance and fertility; the tears of a *true* woman after a scorching week; tears of a soft, soft woman, who has found someone to *protect* her. "He took me in his arms, a woman caressed and now protected"; teardrops glimmering in her eyes, a caress trickling sinuously down her cheeks on to pouting, quivering lips. For a week she had been looking at a fixed point in the distance, with dry and desolate eyes: "they'll kill me." For a week she had been a Marcelle who knew her mind, a hard and sensible

Marcelle, a manly Marcelle. "He says I am a man, and
behold the tears; the weak woman, the streaming eyes.
Why resist? Tomorrow I'll be hard and sensible; once
and for once only, tears, remorse, sweet self-pity, and
humility sweeter still; velvet hands on my sides and on
my hips." She longed to take Mathieu in her arms and ask
his pardon; pardon on her knees: "poor Mathieu, my poor
dear fellow. Once, once only, to be protected and forgiven, it's so comforting." An idea suddenly took her
breath away and filled her veins with vinegar. "This evening when he comes into the room, when I put my arms
round his neck and kiss him, he'll know everything, and
I'll have to pretend not to know that he knows. Ah, we're
deceiving him," she thought in desperation, "we're still
deceiving him; we tell him everything, but our sincerity
is tainted. He knows, he will come in this evening, I shall
see his kind eyes, I shall think to myself: he *knows*, and
how shall I bear it? My poor old fellow, for the first time
in my life I have hurt you—ah, I'll agree to everything,
I'll go to the old woman, I'll destroy the child; I'm
ashamed, I'll do what he wishes, everything you wish."

The telephone bell rang beneath her fingers, she
clutched the receiver.

"Hello!" she said. "Hello! Is that Daniel?"

"Yes," said the fine, calm voice. "Who is that speaking?"

"Marcelle."

"Good morning, my dear Marcelle."

"Good morning," said Marcelle. Her heart was thump-
ing heavily.

"Did you sleep well?"—deep down within her the grave
voice echoed—oh, the exquisite pain of it! "I left you terribly late last evening, Madame Duffet will be furious. But
I hope she didn't know."

"No," gasped Marcelle, "she didn't know. She was fast
asleep when you left. . . ."

"And *you?*" insisted the gentle voice. "Did you sleep?"

"I? Well—not badly. I'm rather upset, you know."

Daniel laughed, a lovely, luscious laugh, a delicate and melodious laugh. Marcelle felt a little easier.

"You mustn't get upset," said he. "Everything went very well."

"Everything—is that true?"

"It is. Even better than I hoped. We have never really appreciated Mathieu, my dear Marcelle."

Marcelle felt a stab of harsh remorse. She said: "I quite agree. We never did appreciate him, did we?"

"He pulled me up at the very start," said Daniel. "He said that he quite understood that something had gone wrong, and that this had been on his mind all yesterday."

"You—you told him that we had been seeing each other?" asked Marcelle in a strangled voice.

"Of course," said Daniel with astonishment. "Wasn't that what we agreed?"

"Yes—yes. . . . How did he take it?"

Daniel appeared to hesitate. "Very well," he said. "Definitely, very well. At first he wouldn't believe it. . . ."

"I expect he said: 'Marcelle tells me everything.'"

"He did"—Daniel seemed amused—"he said it in so many words."

"Daniel!" said Marcelle. "I feel rather remorseful."

Again she heard the deep, exultant laugh. "Ah well, and so does he. He departed in a torment of remorse. If you are both in that sort of mood, I should like to be concealed somewhere in your room when he sees you: it looks like being a delightful scene."

He laughed again, and Marcelle thought with humble gratitude: "He's making fun of me." But the voice had resumed its gravity, and the receiver vibrated like an organ.

"No, seriously, Marcelle, everything is going as well as

possible; I am so glad for your sake. He didn't let me talk, he stopped me almost at once, and said: 'Poor Marcelle, I am deeply to blame, I loathe myself, but I'll make it up to her, do you think there's still time?' And his eyes were quite red. How he does love you!"

"Oh, Daniel!" said Marcelle. "Oh, Daniel! . . . Oh, Daniel!"

A silence followed, then Daniel added: "He told me he would have a frank talk with you this very evening: 'We'll clear it all up.' At present everything is in your hands, Marcelle. He'll do everything you wish."

"Oh, Daniel! Oh, Daniel!" She recovered herself a little and added: "You've been so good, so— I should like to see you as soon as possible, I have so many things to say, and I can't talk to you without seeing your face. Can you come tomorrow?"

The voice, when it came, seemed harsher, it had lost its harmonies.

"Not tomorrow. Of course, I'm most anxious to see you. . . . Look here, Marcelle, I'll ring you up."

"All right," said Marcelle, "ring me up soon. Ah, Daniel, my dear Daniel! . . ."

"Good-by, Marcelle," said Daniel. "Play your cards well this evening."

"Daniel!" she cried. But he had gone.

Marcelle put down the receiver and passed her handkerchief over her damp eyes. "The Archangel! He ran away pretty quick, for fear I might thank him." She approached the window and looked at the passers-by: women, urchins, a few workmen—how happy they looked! A young woman was running down the middle of the street, carrying her child in her arms, talking to him as she ran, gasping and laughing in his face. Marcelle stood watching her, then she approached the mirror and looked at herself with astonishment. On the wash-basin shelf there were three red roses in a tooth-glass. Marcelle paused, picked out one of them, twirled it diffidently in her fingers, then shut her eyes and stuck the rose into her black hair. "A rose in my hair. . . ." She opened her eyes, looked in the mirror, patted her hair, and smiled wryly at herself.

# CHAPTER XV

"PLEASE wait here, sir," said the little man.

Mathieu sat down on a bench. It was a dark waiting-room, redolent of cabbage; on his left a glass-paneled door admitted a faint light. A bell rang, and the little man opened it. A young woman entered, clad with distressful neatness.

"Kindly sit down, madame."

He walked close beside her to the bench, and she sat down, gathering her legs beneath her.

"I've been before," said the woman. "It's about a loan."

"Yes, madame; certainly."

The little man was talking right into her face. "You are in the government service?"

"No; my husband is."

She began to rummage in her bag; she was not bad-looking, but she had a harsh and harassed look; the little man was staring at her greedily. She produced from her bag two or three papers carefully folded; he took them, went up to the glass door to get a better light, and examined them meticulously.

"Quite all right," said he, handing them back to her. "Quite all right. Two children? You look so young. . . ."

We so look forward to having them, don't we? But when they arrive, they rather disorganize the family finances. You are in a little difficulty at the moment?"

The young woman blushed, and the little man rubbed his hands.

"Well," he said genially, "we'll arrange it all, that's what we're here for."

He eyed her for a moment with a pensive, smiling air and then departed. The young woman threw a hostile look at Mathieu and began to fidget with the clasp of her bag. Mathieu felt ill at ease; he had come into the company of people who were really poor, and it was their money he was going to take, gray and tarnished money, redolent of cabbage. He bent his head and looked down at the floor between his feet: again he saw once more the silky, perfumed banknotes in Lola's little trunk; it was not the same money.

The glass door opened and a tall gentleman with white mustaches appeared. He had silver hair, carefully brushed back. Mathieu followed him into his office. The gentleman pointed genially to a rather shabby leather-covered armchair, and they both sat down. The gentleman laid his elbows on the table and clasped his fine white hands. He wore a dark-green tie, discreetly enlivened by a pearl.

"You wish to take advantage of our service?" he asked paternally.

"Yes."

He looked at Mathieu; he had rather prominent, light-blue eyes.

"Monsieur—?"

"Delarue."

"You are aware that the regulations of our society provide solely for a loan service to government officials?"

The voice was fine and white, a little fleshy, like the hands.

"I am a government official," said Mathieu. "A professor."

"Indeed?" said the gentleman with interest. "We are particularly glad to help university men. You are professor at a lycée?"

"Yes. The Buffon."

"Good," said the gentleman suavely. "Well, we will go through the usual little formalities. . . . First, I am going to ask you whether you have about you any evidence of identity—anything will do, passport, army pay-book, electoral card. . . ."

Mathieu produced his papers. The man took them and glanced at them abstractedly.

"Good," he said. "Very good. And what is the amount you have in mind?"

"I want six thousand francs," said Mathieu. He reflected for a moment and said: "Say seven thousand."

He was agreeably surprised. He thought: "I wouldn't have believed it would go through so quickly."

"You know our conditions? We lend for six months, absolutely without renewal. We are obliged to ask twenty per cent interest owing to our heavy expenses and the considerable risks we run."

"That's quite all right," said Mathieu hastily.

The man produced two printed documents from his drawer.

"Would you be so kind as to fill in these forms? And sign your name at the foot of each."

It was an application for a loan, in duplicate, with blanks for name, age, occupation, and address. Mathieu began to write.

"Excellent," said the man, glancing over the documents. "Born in Paris—in 1905—both parents French. . . . Well, that's all for the moment. Upon payment of the seven thousand francs, we shall ask you to sign an acknowledgment of the debt on stamped paper. The stamp will be your liability."

"Upon payment? So you can't let me have the money at once?"

The gentleman seemed very surprised. "At once? But, my dear sir, we shall need at least a fortnight to make our inquiries."

"What inquiries? You have seen my papers. . . ."

The gentleman looked at Mathieu with amused indulgence. "Ah!" he said. "You university men are all alike. All idealists. Please understand, sir, that in this particular case I do not doubt your word. But, speaking generally, what proof have we that the papers shown to us are not false?" He laughed a rueful little laugh. "I fear that those who deal in money inevitably become suspicious. Deplorable, I agree; but we have *no right* to trust people. And so you see," he concluded, "we must conduct our little inquiry: we shall address ourselves directly to your Ministry. Don't worry: with all due discretion, of course. But you know, between ourselves, what officialdom is like. I much doubt if you can reasonably expect our assistance before July 5."

"That's no good," said Mathieu hoarsely. He added: "I need the money this evening, or tomorrow at the latest, it's for an urgent matter. Couldn't it be managed—at a rather higher rate of interest?"

The man seemed scandalized, and lifted his two fine hands. "But we are not usurers, my dear sir! Our society is under the patronage of the Ministry of Public Works. It is, one might almost say, an official organization. We charge a normal rate of interest calculated on a basis of our expenses and our risks, and we could not lend ourselves to any transaction of that kind." He added severely: "If you were in a hurry, you should have come earlier. Haven't you read our notices?"

"No," said Mathieu, getting up. "It was a sudden call."

"Then I regret—" said the man coldly. "Shall I tear up the documents you have just filled in?"

Mathieu thought of Sarah: "She will certainly have induced the man to wait."

"Don't tear them up," he said. "I'll arrange something in the interval."

"Good," said the man affably. "You will surely find a friend who will advance you what you need for a fortnight. This is your permanent address?" he said, pointing a forefinger at the document. "12 rue Huyghens?"

"Yes."

"Well then, at the beginning of July we will send you a reminder."

He got up and accompanied Mathieu to the door.

"Good-by, sir," said Mathieu. "Thank you."

"Glad to be of any service to you," said the gentleman with a bow. "I look forward to seeing you again."

Mathieu strode rapidly through the waiting-room. The young woman was still there; she was biting her glove with a haggard look.

Outside, greenish flashes quivered in the gray air. But, at the moment Mathieu had the persistent impression of being caught between four walls. "Another set-back," he thought. His sole remaining hope was Sarah.

He had reached the boulevard de Sébastopol; he went into a café and asked if he could telephone.

"Telephones at the far end, on the right."

As he dialed his number, Mathieu murmured: "Has she managed it! Oh, has she managed it!" The words were a kind of prayer.

"Hello," said he. "Hello, Sarah?"

"Hello—yes?" said a voice. "It's Weymüller."

"This is Mathieu Delarue," said Mathieu. "Can I speak to Sarah?"

"She's out."

"What a nuisance! You don't know when she'll be back?"

"No, I don't. Do you want to leave a message for her?"

"No. Just say I telephoned."

He hung up the receiver and went out. His life no longer depended on himself, it was in the hands of Sarah; there was nothing left for him to do but wait. He hailed a bus and sat down beside an old woman who was coughing into her handkerchief. "Jews always come to terms," he thought. "He'll agree—he'll certainly agree."

"Denfert-Rochereau?"

"Three tickets," said the conductor.

Mathieu took the three tickets and sat looking out of the window; he thought with gloomy bitterness of Marcelle. The windows shook, the old woman coughed, the flowers danced on her black straw hat. The hat, the flowers, the old woman, Mathieu—all were carried onwards in the huge machine. The old woman did not lift her nose from her handkerchief, she coughed at the corner of the rue aux Ours and the boulevard de Sébastopol, she coughed along the rue Réaumur, she coughed in the rue Montorgueil, she coughed on the Pont-Neuf, above the gray, calm waters. "And if the Jew won't agree?" But even this thought couldn't rouse him from his lethargy; he was no more than a sack upon other sacks, at the bottom of a truck. "Well, that would finish it, I would tell her this evening that I would marry her." The bus, huge, infantile machine, had carried him off; it swung him to the right and left, shook him, bumped him—events bumped him against the back of the seat and up against the window, the speed of his life had dimmed his senses, and he thought: "My life is no longer mine, my life is just a destiny." He watched the heavy, dark buildings of the rue des Saints-Pères leap up one by one into the sky, he watched his life go past. Marry or not marry—"It doesn't concern me now, it's heads or tails."

The brake was suddenly slammed down and the bus stopped. Mathieu stiffened, and threw an agonized look at the driver's back: all his freedom had come back on him once more. "No," he thought, "no, it isn't heads or tails. Whatever happens, it is *by my agency* that everything must happen." Even if he let himself be carried off, in helplessness and in despair, even if he let himself be carried off like an old sack of coal, he would have chosen his own damnation: he was free, free in every way, free to behave like a fool or a machine, free to accept, free to refuse, free to equivocate; to marry, to give up the game, to drag this dead weight about with him for years to come. He could do what he liked, no one had the right to advise him, there would be for him no Good nor Evil unless he brought them into being. All around him things were gathered in a circle, expectant, impassive, and indicative of nothing. He was alone, enveloped in this monstrous silence, free and alone, without assistance and without excuse, condemned to decide without support from any quarter, condemned forever to be free.

"Denfert-Rochereau," cried the conductor.

Mathieu rose and got out; he turned down the rue Froidevaux. He was tired and nervous, he kept on seeing a suitcase at the far end of a dark room, and in the suitcase some soft and odorous banknotes; with a sense of something like remorse. "Ah, I ought to have taken them," he thought.

"There's an express for you," said the concierge. "It has just come."

Mathieu took it and tore open the envelope; in an instant the walls that hemmed him in collapsed, and he was translated into another world. There were four words, in the middle of the page, in a large sloping script: "Flunked. So what? Ivich."

"It isn't bad news, I hope," said the concierge.

"No."

"I'm glad of that. You looked quite upset."

*Flunked. So what? Ivich.*

"It's one of my old pupils who has failed in the examinations."

"Ah, yes, they're becoming more and more difficult, from what I hear."

"Much more."

"And just think! All these young folks that do pass," said the concierge. "There they are with a degree; and then what's to be done with them?"

"Exactly what I say."

He reread Ivich's message for the fourth time. He was disquieted by its phrasing. Flunked. So what? . . . "She's doing some damn-fool thing or other," he thought. "That's as clear as daylight; she's getting herself into a mess."

"What's the time?"

"Six o'clock."

Six. She got the results at two o'clock. For four hours she had been adrift in the streets of Paris. He slipped the telegram into his pocket.

"Madame Garinet, lend me fifty francs," he said to the concierge.

"But I don't know if I've got fifty," said the concierge with some surprise. She rummaged in the drawer of her work-table.

"I've only got a hundred francs, you can bring me the change this evening."

"Right," said Mathieu. "Thanks."

He went out, thinking: "Where can she be?" His head was empty and his hands were trembling. A cruising taxi was passing down the rue Froidevaux. Mathieu stopped it.

"Students' hostel, 173 rue Saint-Jacques. Quick."

"Right," said the chauffeur.

"Where could she be? At best she had already left for Laon; at the worst . . . And I'm four hours behind," he thought. He leaned forward and pressed his right foot hard on the mat, as though he were accelerating.

The taxi stopped. Mathieu got out and rang the bell at the Hostel door.

"Is Mademoiselle Ivich Serguine in?"

The lady looked at him dubiously. "I'll go and see," she said.

She returned almost at once. "Mademoiselle Serguine hasn't been in since this morning. Is there any message?"

"No."

Mathieu got into the cab again. "Hotel de Pologne, rue du Sommerard."

After a moment or two he rapped on the window. "There it is," he said; "on the left."

He jumped out and pushed open the glass door. "Is Monsieur Serguine in?"

The tall albino porter was in the office. He recognized Mathieu and smiled. "He hasn't been back since last night."

"And his sister—a fair-haired young lady—has she been in today?"

"Oh, I know Mademoiselle Ivich quite well," said the man. "No, she hasn't been in, there was only Madame Montero, who telephoned twice to ask Monsieur Boris to come and see her the moment he got back; if you see him, you might tell him."

"I will," said Mathieu.

He went out. Where could she be? At a movie? It was scarcely probable. Wandering about the streets? In any case she had not yet left Paris, otherwise she would have been to the hostel to get her luggage. Mathieu took the express out of his pocket and examined the envelope: it had been sent from the post office in the rue Cujas, but that proved nothing.

"Where to?" asked the chauffeur.

Mathieu looked at him hesitantly and had a flash of enlightenment. "She must have had one or two before she wrote that. She has certainly got drunk."

"Look here," he said, "I want you to drive slowly from the quays up the boulevard Saint-Michel. I'm looking for someone, and I want to see into all the cafés."

Ivich was not at the Biarritz, nor the Source, nor the Harcourt, nor the Biard, nor the Palais du Café. At Capoulade's, Mathieu caught sight of a Chinese student who knew her. He approached the Chinese, who was drinking a glass of port, perched on a high stool at the bar.

"Excuse me," said Mathieu, looking up at him. "I believe you know Mademoiselle Serguine. Have you seen her today?"

"No," said the Chinese, speaking with difficulty. "Some accident has happened to her."

"Some accident has happened to her!" shouted Mathieu.

"No," said the Chinese. "I was asking if any accident had happened to her."

"I don't know," said Mathieu, turning his back on the man.

He no longer even thought of protecting Ivich against herself; he was solely possessed by an anguished and violent desire to see her again. "May she have tried to kill herself? She is quite silly enough for that," he thought savagely. "After all, perhaps she is merely somewhere in Montmartre."

"To the Vavin square," he said.

He re-entered the cab. His hands were trembling; he thrust them into his pockets. The taxi took the turn round the Médicis fountain, and Mathieu caught sight of Renata, Ivich's Italian friend. She was coming out of the Luxembourg, with a portfolio under her arm.

"Stop! Stop!" shouted Mathieu to the chauffeur. He jumped out of the taxi and ran up to her.

"Have you seen Ivich?"

Renata assumed an air of dignity. "Good morning, monsieur," she said.

"Good morning," said Mathieu. "Have you seen Ivich?"

"Ivich?" said Renata. "Yes, I have."

"When?"

"About an hour ago."

"Where?"

"At the Luxembourg. She was in queer company," said Renata rather superciliously. "You know she has failed, poor girl."

"Yes. Where has she gone?"

"They were going to dance somewhere. At the Tarantula, I think."

"Where is that?"

"Rue Monsieur-le-Prince; under a gramophone-record shop, the dance-hall is in the basement."

"Thanks."

Mathieu was hurrying away; then he turned back. "Excuse me, I had *also* forgotten to say good-by."

"Good-by, monsieur," said Renata.

Mathieu returned to his chauffeur. "Rue Monsieur-le-Prince, it's quite near. Drive slowly, I'll stop you." ("If only she's still there. I'll comb all the *thés dansants* in the Latin Quarter.")

"Stop—there it is. Wait a minute or two."

Mathieu went into a record shop.

"The Tarantula," he asked.

"In the basement—down the stairs."

Mathieu walked down a staircase, inhaling a cool mildewy odor, and pushed at one wing of a leather-covered door which swung back on to his stomach. Mathieu stood leaning against the doorpost, and thought: "She's there."

It was a gaunt and antiseptic cellar, completely devoid of shadow. A filtered light descended from oiled-paper fittings in the ceiling. Mathieu saw about fifteen tables covered with cloths, marooned at the far end of this dead sea of light. The beige walls were plastered with bits of multicolored cardboard depicting exotic plants, which had already begun to crackle from the effects of the moisture, and the cacti were bulging with blisters. An invisible radio was broadcasting a *paso doble,* and the potted music made the hall seem even more denuded.

Ivich had laid her head on her partner's shoulder and was pressing close against him. He was a good dancer. Mathieu recognized him as the tall, dark-haired young man who had been with Ivich on the previous evening in the boulevard Saint-Michel. He was breathing into Ivich's hair and kissing it from time to time. Then she would throw her head back and laugh, her face drained of color, her eyes closed, while he whispered in her ear; they were alone in the middle of the dance-floor. At the far end of the room four young men and a girl violently made-up clapped their hands and shouted: "Bravo!" The tall dark fellow brought Ivich back to their table, with his arm round her waist, while the students buzzed around her; but there was an oddly awkward touch in their familiarity. They greeted her with warm, embracing gestures, but they kept their distance. The made-up lady held herself aloof. She stood, a heavy, listless figure, with a fixed look in her eyes, lit a cigarette, and said pensively:

"Bravo."

Ivich dropped into a chair between the girl and a short, fair-haired man with a frill of beard. She was laughing hysterically.

"No, no," she said, waving a hand in front of her face. "No alibi! No need of an alibi!"

The bearded gentleman promptly rose to surrender his chair to the handsome dark-haired dancer. "That settles it," thought Mathieu. "They recognize his right to sit beside her." The dark handsome gentleman seemed to find this quite natural; he was, indeed, the only member of the party who seemed at ease.

Ivich pointed a finger at her bearded escort. "He's trying to escape, because I've promised to kiss him," she said, laughing.

"Excuse me," said the bearded one with dignity, "you did not promise, you threatened."

"Well, I shan't kiss you," said Ivich. "I shall kiss Irma."

"Do you really want to kiss me, Ivich darling?" said the girl, surprised and flattered.

"Yes, come here," she grasped her imperiously by the arm.

The others drew back, looking rather shocked, and someone said: "Look here, Ivich!" in a gently remonstrative tone. The handsome, dark-haired gentleman was watching her with a thin-lipped, chilly smile; he was estimating her. Mathieu felt humiliated: to this elegant young man, Ivich was merely a victim; he undressed her with a knowing sensual air, she was already naked to his vision, he had guessed the contours of her breasts and thighs, and the odor of her flesh. . . . Mathieu shook himself abruptly and walked towards Ivich, feeling rather weak at the knees: he had realized that he for the first time desired her, though little to his credit, through another man's desire.

Ivich, after a good deal of attitudinizing, took the girl's head in both hands, kissed her on the lips, and then repulsed her violently.

"You smell of cachous," she said indignantly.

Mathieu planted himself beside their table.

"Ivich," he said.

She looked at him open-mouthed, and he wondered if she recognized him. Slowly she raised her left hand and held it out:

"So it's you," she said. "Just look at that." She had torn off her bandages. Mathieu saw a reddish, sticky scar, edged with little dabs of yellow pus.

"You've kept yours on," said Ivich in a voice of disappointment. "I forgot—you are a careful man."

"She tore it off in spite of us," said the girl in a pleading tone. "She's a little devil."

Ivich rose abruptly and looked darkly at Mathieu.

"Take me away from here. I feel degraded."

The young people looked at each other.

"We haven't been making her drink, you know," said the bearded youth to Mathieu. "Actually, we have tried to stop her."

"True enough," said Ivich with disgust. "Children's nurses—that's what they are."

"Except me, Ivich," said the handsome dancer. "Except me."

He looked at her with an air of secret understanding. Ivich turned to him and said: "Except this fellow, and he's a cad."

"Come along," said Mathieu quietly.

He put an arm round her shoulders and drew her away; behind him rose a hum of consternation.

Halfway upstairs Ivich began to droop.

"Ivich!" he pleaded.

She shook her curls mirthfully. "I want to sit down right here," she said.

"Please!"

Ivich began to gurgle and pulled her skirt up above her knees.

"I want to sit down right here."

Mathieu gripped her by the waist and dragged her out. When they were in the street, he let her go; she had not resisted. She blinked and looked sullenly about her.

"Do you want to go back to your place?" suggested Mathieu.

"No!" said Ivich emphatically.

"Would you like me to take you to Boris's?"

"He isn't there."

"Where is he?"

"God knows."

"Then where do you want to go?"

"How should I know? It's for you to say, you took me away."

Mathieu pondered for a moment.

"All right," he said.

He gave her an arm as far as the taxi, and said: "Twelve rue Huyghens."

"I'm taking you home with me," he said. "You can lie down on my sofa, and I'll make you some tea."

Ivich did not protest. She climbed stiffly into the cab and collapsed on the cushions.

"Anything wrong?" she was livid.

"I'm ill," she said.

"I'll tell him to stop at a drugstore," said Mathieu.

"No!" she said, violently.

"Then lie back and shut your eyes," said Mathieu; "we shall soon be there."

Ivich groaned a little. Suddenly her face turned green, and she leaned out of the window. Mathieu saw her small thin back shaken by gusts of vomiting. He reached out a hand and quietly grasped the latch of the door: he was afraid that it might swing open. In a few moments the coughing stopped. Mathieu drew back quickly, took out his pipe, and filled it with an abstracted air. Ivich collapsed once more on the cushions, and Mathieu put his pipe back in his pocket.

"Here we are," he said.

Ivich sat up with an effort. "I feel so ashamed!" she said.

Mathieu got out first and held out his arms to her. But she pushed him aside and jumped briskly out on the pavement. He hurriedly paid the chauffeur and turned towards her. She was watching him with a noncommittal air; a faint, sour reek of vomit came from her delicate mouth. Mathieu inhaled it ecstatically.

"Are you feeling better?"

"I'm sober now," said Ivich gloomily. "But my head's throbbing."

Mathieu made her walk slowly upstairs.

"Every step I take seems to go through my head," she

said with a hostile air. On the third landing she stopped for a moment to recover her breath.

"Now I remember everything."

"Ivich!"

"Everything. I've been trailing about with those brutes and making an exhibition of myself. And I—I flunked the P.C.B."

"Come along," said Mathieu. "There's only one flight more."

They walked on in silence. Suddenly Ivich said: "How did you find me?"

Mathieu bent down to insert the key in the lock.

"I was looking for you," he said, "and then I met Renata."

Ivich muttered behind his back: "I was hoping all the time that you would come."

"In you go," said Mathieu, standing on one side. She brushed against him as she passed, and he longed to take her in his arms.

Ivich tottered as she entered the room. She looked around her drearily.

"So this is where you live?"

"Yes," said Mathieu. It was the first time that she had come to his flat. He looked at his green leather armchairs and his writing-table. He saw them with Ivich's eyes, and he was ashamed of them.

"There's the sofa," he said. "Now you must lie down."

Ivich flung herself on the sofa without a word.

"Would you like some tea?"

"I'm cold," said Ivich.

Mathieu fetched his coverlet and folded it over her legs. Ivich shut her eyes and laid her head on a cushion. She was in pain; there were three vertical wrinkles from her forehead to the root of her nose.

"Would you like some tea?"

She did not answer. Mathieu picked up the electric

kettle and went to fill it at the sink faucet. In the pantry he found a stale half lemon, with the rind dried up and the pulp congealed, but he thought that by squeezing it very hard he could extract a drop or two of juice. He put it on a tray, with two cups, and came back into the room.

"I've put the water on to boil."

Ivich did not answer: she was asleep. Mathieu drew a chair up to the sofa and sat down very quietly. Ivich's three wrinkles had vanished, her forehead was smooth and clear; she was smiling, with eyes closed. "How young she is!" he thought. He had set all his hopes upon a child. She looked so light and fragile, lying on the sofa. She could give no help to anyone; on the contrary, she would have to be helped to carry on her own life. And Mathieu could not help her. Ivich would go off to Laon, she would vegetate there for a winter or two, and then some man would come along—a young man—and take her off. "For my part, I shall marry Marcelle." Mathieu got up and tiptoed out to see if the water was boiling, then returned and sat down again beside Ivich; he looked tenderly at that little sick, soiled body, still so fine in slumber; he realized that he loved Ivich, and was surprised. Love was not something to be felt, not a particular emotion, nor yet a particular shade of feeling, it was much more like a lowering curse on the horizon, a precursor of disaster. The water began to bubble in the kettle, and Ivich opened her eyes.

"I'll make you some tea," said Mathieu. "Would you like some?"

"Tea?" said Ivich with an air of perplexity. "But you don't know how to make tea." With the flat of her hand she drew her curls back over her cheeks and got up, rubbing her eyes. "Give me the package," she said. "I'll make you some Russian tea. Only I shall want a samovar."

"I've only got a kettle," said Mathieu, handing her the package of tea.

"Oh dear, and it's Ceylon tea. Well, it can't be helped."

She busied herself over the kettle. "Where's the teapot?"

"Sorry," said Mathieu. And he ran to fetch the teapot from the kitchen."

"Thank you."

She still looked rather glum, but a little more animated. She poured the water into the teapot and then came back and sat down.

"We must let it stand," she said.

A silence followed, then she went on: "I don't like your apartment."

"So I thought," said Mathieu. "If you are feeling a bit better, we might go out."

"Where to?" said Ivich. "No," she went on, "I'm glad to be here. All those cafés were revolving round me; and the people are a nightmare. It's ugly here, but it's quiet. Couldn't you draw the curtains? What about lighting that little lamp?"

Mathieu got up. He closed the shutters and unhooked the curtain-loops. The heavy green curtains swung together. He lit the lamp on his writing-table.

"It's like night," said Ivich delightedly.

She set her back against the sofa cushions. "How nice this is! I feel as if the day were over. I want it to be dark when I leave here, I'm afraid of going back into daylight."

"You can stay as long as you like," said Mathieu. "No one is likely to come, and besides, if anyone does come, we'll let them ring without opening the door. I am entirely free."

It was not true. Marcelle was expecting him at eleven o'clock. He said to himself rather maliciously: "Let her wait."

"When are you leaving?"

"Tomorrow. There's a train at noon."

Mathieu stood for a moment silent. Then he said, carefully controlling his voice: "I'll go with you to the station."

"No!" said Ivich. "I loathe being seen off, it always

means a lot of feeble good-bys that stretch out like a length of indiarubber. Besides, I shall be utterly exhausted."

"As you like," said Mathieu. "Have you telegraphed to your parents?"

"No. I—Boris wanted to, but I wouldn't let him."

"So you'll have to tell them yourself."

Ivich bent her head. "Yes."

A silence followed. Mathieu looked at Ivich's bent head and fragile shoulders: he felt as though she were leaving him bit by bit.

"So," he said, "this is our last evening in the year."

"Ha!" she said, with an ironic laugh—"in the year!"

"Ivich," said Mathieu, "you really ought not. . . . In the first place, I'll come and see you at Laon."

"I won't have it. Everything connected with Laon is defiled."

"Well, you will come back."

"No."

"There's a course in November, your parents can't—"

"You don't know them."

"No. But they can't possibly wreck your whole life to punish you for having failed in an examination."

"They won't think of punishing me," said Ivich. "It will be worse than that; they will ignore me, I shall simply fade out of their minds. However, it's what I deserve," she said passionately. "I'm not capable of learning a job, and I would sooner stay at Laon all my life than begin the P.C.B. all over again."

"Don't say that," said Mathieu in alarm. "Don't resign yourself already. You loathe Laon."

"Indeed yes, I loathe it," she said with clenched teeth.

Mathieu got up to get the teapot and the cups. Suddenly the blood surged into his face; he turned towards her and murmured without looking at her:

"Look here, Ivich, you're going off tomorrow, but I give

you my word that you'll come back. At the end of October. Until then I'll see what can be done."

"You'll see what can be done?" said Ivich with weary astonishment; "but there's nothing to be done. I tell you I'm incapable of learning a job."

Mathieu turned his eyes to her doubtfully, but did not feel reassured. How was he to find words that would not irritate her?

"That's not what I meant to say. . . . If— If you had been willing to let me help you—"

Ivich still looked as if she did not understand.

Mathieu added: "I shall have a little money."

Ivich gave a sudden start. "So that's it," she said. And she added curtly: "Quite impossible."

"Not at all," said Mathieu warmly. "It's not by any means impossible. Listen: during the vacation I shall put a little money on one side. Odette and Jacques invite me every year to spend August at their villa at Juan-les-Pins. I have never been there, but I must accept some time. I'll go this year, it will amuse me, and I shall save money. . . . Don't refuse offhand," he said eagerly, "it would just be a loan."

He stopped. Ivich sat huddled on the sofa and was looking rather malevolently up at him.

"Don't look at me like that, Ivich."

"I don't know how I'm looking at you, but I know I've got a headache," said Ivich peevishly. She dropped her eyes and added: "I ought to go home to bed."

Ivich, do please listen: I'll find the money, you shall live in Paris—now don't say no. I beg you not to refuse without thinking it over. It can't inconvenience you in the least: you will pay me back when you are earning your living."

Ivich shrugged her shoulders, and Mathieu added eagerly: "Very well then, Boris shall repay me."

Ivich did not answer, she had buried her head in her

hands. Mathieu remained planted in front of her, angry and distraught.

"Ivich!"

She was still silent. He felt like taking her by the chin and forcing her head up.

"Ivich, you must answer me. Why don't you answer me?"

Ivich was silent. Mathieu began to pace up and down the room. He thought: "She will accept, I shan't let her go before she accepts. I—I'll do tutoring, or correct proofs."

"Ivich," he said, "you are please to tell me why you won't accept." It was sometimes possible to wear Ivich down: the method was to harry her with questions each pitched in a different key.

"Why won't you accept?" he said. "Say why you won't accept."

Ivich at last murmured, without lifting her head: "I won't accept your money."

"Why? You accept your parents' money willingly enough."

"That isn't the same thing."

"It certainly isn't the same thing. You have told me a hundred times that you detest them."

"I have no reason for accepting your money."

"Have you any reason for accepting theirs?"

"I don't want people to be generous to me," said Ivich. "When it's my father, I don't need to be grateful."

"Ivich," cried Mathieu, "what sort of pride is this? You haven't the right to wreck your life for a matter of dignity. Think of the life you will lead down there. You will regret every day and every hour that you refused."

Ivich's face became convulsed. "Let me go," she said, "let me go." And she added in a low, hoarse voice: "What a torment it is not to be rich! It gets one into such abject situations."

"But I don't understand you," said Mathieu quietly.

"You told me last month that money was something vile that one shouldn't bother about. You said you didn't care where it came from provided you had some."

Ivich shrugged her shoulders. Mathieu could no longer see anything but the top of her head and a patch of neck between the curls and the collar of her blouse. The neck was browner than the skin of her face.

"Didn't you say that?"

"I won't allow you to give me money."

Mathieu lost patience. "Oh, so it's because I'm a man," he said, with a sharp laugh.

"I beg your pardon?" said Ivich.

She looked at him with cold aversion. "That's offensive. I never thought of such a thing—and I certainly wouldn't let that worry me. I don't even imagine—"

"Very well, then. Think: for the first time in your life you would be absolutely free; you could live where you liked; you could do exactly as you pleased. You once told me you would like to take a degree in philosophy. Well, why not try? Boris and I would help you."

"Why do you want to do all this for me? I've never done anything for you. I—I've always been horrid to you, and now you're taking pity on me."

"I'm not taking pity on you."

"Then why do you offer me money?"

Mathieu hesitated; then he said, turning away: "I can't endure the idea of not seeing you again."

A silence fell; then Ivich said in a faltering voice: "You —you mean that your—motive for offering me the money is a selfish one?"

"Purely selfish," said Mathieu curtly. "I want to see you again, that's all."

He turned nervously towards her. She was looking at him with eyebrows uplifted and parted lips; then suddenly her tense mood seemed to relax.

"Perhaps I will," she said with indifference. "In that

case, it's your affair; we'll see. After all, you are right: it doesn't matter whether the money comes from here or elsewhere."

Mathieu drew a deep breath. "I've done it," he thought. But he did not feel much relieved: Ivich retained her sullen look.

"How are you going to get your parents to swallow all this?" he asked, by way of committing her yet further.

"I'll say something or other," said Ivich vaguely. "They'll believe me or they won't. What does it matter, since they won't be paying out any more money?"

She hung her head gloomily. "I shall have to go back home," she said.

Mathieu did his best to mask his irritation. "But you will be returning here."

"Oh," she said, "that's all in the air. I say no, I say yes, but I don't really believe in it at all. It's too remote. Whereas I know I shall be in Laon tomorrow evening."

She touched her throat and said: "I feel it there. I must go and pack soon. It will take me all night."

She got up. "The tea must be ready. Come and drink it."

She poured the tea into the cups. It was as black as coffee.

"I'll write to you," said Mathieu.

"I'll write too," she said, "but I shall have nothing to say."

"You can describe your house, and your room. I should like to be able to imagine you there."

"Oh, no!" she said. "I wouldn't care to talk about all that. It's quite enough to have to live there."

Mathieu thought of the curt little letters that Boris sent to Lola. But it was only for an instant: he looked at Ivich's hands, her crimson, pointed nails, and he thought: "I shall see her again."

"What strange tea!" said Ivich, putting her cup down.

Mathieu started: there was a ring at the front-door bell. He said nothing: he hoped that Ivich had not heard.

"Wasn't that a ring at the bell?" she asked.

Mathieu laid a finger on his lips. "We said just now that we wouldn't open the door," he whispered.

"Oh, but you must—you must," said Ivich in a high voice. "Perhaps it's important; open the door, quick."

Mathieu made his way to the door, thinking: "She hates the idea of any sort of bond between us." He opened the door just as Sarah was about to ring a second time.

"Good afternoon," said Sarah, quite out of breath. "You do keep me on the go. The little Minister told me you had telephoned, and here I am; I didn't even stop to put on a hat."

Mathieu looked at her with alarm: arrayed in an appalling apple-green dress, laughing with all her carious teeth, her hair in disorder, and beaming with unwholesome kindness, she reeked of catastrophe.

"Good afternoon," he said cheerfully. "I've got some-one—"

Sarah pushed him amicably aside and craned her head over his shoulder.

"Who is it?" she asked with greedy curiosity. "Oh, it's Ivich Serguine. How are you?"

Ivich got up and made a sort of bow. She looked rather put out. So, indeed, did Sarah. Ivich was the only person whom Sarah could not stand.

"How dreadfully thin you are!" said Sarah. "I'm sure you aren't eating enough, you don't look after yourself."

Mathieu confronted Sarah and eyed her fixedly. Sarah began to laugh.

"There's Mathieu looking very sternly at me," she said with a lively laugh. "He won't have me talk to you about diet." She turned towards Mathieu. "I came back late," she said. "Waldmann was not to be found anywhere. He hasn't been three weeks in Paris, and he's already involved in all sorts of shady affairs. It was six o'clock before I could get hold of him."

"How kind you are, Sarah—I'm truly grateful," said Mathieu. And he added briskly: "But we'll talk about all that later on. Will you have a cup of tea?"

"Indeed, no. I can't even sit down," she said; "I must dash along to the Spanish bookshop, they want to see me urgently, there's a friend of Gomez who has just arrived in Paris."

"Who is it?" asked Mathieu, by way of gaining time.

"I don't yet know. I was merely told a friend of Gomez. He comes from Madrid."

She gazed affectionately at Mathieu. There was a look of agonized kindness in her eyes.

"My poor Mathieu, I've got some bad news for you: he refuses."

"Hm!" But all the same Mathieu did bring himself to say: "You would like a word with me in private, no doubt?"

He frowned meaningly. But Sarah was not looking at him. "Oh, it's hardly worth while," she said gloomily. "I have almost nothing to tell you." And she added in a voice that vibrated with mystery: "I pressed him as hard as I could. Nothing doing. The person in question must be at his place tomorrow morning, with the money."

"All right. Well, it can't be helped; don't let's talk about it any more," said Mathieu briskly.

He stressed the last words, but Sarah was anxious to justify herself, and said:

"I did everything I could—I implored him to agree. He said: 'Is she a Jewess?' I said no. Then he said: 'I don't give credit. If she wants my help, she must pay for it. Otherwise, there are plenty of clinics in Paris.' "

Mathieu heard the sofa creak behind his back. Sarah continued: "He said: 'I will never give *them* credit, *they* made us suffer too much.' And it's true, you know, I can almost understand his attitude. He spoke of the Jews in Vienna, and the concentration camps. I wouldn't believe it. . . ." Her voice almost failed her. "They were martyred."

She paused, and a heavy silence followed. Then she continued, shaking her head: "So what will you do?"

"I don't know."

"You are not thinking of—"

"Yes," said Mathieu gloomily; "I imagine it will end in that."

"My dear Mathieu," said Sarah with emotion.

He looked at her coldly, and she, embarrassed, said no more; he observed something like a gleam of awareness kindle in her eyes.

"Very well, then," she said after a moment or two; "I must run away. Ring me up tomorrow morning without fail, I shall want to know."

"I will," said Mathieu. "Good-by, Sarah."

"Good-by, Ivich darling," cried Sarah from the door.

"Good-by, Madame," said Ivich.

When Sarah had gone, Mathieu went on pacing up and down the room. He was cold.

"That good creature," he said with a laugh, "is a hurricane. She comes in like a squall of wind, flings everything on the floor, and then whirls out again."

Ivich said nothing. Mathieu knew she would not answer. He came and sat down beside her and said, with averted eyes: "Ivich, I'm going to marry Marcelle."

There was a further silence. Mathieu looked at the heavy green curtains that masked the window. He was tired. He bent his head and went on, by way of explanation:

"She told me two days ago that she was pregnant."

The words emerged with difficulty. He did not venture to turn towards Ivich, but he knew she was looking at him.

"I wonder why you tell me," she said in a frozen voice. "These are your affairs."

Mathieu shrugged his shoulders and said: "You knew she was—"

"Your mistress?" said Ivich disdainfully. "I had better tell you that I don't pay much attention to that sort of thing." She hesitated, and then said, with a listless air: "I don't see why you should assume that devastated look. If you marry her, it's presumably because you want to. Otherwise, from what I hear, there are all sorts of ways—"

"I haven't any money," said Mathieu. "I have tried to raise some everywhere. . . ."

"So that's why you asked Boris to borrow five thousand francs from Lola?"

"Ah! You know? I didn't—well, yes, if you like, it was for that."

Ivich said in a toneless voice: "How sordid!"

"Yes."

"Anyway, it doesn't concern me," said Ivich. "You ought to know what you're about."

She drank up her tea and asked: "What time is it?"

"A quarter to nine."

"Is it dark?"

Mathieu went to the window and lifted the curtain. A murky light still filtered through the shutters.

"Not quite."

"Oh well, never mind," said Ivich, getting up; "I shall go all the same. I've got all my packing to do," she said in a tone of lamentation.

"Well—good-by," said Mathieu.

He felt no desire to detain her.

"Good-by."

"I shall see you again in October?"

It came out unawares. Ivich gave a violent start

"In October!" she said with flashing eyes. "In October No indeed!" She began to laugh. "Excuse me," she said, "but you look so odd. I never really thought of taking your money: you will need all you have to start housekeeping."

"Ivich!" said Mathieu, grasping her arm.

Ivich uttered a cry and shook his hand off.

"Let me go," she said. "Don't touch me."

Mathieu dropped his arms. He felt a desperate anger rising up within him.

"I suspected something of the kind," Ivich went on breathlessly. "Yesterday morning—when you had the impertinence to touch me—I said to myself: that's the way a married man behaves."

"That's enough," said Mathieu roughly. "You needn't say any more. I understand."

There she stood, face to face with him, red with anger, an insolent smile upon her lips; he was afraid of himself. He thrust her aside, flung himself out of the apartment, and slammed the front door behind him.

# CHAPTER XVI

*You know not how to love, you know not how.*
*In vain I love you so.*

THE Three Musketeers café gleamed through the faltering dusk with all its lights ablaze. A desultory crowd had assembled on the terrace outside. Soon the luminous network of the night would be stretched above Paris; these people were waiting for the night, listening to the band, and looking happy enough as they gathered gratefully round this first red glimmer of the night to come. Mathieu kept well away from this lyric crowd: the charm of the evening was not for him.

*You know not how to love, you know not how.*
*And you will never know.*

A long, straight street. Behind him, in a green room, a little malevolent consciousness obdurately repulsed him. Before him, in a pink room, a motionless woman awaited him with a smile of hope. In an hour's time he would walk softly into that pink room and gradually become enmeshed by all the gentle hope, the gratitude and love that he would find there. Men have drowned themselves for less than that.

"Look out, you damn fool!"

Mathieu flung himself forward to avoid the car; he tripped against the pavement and found himself on the ground. He had fallen on his hands.

"God damn it all!"

He got up, with smarting palms. Gravely he contemplated his muddy hands: the right one was quite black and bruised, the left was aching badly; his bandage was spattered with mud. "That's the last straw," he murmured solemnly. "That's the last straw." He pulled out his pocket-handkerchief, wetted it in his mouth, and rubbed the palms of his hands with a kind of odd solicitude; he felt like shedding tears. There followed a moment of suspense, in which he looked himself over with amazement. Then he burst out laughing. He laughed at himself, at Marcelle, at Ivich, at his own ridiculous clumsiness, his life, his shabby passions; he recalled his former hopes and laughed at them too, because they had culminated in *this*, in this solemn personage who had been on the point of shedding tears because he had fallen down; he looked at himself with no sort of shame, with a cold intense amusement, and he thought: "To think I used to take myself seriously." The laughter stopped after a few final gasps: there was no one left to laugh.

Empty space. The body started off again, heavy and hot, with tremors and flushes of anger assailing the throat and stomach. But no one inhabited that body now. The streets were emptied as though their contents had been poured down a sink; something that awhile ago had filled them had been swallowed up. The usual objects were still there, intact, but they had all become disrupted, they hung down from the sky like enormous stalactites, or towered upwards like fantastic dolmens. All their usual little appeals, their shrill cicada-chirpings, had vanished into thin

air and were silent. A man's future had once challenged
them, and they met it with a scatter of diverse temptations.
That future was dead.

The body turned to the right and plunged into a luminous haze at the far end of a noisome cleft, between ice-
blocks streaked by intermittent flashes. Dark masses
creaked as they crawled past. At the level of the eyes
swung a line of furry flowers. Between these flowers, in
the depths of the crevasse, glided a transparency that contemplated itself with frozen fury.

"I'll go and get it!" The world resumed its shape—a
noisy, bustling world, of cars and people and shop-
windows. Mathieu discovered himself in the middle of
the rue du Départ. But it was no longer the same world,
nor quite the same Mathieu. At the far end of the world,
beyond the buildings and the streets, there was a closed
door. He searched in his pocketbook and produced a key.
Yonder the closed door, here the small flat key: these were
the sole objects in this world; between them, nothing but
a medley of obstacles and distances. "In one hour. There's
time for me to walk." One hour; just time to get to the door
and open it; beyond that hour there was nothing. Mathieu
walked with a measured stride, inwardly at peace, intent
upon evil and yet unperturbed. "Suppose Lola had stayed
in bed?" He put the key back into his pocket and said:
"Oh well, it can't be helped: I should take the money just
the same."

The lamp shone dimly. Near the attic window, between
the photos of Marlene Dietrich and of Robert Taylor,
hung an advertisement-calendar bearing a small and
rather tarnished mirror. Daniel approached it and, bending down a little, set about retying the knot of his necktie;
he was in a hurry to get himself dressed. In the mirror,
behind him, almost effaced by the half-darkness and the
white discolorations on the mirror, he could see Ralph's

haggard, harsh profile, and his hands began to tremble: he longed to squeeze that thin neck with its protuberant Adam's apple and feel it crack beneath his fingers. Ralph turned his head towards the glass—he did not know that Daniel was looking at him—and eyed him with a queer expression. "He's looking positively murderous," thought Daniel with a shiver—almost, in fact, almost a shiver of enjoyment—"he's hurt in his little masculine pride, he hates me." He took time over knotting his tie. Ralph was still looking at him, and Daniel was enjoying the hatred that united them, a rejuvenated hatred that seemed to date back twenty years, a veritable possession; he felt the purer for it. "One day a fellow like that will come and knock me out from behind." The youthful face would expand in the mirror, and that would be the end—the infamous death that was his due. He swung suddenly around, and Ralph promptly lowered his eyes. The room was a furnace.

"You haven't got a towel?"

Daniel's hands were moist.

"There may be one in the water-jug."

In the water-jug there was in fact a dirty towel. Daniel wiped his hands carefully.

"There has never been any water in that water-jug. You don't appear to wash much, either of you."

"We wash under the faucet in the passage," said Ralph in a surly tone. After a pause he added: "It's more convenient."

He slipped on his shoes, sitting on the edge of the truckle bed, his torso bent and his right knee raised. Daniel looked at the slim back, and the young muscular arms protruding from the short-sleeved Lacoste shirt: "he has charm," he thought dispassionately. But he loathed that very charm. In an instant he would be outside, and all this would be over. But he knew what awaited him outside. Just as he was putting on his jacket he hesitated; his shoulders and chest were bathed in sweat, he realized with annoyance that the weight of the coat would make his linen shirt stick to his damp flesh.

"It's disgustingly hot in here," he said to Ralph.

"We're right under the roof."

"What time is it?"

"Nine o'clock. Just struck."

Ten hours to kill before daylight. He could not go to bed after that sort of episode, it always upset him much more if he did. Ralph looked up.

"I wanted to ask you, Monsieur Lalique—was it you who advised Bobby to go back to his druggist?"

"Advised? No. I told him he was a fool to have walked out on him."

"Aha! That's not the same thing. He came and told me this morning that he was going to apologize, that it was you who wanted him to, but he didn't look as though he was telling the truth."

"I don't want him to do anything," said Daniel, "and I certainly didn't tell him to apologize."

They both smiled contemptuously. Daniel was on the point of putting on his jacket, but his heart failed him.

"I said do as you like," said Ralph, bending down again. "It's not my business. If that's what Monsieur Lalique advised—but I see what it is now."

He tugged savagely at the lace of his left shoe.

"I shan't say anything to him," said he, "he's like that, he can't help telling lies. But there's one chap I swear I'll catch by the short hairs."

"The druggist?"

"Yes. Not the old one. The young chap."

"The assistant?"

"Yes. That's the brute. You know what he said about Bobby and me. Bobby can't have much pride to go back to that hole. Mark my words, I'll be waiting for that chap one evening when he leaves the shop."

He smiled an evil smile, in enjoyment of his own anger.

"I'll just stroll up with my hands in my pockets and a nasty look in my eye. 'You recognize me, do you? Good! What's this you've been saying about me, eh? What have you been saying about me?' And the chap will answer: 'I didn't say anything. I didn't say anything.' 'Oh, didn't you!' Then a jab in the stomach that'll knock him over, and I'll jump on him and bash his mug against the pavement."

Daniel eyed him with ironical disfavor; he thought: "They're all alike." All. Except Bobby, who was a female. *Afterwards* they always talked about smashing someone's face. Ralph was becoming excited, his eyes were gleaming and his ears were scarlet; he felt impelled to make abrupt and vivid gestures. Daniel could not resist the desire to humiliate him still further.

"But perhaps he'll knock you out."

"Ha?" jeered Ralph. "Let him come along. You've only got to ask the waiter at the Oriental; he'll tell you. A chap about thirty with tremendous arms. He said he was going to throw me out."

Daniel smiled offensively. "And you just ate him up, of course."

"Ask anyone you like," said Ralph indignantly. "There were about ten of them looking on. 'You come outside,' I said to him. There was Bobby and a big chap, I've seen you with him—Corbin, works at the slaughterhouse. So he went out. 'Want to teach a grown man how to behave, eh?' says he to me. So I let him have it. I socked him one in the eye to begin with and then when he came back for another, jabbed him with my elbow. Just like that. Flat on the nose." He had got up and began to mimic the episodes of the encounter. He swung around, displaying his firm small buttocks under his tight-fitting blue trousers. Daniel was seized by an access of rage and longed to knock him down. "He was pissing blood," continued Ralph, "so I grabbed his legs and tipped him over. And my friend, the grown man, didn't know where he was when I'd done with him."

He paused, malevolent and swollen with pride, sheltering now behind his deed of glory. He looked like an insect. "I wish I could kill him" thought Daniel. He did not really believe these stories, but it none the less humiliated him to think that Ralph had knocked down a man of thirty. He began to laugh.

"Mind how you throw your weight about," he said slowly. "You'll get what's coming to you one of these days."

"I don't throw my weight about," he said, "but it isn't the big chaps I'm afraid of."

"So," said Daniel, "you aren't afraid of anyone, eh? Not of anyone?"

Ralph flushed. "The big chaps aren't the strongest," he said.

"And what about you? Let's see how strong you are," said Daniel, pushing him. "Just let's see."

Ralph stood for a moment with his mouth open, then his eyes glittered.

"As it's you, I don't mind. For fun, of course," he said in a sibilant voice. "And no dirty business. You won't get the best of it."

Daniel grabbed him by the belt. "I'll show you, baby mine."

Ralph was lithe and sinewy; his muscles rippled under Daniel's hands. They wrestled in silence, and Daniel began to pant, he figured himself somehow as a tall fellow wearing a mustache. Ralph finally managed to lift him off his feet, but Daniel thrust both hands into his face, and Ralph let go. They stood confronting each other, each with a venomous smile upon his face.

"So you would, would you!" said Ralph in a strange voice. He made a sudden dash at Daniel with his head down. Daniel dodged his head and grabbed him by the back of the neck. He was already out of breath. Ralph did not look in the least tired. They clinched again and began to revolve in the middle of the room. Daniel was aware of a sour and feverish taste at the back of his mouth. "I must finish him off or he'll do me in." He pushed at Ralph with all his strength, but Ralph resisted. Daniel was possessed by a maniacal fury as he thought: "I'm making a fool of myself." He bent down suddenly, seized Ralph by the small of his back, lifted him, flung him on the bed, and with the same impulse fell on top of him. Ralph struggled and tried to scratch, but Daniel seized his wrists and held them down on the bolster. Thus they remained for several moments. Daniel was too exhausted to get up. Ralph lay immovable and helpless, with the weight of a man—another grown man—flattening him out.

"Well, who had the best of that?" gasped Daniel. "Who had the best of that, my little friend?"

Ralph promptly smiled and said slyly: "You're a strong fellow, Monsieur Lalique."

Daniel released him and rose to his feet. He was out of breath and felt humiliated. His heart was throbbing violently.

"I used to be a strong fellow," he said. "At the moment I can hardly get my wind."

Ralph was on his feet, straightening his collar, and breathing naturally. He tried to laugh, but he evaded Daniel's eyes.

"Wind isn't what matters," he said generously. "It's training."

They both grinned with an air of embarrassment. Daniel longed to take Ralph by the throat and dash his fist into his face. He slipped on his coat again; his shirt, soaked as it was with sweat, stuck to his skin.

"Well," he said, "I must be off. Good-by."

"Good-by, Monsieur Lalique."

"I've hidden something for you in the room," said Daniel. "Look for it carefully and you'll find it."

The door closed. Daniel walked rather unsteadily downstairs. "First and foremost I must get a wash," he thought; "wash myself from head to foot." As he emerged into the street, a thought suddenly came upon him and brought him up short: he had shaved that morning before going out, and he had left his razor on the mantelpiece, wide open.

As he opened the door, Mathieu released the muffled tinkle of a bell. "I didn't notice it this morning," he thought: "I suppose they connect it up in the evening, after nine o'clock." He flung a sidelong glance through the glass door of the office and saw a shadow: there was someone there. He walked sedately up to the keyboard. Room 21. The key was hanging from a nail. Mathieu took it quickly and slipped it into his pocket, then turned and approached the staircase. A door opened behind his back. "They're going to stop me," he thought. He was not afraid: this had been foreseen.

"Hello there! Where are you going?" said a harsh voice.

Mathieu turned. It was a tall thin woman with eyeglasses. She looked important and suspicious. Mathieu smiled at her.

"Where are you going?" she repeated. "Couldn't you inquire at the office?"

Bolivar. The Negro's name was Bolivar.

"I'm going to see Monsieur Bolivar, on the third floor," said Mathieu quietly.

"Ah! And why were you nosing round the keyboard?" said the woman suspiciously.

"I was looking to see if his key was there."

"And isn't it?"

"No. He's in," said Mathieu.

The woman went up to the board. One chance in two.

"Yes," she said, with an air of disappointment and relief. "He's in."

Mathieu walked upstairs without replying. On the third landing he stopped for a moment, then he slipped the key into the lock of number twenty-one and opened the door. The room was plunged in darkness. A red darkness that smelt of fever and scent. He locked the door behind him and went up to the bed. At first he held out his hands in front of him so as not to bump into anything, but he soon became accustomed to the dimness. The bed was unmade; there were two pillows on the bolster, still hollowed by the weight of heads. Mathieu knelt down by the suitcase and opened it; he was aware of a faint desire to be sick. The bills he had dropped that morning had fallen on the packages of letters: Mathieu took five; he did not want to steal anything for his own benefit. "What am I going to do with the key?" He hesitated for a moment and then decided to leave it in the lock of the suitcase. As he got up he noticed, at the far end of the room, a door that he had not seen that morning. He went and opened it: it was a dressing-room. Mathieu struck a match and saw his face, gilded by the flame, appear in a mirror. He looked at himself until the flame went out, then he dropped the match and went back into the bedroom. He could now clearly distinguish the furniture, Lola's clothes, her pajamas, her dressing-gown, her coat and skirt, carefully laid out on chairs and suitcases; he laughed a curt, malicious laugh and went out.

The corridor was deserted, but he could hear the sound of footsteps and laughter, there were people coming upstairs. He half-turned to go back into the room; but no: he did not in the least mind if he were caught. He slipped the key into the lock and double-locked the door. When he stood up again, he saw a woman followed by a soldier.

"It's on the fourth floor," said the woman.

And the soldier said: "It's a long way up."

Mathieu let them pass and then went down. He reflected with amusement that the hardest part was yet to come: the key would have to be replaced on the board.

On the first floor he stopped and leaned over the banisters. The woman was standing in the entrance doorway, with her back towards him, and looking out into the street. Mathieu walked noiselessly down the last few stairs, hung the key on its nail, then tiptoed up again to the first landing, waited a moment, and marched heavily down the staircase. The woman turned, and he greeted her as he passed.

"Good evening, madame."

"Evening," she mumbled.

He went out, feeling the weight of the woman's look upon his back, and he wanted to laugh.

*Dead the beast, dead the poison.* He walks with long strides, feeling rather weak in the legs. He is afraid, his mouth is dry. The streets are too blue, the air is too soft. *The flame runs along the fuse, with a barrel of powder at the end of it.* He dashes upstairs four steps at a time. He finds it difficult to put the key into the lock, his hand shakes. Two cats dart between his legs; they are afraid of him just now. *Dead the beast. . . .*

The razor is there, on the night-table, wide open. He picks it up by the handle and looks at it. The handle is black, the blade is white. *The flame runs along the fuse.* He slips his finger down the edge of the blade, he feels at the tip of his finger the acid savor of a cut, he shudders: it is *my hand* that must do it all. The razor does not help, it lies inert, weighing no more than an insect in the hand. He takes a few steps into the room, looking for support or for a sign. Everything is inert and silent. Table and chairs are all inert, afloat in a motionless light. He alone is erect, he alone alive in the oppressively blue light. Nothing will help me, nothing will happen. The cats are scratching in the kitchen. He leans his hand upon the table, it responds to his pressure with an equal pressure, no more, no less. Objects are servile. Submissive. Subject to control. *My hand* will do it all. He yawns, from anguish and from boredom; but mainly from boredom. He is alone upon the scene. Nothing impels him to decide, nothing stops him from doing so: he alone must decide. His act is purely negative. That red flower between his legs— *it is not there;* that red stain on the floor, *it is not there.* He looks at the floor. The floor is an even, smooth expanse: nowhere is there room for any mark. *I shall be lying on the floor, inert, my trousers torn and sticky; the razor will be on the floor, red, jagged, and inert.* He is spellbound by the razor, by the floor: if only he could picture them vividly enough—the red stain and the gash, vividly enough to bring them into being without his having to commit that act. Pain—I can bear it. I long for it, I welcome it. But it's the act—*that act.* He looks at the floor, then at the blade. In vain: the air is soft, the room is softly lit, the razor gleams softly, weighs softly in his hand. An act, an act is needed, the moment rocks upon the first drop of blood. It is my hand, *my hand* that must do it all.

He goes to the window, he looks at the sky. He draws the curtains: with his left hand. He switches on the light: with his left hand. He transfers the razor to his left. He takes out his pocketbook and produces five thousand-franc notes. He takes an envelope from his desk and puts the money into the envelope. He writes on the envelope: "For M. Delarue, 12 rue Huyghens." He places the envelope conspicuously on the table. He gets up, he walks, the beast is lying close against his stomach, the beast is sucking at him, he can feel it. Yes or no. He is caught in the trap. He must decide. He has all night for doing so. Alone in confrontation with himself. All night. His right hand recovers the razor. He is afraid of his hand, he watches it: quite stiff at the extremity of his arm. And he says: "Now!"

A little laughing shiver runs up him from the small of the back to his neck. "Now—finish it!" If only he could *find himself with his throat cut*, as a man finds himself on his legs in the morning, when the alarm has sounded, without knowing how he got there. But first that foul and filthy act must be done, carefully and patiently he must undo his buttons. The inertness of the razor passes into his hand, into his arm. A warm and living body with an arm of stone. The huge arm of a statue, inert, frozen, with a razor at the tip of it. He loosens his grip. The razor falls on the table.

The razor is there, on the table, open. Nothing has changed. He can reach out a hand and pick it up. The razor, inert still, will obey. There is yet time; there will be plenty of time, I have all night. He walks across the room. He does not hate himself, he now wants nothing, he is adrift in a void. The beast is there, between his legs, erect and rigid. How loathsome! Well, my young friend, if it disgusts you too much, the razor lies there, on the table. *Dead the beast.* . . . The razor. The razor. He walks round and round the table without taking his eyes off the razor. Will nothing stop me from picking it up? Nothing. The room and all in it are inert and quiet. He reaches out a hand, he touches the blade. *My hand will do it all.* He leaps back, opens the door, and dashes out on the staircase. One of his cats darts wildly downstairs in front of him.

Daniel ran out into the street. Up above, the door stood wide open, the lamp was still alight, and the razor on the table: the cats were prowling about the dark stairway. There was nothing to prevent him from retracing his steps and going back. The room was awaiting him, submissive to his will. Nothing had been decided, nothing ever would be decided. He must run, he must get away as far as possible, immerse himself in noise and light, in a throng of people. he must become a man among his fellows and feel the eyes of other men upon him. He ran all the way to the Roi Olaf and pushed open the door, gasping for breath.

"Bring me a whisky," he panted.

His heart was shaken by heavy throbs that reached to the tips of his fingers, there was an inky taste in his mouth. He sat down in an alcove at the far end.

"You look tired," said the waiter with a respectful air. He was a tall Norwegian who spoke French without a trace of accent. He looked genially at Daniel, and Daniel felt himself transformed into a rich, eccentric client who could be relied on for a good tip. He smiled.

"I'm rather out of sorts," he explained, "a little feverish."

The waiter nodded and departed. Daniel relapsed into his solitude. His room awaited him up yonder, all prepared, the door stood wide open, the razor glittered on the table. "I shall never be able to go back home." He would drink for as long as he felt inclined. On the stroke of four the waiter, assisted by the bartender, would put him into a taxi, as always happened on these occasions.

The waiter returned with a half-filled glass and a bottle of Perrier water.

"Just as you like it," he said.

"Thank you."

Daniel was alone in this very ordinary, quiet café, all around him a froth of amber light, and amber gleams from the wood of the partitions, which were plastered with thick varnish, sticky to the touch. He poured the Perrier water into his glass, the whisky sparkled for a moment, busy bubbles mounted to the surface, like a throng of eager gossips, and then the little agitation subsided, Daniel eyed the yellow, viscous liquid, still faintly flecked with effervescence: it looked very like flat beer. At the bar, out of his sight, the waiter and the bartender were talking in Norwegian.

"More drink!"

With a sudden stroke he swept the glass off the table, and sent it crashing to the floor. The bartender and the waiter promptly stopped their conversation; Daniel leaned down beneath the table: the liquid was oozing slowly over the tiled floor, thrusting out tentacles towards the foot of an adjacent chair.

The waiter hurried up.

"How clumsy of me!" lamented Daniel with a smile.

"Shall I get you another?" asked the waiter. He had bent down with back outstretched to mop up the liquid and collect the fragments of the glass.

"Yes.—No," said Daniel brusquely. "It's a warning," he added in a jocular tone. "I mustn't take any liquor this evening. Bring me another small Perrier with a slice of lemon."

The waiter departed. Daniel felt more composed. An impenetrable present had begun to encompass him once more. The smell of ginger, amber light, and wood partitions.

"Thanks."

The waiter had opened the bottle and half-filled the glass. Daniel drank and put the glass down. "I knew it," he thought. "I knew I wouldn't do it." While he was striding through the streets and dashing upstairs four steps at a time, he knew he would not actually do the deed; he knew it when he picked up the razor, he had not deceived himself for one second—wretched comedian that he was! All that had happened was that, in the outcome, he had succeeded in frightening himself and had fled in disorder. He picked up his glass and gripped it: with all his might he longed to loathe himself, he would never find so good an opportunity. "Beast!—coward and comedian: beast!" For an instant he thought he would succeed, but no— these were mere words. He ought to have— Ah, no matter who it was, he would have accepted any person's judgment, no matter whose, so it were not his own, not that ghastly self-contempt, that utterly futile, weak, moribund self-contempt, which seemed at every moment on the point of self-annihilation, but always survived. If only someone knew, if he could feel upon him the weight of *someone else's* contempt. "But I never shall, I would sooner castrate myself." He looked at his watch, eleven o'clock, eight more hours to kill before morning. Time no longer flowed on.

Eleven o'clock! He gave a sudden start. "Mathieu is with Marcelle. She's talking to him. At this very moment, she is talking to him, she puts her arms round his neck and thinks him deplorably slow in declaring himself. . . . This too; I did it." He began to tremble all over: "he will give way, he will end by yielding, I have wrecked his life."

He had relinquished his glass, he was on his feet, staring into vacancy, he cannot despise himself nor yet forget himself. He wishes he were dead and he exists, he obstinately maintains his own existence. He wants to be dead, he thinks he wants to be dead, he thinks that he thinks he wants to be dead. . . . *There is a way.*

He had spoken aloud, the waiter hurried up.

"Did you call me?"

"Yes," said Daniel, absent-mindedly. "That's for yourself."

He threw a hundred francs on the table. There is a way. A way to settle everything. He stood erect and walked briskly towards the door. "An admirable way." He laughed shortly: he was always amused when he found occasion to play a little trick upon himself.

# CHAPTER XVII

MATHIEU closed the door quietly, lifting it slightly on its hinges so that it should make no noise, then he set his foot on the first step of the staircase, bent down, and unlaced his shoes. His chest was almost touching his knee. He removed his shoes, held them in his left hand, got up, and laid his right hand on the banisters, looking upwards at the pale pink haze that seemed to hover in the shadows. He passed no more judgments on himself. Slowly he climbed up into the darkness, treading carefully to avoid making the stairs creak.

The door of the room was ajar; he pushed it open. The room smelt oppressive. All the heat of the day had settled into its depths, like the lees in a bottle. On the bed sat a woman watching him with a smile: Marcelle. She had put on her elegant white dressing-gown with the gilded cord, she was carefully made-up, and her expression was composed and cheerful. Mathieu shut the door behind him and stood motionless, his arms hanging loosely by his sides, the unbearable delight of mere existence had caught him by the throat. He was *there*, he was finding his fulfillment *there*, in the presence of this smiling lady, immersed in this odor of sickness, candy, and love. Marcelle had thrown her head back and was now surveying him maliciously through half-closed eyelids. He returned her smile and deposited his shoes in the wardrobe. A voice swollen with affection sighed at his back:

"Darling."

He turned abruptly around and leaned back against the wardrobe.

"Hello!" he said in an undertone.

Marcelle raised a hand to the level of her temple and flickered her fingers. "Hello, hello!"

She got up, came and put her arms round his neck, and kissed him, slipping her tongue into his mouth. She had darkened her eyelids.

"You are hot," she said, stroking his neck.

She looked him up and down, her head tilted slightly back, darting her tongue out between her teeth, with an air of vivacity and joy; she was beautiful. Mathieu gloomily recalled Ivich's emaciated plainness.

"You are very gay," he said. "Yesterday, on the telephone, you didn't sound as if things were going at all well."

"No. I was being silly. But they are going well enough today, very well indeed, in fact."

"Did you have a good night?"

"I slept like a dormouse."

She kissed him again, he felt upon his lips the rich velvet of her mouth, and then that smooth, warm, darting nakedness—her tongue. Gently he disengaged himself. Marcelle was naked under her dressing-gown, he could see her shapely breasts, and there was a taste of sugar in her mouth. She took his hand and drew him towards the bed.

"Come and sit beside me."

He sat down at her side. She still held his hand in hers, squeezing it with little awkward jerks, and Mathieu felt as though the warmth of those hands was penetrating to his armpits.

"It's very hot in here," he said.

She did not reply, she devoured him with her eyes, her lips were parted, and there was a humble and appealing look upon her face. He slipped his left hand across his stomach and stealthily felt in his right-hand hip pocket for his tobacco. Marcelle noticed the hand in transit and uttered a little cry:

"Oh! But what's the matter with your hand?"

"I cut myself."

Marcelle let go Mathieu's right hand and grabbed the other as it passed; she turned it over like a pancake and looked at the palm.

"But your bandage is horribly dirty, you'll get blood-poisoning! And there's mud on it, how did that get there?"

"I fell down."

She laughed a shocked, indulgent laugh. " 'I cut myself, I fell down'! Silly boy! What on earth have you been up to? Wait a minute, I'll put that bandage straight for you; you can't go about like that."

She unbound Mathieu's hand and nodded. "It's a nasty wound, how did it happen? Have you been fighting?"

"Of course not. It was yesterday evening, at the Sumatra."

"At the Sumatra?"

Broad, pale cheeks, golden hair; tomorrow—tomorrow I'll do my hair like that to please you.

"It was some nonsense of Boris's," he replied. "He had bought a dagger, and challenged me to stick it in my hand."

"And you, of course, promptly did so. But you're completely dotty, my poor darling, these rotten friends of yours will make an utter fool of you if you aren't careful. Look at that poor ravaged paw."

Mathieu's hand lay inert between her two burning hands; the wound looked repulsive, with its black and pulpy scab. Marcelle slowly lifted the hand to the level of her face, looked at it fixedly, then suddenly bent down and laid her lips upon the wound in a transport of humility. "What can be the matter with her?" he wondered. He drew her towards him and kissed her on the ear.

"Are you loving me?" asked Marcelle.

"Of course."

"You don't look as if you were."

Mathieu smiled and did not answer. She rose and went to get her box of dressings from the wardrobe. She had her back to him, she was standing on tiptoe and lifting her arms to reach the top shelf; her sleeves had slipped down her arms. Mathieu looked at the lovely arms he had so often caressed, and all the old desires awakened within him. Marcelle came towards him with a sort of cumbrous briskness.

"Give me your paw."

She had poured some alcohol on a small sponge and began to clean his hand. He felt against his hip the faint glow of that too familiar body.

"Now lick that!"

Marcelle held out to him a bit of sticking plaster. He put out his tongue and obediently licked the pink transparency. Marcelle applied the patch of plaster to the skin; she then picked up the old bandage and held it for a moment in her fingertips, eying it with amused disgust.

"What am I to do with this loathsome object? When you have gone, I'll go and throw it in the rubbish bin."

She deftly bound up the hand with a length of clean white gauze.

"So Boris challenged you, did he? And you made a mess of your hand. You silly old boy! And did he do the same?"

"Not he!" said Mathieu.

Marcelle laughed. "So he made a pretty sort of fool of you!"

She had stuck a safety-pin in her mouth, and was tearing the gauze with both hands. She said, compressing her lips on the pin: "Was Ivich there?"

"When I cut myself?"

"Yes."

"No. She was dancing with Lola."

Marcelle stuck the pin into the bandage. There was a smear of vermilion from her lips on the steel shank.

"There. That's all right now. Did you have a good time?"

"Not bad."

"Is the Sumatra a nice place? I do wish you would take me there one of these days."

"But it would tire you," said Mathieu rather irritably.

"Oh, just for once—we would make an occasion of it, it's so long since I've had an evening out with you anywhere."

An evening out! Mathieu angrily repeated the too conjugal phrase: Marcelle was not tactful in her choice of words.

"Will you?" said Marcelle.

"Look here," he said, "it couldn't be before autumn anyway: you must look after yourself properly just now, and besides the place will soon be closing for the summer as usual. Lola is going on tour in North Africa."

"Well, then, we'll go in the autumn. Is that a promise?"

"Yes."

Marcelle coughed with embarrassment. "I can see you're a bit annoyed with me."

"Annoyed?"

"Yes. . . . I was very tiresome the day before yesterday."

"Not at all. Why?"

"Indeed I was. I was upset."

"Well, that was natural. It's all my fault, my poor darling."

"You're not in the least to blame," she exclaimed cheerfully, "you never have been."

He did not dare to look at her, he could picture only too clearly the expression on her face, he could not endure that inexplicable and unmerited air of confidence. There was a long silence: she certainly expected a word of affection, a word of forgiveness. Mathieu could hold out no longer.

"Look," he said.

He produced his pocketbook and laid it open on his knees. Marcelle craned her neck to look and set her chin on Mathieu's shoulder.

"What am I to look at?"

"This."

He took the notes out of the pocketbook:

"One, two, three, four, five," said he, crackling them triumphantly. They were still odorous of Lola. Mathieu waited a moment, with the notes on his knees, and as Marcelle did not utter a word, he turned towards her. She had raised her head, she was looking at the notes and blinking. She did not seem to understand. Then she said slowly:

"Five thousand francs."

Mathieu airily dropped the notes on the table by the bed.

"Yes indeed," he said. "Five thousand francs. I had some trouble in raising the money."

Marcelle did not answer. She bit her under lip and looked at the notes with an air of incredulity; she had suddenly aged. She looked at Mathieu with a sad but still confiding air. And she said: "I thought—"

Mathieu interrupted her and said briskly: "You'll be able to go to the Jew. It seems he's famous. Hundreds of women in Vienna have been through his hands. Women in good society, wealthy patients."

The light in Marcelle's eyes went out. "Good," she said. "Good."

She had taken a safety-pin out of the box of dressings and was nervously opening and shutting it.

Mathieu added: "I'll leave the money with you. I imagine Sarah will take you to him, and you will pay the fee, he wants to be paid in advance, confound him."

There was silence, and then Marcelle asked: "Where did you get the money?"

"Guess," said Mathieu.

"Daniel?"

He shrugged his shoulders: she knew quite well that Daniel had refused to lend a penny.

"Jacques?"

"Certainly not. I told you yesterday on the telephone."

"Then I give it up," she said curtly. "Who?"

"No one *gave* it to me," he said.

Marcelle smiled faintly: "You're not going to tell me that you stole the money?"

"That's just what I did."

"You stole it," she replied with bewilderment. "It isn't true?"

"It is. From Lola."

A silence followed. Mathieu wiped the perspiration from his forehead.

"I'll tell you all about it," he said.

"You stole it!" repeated Marcelle slowly.

Her face had turned gray; with eyes averted, she said: "How you must have wanted to get rid of the child!"

"What I did want was to prevent you going to that old woman."

She pondered; her mouth had resumed its hard and cynical expression.

"Do you blame me," he asked, "for having stolen the money?"

"Good heavens, no."

"Then what's the matter?"

With a sudden movement of her hand Marcelle knocked the box of dressings on to the floor. They both looked at it, and Mathieu thrust it aside with his foot. Slowly Marcelle turned her head towards him, she looked astonished.

"Tell me what's the matter," repeated Mathieu.

She laughed shortly.

"What are you laughing at?"

"At myself," she said.

She had taken the flower from her hair and was twirling it in her fingers. She murmured: "What a fool I've been!"

Her face had hardened. She sat with her mouth open as though she wanted to speak to him, but the words would not come: she seemed to be afraid of what she had in mind to say. Mathieu took her hand, but she drew it away. She said, without looking at him: "I know you have seen Daniel."

It was out! She had jerked herself backwards and was convulsively clutching the sheets; she looked both frightened and relieved. Mathieu also felt relieved: all the cards were on the table; they must go through with it now. They had all night before them.

"Yes, I've seen him," said Mathieu. "How did you know? I suppose it was you who sent him? You fixed it all up between you, eh?"

"Don't talk so loud," said Marcelle, "you'll wake my mother. It wasn't I who sent him, but I knew he wanted to see you."

"How rotten of you!" said Mathieu regretfully.

"Oh yes; it was rotten of me," said Marcelle bitterly.

They were silent: Daniel was there, he was sitting between them.

"Well," said Mathieu, "we must have a frank explanation. That's all we can do now."

"There's nothing to explain," said Marcelle. "You have seen Daniel. He told you what he had to tell you, and you promptly went off and stole five thousand francs from Lola."

"Yes. And you have been receiving Daniel secretly for

months past. There are plenty of things to be explained, you see. Look here," he said, brusquely, "what went wrong the day before yesterday?"

"The day before yesterday?"

"Don't pretend not to understand. Daniel told me that you were hurt by my attitude on that day."

"Never mind now," she said. "Don't you worry about that."

"Please don't be obstinate, Marcelle," said Mathieu. "I assure you I mean well, I'll admit anything that I shouldn't have done. But tell me what went wrong the day before yesterday. We should get on so much better if we could recover a little confidence in each other."

She hesitated; she was looking sullen and rather listless.

"Please," he said, taking her hand.

"Well—it was just as usual, you couldn't be serious about what was in my mind."

"And what was in your mind?"

"Why do you want to make me say? You know quite well."

"Yes," said Mathieu, "I think I know."

He thought: "That's done it, I shall marry her." All was now clear. "I must indeed have been a swine to imagine I could get out of it." She was there, she was in distress, she was wretched and resentful, only one gesture was needed to restore her peace of mind. He said:

"You want us to get married, don't you?"

She snatched her hand away and leaped to her feet. He looked at her with bewilderment: she had turned sickly pale and her lips were quivering:

"Yes. . . . Was it Daniel told you that?"

"No," said Mathieu, disconcerted. "But that's what I assumed."

"That's what you assumed!" she laughed. "That's what you assumed! Daniel told you I was upset, and you assumed I wanted to get married. So that's what you think of me, Mathieu, after seven years."

Her hands too had now begun to tremble. Mathieu longed to take her in his arms, but did not dare.

"You are right," he said. "I oughtn't to have thought that."

She seemed not to hear.

"Look here," he went on; "there were excuses for me: Daniel had just told me you were seeing him without letting me know."

She still did not answer, and he added gently: "I suppose you want to have the baby?"

"That," said Marcelle, "is no concern of yours. What I want is no longer any concern of yours."

"Please," said Mathieu. "There is still time. . . ."

She shook her head. "That's not true, there isn't time."

"But why, Marcelle? Why won't you talk things over with me quietly? An hour would be enough: everything could be settled and cleared up. . . ."

"I won't."

"But why? Why?"

"Because I no longer respect you. And also because you don't love me any more."

She had spoken with assurance, but she herself was surprised and frightened by what she had just said; there was nothing now in her eyes but an uneasy interrogation. She continued in a melancholy voice: "If you think like that of me, you must have completely ceased to love me. . . ."

It was almost a question. If he took her in his arms, if he told her that he loved her, the situation might yet be saved. He would marry her, they would have the child, they would live side by side for the rest of their lives. He had got up; he was about to say to her: "I love you." He swayed slightly, and then said in a clear voice:

"Well, it's true—I no longer love you."

Some while after the words had been spoken he still heard them, to his amazement. And he thought: "That's the end of everything." Marcelle had started back, uttering a cry of triumph, but almost immediately she laid her hand to her mouth and signed to him to be silent.

"Mother—" she murmured anxiously.

They both stood listening, but could hear no sound but the distant mutter of traffic.

"Marcelle," said Mathieu, "I still care for you very deeply. . . ."

Marcelle laughed disdainfully. "Of course. Only you care—differently. Is that what you mean?"

He took her hand and said: "Listen. . . ."

She jerked her hand away. "That's enough," she said. "That's enough. I know what I wanted to know."

She brushed back from her forehead a few meshes of hair now soaked in perspiration. Suddenly she smiled, as though at a recollection.

"But look here," she resumed with a flash of malicious joy; "that isn't what you said yesterday, on the telephone. You said in so many words: 'I do love you,' though no one asked you the question."

Mathieu did not answer. She said with a crushing look: "The fact is—you despise me."

"I don't despise you," said Mathieu. "I—"

"Go," said Marcelle.

"You're crazy," said Mathieu. "I won't go, I really must explain to you that I—"

"Go," she repeated hoarsely, her eyes closed.

"But I still care for you deeply," he exclaimed in desperation; "I have no notion of giving you up. I want to stay with you all my life, I'll marry you, I—"

"Go," she said. "Go, I can't see you any more; go or I won't answer for myself, I'll start screaming."

She had begun to quiver all over. Mathieu took one step towards her, but she repulsed him violently.

"If you don't go, I shall call Mother."

He opened the wardrobe and took out his shoes; he felt ridiculous and detestable. Addressing his back, she said: "Take your money with you."

Mathieu turned around. "No," he said, "that's a separate matter. There's no sense in—"

She took the notes from the night-table and flung them in his face. They fluttered across the room and dropped beside the bed, near the box of dressings. Mathieu did not pick them up; he looked at Marcelle. She had begun to laugh in hysterical paroxysms, her eyes still closed.

"Oh, how funny it all is! And I who thought—"

He made as though to approach her, but she opened her eyes and leaped backwards, pointing to the door. "If I stay, she'll begin to scream," he thought. . . . He turned on his heel and went out of the room in his socks, carrying his shoes in his hand. When he reached the bottom of the staircase, he put on his shoes, paused for an instant, his hand on the latch of the front door, and listened. He suddenly heard Marcelle's laugh, a low-pitched ominous laugh that gradually shrilled into something like a horse's neigh and then cascaded downwards. A voice cried: "Marcelle! What's the matter? Marcelle!"

It was her mother. The laugh broke off short, and silence fell. Mathieu listened for an instant longer, and, as he could hear nothing more, he quietly opened the door and went out.

# CHAPTER XVIII

H E THOUGHT: "I'm a swine," and was vastly astonished at the fact. There was nothing left in him but exhaustion and amazement. He stopped at the second-floor landing to get his breath. His legs were unsteady; he had only had six hours' sleep for three days, perhaps not even that. "I'll go to bed." He would throw his clothes down anyhow, stagger to his bed, and fall into it. But he knew he would stay awake all night, staring into the darkness. He went on upstairs: the door of his apartment was still open. Ivich must have fled; the reading-lamp was still alight in his study.

He went in and saw Ivich. She was sitting on the sofa, stiffly upright.

"I didn't go," she said.

"So I see," said Mathieu, dryly.

They remained for a moment silent; Mathieu could hear the strong and steady pulse of his own breathing.

Ivich said, with eyes averted: "I was horrid."

Mathieu did not answer. He looked at Ivich's hair and thought: "Is it for her I did it?" She had bent her head, he looked at her soft brown neck with laborious affection: he wanted to feel that he was more fond of her than of anyone else in the world, so that his act might at least have had so much justification. But he was conscious of nothing but an aimless anger, and the act was behind him, naked, elusive, incomprehensible: he had committed a theft, he had deserted Marcelle in her pregnancy, *for nothing*.

Ivich made an effort and said politely: "I oughtn't to have intruded my advice on you. . . ."

Mathieu shrugged his shoulders. "I have just broken with Marcelle."

Ivich raised her head and said in a toneless voice: "You have left her—without money?"

Mathieu smiled. "Of course," he thought. "If I had done so, she would be blaming me for it now."

"No, I fixed that up."

"You got the money?"

"Yes."

"Where from?"

He did not answer. She looked at him uneasily. "But you didn't—"

"I did. I stole it, if that's what you mean. From Lola. I went up to her room when she wasn't there."

Ivich blinked, and Mathieu added: "I shall return it to her, of course. It's a forced loan, that's all."

Ivich looked bewildered; she repeated slowly, as Marcelle had done not long before: "You stole it from Lola."

Her shocked expression annoyed Mathieu, and he said briskly: "Yes, it wasn't much of an achievement, you know: just a staircase to climb and a door to open."

"Why did you do it?"

Mathieu laughed shortly. "If I only knew!"

She stiffened abruptly and her face assumed the hard, remote look that came over it when she turned around in the street to look at a pretty woman or a young man who had just passed by. But this time it was Mathieu she was looking at. Mathieu realized that she was blushing. He continued conscientiously:

"I didn't want to leave her in the lurch. Just to give her the money so that I shouldn't have to marry her."

"Yes, I understand," said Ivich.

She didn't in the least look as if she understood, her eyes were still upon him. He went on, with eyes averted: "It was pretty rotten, you know: it was she who sent me away. She took it very badly, I don't know what she expected."

Ivich did not answer, and Mathieu was silent, in a sudden access of anguish. "I don't want her to make it up to me," he thought.

"You are a fine fellow," said Ivich.

Mathieu was appalled to feel his bitter love revive within him. It seemed to him that he was deserting Marceile for the second time. He said nothing, he sat down beside Ivich and took her hand. She said: "You look so terribly alone."

He felt ashamed, and after a while he said: "I wonder what you really think, Ivich? This was a dreadful business, you know: I was half crazy when I stole the money, and now I feel remorseful."

"I can see you do," said Ivich, with a smile. "I think I should feel remorseful in your place: one can't help it for a day or so."

Mathieu squeezed the small rough hand with its pointed nails.

"You are wrong, I'm not—"

"Say no more," said Ivich.

She abruptly drew her hand away and smoothed her hair back, uncovering her cheeks and ears. A few rapid movements sufficed, and when she withdrew her hands, her hair stayed back, leaving her face bare.

"There!" said she.

Mathieu thought: "She wants to rob me even of my remorse." He stretched out his arms and drew Ivich towards him, unresisting; he could hear within himself a little gay and lively tune that he thought had long since faded from his memory. Ivich's head tilted a little on to one shoulder and she smiled at him with parted lips. He returned her smile and kissed her lightly; then he looked at her, and the little tune stopped short. "Why, she's nothing but a child," he said to himself. He felt absolutely alone.

"Ivich," he said gently.

She eyed him with surprise.

"Ivich, I—I was wrong."

She was frowning, and her head was shaken by faint tremors. Mathieu let his arms fall and said wearily: "I don't know what I want from you."

Ivich gave a sudden start and quickly drew away from him. Her eyes began to glitter, but she closed them and assumed an air of gentle melancholy. Her hands alone retained her wrath: they fluttered around her, patted the top of her head, and tugged at her hair. Mathieu's throat was dry, but he watched this anger with indifference. "Well," he thought, "I've wrecked this business too," and he was almost glad. It was a sort of expiation. And he continued, seeking the gaze that she kept obstinately averted:

"I mustn't touch you."

"Oh, it doesn't matter now," she said, crimson with rage. And she added in a lilting tone: "You looked so proud of having made a decision that I thought that you had come for a reward."

He again sat down beside her and gently grasped her arm, a little above the elbow. She did not disengage herself.

"But I love you, Ivich."

Ivich stiffened. "I shouldn't like you to think—" she said. "Think what?"

But he guessed. He relinquished her arm.

"I—I don't love you," said Ivich.

Mathieu did not answer. He thought: "She is revenging herself, quite naturally." Moreover it was probably true: why should she have loved him? All he wanted was to sit for a while silently at her side and then to let her go without another word. But he said:

"You will come back next year?"

"I shall."

She smiled at him with something like affection, she must have considered her honor satisfied. It was the same face she had turned towards him on the previous evening, when the lavatory dame was bandaging her hand. He eyed her dubiously, he felt his desire revive. That sad and resigned desire which was a desire *for nothing*. He took her arm, he felt the cool flesh beneath his fingers. And he said:

"I—you—"

He stopped. There was a ring at the outer door: one ring first, then two, then an unbroken peal. Mathieu felt frozen. "Marcelle," he thought. Ivich had paled, she had certainly had the same idea. They looked at each other.

"You must open the door," she whispered.

"I think I must," said Mathieu.

He did not move. Then came a violent hammering on the door.

Ivich said with a shudder: "It's dreadful to think that there's someone on the other side of that door."

"Yes," said Mathieu. "Will you—will you go into the kitchen? I'll shut the door, no one will see you."

Ivich looked at him with an air of calm authority: "No. I shall stay here."

Mathieu went to the door and opened it; in the half-light he saw a large grimacing head, not unlike a mask: it was Lola. She pushed him aside and dashed into the apartment.

"Where is Boris?" she demanded. "I heard his voice."

Mathieu did not even stay to shut the outer door, he hurried after her into the living-room. Lola had advanced on Ivich with a menacing air.

"You must tell me where Boris is."

Ivich looked at her with stricken eyes. And yet Lola did not appear to be speaking to her—or to anyone—and she wasn't even sure that she had seen her. Mathieu slipped between them.

"He isn't here."

Lola turned her ravaged face upon him. She had been crying.

"I heard his voice."

"Apart from this room," said Mathieu, trying to catch Lola's eye, "there's only a kitchen and a bathroom in the apartment. You can search anywhere you like."

"Then where is he?"

She was still wearing her black silk frock and her professional make-up. There was a sort of curdled look in her great dark eyes.

"He left Ivich about three o'clock," said Mathieu. "We don't know what he has been doing since."

Lola began to laugh hysterically. Her hands were clutching a little black velvet bag, which seemed to contain one sole object, something hard and heavy. Mathieu noticed the bag and felt afraid; he must get Ivich out of the place at once.

"Well, if you don't know what he has been doing, I can inform you," said Lola. "He came up to my room about seven, just after I had gone out; he opened my door, forced the lock of a suitcase, and stole five thousand francs."

Mathieu did not dare to look at Ivich; he said to her quietly, keeping his eyes fixed on the floor:

"Ivich, you had better go away; I must talk to Lola. Can I—can I see you again this evening?"

Ivich looked distraught. "Oh no!" she said. "I must go

back, I've got my packing to do, and I must get some sleep. I do so need some sleep."

"Is she going away?" asked Lola.

"Yes," said Mathieu; "tomorrow morning."

"Is Boris going away too?"

"No."

Mathieu took Ivich's hand. "Mind you get some sleep, Ivich. You have had a rough day. I suppose you wouldn't like me to see you off?"

"No. I'd rather not."

"Well, then, good-by till next year."

He looked at her, hoping to discover a flicker of affection in her eyes, but all he could read in them was panic fear.

"Till next year," she said.

"I'll write to you, Ivich," said Mathieu dismally.

"Yes. Yes."

She was just going out when Lola barred the way. "One moment! How am I to know she isn't going to join Boris?"

"And what then?" said Mathieu. "She is free, I suppose."

"Stay here," said Lola, grasping Ivich's wrist with her right hand.

Ivich uttered a cry of pain and anger.

"Let me go," she cried. "Don't touch me, I won't be touched."

Mathieu thrust Lola aside, and she drew back a few steps, muttering indignantly. He looked at her bag.

"Disgusting woman," muttered Ivich between her teeth. She felt her wrist with her thumb and forefinger.

"Lola," said Mathieu, without taking his eyes off the bag, "let her go. I have many things to say to you, but let her go first."

"Will you tell me where Boris is?"

"No," said Mathieu, "but I'll explain how the money was stolen."

"Very well, go along," said Lola. "And if you see Boris, tell him I've made a charge against him."

"The charge will be withdrawn," said Mathieu in an undertone, his eyes still fixed upon the bag. "Good-by, Ivich, off you go."

Ivich did not answer, and Mathieu heard with relief the light patter of her feet. He did not see her go, but the sound ceased, and for an instant he felt his heart contract. Lola took a step forward and exclaimed:

"Tell him he's got in wrong this time. Tell him he's too young to fool me!"

She turned towards Mathieu: still with the same baffling look, which seemed to see nothing.

"Well?" she said harshly. "And now for your story."

"Listen, Lola!" said Mathieu.

But Lola had begun to laugh again. "I wasn't born yesterday," she said, laughing. "I certainly wasn't. I'm sick of being told I might be his mother."

Mathieu advanced towards her. "Lola!"

"I can hear him saying: 'The old girl is daffy about me; she won't mind my pinching a little cash, she'll even thank me.' He doesn't know me! He doesn't know me!"

Mathieu seized her arm and shook her like a plum tree, while she still laughed and shrieked:

"He doesn't know me!"

"Be quiet!" he said roughly.

Lola became calmer and, for the first time, seemed to see him. "Well, what have you got to say?"

"Lola," said Mathieu, "have you *really* made a charge against him?"

"Yes. What then?"

"It was I who stole the money."

Lola looked at him blankly. He had to repeat: "It was I who stole the five thousand francs!"

"Oh!" she said, "it was you?"

She shrugged her shoulders. "The manageress saw him."

"How could she have seen him? I tell you it was I."

"She saw him," said Lola irritably. "He slipped upstairs at seven o'clock. She let him pass because I had told her to. I had been waiting for him all day, and I had only gone out ten minutes before. He must have been watching for me at the corner of the street and gone up as soon as he saw me go."

She spoke in a quick, dejected tone that seemed to express an unshakable conviction. "It's as though she wanted to believe it," thought Mathieu wearily. And he said: "Listen. At what time did you get back?"

"The first time? Eight o'clock."

"Well, the notes were then still in the suitcase."

"I tell you Boris went up at seven o'clock."

"He may have done so, perhaps he was coming to see you. But you didn't look in the suitcase, did you?"

"Yes, I did."

"You looked in it at *eight o'clock?*"

"Yes."

"Lola, you're not being straightforward," said Mathieu. "I know you didn't look. I *know*. At eight o'clock I had the key on me, and you couldn't have opened the suitcase. Besides, if you discovered the theft at eight o'clock, how are you going to get me to believe that you would have waited until midnight before coming to see me? At eight o'clock you made your face up, you put on your black frock, and you went to the Sumatra. Isn't that so?"

Lola looked at him with an impenetrable air. "The manageress saw him go up."

"Yes, but *you*—you didn't look in the suitcase. At eight o'clock the money was still there. I went up at ten o'clock and took it. There was an oldish woman in the office, she saw me, she can bear me out. You noticed the theft at midnight."

"Yes," said Lola wearily. "It was at midnight. But it's

the same thing. I felt unwell at the Sumatra and went back to my hotel. I lay down, and I put the suitcase on the bed beside me. There were—there were letters in it I wanted to read over."

Mathieu thought: "That's true: the letters. Why does she want to conceal the fact that they've been stolen too?" They both fell silent; now and then Lola swayed to and fro, like a sleepwalker standing. She appeared to wake up at last.

"*You*—you stole the money?"

"Yes."

She laughed curtly. "Keep your patter for the magistrates, if you want to pick up six months instead of him."

"Look here, Lola: why on earth should I risk imprisonment for Boris's sake?"

She made a wry face. "How am I to know what you and he are up to?"

"That's just silly! Listen, I give you my word it was I: the suitcase was by the window, under a valise. I took the money and left the key in the lock."

Lola's lips quivered, she fingered her bag nervously. "Is that all you've got to tell me? Then let me go."

She tried to pass, but Mathieu stopped her.

"Lola, you just *won't* be convinced."

Lola gripped his shoulders and thrust him aside.

"Don't you see the state I'm in? Do you think I'm going to swallow your story about the suitcase? 'It was under a valise by the window,' she repeated, aping Mathieu's voice. Boris has been here, and you think I don't know it? You've agreed together what the old woman should be told. Now let me go," she said with a venomous look; "let me go."

Mathieu tried to take her by the shoulders, but Lola recoiled and fumbled with her bag: Mathieu snatched it from her and flung it on the sofa.

"Beast!" said Lola.

"Is it vitriol or a revolver?" asked Mathieu with a smile.

Lola began to tremble all over. "Oh Lord," thought Mathieu: "she's going to have hysterics." He felt as though he were plunged in a sinister and preposterous dream. But she *must* be convinced. Lola stopped trembling. She had retreated to the window and watched him; her eyes were glittering with impotent hatred. Mathieu looked away· he was not afraid of her hatred, but on her face there was an expression of bleak desolation that was more than he could bear.

"I came up to your room this morning," he said in a measured tone. "I took the key from your bag. When you woke up, I was just going to open the suitcase. I hadn't time to replace the key and that is what put it into my head to go up to your room again this evening."

"It's no good," said Lola curtly. "I saw you come in this morning. When I spoke to you, you hadn't even got to the foot of my bed."

"I had come in once before and gone away again."

Lola grinned, and he added reluctantly: "To get the letters."

She did not seem to hear: it was quite useless to talk to her about the letters, she could only think of the money, and she needed to think of it in order to keep her anger burning, that being her sole resource. At last she said with a short dry laugh:

"Unfortunately for your story, he asked me for the five thousand francs yesterday evening. That, actually, is what we quarreled about."

Mathieu realized his helplessness: it was clear that the culprit *could be* no other than Boris. "I ought to have thought of it," he said to himself dejectedly.

"Don't you worry," said Lola with a malignant smile. "I'll get him. If you succeed in bamboozling the judge, I'll get him in another way, that's all."

Mathieu looked at the bag on the sofa. Lola looked at it too.

"It was for me that he asked you for the money," he said.

"Yes. And I suppose it was for you that he stole a book from a bookshop yesterday afternoon. He boasted of that while he was dancing with me."

She stopped short, and suddenly continued with ominous calm:

"Very well, then. It was you who robbed me?"

"Yes."

"Then give me back the money."

Mathieu stood abashed; and Lola added in a tone of ironical triumph:

"Give it back to me at once and I'll withdraw my charge."

Mathieu did not answer, and Lola said: "That'll do. I understand."

She picked up her bag, and he made no attempt to prevent her.

"Anyway, even if I had it, that would prove nothing," he said with difficulty. "Boris might have given it to me."

"I'm not asking you that. I'm asking you to give it back to me."

"I no longer have it."

"Are you serious? You stole it from me at ten o'clock, and at midnight you no longer have it? I congratulate you."

"I've given it to someone."

"To whom?"

"I shan't tell you." He added sharply: "It wasn't to Boris."

Lola smiled without replying; she made her way to the door and he did not stop her. He thought: "Her local police station will be the one in the rue des Martyrs. I'll go there and explain." But when he saw the back of that tall black figure moving with the blind momentum of catastrophe, he was afraid; he thought of the bag and made a last attempt:

"After all, I can very well tell you whom it was for: it was for Mademoiselle Duffet, a friend of mine."

Lola opened the door and went out. He heard her utter a cry as she stepped into the outer room, and his heart leaped. Lola suddenly reappeared, looking like a mad-woman.

"There's someone there," she said.

And Mathieu thought: "It's Boris."

It was Daniel. He marched in with a flourish and bowed to Lola.

"Here are the five thousand francs, madame," he said, handing her an envelope. "Will you kindly verify that they are in fact yours?"

Two thoughts came simultaneously into Mathieu's mind: "It's Marcelle who sent him," and "He was listening at the door." Daniel was rather in the habit of listening at doors so as to stage his entrances.

"Has she—" Mathieu began.

Daniel reassured him with a gesture. "All is well," he said.

Lola looked at the envelope with a peasant woman's sly, suspicious eyes.

"There are five thousand francs inside it?" she asked.

"Yes."

"How can I be sure they're mine?"

"Didn't you take the numbers?" asked Daniel.

"As if I should!"

"Ah, madame," said Daniel with a reproachful air, "you ought always to take the numbers of notes."

Mathieu had a sudden inspiration: he recalled the heavy odor of chypre and mustiness that had emerged from the suitcase.

"Smell them," he said.

Lola hesitated for a moment, then she grabbed the envelope, tore it open, and put the notes to her nose. Mathieu was afraid that Daniel would burst out laughing. But Daniel was impeccably serious and eyed Lola with a blandly comprehending air.

"So you forced Boris to give them back?" she said.

"I know no one by the name of Boris," said Daniel. "It was a friend of Mathieu, a woman, who gave them to me to bring them back to you. I hurried round here and broke in upon the end of your conversation; I offer you my excuses, madame."

Lola stood motionless, her arms close at her sides, holding her bag tightly in her left hand, her right hand clutching the notes; she looked uneasy and bewildered.

"But why should you have done it—*you?*" she asked abruptly. "What are five thousand francs to you?"

Mathieu smiled a mirthless smile. "A good deal, apparently." And he added quietly: "You must withdraw your charge, Lola. Or, if you like, bring it against me."

Lola averted her eyes and said quickly: "I hadn't made any charge."

She stood rigid in the center of the room, with a set look on her face. Then she said: "What about the letters?"

"I no longer have them. I took them this morning, for Boris, when you were thought to be dead. That's what gave me the idea of coming back to take the money."

Lola looked at Mathieu without hatred, but with an immense astonishment and a sort of curiosity.

"You stole five thousand francs from me!" she said: "What—what a scream!"

But the light quickly vanished from her eyes, and her face hardened. She seemed to be in pain.

"I'm going," she said.

They let her depart in silence. In the doorway she turned. "If he hasn't done anything wrong, why doesn't he come back?"

"I don't know."

Lola uttered a brief sob and leaned against the frame of the door. Mathieu took a step towards her, but she had recovered herself.

"Do you think he will come back?"

"I think so. He's one of those who can't make people happy, but can't throw them over—they find that even more difficult."

"Yes," said Lola. "Yes. Well—good-by."

"Good-by, Lola. You—you aren't in need of anything?"

"No."

She went out. They heard the door close.

"Who is that old party?" asked Daniel.

"It's Lola, Boris Serguine's friend. She's a little cracked."

"She looks it," said Daniel.

Mathieu felt embarrassed at being left alone with him; he felt as though he had been thrust abruptly into the presence of his misdeed. It was there, face to face with him, *alive*, it lived in the depths of Daniel's eyes, and God alone knew what form it had assumed in that capricious and artificial consciousness. Daniel seemed inclined to take unfair advantage of the situation. His demeanor was ceremonious, insolent, and funereal, as it always was on his most disagreeable days.

Mathieu stiffened, and held his head erect; Daniel was livid.

"You look pretty rotten," said Daniel with a malicious smile.

"I was going to say the same to you," said Mathieu. "We're quits."

Daniel shrugged his shoulders.

"Do you come straight from Marcelle?" asked Mathieu.

"Yes."

"It was she who gave you the money?"

"She didn't need it," said Daniel evasively.

"She didn't need it?"

"No."

"You might at least tell me if she can manage—"

"There's no longer any question of that, my dear fellow," said Daniel. "All that is ancient history."

He had raised his left eyebrow and was gazing ironically at Mathieu as though through an imaginary monocle. "If he wants to impress me," thought Mathieu, "he had better keep his hands steady."

Daniel observed nonchalantly: "I'm going to marry her. We shall keep the child."

Mathieu took a cigarette and lit it. His skull was vibrating like a bell. He said calmly: "So you were in love with her?"

"Why not?"

"It is Marcelle we are talking about," thought Mathieu. *Marcelle!* He could not fully grasp that fact.

"Daniel," he said, "I don't believe you."

"Wait a bit and you'll see."

"No, what I mean is—you won't make me believe that you're in love with her, and I'm wondering what's behind all this."

Daniel looked tired, he had sat down on the edge of the desk, with one foot on the floor and nonchalantly dangling the other. "He's making fun of me," thought Mathieu angrily.

"You would indeed be astonished if you knew how matters stand," said Daniel. And Mathieu thought: "Why of course! She was his mistress."

"If you oughtn't to tell me, don't," he said, curtly.

Daniel looked at him for an instant as though he enjoyed mystifying him, then he suddenly got up and passed a hand over his forehead. "It's a bit awkward," he said. He eyed Mathieu with surprise. "That's not what I came to talk to you about. Look here, Mathieu, I'm—" He laughed constrainedly. "What I have to say may upset you a bit."

"Never mind. Tell me or not, as you like," said Mathieu.

"Well, I'm—" He stopped again, and Mathieu, growing impatient, finished for him:

"You are Marcelle's lover. That's what you want to say."

Daniel opened his eyes wide and emitted a faint whistle. Mathieu felt himself blushing crimson.

"Not a bad guess," said Daniel with an admiring air. "Just what would suit your book, eh? No, my dear fellow, you haven't even that excuse."

"Hadn't you better tell me?" said Mathieu, rather dashed.

"Wait," said Daniel. "You haven't got anything to drink, have you? Whisky?"

"No," said Mathieu, "but I've got some rum. An excellent idea," he added; "we'll have a drink."

He hurried into the kitchen and opened the cupboard. "I've been behaving disgracefully," he thought. He returned with two claret glasses and a bottle of rum. Daniel took the bottle and filled the glasses to the brim.

"It comes from the Martinique shop?" he said.

"Yes."

"You still go there sometimes?"

"Sometimes," said Mathieu. "Here's your good health."

Daniel looked at him with an inquisitorial air, as though Mathieu were concealing something from him. "To the beloved," he said, raising his glass.

"You're drunk," said Mathieu furiously.

"It's true I've had a drink or two," said Daniel. "But don t worry. I was sober when I went to see Marcelle. It was after—"

"Have you just come from her?"

"Yes. Except that I looked in at the Falstaff on the way."

"You—you must have arrived just after I had gone?"

"I was waiting for you," smiled Daniel. "I saw you turn the corner of the street, and I went in."

Mathieu could not suppress a gesture of annoyance.

"You were watching for me?" he said. "Oh, just as well, I dare say; Marcelle won't have wanted to be alone. Now what is it you wanted to tell me?"

"Nothing at all, my dear fellow," said Daniel with sudden cordiality. "I simply wanted to inform you of my approaching marriage."

"Is that all?"

"That's all.— Yes, that's all."

"As you please," said Mathieu coldly. They were silent for a moment, and then Mathieu said:

"How—how is she?"

"Do you want me to tell you she's delighted?" asked Daniel ironically. "Spare my modesty."

"I beg your pardon," said Mathieu dryly. "Quite true, I have no right to ask. . . . But, after all, you did come here. . . ."

"Well," said Daniel. "I thought I should have had more trouble in persuading her: but she fairly jumped at my proposal."

Mathieu saw something like a flash of resentment gleam for an instant in his eyes; he said sharply, by way of excusing Marcelle:

"She was drowning. . . ."

Daniel shrugged his shoulders and began to pace up and down. Mathieu dared not look at him. Daniel was keeping a close hold upon himself, he spoke quietly, but he looked like a man possessed. Mathieu clasped his hands and fixed his eyes upon his shoes. He continued painfully:

"So it was the baby she wanted. I didn't understand that. If she had told me—"

Daniel said nothing.

Mathieu went on laboriously: "It was the baby. Very well. It will be born. I—well, I wanted to get rid of it. I suppose it's better that it should be born."

Daniel did not answer.

"I shall never see it, of course," said Mathieu.

It was scarcely a question; he added, without waiting
for an answer: "Well, there we are; I suppose I ought to
be glad. In one sense, you are saving her . . . but I don't
understand it at all—why are you doing it?"

"Certainly not from philanthropic motives, if that's what
you mean," said Daniel dryly. "Your rum is filthy," he
added; "but give me another glass."

Mathieu filled the glasses and they drank.

"And what are you going to do now?" asked Daniel.

"Nothing. Nothing more."

"That little Serguine girl?"

"No."

"But you're free now."

"Pah!"

"Well, good night," said Daniel, getting up. "I came to
give you back the money and to reassure you a bit. Marcelle has nothing to fear, she trusts me. All this business
has shaken her terribly, but she isn't really unhappy."

"You're going to marry her!" repeated Mathieu. "She
hates me," he added in an undertone.

"Put yourself in her place," said Daniel severely.

"I know. I have done so. Did she say anything about
me?"

"Not much."

"The fact is," said Mathieu, "it seems to me queer that
you should be marrying her."

"Have you any regrets?"

"No. I find it rather sinister."

"Thanks."

"Oh, for both of you. I don't know why."

"Don't you worry, everything will be all right. If it's a
boy, we'll call him Mathieu."

Mathieu stiffened, and clenched his fists. "That will do!"
he said.

"Now, don't get angry," said Daniel. And he repeated

with an abstracted air: "Don't get angry. Don't get angry."
He could not make up his mind to go away.

"In short," said Mathieu, "you came to see what I should
look like after all this."

"That was one reason," said Daniel. "Frankly, that was
one reason. You always look—so solid: you annoyed me."

"Well, and now you've seen me," said Mathieu. "I'm
not so solid after all."

"No."

Daniel took a few steps towards the door, and came
brusquely back to Mathieu; he had shed his ironic expression, but he looked no more amiable.

"Mathieu, I am a homosexual," he said.

"I beg pardon?" said Mathieu.

Daniel had flung himself backwards and was looking at
him with amazement, his eyes sparkling with anger.

"That disgusts you, I suppose?"

"You are a homosexual?" repeated Mathieu slowly.
"No, it doesn't disgust me; why should it disgust me?"

"Look here," said Daniel, "don't feel obliged to assume
a broad-minded attitude. . . ."

Mathieu did not answer. He looked at Daniel and
thought: "He is a homosexual." He was not greatly astonished.

"You say nothing," pursued Daniel in a hissing tone.
"You are right. You have the proper reaction, I am sure,
such as every sound man ought to have, and you do
equally well to keep it to yourself."

Daniel stood motionless, his arms stiff against his sides,
he seemed to have dwindled.

"Why on earth did he come to torment himself in my
flat?" Mathieu asked himself resentfully. He thought he
ought to have found something to say, but he was plunged
in a profound and paralyzing indifference. Besides, it
seemed to him so natural, so normal: he was a swine,

Daniel was a homosexual, all this was in the order of things. In the end he said:

"You can be what you like, it's no concern of mine."

"True," said Daniel with a supercilious smile; "true indeed, it's no concern of yours. You have your hands full dealing with your own conscience."

"Then why do you come to tell me all this?"

"Well, I—I wanted to see the effect it would produce on a fellow like you," said Daniel, clearing his throat. "Also, now that there's someone who *knows*, I—I shall perhaps succeed in believing it."

He had turned a little green and spoke with difficulty, but he was still smiling. Mathieu could not endure that smile and turned his head away.

Daniel grinned. "Does it surprise you? Does it upset your conception of inverts?"

Mathieu raised his head abruptly. "Don't throw your weight about," he said. "It's distressing. There's no need to do that for my benefit. You are disgusted with yourself, I suppose, but not more so than I am with myself, there's nothing much to choose between us. Besides," he said after a moment's reflection, "that's why you tell me all this. It must be much easier to confess to a derelict like me; and you get the advantage of the confession just the same."

"You're a sly little devil," said Daniel in a coarse voice that Mathieu had never heard him use before.

They were silent. Daniel was staring straight into vacancy with an expression of fixed bewilderment, as old men do. Mathieu felt an agonizing stab of remorse.

"If it's like that, why are you marrying Marcelle?"

"That has nothing to do with it."

"I—I can't let you marry her," said Mathieu.

Daniel stiffened, and dark red blotches appeared on his drowned-corpse countenance.

"*Can't* you indeed?" he demanded haughtily. "And how are you going to stop me?"

Mathieu got up without answering. The telephone was on his desk. He picked up the receiver and dialed Marcelle's number. Daniel watched him ironically. There was a long silence.

"Hello?" came Marcelle's voice.

Mathieu gave a start.

"Hello," he said, "it's Mathieu. I—look here, we were behaving idiotically just now. I want— Hello! Marcelle? Are you there? Marcelle!" he said savagely. "Hello!"

No answer. He lost his head and shouted into the instrument: "Marcelle, I want to marry you!"

There was a brief silence, then a yapping sound at the end of the line, and a concluding click. Mathieu gripped the receiver for a moment, then gently replaced it. Daniel eyed him without uttering a word, his expression was in no sense triumphant. Mathieu took a drink of rum and sat down in the armchair.

"Well, that's that," he said.

Daniel smiled. "Don't you worry," he said by way of consolation. "Homosexuals have always made excellent husbands—that's well known."

"Daniel! If you are marrying her as a sort of gesture, you will ruin her life."

"You ought to be the last person to tell me so," said Daniel. "Besides, I'm not marrying her as a sort of gesture. The fact is, what she wants above all is the baby."

"Does she—does she know?"

"No."

"Why are you marrying her?"

"Because I'm fond of her."

The tone was not convincing. They refilled their glasses, and Mathieu said doggedly:

"I don't want her to be unhappy."

"I swear she won't be."

"Does she believe you're in love with her?"

"I don't think so. She suggested I should come and live in her place, but that wouldn't suit me at all. I shall bring her to my apartment. It is agreed that any emotional relation shall come gradually." And he added with laborious irony: "I mean to fulfill all my marital duties."

"But—" Mathieu blushed violently. "Do you like women too?"

Daniel emitted an odd sniff and said: "Not much."

"I see."

Mathieu bent his head, and tears of shame came into his eyes. He said: "I'm even more disgusted with myself because I know you're going to marry her."

Daniel drank. "Yes," he said with a nonchalant, absent-minded air. "I suppose you must be feeling pretty rotten."

Mathieu did not answer. He was looking at the floor between his feet. "He's a homosexual, and she's going to marry him."

He unclasped his hands and scraped his heel against the floor: he felt like a hunted quarry. Suddenly the silence grew burdensome; he said to himself: "Daniel is looking at me," and he hurriedly raised his head. Daniel was indeed looking at him, and with so venomous an expression that Mathieu's heart contracted.

"Why are you looking at me like that?" he asked.

"You *know*," said Daniel. "There is someone who *knows!*"

"You wouldn't be sorry to put a bullet through me?"

Daniel did not answer. Mathieu was suddenly scorched by an unendurable idea. "Daniel," he said, "you are marrying her to make a martyr of yourself."

"What then?" said Daniel in a toneless voice. "That's nobody's concern but mine."

Mathieu laid his head in his hands. "My God!" he said.

Daniel added rapidly: "It's of no importance. *For her* it's of no importance."

"Do you hate her?"

"No."

And Mathieu reflected sadly: "No, it's me he hates."

Daniel had resumed his smile. "Shall we finish the bottle?"

"By all means," said Mathieu.

They drank, and Mathieu became aware that he wanted to smoke. He took a cigarette from his pocket and lit it.

"Look here, what you are is none of my business. Even now that you've told me about it. But there is one thing I should like to ask you: why are you ashamed?"

Daniel laughed dryly. "I was waiting for that, my dear fellow. I am ashamed of being a homosexual *because I am* a homosexual. I know what you're going to say: 'If I were in your place, I wouldn't stand any nonsense. I would claim my place in the sun, it's a taste like any other,' and so forth and so on. But that is all entirely off the mark. You say that kind of thing precisely because you are not a homosexual. All inverts are ashamed of being so, it's part of their make-up."

"But wouldn't it be better—to accept the fact?" asked Mathieu timidly.

This seemed to annoy Daniel. "You can say that to me, when you have accepted the fact that you're a swine," he answered harshly. "No. Homosexuals who boast of it or proclaim it or merely acquiesce—are dead men. Their very sense of shame has killed them. I don't want to die that sort of death."

But his tense mood seemed to have relaxed and he looked at Mathieu without hatred.

"I have accepted myself only too thoroughly," he continued quietly. "I know myself inside out."

There was nothing more to say. Mathieu lit another

cigarette. There was a drain of rum left in his glass and he drank it off. Daniel filled him with horror. He thought: "In two years, in four years . . . shall I be like that?" And he was suddenly seized with the desire to talk to Marcelle about it: it was to her alone that he could talk about his life, his fears, his hopes. But he remembered that he would never see her again, and his desire, not yet actual or defined, slowly dissolved into a kind of anguish. He was alone.

Daniel seemed to be reflecting: his eyes were set, and from time to time his lips parted. He uttered a faint sigh, and something in his face seemed to give way. He passed a hand over his forehead: he looked astonished.

"Today, all the same, I did surprise myself," he said in an undertone.

He smiled a strange, almost childlike smile, which looked out of place on his sallow face, on which a hasty shave had left blue blotches. "It's true," thought Mathieu; "he went right through with it this time." Suddenly an idea came to him that made his heart turn over. "He is free," he thought. And the horror with which Daniel inspired him was suddenly combined with envy.

"You must be in a strange state," he said.

"Yes, in a very strange state," said Daniel.

He was still smiling genially, and he said: "Give me a cigarette."

"Are you smoking now?" asked Mathieu.

"One. This evening."

"I wish I were in your place," said Mathieu abruptly.

"In my place?" said Daniel, without much surprise.

"Yes."

Daniel shrugged his shoulders. "In this affair," he said, "you've been a winner all round."

Mathieu laughed dryly, and Daniel explained: "You are free."

"No," said Mathieu, shaking his head. "It isn't by giving up a woman that a man is free."

Daniel looked at Mathieu with curiosity. "You looked as if you believed it this morning."

"I don't know. It wasn't clear. Nothing is clear. The truth is that I gave up Marcelle *for nothing.*"

He gazed at the window curtains, which were faintly stirring in the night breeze. He was tired.

"For nothing," he repeated. "In all this affair I have been a sort of embodied refusal, a negation. Marcelle is no longer in my life, but there's all the rest."

"What do you mean?"

Mathieu pointed to his desk with a vague embracing gesture. "All that—all the rest."

He was intrigued by Daniel. "Is that what freedom is?" he thought. "He has *acted;* and now he can't go back: it must seem strange to him to feel behind him an unknown act which he has already almost ceased to understand and which will turn his life upside down. All I do, I do *for nothing.* It might be said that I am robbed of the consequences of my acts; everything happens as though I could always play my strokes again. I don't know what I would give to do something irrevocable."

He said aloud: "Two evenings ago I met a fellow who had wanted to join the Spanish militia."

"Well?"

"Well, and then he became deflated. He's down and out now."

"Why do you tell me that?"

"I don't know. It just came into my head."

"Do you want to go to Spain?"

"Yes; but not enough."

They were silent. After a moment or two Daniel threw away his cigarette and said: "I should like to be six months older."

"I wouldn't," said Mathieu. "In six months I shall be the same as I am now."

"Minus the remorse," said Daniel.

He got up. "Come and have a drink at Clarisse's."

"No," said Mathieu. "I don't want to get drunk this evening. I don't quite know what I should do if I were to get drunk."

"Nothing very sensational," said Daniel. "So you won't come?"

"No. Won't you stay a little longer?"

"I must drink," said Daniel.

"Good-by. I—shall see you soon?" asked Mathieu.

Daniel seemed embarrassed.

"I feel it will be difficult. Marcelle certainly told me that she didn't want to alter anything in my life, but I doubt if she would care for me to see you again."

"Indeed? All right," said Mathieu dryly. "In that case, good luck."

Daniel smiled at him without replying, and Mathieu added brusquely: "You hate me."

Daniel went up to him and laid a hand on his shoulder with an awkward, diffident little gesture. "No, not at this moment."

"But tomorrow—"

Daniel bent his head and did not answer.

"Good-by," said Mathieu.

"Good-by."

Daniel went out; Mathieu walked up to the window and drew the curtains. It was a lovely night, a lovely blue night; the wind had swept the clouds away, the stars were visible above the roofs. He laid his elbows on the balcony and yawned. In the street below, a man was walking quietly along; he stopped at the corner of the rue Huyghens and the rue Froidevaux, raised his head, and looked at the sky: it was Daniel. The sound of music came in gusts from the avenue du Maine, the white shaft of a headlight slid across the sky, lingered above a chimney, and plunged down behind the roofs. It was a sky for a village fête, sparkling with ribbons and rosettes, redolent of holidays and dancing in the open air. Mathieu watched Daniel disappear and thought: "I remain alone." Alone but no freer than before. He had said to himself last evening: "If only Marcelle did not exist." But in so saying he deceived himself. "No one has interfered with my freedom; my life has drained it dry." He shut the window and went back into the room. The scent of Ivich still hovered in the air. He inhaled the scent and reviewed that day of tumult. "Much ado about nothing," he thought. For nothing: this life had been given him for nothing, he was nothing and yet he would not change: he was as he was made. He took off his shoes and sat motionless on the arm of the easy chair; he could still feel at the back of his throat the amber, sugared pungency of rum. He yawned: he had finished the day, and he had also finished with his youth. Various tried and proved rules of conduct had already discreetly offered him their services: disillusioned epicureanism, smiling tolerance, resignation, flat seriousness, stoicism—all the aids whereby a man may savor, minute by minute, like a connoisseur, the failure of a life. He took off his jacket and began to undo his necktie. He yawned again as he repeated to himself: "It's true, it's really true: I have attained the age of reason."

## VINTAGE WORKS OF SCIENCE AND PSYCHOLOGY

# VINTAGE POLITICAL SCIENCE AND SOCIAL CRITICISM